W9-BCS-699

THE LIBRARIAN OF BOONE'S HOLLOW

THE LIBRARIAN OF BOONE'S HOLLOW

A NOVEL

KIM VOGEL SAWYER

THORNDIKE PRESS
A part of Gale, a Cengage Company

LIBRARY OF CONGRESS CIP DATA ON FILE.
CATALOGUING IN PUBLICATION FOR THIS BOOK
IS AVAILABLE FROM THE LIBRARY OF CONGRESS.

ISBN-13: 978-1-4328-8368-3 (hardcover alk. paper)

Published in 2021 by arrangement with WaterBrook, an imprint of Random House, a division of Penguin Random House LLC.

Printed in Mexico
Print Number: 01   Print Year: 2021

In memory of *Mom,* who taught me
to love books, to follow Jesus, and
to always be kind (even to those who
don't "deserve" it)

I say unto you which hear,
love your enemies, do good to them
which hate you.

— Luke 6:27

ONE

Mid-May 1936
Lexington, Kentucky
Addie Cowherd

During her three years as a student at the University of Kentucky, Addie had never been summoned to a dean's office. Until today. Her roommate, Felicity, had proclaimed with typical dramatic flair that being asked to meet with Dean Crane first thing on a Friday morning would have cast her into an endless pit of nervousness. Addie wasn't nervous. Curious? Most certainly. But not nervous. At least not much.

She traveled the wide hallways of the campus's main building, the heels of her freshly polished black patent pumps clicking a steady rhythm on the marble tile. Why did Dean Crane want to see her? Felicity suggested perhaps she'd been voted one of the campus beauties. Last night before bed, she had fluffed Addie's hair with her hands

9

and exclaimed, "Oh, to have hair that lays in such delightful waves, all on its own accord! And what a wondrous color — blended pecan and caramel. Mine's as straight as a pin and so blond it's almost white. Surely I'm not the only one who's taken note of your physical attributes."

Addie's heart now gave a little flutter. Could it be? What girl wouldn't be flattered by the title of campus beauty? But then she dismissed the idea. She was too tall, too thin, too . . . bookish to be a beauty. The petite girls with button noses, sparkling blue eyes, and infectious giggles — the ones like Felicity — always seemed the top picks for popularity. Besides, senior girls were chosen as campus beauties, and Addie was only a junior.

She climbed the stairs to the building's second level, other possibilities creeping through her brain. Were her latest test scores the top in her class? Did he want her to mentor a younger, less confident student? Probably not the latter, as the year was nearly over, but the former could be true. Wouldn't Mother and Daddy be proud when she told them? She rounded the final corner and approached the secretary's desk positioned outside the dean's office door.

She smiled at the gray-haired, thin-faced

woman sitting behind the oversized desk. "Hello, I'm Addie — er, Adelaide — Cowherd. Dean Crane sent a message saying he wishes to speak to me."

"Adelaide Cowherd . . ." The woman checked a notebook lying open on the desk's pull-out shelf. "Yes, his nine-fifteen appointment. You're right on time." She pressed a button on a little box and leaned close to it. "Dean Crane, Miss Cowherd is here."

"Send her in," a voice crackled from the box.

The secretary gestured to the richly stained raised-panel wooden door behind her. "Right through there, young lady."

Addie took one step and then paused. Should she have worn her Sunday suit? Although at least two years old, the navy-and-white plaid shirtwaist she'd selected from her array of everyday dresses showed no frays or stains. Even so, perhaps it was too casual an outfit for meeting with someone as important as the dean of students.

"Miss Cowherd, Dean Crane has a busy morning ahead. Please don't keep him waiting."

"Yes, ma'am." Too late to worry about her dress. She'd have to go in. But she smoothed the front of her pleated skirt, centered her

11

belt buckle, and straightened her spine — no slouching, Mother always said, even if she was tall for a girl — before giving the brass doorknob a twist. The door swung open on silent hinges, and she crossed the threshold. She sucked in a startled breath. Built-in bookcases packed with books, some standing vertically and others stacked horizontally, filled three walls all the way from the floor to the ceiling in the spacious, windowless office. She'd thought Daddy's study at home and his collection of printed works impressive, but Daddy had only two stacks of barrister shelves, four sections each. A desire to peruse the dean's shelves made her insides twitch.

"Miss Cowherd?"

Addie forced her attention to the dean, who stood beside a gleaming mahogany desk in a slash of pale lamplight, his pose as dignified as that of a judge overseeing a courtroom. Some of the rowdier students called Dean Crane Ol' Ichabod, a title Addie had always found offensive, but seeing the unusually tall, thin man up close, she understood the nickname. "Yes, sir?"

The dean peered at her over the top of a pair of wire-rimmed half-moon glasses, which sat precariously at the end of his narrow, hooked nose. "Please close the door and have a seat."

Addie snapped the door into its casing, shutting out the bright light from the hallway's many hanging pendants, and crossed the thick carpet to a pair of matching round-back, padded armchairs facing his desk. She perched on the brocade seat of the one on the right and placed her laced hands in her lap. She offered the dean a smile.

Fine tufts of white hair that stuck up like dandelion fluff on top of his head and bushy salt-and-pepper muttonchop whiskers gave him an almost comical appearance. But his stern frown spoiled any cheerful effect. A curtain of dread fell around her, and her stomach performed little flip-flops. A man who appeared so dire wouldn't deliver good news. Felicity's endless pit of nervousness suddenly seemed less far fetched.

He settled in his chair. "Thank you for coming, Miss Cowherd. I know this is a busy time for students, preparing for final examinations."

"Yes, sir, it is." She forced herself to speak calmly. "But I presumed it was something important."

"You presumed correctly." He opened a folder that lay on an exceptionally large blotter, his movements slow and painstaking, giving the impression the card stock folder was actually formed from a slab of stone. He tapped the top page of the short stack of papers inside the folder with his long, bony finger. "Your academic achievements are impressive, Miss Cowherd. Yours are among the highest scores in the junior class."

The acrobats in her stomach slowed their leaping. Perhaps his grim countenance was by habit. Even Preacher Finley back home in Georgetown was a somber man who rarely smiled but had a very kind heart. She placed her hands on the chair's carved wooden armrests and crossed her ankles, allowing her tense muscles to relax. "Thank you, sir."

He slid the sheet of paper aside, his gaze seeming to follow its path, then lifted a second page and squinted at it. "Every report from your professors is positive, praising your deportment, responsibility, and morals."

Addie lowered her chin, battling a wave of pride. Her mother stressed humility. She wouldn't shame Mother by gloating, but it surely sounded as if she were about to receive some sort of award. She coached herself to respond appropriately when the dean finally explained why he'd called her to his office.

"Which is why it saddens me to dismiss you as a student."

She jerked her head upright so abruptly her neck popped. A spot below her left ear burned as if someone had touched a match to her flesh. She rubbed the spot and gaped at the man. "Dismiss me? But why?"

He closed the folder. "Lack of payment."

Addie's jaw dropped. "L-lack . . ." She shook her head. "There must be a mistake."

"There's no mistake, Miss Cowherd. The tuition and board payments ceased to arrive in February. Your parents were allowed our standard three-month grace period, but despite repeated letters requesting payment, no monies were sent. Thus, we have no choice but to prohibit you from attending classes."

"But it's only a week to the end of the term. Won't I be allowed to take my final examinations?"

"I'm afraid not." The man's expression and tone revealed he took no pleasure in delivering the mandate, but that recognition did little to comfort her. "Campus personnel and each of your instructors have been informed of the decision. Any attempts to enter classrooms or the cafeteria will be met with an immediate response from security

15

officers."

Who would escort her away in humiliation. She'd witnessed such happenings more times than she cared to recall during her years at the college. With so many families struggling financially due to the stock market crash of '29, college was a luxury many couldn't afford. She never thought she'd be one of the unfortunate ones, though.

She shifted to the edge of the chair and implored the man with her eyes. "Dean Crane, there must be some sort of mistake. I'll call my parents. I'm positive they'll send the money right away." They'd never denied her anything she truly needed. And she needed her degree. "If they promise to do so, may I stay?"

"It's been three months, Miss Cowherd."

Fear and worry battled for prominence. "But my father never lets bills go unpaid. Not ever. The payments must have gotten lost in the mail. Or stolen." Yes, that had to be it. She stood. "Aren't there desperate people everywhere? Someone must have known there was money in the envelopes and taken them before they could reach the college. There can be no other explanation."

Dean Crane stared at her for several seconds, lips set in a grim line, beady eyes

16

narrowed. Finally, he sighed. "Very well. Contact your parents. Ask if they sent payments for March, April, or May." He pulled a gold watch from his vest pocket and scowled at it. "Come back at three o'clock and apprise me of their response. If there's been, as you suspect, a mistake, I'll speak with the committee about making an exception."

Addie nearly collapsed from relief. "Thank you, sir."

"Although you may not attend classes or take meals in the cafeteria until the financial matter is rectified, you may remain in the dormitory until the end of term. I understand from the business office manager that your room bill is current."

"Yes, sir. I work all day Saturday and a few hours each Monday, Wednesday, and Thursday cataloging books at the city library to pay for my room."

"Very commendable."

"Thank you." Daddy had insisted she contribute toward her education, claiming she would appreciate it more if she helped pay the bill. She'd resented it at first, but she'd come to realize he was right. Even though she had to give nearly every penny she earned to the college, it gave her a sense of pride and satisfaction to know she was helping to pay her way.

"Dean Crane," the secretary's voice intruded from the little box on the corner of the dean's desk, "your next appointment is here."

He rose with a slow unfolding of his legs and rounded the desk, gesturing for Addie to precede him. At the door, he offered the closest thing to a smile she'd seen since she entered the room. "I wish you well in your search for answers, Miss Cowherd. I'll see you at three."

Addie scurried out, avoiding eye contact with the student waiting to enter. Was he facing a similar fate? She set a quick pace up the hallway, grateful the pleats in her skirt allowed her to take long strides. The sooner she reached a public telephone and called Mother, the sooner this embarrassing situation would be put to right.

She pattered down the stairs to the first floor and joined the flow of students. The scent of waffles and syrup wafted from the cafeteria. Her stomach growled, and she placed her hand against her belly, grimacing. She'd skipped breakfast after taking a little extra time preparing for her meeting with the dean. If she'd gone with Felicity for her customary coffee and toast with jam earlier that morning, would she have been barred from entering the cafeteria? Imagining the humiliating scene was enough to make her cheeks burn. She needed to straighten out this embarrassing situation as quickly as possible.

She wove between others, perspiration prickling her skin. Not yet ten o'clock, and already the air creeping through the open windows was hot and humid. She'd likely need a change of clothes before she met with Dean Crane again. At the very least, she'd give herself a quick wash in the dormitory lavatory. What a relief to know she wouldn't be booted from the campus, thanks to her paying her room bill separately. She wouldn't receive another paycheck from the library until the end of the month, and she didn't have enough money for train fare to go home to Scott County. But how could she remain on the campus and not attend classes without feeling completely out of place? Although only five and a half years old when she was ushered through the door of the Kentucky Orphans' Asylum, she'd never forgotten the feeling of displacement, of knowing she didn't belong. She had no desire to revisit that uncomfortable feeling.

She reached the section of the building that housed the business office. Swiping away the perspiration tickling her temples, she trotted the last few yards to the end of the wide hallway, where a row of booths holding telephones were available for the students' use. A female student stood in the far right booth, chattering animatedly about attending a recent fraternity dance. Addie took the booth at the far left. She sent up a quick prayer that the girl wouldn't overhear her conversation, then lifted the handset from its cradle. Placing it to her ear, she poked her finger in the little circle for 0 and rotated the dial. She cringed at the discordant *ack-ack-ack* as the dial spun back into place.

An operator answered.

Addie cupped her hand around her mouth. "Yes, would you please connect me to the operator in Georgetown, Kentucky?"

"One moment, miss."

Addie tapped her foot and sent surreptitious glances over her shoulder while she waited for a connection. When she thought her chest might burst from impatience, a voice crackled in her ear. "Georgetown. Your number, please."

Addie recited her family's number and pressed the phone tight against her ear while shifting from foot to foot. She willed Mother to answer quickly and ease her fears, as she'd done since Addie was a child of six. Even though she hadn't been born to Penrose and Fern Cowherd, they'd always treated her as if she had. How she loved and appreciated them for taking in a sad little orphaned girl and giving her such a grand life.

"Miss?"

Addie groaned. The operator's voice again. Which meant the line must be busy. Sociable Mother was probably talking to one of her many friends.

"That number is not in service."

Addie drew back and frowned at the telephone. Had she given the wrong series of numbers? Granted, she hadn't called for quite a while, but surely she hadn't forgotten her parents' number. She closed her eyes and searched her memory. No, she'd been correct. "Are you sure you connected it properly?"

A huff met her ear. "Yes, miss, I'm sure. The number is not in service."

Maybe the telephone was broken. Telephones could break, couldn't they? Addie took a slow breath, forcing her racing pulse to calm. Daddy would be at the bank. Although she hated to bother him at work, this was an emergency. "All right, then, please dial Georgetown Citizens Bank." She

21

gave the number and gnawed a hangnail on her thumb, her pulse galloping.

"Citizens Bank. May I help you?"

Addie didn't recognize the man's voice, but she'd been away long enough to forget many of her father's coworkers. At least she'd reached the right place. "Yes. I'd like to speak to Mr. Cowherd, please."

"Penrose Cowherd?"

How many men with the surname Cowherd worked at the bank? "Yes, Penrose Cowherd."

"He's no longer employed here, miss."

Addie's legs turned to jelly. She slumped against the wall and slid down until her bottom met the narrow bench. She clung to the telephone receiver the way a drowning man gripped a life preserver. "What do you mean he isn't employed there? He's been employed there my whole life." Except for the two-year period when the bank was forced to close its doors. But the moment they'd opened again, the president had put Daddy back to work.

"Am I speaking to Addie?"

She managed a raspy yes.

"Addie, this is Mr. Bowles."

Oh, yes, Mr. Bowles — a middle-aged man with coal-black hair and a mustache to match. He'd given her clove-flavored candy sticks on visits to the bank when she was a little girl. She could speak freely with him. "Mr. Bowles, I don't understand. Why is Daddy not employed there anymore?"

"The bank got bought out. The new owner let go any man older than fifty-five. Your daddy's in his sixties, so . . ."

"When did this happen?"

"Last October."

"October?" She squawked the word. Seven months ago? How could she not have known? Yes, Daddy had been home her entire Christmas break. But when she asked why he wasn't going to work, he kissed her cheek and said, "I'd rather spend the time with you, sugar dumplin'." She'd never suspected he wasn't telling the full truth. "They probably can't afford to keep the telephone connected."

She didn't realize she'd spoken the thought until Mr. Bowles's voice rumbled in her ear. "They lost the house a month ago. According to bank gossip, they took a room in Mrs. Fee's boardinghouse."

Addie envisioned the huge clapboard building on a rise at the edge of town. With peeling paint, missing spindles on its porch railing, and a dirt yard dotted with weeds, the Fee boardinghouse was the saddest looking dwelling Addie had ever seen. Even

23

sadder than the ramshackle orphans' home where she'd spent a dismal nine months before Mother and Daddy adopted her. Tears pricked, and she bit the inside of her lip — the tactic she'd used since childhood to prevent herself from crying.

"I can give you the number there, if you want it."

She closed her eyes and rested her forehead against the wooden barrier. Her chest ached. She could hardly bear to think of her beloved parents residing in a room in the Fee boardinghouse.

"Addie? Do you want the boardinghouse's number?"

If she didn't say something, Mr. Bowles would think she'd hung up. She swallowed a knot of agony and forced her tight vocal cords to speak. "Yes. Thank you." She didn't have anything on which to write, but she chanted the number to herself as she hung up and then hooked her finger in the dial.

But she didn't turn it. She stared at the wall, puckering her brow.

Why hadn't Daddy let her know things were so bad? Why hadn't Mother told her they'd moved? Anger churned in her belly. She wasn't a child to be coddled anymore. They should have been honest with her. How cruel to let her find out on her own.

24

She expected better from her ordinarily loving parents. Even if they couldn't call, they could have written. They should have —

She jolted. Maybe they *had* written. When had she last visited her mail cubby? She cringed. Six weeks ago, at least. Caught up in sorority activities, studying, and other end-of-year programs and events, she hadn't even thought about checking for letters from home.

Guilt chased away the anger. She smacked the receiver into its cradle, bolted from the telephone booth, and headed for the mail cubbies.

TWO

Addie

Holding her breath, Addie leaned down and peered into her mail cubby. Three letters waited in her box. Her breath burst free on a little cry of regret.

She pulled them out. A quick glance confirmed all were from her parents. She pressed the envelopes to her aching chest and bit the inside of her lower lip. Hard. Punishingly hard. When they hadn't received a reply to their missives, Mother and Daddy must have thought she didn't care at all. And they were right to make such a presumption. How could she have been so neglectful?

She arranged the envelopes in chronological order according to the post office date stamps but then impulsively slapped the most recent one, sent the third of May, on top. She would read it first, although she already surmised what she would find

26

inside, given her conversations with Dean Crane and Mr. Bowles.

Likely, the letter would confirm no money was coming. She wouldn't be allowed to take her final examinations. The entire semester, all the studying and completed assignments, was wasted. Sadness — or was it anger? — struck with force. Facing Dr. Crane and admitting that her parents were unable to pay the bill would require courage. Maybe she wouldn't meet with him after all. What was the use?

With the letters gripped firmly in her hand, she set a straight path for Patterson Hall, ignoring the winding sidewalks and crossing the recently mowed grass instead. Students were discouraged from treading upon the lush lawns, and she'd always made use of the established walkways. But she wasn't a student any longer, and therefore, the rules didn't apply to her. Besides, if she didn't reach her room quickly, she might not be able to hold back the tears pressing for release. She'd nearly bitten through the tender skin behind her lip, and it wasn't helping. If she was going to cry, she would do it in private.

She reached the women's dormitory, trotted through the foyer, clattered up the staircase, then burst into her room. Felicity leaped up from the desk in the corner and spun toward the door, her blue eyes wide and her slender hand pressed to her lace bodice.

"What are you doing here?"

They asked the question at the same time. Felicity sounded confused, but aggravation tinged Addie's tone. She tamped down the unwelcome emotion and spoke more kindly. "Why aren't you in class?"

"Professor Dunbright had a toothache and canceled. So I decided to study for my biology examination, even though the subject positively bores me to tears." Felicity perched sideways on the chair, draped her hands over the chair's ladder back, and rested her chin on her knuckles. "Tell me about your meeting with Dean Crane. Was his office as dark and spooky as my guys say?" Felicity always referred to the half dozen boys who regularly ran in their circle of friends as her guys. Sometimes Addie found it endearing, and other times childish. In her present mood, the reference rankled.

"It was dark but hardly spooky." Addie plopped onto the corner of her unmade bed, sliding the letters from Mother under the rumpled sheets. "I keep telling you not to listen to the guys. They like to exaggerate."

"I know." Felicity wrinkled her nose, giggling. "But they're so cute. I can't ignore them."

Addie lowered her head and fiddled with the envelopes, stifling a sigh. How had she and Felicity formed such a tight bond, given their many differences? Felicity was an active member of the arts-and-theater sorority, while Addie had pledged the literary sorority. Felicity was flighty and prone to giggles, but Addie — having been raised by loving but older, no-nonsense parents — rarely indulged in giggling or impulsive behavior. If thinking before speaking was a sport, Felicity would always be at the bottom of the heap. Even so, Addie had grown to love her roommate as a sister, and she didn't doubt Felicity felt the same way about her. Could she trust her with this recent, unsettling news?

She looked up and started to speak, but Felicity was bent over the desk again, apparently studying. Knowing how difficult it was for the girl to stay focused for any length of time, she chose not to disturb her. She slid the latest letter from beneath the sheets and carefully opened the flap. After stretching out on her side with her back to

Felicity, she removed the sheets of Mother's flowered stationery from the envelope and unfolded them.

Our dearest Adeladybug . . .

The childhood nickname took her back to rosy days of love and laughter. How writing this letter must have pained Mother, whose kindness was such that she couldn't even swat a fly without feeling guilty for ending its life. Tears filled Addie's eyes, and she blinked to clear them.

I'm sorry to send so many dismal missives. We are sure you are reeling and uncertain how to respond. Yet your daddy and I believe you are old enough to accept these realities and need to be aware of how our lives have so rapidly changed. Or perhaps not so rapidly, as we have been on a slow descent for quite some time.

You likely noticed the new address on the envelope. We no longer have our house on Briar Drive. The bank foreclosed on it. We are sad, but we aren't bitter. After all, we had many happy years there, and the bank is only doing what it must to recover its money. If we'd more prudently used our reserve when Daddy lost his job in '30, perhaps things would be different, but one cannot go back in time. So we choose to move forward and look for the blessings.

Addie smiled. So many times she'd heard Mother say, "Look for the blessings, Addie." Mother believed the promise in Romans 8:28 that all things — even the hard things of life — worked for the good of the believer. Mother was the most steadfast believer Addie knew. She'd taught Addie to pray and instilled in her the habit of reading from God's Word at the start of the day. Maybe when Addie grew up all the way, she would be as strong in faith as her mother.

Her smile faded, though, when she reread, *"If we'd more prudently used our reserve when Daddy lost his job in '30 . . ."* During those two years, when the bank's doors remained locked and Daddy was without a job, they had continued to pay for her ballet and piano lessons, allowed her sweets from the candy shop every Saturday, bought her new dresses each season. Had they not indulged her, would they have had the funds to save the house? Guilt nibbled at her, and she lifted the letter again.

Our biggest concern now is for you. Our room here at the boardinghouse is spacious enough to accommodate our bedroom furniture and our favorite chairs from the parlor, so we have a sitting area in which to relax. With photographs and a few favorite pieces of bric-a-brac surrounding us, we've made it a cheerful place, but it is only one room. If you were a little girl, we could tuck a cot in the corner for you; however, you're far too grown up to share a room with your parents. The boardinghouse is full — we were fortunate to secure this room. My tears flow as I write, but I don't know where you will stay when you return to Georgetown.

Daddy is searching for employment, and you know how determined he is. As soon as he is working and we've been able to save a little money, we will move into a house with a second bedroom for our sweet little ladybug. You haven't been cast out forever. (Daddy says to assure you that the books from his study, all your belongings, and the furniture from your room are safely stored in the loft of Preacher Finley's barn. We sold many items from the house, but Daddy adamantly refused to sell your beloved books or anything else of importance to you, and I agreed with him.)

An image formed in her head of her parents — gentle Mother, proud Daddy — carefully saving the things that mattered to her but selling their furniture and personal effects to strangers or, even worse, to their neighbors. The indignity of such an event . . . Why had God allowed them to suffer so? Tears filled her eyes again. She bit down until she tasted blood, but no amount of biting on her lip could stem the tide. A sob broke from her throat, a second burst out behind it, and she dissolved into a wailing mess.

Feet pattered on the floor, and warm arms surrounded her. "Addie, Addie . . ." Felicity rocked her the way Mother had when Addie was small and frightened by a storm. "What is it, dear one? Did Dean Crane say something to frighten you? Oh, I should have paid more attention to you than to my silly biology book. I'm so sorry."

Her parents were burdened with a guilt they shouldn't have to bear. She wouldn't leave Felicity to suffer self-recrimination. She pulled loose and wiped her face with the corner of her sheet. "It isn't your fault. Of course you need to study. I'm sorry I

33

disturbed you."

"Don't be ridiculous. You're more important to me than any old test ever could be." Felicity pushed a strand of hair from Addie's cheek, then caught hold of her hands. Her full lips formed a sympathetic pout. "I've never seen you cry. Something must be horribly wrong. Please tell me. I'll do whatever I can to help."

Addie sniffed hard, her lower lip wobbling. "I doubt there's anything you can do, but I'll tell you anyway." She relayed her conversations with the dean and Mr. Bowles and details from Mother's letter. As Addie spoke, Felicity's mouth fell open and her eyebrows shot so high they nearly disappeared beneath her carefully coiffed bangs. Her explanation complete, Addie hung her head and shrugged. "So, there you have it. I'm . . . expelled, and I have nowhere to go."

"Barred from class and even from the cafeteria? How uncivilized! What do they expect you to do, starve to death?" Felicity bolted to her feet and paced back and forth in the narrow space between the beds, waving her arms. "The dean of students is supposed to defend students, not defeat them. If Ol' Ichabod won't do his job, then I'll start a petition. I'll organize a protest. I'll paint banners and assign students to march in front of the administration building while calling for —"

Addie grabbed Felicity's arm and pulled her onto the mattress. "You'll do no such things."

"But when people know what's happened to you, they'll —"

"No, Felicity."

Felicity twisted loose and glared. "Yes, Addie. It must be done. You must be vindicated."

Addie took hold of Felicity's shoulders. "Listen to me. The school can't allow me to attend classes or eat meals for free. How would that be fair to the students who are paying?" What about the balance she still owed? How would she pay the outstanding bill? She dropped her hands to her lap and heaved a huge sigh. "It's not Dean Crane's fault. He's only doing his job."

Felicity blinked rapidly. "But, Addie, you're my best friend in the whole wide world. How can I sit here and do nothing to help?"

Addie sent her a sidelong look. "Do you really want to help?"

"You know I do!"

"Then" — Addie offered a weak grin — "could you maybe sneak me a sandwich from the cafeteria? I didn't have breakfast, and I'm famished."

Felicity rose so quickly the mattress bounced. "A sandwich? Oh, no, my dear, I'll bring you something hot and hearty, even if I have to carry it out in my pockets." She marched to the door, hands clenched into fists and arms pumping. "Wait here. I'll be back in two shakes of a lamb's tail." She paused in the doorway and cast a sorrowful look over her shoulder. "I wish I had lots of money. I'd pay your bill."

Addie's heart rolled over in her chest. "You're a good friend, Felicity. Thank you."

With a nod, she scurried out of the room.

Addie picked up Mother's letter. She sniffed, cleared the moisture from her eyes with a sweep of the back of her hand, and focused on Mother's precise penmanship.

Your daddy and I are praying for you, asking God to comfort your aching heart and to provide for you. We remind ourselves that He is better equipped to meet your needs than we are, and we trust Him to guide and protect you. I do hope you'll find the time to write. Even if you only want to rail at us and com-

plain, we still want to hear from you.
                    We love you forever and always,
                                            Mother

Addie read the other two letters, then folded them all together. She held the stack against her bodice and eased backward until her spine met the mattress. Her feet dangling toward the floor, she stared at the painted ceiling. When she was very young, before Mother and Daddy adopted her from the orphanage, she often lay awake at night and stared out the window at the sky, searching for a falling star on which to make a wish. The wish was always the same. She whispered it now. "I wish I had a daddy and mama to love me."

God had heard her little-girl wish and sent Penrose and Fern Cowherd to rescue her from that dreary place. Mother and Daddy often said God chose her specially just for them, but she knew the opposite was true. She had a few fuzzy memories of the parents who'd birthed her, and they had been good people, but she couldn't imagine better parents than the ones who'd adopted her.

"Even if you only want to rail at us and complain, we still want to hear from you."

Addie pushed off the bed and hurried to the desk. She slid Felicity's books aside, retrieved paper and a pen from the drawer, and smacked them onto the desktop. A letter formed in her mind. She would not rail at and complain to the wonderful people who'd taken her into their home and loved her as their own. First, she would apologize for not writing sooner. Then she would thank them for everything they'd done for her. Finally, she would promise to get them out of that awful boardinghouse. They didn't belong there any more than she had belonged in the orphans' asylum.

A plan unfolded. She would find a job, save every cent possible, and send it to Mother and Daddy. Lexington was larger than Georgetown. Surely there were opportunities here for a girl to make an honest wage. It meant putting off her own plans for her future, but what kind of daughter would she be if she gave in to her selfish wants and left her parents in need? They'd rescued her. Now she would rescue them.

She took up the pen and wrote, "Dearest Mother and Daddy . . ."

THREE

Addie

After she finished the flavorful chicken and dumplings Felicity brought from the cafeteria — which she carried in a bowl, thank goodness, and not in her pocket — Addie set off for the Lexington Public Library. She needed solace and would find it there. Had she really awakened only a few short hours ago lighthearted, secure in her world, and with a carefree summer stretching before her? So quickly her life had changed, and the uncertainties now looming ahead rested heavily on her shoulders. Even so, she caught herself walking with a bounce in her step. And why not? How could anyone, even someone burdened with cares and woes, trudge along when something as wondrous as a library waited at the end of the pathway?

She'd thanked God dozens of times in the past three years for the opportunity to work in the beautiful neoclassical building that was constructed at the edge of Gratz Park thirty years ago, thanks to a generous donation from Andrew Carnegie. The one-mile route from the university campus led more directly to the library's back door, but Addie always walked the additional yards needed to enter from the front. Every time she ascended the library's concrete steps and crossed between a pair of its two-story-high fluted columns, she experienced a chill of delight. Books! How she loved books. The clean or musty smell, depending on the book's age. The weightiness in her hands. The joy of discovery as the words printed on a piece of paper formed pictures in her mind. Was there anything more magical or satisfying than a book?

Had her fascination begun with the stories Mother read to her each bedtime from the first day of her adoption on, or did it go back even further to the short years before she became Adelaide Cowherd? She couldn't be sure. All she knew was that books were a marvelous invention, and a novel bearing the name A. F. Penrose — didn't combining her and her parents' names create an authorly ring? — on its cover would stand proud one day on library shelves across the state. Perhaps across the entire nation.

She ran the last few feet to the wide stairway and pattered up the center, as she always did, taking a direct shot to the tall door framed in its ostentatious plaster casing. She entered the building, closed the door with care to avoid even so much as a muffled snap, then paused on the mosaic floor of the vestibule. Silence engulfed her. Peace wove its way through her frame. She drew in a deep breath, and as she exhaled, her worries seemed to drift away. Ah, such a haven.

Today's desk librarian, a middle-aged spinster named Miss Collins, looked up from behind the half-octagon-shaped desk that filled the floor space near the open, railed staircase leading to the second story. Her gaze met Addie's, and she smiled, then beckoned with her fingers.

Addie crossed to the desk and rested her arms on its cool marble top. "Good afternoon." She spoke in a whisper. Mother had taught her that one never desecrated the studious atmosphere of a library by speaking loudly.

"Good afternoon, Addie. I'm glad to see you." Miss Collins also whispered, and her breath held the scent of peppermint. Daddy sucked Reed's peppermint discs because he said they settled his stomach. Miss Collins must suffer frequent tummy upset, because Addie had never seen her without a white disc tucked in her cheek. She lifted a thick book from a built-in cubby and placed it upside down between Addie's elbows. "Look what came in, fresh from the publisher."

Addie turned the book over and gasped. "A new Christie novel!"

The librarian grinned. "Yes. The way you raved over *Murder on the Orient Express* and *Death in the Clouds,* I was certain you'd want to be the first to check out *The A.B.C. Murders.*" Then her bright expression faded. "Oh . . . You're preparing for final examinations, aren't you? You probably don't have time to engage in reading for enjoyment."

Addie swallowed. She hadn't intended to divulge the news of her expulsion to anyone except the head librarian, Mrs. Carrie Hunt, but Miss Collins might take the book back if Addie didn't admit the truth. She smoothed the glossy dustcover, relishing the fresh newness beneath her fingers. The book hadn't even been cataloged yet or the dustcover would have been removed.

Desire to be the very first person to crack the pages of Mrs. Christie's newest novel rose and spilled out. "I'll have time. My studies are all complete." Strange how one could speak the truth without sharing the entire truth. Strange, too, how the statement left her feeling a little sneaky and guilty.

"Good for you. I'll get a card ready, and you can be the first to sign it."

"Thank you." She observed Miss Collins's activities, trying not to fidget. The woman was very knowledgeable and adept at her job, but sometimes she reminded Addie of a sloth. "Is Mrs. Hunt in her office?"

"She should be." Miss Collins meticulously dabbed glue onto the back of a yellow manila library envelope. "I didn't see her come in, but she always returns from lunch promptly at half past twelve." The tip of her tongue poked out the corner of her mouth as she pressed the envelope inside the back cover.

"I'll go up and talk to her, then come for the book."

"That sounds fine."

Addie mounted the stairs on her tiptoes, unwilling for her shoes' metal heel protectors to click on the marble treads. She entered her favorite room in the library, the reading room, and moved past tables, each lit by a hanging chandelier and set in a neat configuration around the rails that opened to the floor below. A half dozen patrons sat at various tables, but none even glanced up at Addie's passage. All engrossed in their reading, it seemed. A smile trembled on her lips. Such a glorious gift authors gave to readers — an escape into another world. Writers enlightened and entertained and excited simply by stringing words together. Having discovered the joy books provided, she longed to offer a similar delight to others. And she would. Someday.

On the left side of the room, short hallways sprouted in opposite directions and led to smaller rooms. Addie chose the rear hallway, which took her to the library director's office. A pair of raised-panel doors, nearly ten feet high, stood open in silent invitation, but Addie paused and tapped lightly on the doorjamb.

"Come in."

She stepped over the threshold into the long, narrow office. Mrs. Hunt sat at her desk. The height of the ceiling dwarfed every piece of furniture in the room, giving the space a dollhouse-like appearance. The woman was busily writing in a journal of some sort, so Addie waited beside the door until Mrs. Hunt set the pen aside and looked up. Surprise registered on her face.

"Why, Addie, I didn't realize you were on

the schedule today."

"I'm not. I n-needed to talk to you." The stutter surprised her. Perhaps this conversation would be more difficult than she'd originally imagined.

A frown creased Mrs. Hunt's forehead. "Is something wrong?"

"Yes, ma'am." Her legs suddenly felt shaky. She wished she could sit, but the only other chair in the room was in the corner, which would put far too much distance between them. Addie forced her feet to carry her over the unstained maple floorboards. She stopped on the opposite side of the desk, sucked in a fortifying breath, and blurted, "My daddy lost his job. He couldn't pay my tuition bill, so I can't finish the semester. He and Mother moved into a boardinghouse, and there isn't room for me there. Thus, I need to secure a job in Lexington. May I hire on here full time?"

Mrs. Hunt stared at her blankly for several seconds, eyeglasses glinting from the bulbs in the chandelier hanging above her desk. Then she abruptly rose, rounded the desk, and gripped Addie's upper arms. "My dear, I wish I could say yes. You've been a very dependable worker. But my operating budget has been cut twice in the past three years. This economic depression — it affects so many things, you know."

Yes, Addie knew. She offered a weak smile. "I understand."

The library director released Addie and folded her arms over her chest. "I would happily write you a recommendation for any potential employers if that would be helpful."

Given the woman's fine reputation in town, her recommendation was worth a great deal. Addie nodded. "Thank you, ma'am, I would appreciate that very much."

Mrs. Hunt started around the desk, her steps brisk. "Then I shall write it this afternoon and give it to you tomorrow at the end of your shift." She stopped and aimed a mild frown in Addie's direction. "You do intend to continue your part-time position here until the end of the month, as originally planned?"

"Yes, ma'am. I made a commitment, and Daddy says we should always honor our commitments." Not to mention she needed the money.

A smile softened the woman's expression. "You have a wise daddy who raised a fine, responsible daughter." Mrs. Hunt settled in her chair and linked her hands on top of the open journal. She angled her head and fixed a solemn look on Addie. "I'll be honest. Most young women, if faced with your situation, would wallow in self-pity or spew with anger. I'm proud of the way you're approaching the problem. I'm sure your parents are proud of you, too."

A knot filled Addie's throat, hindering her from speaking. She gave a quick nod, which she hoped Mrs. Hunt would interpret as a thank-you. She turned toward the door.

"Addie, just a moment."

Addie looked back.

"Whatever decent employment opportunities exist in Lexington will be listed in the classified section of the *Lexington Herald.*"

"Yes, I planned to buy a paper and look through the classifieds for a room to let." Panic tried to attack. The dormitories would close after graduation. Only one week away. Where would she go if she couldn't find a place to live? *"Your daddy and I are praying for you . . ."* Part of Mother's letter whispered in Addie's memory and encouraged her to remain hopeful. "I'll search the help wanted section, too."

"Well, please make use of the library's copy rather than unnecessarily spending a nickel."

Addie wouldn't argue about saving her money. "Thank you, ma'am. I'll do that." She left Mrs. Hunt's office and returned to the reading room.

Those poring over books seemed so peaceful. Temptation to go down to the first floor and retrieve the copy of *The A.B.C. Murders* tugged hard. She'd find blissful escape in an Agatha Christie mystery. How she needed an escape from the harsh reality that had befallen her like an unexpected thunderstorm. But Mrs. Hunt had called her responsible. A responsible person would see to business first and pleasure second. Setting aside the selfish desire, she tiptoed between tables to the door that opened into the periodical room.

One quarter the size of the reading room, crowded with freestanding shelves and sporting only one overhead chandelier above the center of three tables jammed end to end, the periodical room seemed gloomy — much like Dean Crane's office — in comparison. She'd take the newspaper to the reading room for examination. She hurried to the rack of stained dowel rods, where the latest issues of the five newspapers purchased by the library could be displayed.

Four of the five rods held folded sheets of newsprint. Addie scanned the titles — *Mount Vernon Signal, Public Ledger, Kentucky Irish American, Lexington Leader* — and stifled a little huff of irritation. Where was the *Lexing-*

48

ton Herald? Sometimes patrons didn't return items to their rightful places. How many times had she found books on the wrong shelves or magazines lying on chairs? She scanned the room, seeking a newspaper discarded on a desk or tucked on a shelf. At the far end of the row of tables, in front of the single tall window in the corner of the room, a lone figure hunched over a newspaper. No doubt the very newspaper Addie needed.

She remained in place for several seconds, observing the man. His stiff pose and unwavering focus on the newsprint in front of him spoke of deep concentration. She wanted to ask if he was nearly finished, but she'd been taught to treat others the way she wished to be treated. She didn't appreciate people interrupting her reading, so she'd have to be patient and wait her turn. In the meantime, Agatha Christie's new novel was waiting.

Addie spun on her heel and returned to the checkout desk, moving as swiftly yet as quietly as possible. Miss Collins slid the crisp new checkout card across the desk with a smile, and Addie wrote her name on the first line. Then, with the book tucked safely in the crook of her arm, she hurried up the stairs and chose the table closest to the periodical room door. She sat facing the door so she'd be sure to notice the gentleman leaving, and she opened the book.

It was in June of 1935 that I came home from my ranch in South America for a stay of about six months . . .

As expected, she was pulled immediately into the story's world. She turned page after page, eyes swallowing paragraphs of text. Sometimes smiling, sometimes nodding, occasionally biting her thumbnail or pressing her hand to her chest. She flipped a page and encountered the heading, *Six: The Scene of the Crime.* She gave a start. Chapter six already? How long had she been reading?

A tall grandfather clock, its chime silenced, stood sentry in the corner of the room. She glanced at its face and gasped. Almost three o'clock? She'd been caught up in the book for well over an hour. Was the man still reading the newspaper?

She leaped up and darted around the table and into the periodical room. The table near the window was empty, and the newspaper was draped neatly over the top rod of the rack. Inwardly berating herself for being so unaware of her surroundings, she yanked the paper from its rod and flopped it open on the closest table. She turned to the final section, where the classified ads were always printed.

The entire page where help wanted and rooms-to-let posts should be was missing.

"That creep!" She clapped her hand over her mouth and sent a quick look left and right. Not another soul in the room. She smacked the tabletop and spoke aloud again. "What an absolute creep."

FOUR

Emmett recorded the address for the last job opportunity listed — feather plucker at a chicken plant outside town — then wadded up the sheet of newsprint. He started to toss it into the small wastebasket next to his desk but paused, his hand in midair. Maw would say he'd stolen the section from the library's newspaper, and she'd be right. Paw would snort and say, "A feller who's s'posed to be so smart can sure act dumb." It pained Emmett to admit it, but Paw would be right. All his studying for final examinations must have numbed his brain if he forgot to take something as basic as paper and a pen to the library.

He balanced the crumpled ball of paper on his palm, frowning. Should he return the page to the library? He didn't care to make that long walk from his room in Bradley Hall to the library for a second time in one day. Especially with it being so hot and muggy out. Still, someone else might need to read the help wanted ads. Not that there were countless options. He smoothed the page as flat as possible on the desk. Wrinkles, smudges, and little tears on the edges marred the sheet of newsprint. The library wouldn't want it now. He turned it into a ball, lobbed it into the wastebasket, then put his head in his hands and groaned. He might as well wad up his hard-earned college diploma, too. What use was his degree if no businesses were hiring managers?

When Mr. Halcomb, the teacher back in Boone's Hollow, first mentioned going to college, Emmett had thought the man addlebrained. Nobody from Emmett's family, nor anyone from Boone's Hollow as far as he knew, had ever gone to a university. Most men either put in an honest day's work in the coal mines or dodged revenuers and sold distilled whiskey. Paw had wanted Emmett to sign on at the mine as soon as he turned fifteen to help support the family. But Mr. Halcomb said a mind like his shouldn't be wasted. So, to Paw's chagrin, Emmett had stayed in school all the way to twelfth grade and, mostly to make the teacher happy, took the scholarship test. He was more surprised than Paw when he got the letter from the university telling him he'd won.

Every year for four years straight, he'd received scholarship money to pay for tuition, room, board, and books. A waste of time, Paw called it. A blessing, Maw called it. He heard her proud voice in his head. "The Almighty has big plans for you if He's rainin' down such a blessin'." Emmett had always thought Maw was right. Until now. He glared at the list of possible jobs he'd written on his notepad. Not one of them looked like the means to fulfill big plans. Each looked more like a joke.

He shoved the list aside. "I should've stayed put, gone to the mines, like Paw said."

"What was that, ol' bloke?"

Emmett jerked sideways in the chair and looked over his shoulder. His roommate stood in the open doorway, grinning like the hills men did after sampling too much of their homemade corn liquor. Emmett gritted his teeth. How long had Spence been standing there watching him?

" 'Fraid you'll need to repeat it. I didn't catch it the first time."

"Never mind. Was talking to myself." Embarrassment gruffed Emmett's voice.

Spence caught the edge of the door with

his heel and sent it into its frame. "Talkin' to yourself's fine. So long as you don't ask questions and then answer yourself. That's plain loco." He dropped his armload of books on the bed and shrugged out of his suit coat. He tossed the coat on top of the books, then ambled to the desk.

Spence leaned on the corner, crossed his arms, and frowned at Emmett. "Studyin' again? You put the rest of us to shame, y'know, with your read, read, read. You've gotta be more ready for next week's final exams than any other fella on the whole campus. Why not let up on yourself some, Tharp?"

Emmett fiddled with the corner of the page where he'd recorded the list of jobs. "Wasn't studying. More like thinking. Planning." And coming up empty.

"Plannin' what?"

Emmett tilted his head and met Spence's grin. The color of his roommate's eyes, eyebrows, and hair matched the reddish-brown freckles dotting his entire face. Even though Spence was twenty-two years old, same as Emmett, all those freckles made him look a lot younger. He acted younger, too. Or maybe Emmett acted old. Sometimes he sure felt old.

Spence bumped Emmett's shoulder with

his elbow. "Hey, I asked a question. Plannin' what?"

Even if Emmett told Spence how bleak the future looked, the other man wouldn't understand. His family lived on a horse ranch outside Lexington, and he'd confessed early on that he only enrolled in college to get out of working all day in the stables. He said he'd rather take tests than take care of the thoroughbred quarter horses his daddy raised. Did he know how lucky he was to have a family business he could step into? Probably not.

Emmett shrugged. "It's not important."

Spence stared hard at Emmett for several seconds, then pushed off from the desk. "Well, I'm fixin' to get some supper." Grinning, he rubbed his flat belly. "Skipped lunch so I'd have plenty of room. Friday night fish fry in the cafeteria. My favorite. You ready to go?"

If Spence'd had to gut and scrape scales from fish as often as Emmett had while growing up, he might not find the weekly fried fish so appealing. Besides, the dismal opportunities written in black pen on white paper had robbed Emmett of his appetite. He waved his hand. "Go ahead. I'll see you later."

Spence gave him a hearty smack on the

shoulder and took off toward the door. "Suit yourself. You're goin' to the bonfire later, though, aren't you?"

Emmett had forgotten about the traditional end-of-year bonfire, when students burned old reports or tests or whatever else they took a mind to. Students loved the bonfire, loved the chance to blow off steam before the pressure of finals week. They made it a rowdy affair. The whole thing seemed silly to him, but he went because his fraternity organized the event. This year he'd served as secretary for Delta Sigma Phi, so it'd look plenty funny if he didn't show. He gave a weak nod. "I'm going."

Spence saluted. "Good! See you there, then." He sauntered out, leaving the door open behind him.

Emmett slumped low in the chair and pinched his chin. If he already had his diploma, maybe he'd burn it. Seemed a fitting act, considering how worthless the sheepskin was turning out to be.

Addie

Why had she let Felicity talk her into attending the bonfire? Addie stood well away from the crackling flames and the milling throng of laughing, shouting, celebrating students. She'd wanted to post her letter to

57

her parents, but Felicity had said she could walk to the post office any old time, but when else could she attend the end-of-year bonfire? The question had stung. Unless Daddy found a good-paying job quickly, she might never return to the university.

Felicity had encouraged her to try for a scholarship, and she appreciated her friend's confidence in her, but she couldn't bank on receiving one. Not when so many students applied and only a few were awarded. No, she needed to accept the probability that there would be no more classes, no more sorority get-togethers, no more bonfires. So she'd accompanied Felicity to the sporting arena. But she found no joy in the celebration. Maybe she should return to her room, where it would be quiet, and read some more chapters from the Christie novel.

The desire for escape won. Inching sideways around the periphery of the group, she searched the crowd of revelers for Felicity. Her roommate's shining cap of hair should be easy to spot, even under the moonlight, but Addie made a complete circle without spotting her. Well, she'd given it her best try. She turned in the direction of the women's dormitories, but a young man stood in her way. He seemed oblivious to her presence, his focus locked on the bonfire. She started to excuse herself and step around him, but something about him seemed vaguely familiar.

She tipped her head and examined him from head to toe. Short-cropped brown hair — or maybe closer to blond — shone with oil and lay combed away from his forehead. His square, clean-shaven face wore a solemn, almost-melancholy expression as he peered beyond her. Attired in brown trousers and a matching double-breasted suit coat with a white shirt, no tie, he resembled any number of male students on campus. Except those attending the bonfire had shed their jackets and piled them in a heap at the edge of the field. This student held a formal pose, as if removing his jacket and joining in the fun were beyond his ability.

Her gaze landed on the scuffed toes of his lace-up shoes, then traveled slowly upward again. When it reached his eyes, it collided with his intense scrutiny. Heat completely unrelated to the roaring flames a few yards away seared her face. She took a single step to the right, eager to flee.

His brows pulled into a puzzled frown. "Do I know you?"

She paused. "I . . . I don't think so." His question gave her permission to stare into his eyes. Firelight bounced on his face, giving her sporadic glimpses of his features. She couldn't be sure if his eyes behind the glass of his round wire spectacles were green or blue, but his attention was unwavering. She almost squirmed beneath it. Within seconds she'd determined he wasn't in any of her classes. She was equally certain she'd never seen him at any of the combined sorority and fraternity gatherings, nor in the cafeteria.

Suddenly, he gave a little jolt and snapped his fingers. "I know where I've seen you. You were at —"

Her mouth fell open, realization dawning. "The library," she chorused with him.

A smile broke over his face, completely transforming him. "You were there reading today, weren't you?"

She nodded. And he was the creep who'd stolen the most important part of the newspaper. Or maybe he hadn't. Maybe someone else had taken it before he got to it. Maybe he wasn't a creep after all. He didn't seem like a creep, with firelight rippling across his face and tall, solid frame.

"I'm Emmett Tharp."

"I'm Addie Cowherd." Addie extended her hand, and his warm fingers encased it for only a brief second — a perfect gentlemanly handshake, Mother would say.

"It's nice to meet you." He slipped his hands into his jacket pockets, as if settling in for a lengthy chat. "I didn't know you were a student here."

Given the size of the campus and the number of students attending classes, she wasn't surprised their paths hadn't crossed before. What did surprise her was the niggle of regret settling in her chest. Here they were at the end of the year, and she most likely wouldn't return next year. And somehow she'd failed to make his acquaintance earlier. Getting to know him now presented a challenge for more reasons than the short amount of time remaining in the semester. The bonfire, with all its noise and revelry, made a less-than-ideal setting for conversation.

She linked her hands behind her back and raised her voice. "I'm a junior in the College of Education."

"You want to be a teacher?"

She shrugged. The courses offered the best preparation for becoming an author, but she hadn't shared her dream with anyone besides her parents and a trusted teacher or two, and she certainly wouldn't open up that secret part of herself to someone she'd recently met, no matter how kind and charming he appeared. "What degree

61

are you seeking?"

An odd look creased his face — half frustration, half sorrow. "I'm a senior, graduating with a bachelor of science in commerce."

A senior. So he wouldn't be back next year either, although for a different reason. She wanted to ask whether he intended to open his own business, but a rousing cheer rose from the crowd behind her. He angled his frame slightly and peered past her, and she turned around.

The crowd was separating, forming a circle around the dying flames. They slung their arms around one another's shoulders and gently swayed to and fro. A male voice began to sing, " 'Should auld acquaintance be forgot . . .' "

Dozens of others joined. " 'And never brought to mind?' "

A lump filled Addie's throat. Was it too late to join the circle? She wanted the kinship the others were experiencing. Did Emmett Tharp also wish to join in? If he went, she would go, too, and they could become part of the singing and swaying. She glanced over her shoulder, hoping to see the same longing that twined through her reflected in his expression.

But he wasn't there.

She spun and surveyed the area. Finally, in the waning shadows, she spotted his retreating figure. With his hands still in his pockets, his head low and feet scuffing through the grass, his dismal posture increased the sadness settling in her heart.

FIVE

Addie

"Hurry now. We don't want to let in any flies."

"Yes, ma'am." Addie held one suitcase in front and the other behind her, watching both front and back as she crossed Miss Collins's back door threshold. If she bumped the doorjamb, she might damage what appeared to be a recent coat of white paint. Miss Collins was kind enough to allow Addie to stay with her temporarily, so she'd strive to be the best houseguest ever.

She entered a small kitchen, and Miss Collins snapped the door closed behind her. Addie placed her suitcases on the shiny clean linoleum floor. A sigh of relief eased from her throat. Carrying the packed cases the entire half-mile walk from the university to Miss Collins's little bungalow on South Upper Street had taxed her muscles. She might not be able to lift so much as a magazine come Monday morning. At least her walk to work would now be cut in half.

Miss Collins stepped past the suitcases and faced Addie, hands on her hips. "Are you all checked out at the dormitory?"

"Yes, ma'am."

"And you made your way here with no problems?"

"Yes, ma'am." Addie blinked several times, wincing. An uncovered bulb hung from the center of the papered ceiling on a strand of brown twisted wire. Its light glared off the white painted cabinets, white enamel stove, and white electric refrigerator. Were it not for the mottled-green linoleum covering both the floor and countertops and the green gingham curtains gracing the single window, the room would have no color at all. So different from Mother's cheery red, yellow, and blue kitchen at home.

Home . . . She no longer had a home. She swallowed a knot of sorrow.

"I imagine it feels good to be done with another school year."

Addie contemplated an appropriate response. She couldn't honestly say she felt *good.* After all, a half year's efforts were lost, she had no idea when or if she'd be able to return to school, and her entire future looked bleak. Felicity had fussed at her, claiming Addie would wither up and die if she didn't do something fun, but she'd avoided closing activities. Instead, she'd spent the last days of the school year seeking a place of employment. And failing. What would she have done if Miss Collins hadn't offered to host her for a while? Her active imagination painted pictures in her head, and she shuddered. "I really appreciate you taking me in. I promise I won't be a nuisance."

The woman laughed. "If I'd feared such, I wouldn't have offered you a room. Let me show you where you'll stay." She turned and moved at a brisk pace.

Addie grabbed the handles of her suitcases and straightened, stifling a groan as her arm muscles complained, and followed the librarian into a sparsely furnished dining room. A wide doorway on the opposite side of the room revealed a parlor with a sofa and pair of chairs, all upholstered in a dreary green velvet. The walls were papered, but the paper was so old the color had nearly faded away, leaving behind only muted smudges of what Addie surmised had once been flowers. Although the rooms appeared drab in comparison to her childhood home, she didn't spot a speck of dust anywhere. She'd need to be extra fastidious and not offend her hostess.

Miss Collins entered the opening of a narrow hallway, then came to a halt and turned a rueful grimace on Addie. "There are only two bedrooms in my house. When my mother passed away, bless her departed soul, I moved the sewing machine from the corner of the dining room to her bedroom. I confess there isn't a great deal of space in there. You'll be crammed in tight as a cork in a bottle."

Memories of her spacious bedroom in the house on Briar Drive in Georgetown flooded Addie's mind. She forced herself to smile. "I'm sure it will be fine."

Miss Collins patted Addie's arm. "Anything's better than a cot at the YWCA, hmm?"

"Yes, ma'am."

"And as for calling me ma'am, for the duration of your stay, I'd prefer you use my given name, which is Griselda Ann." The woman's dark eyebrows lowered. "When we're not at work, of course."

"Of course." Addie wouldn't have guessed the plain woman living in a plain house would have such a lovely name. "Thank you, Griselda."

"Griselda Ann."

"Griselda Ann," Addie repeated, commanding herself not to chortle. The only time anyone used her own full name was when she'd been up to mischief, which wasn't often. She was willing to wager Griselda Ann never got up to mischief.

"Well, come along now, Addie." Griselda Ann entered the dark hallway and turned right. Addie trailed her to a closed door. Her hostess opened the door, revealing a shadowed space. She reached inside, a click sounded, and the room lit up. Griselda Ann plastered herself to the wall and held her hand in invitation for Addie to enter the bedroom-turned-sewing room.

Addie inched sideways to the doorway, suitcases bouncing against her legs, then stopped. Her mouth fell open, and she gawked, hardly able to believe her eyes. Color — every color imaginable — exploded from all corners of the room. She took a stumbling step forward, gaze darting from ceiling-high stacks of what seemed to be articles of clothing to the sewing machine, which held a partially completed quilt, to a basket overflowing with fabric pieces, to a table wedged in the corner at the foot of the bed and weighted down with . . . something. Curiosity coiling through her, Addie placed her suitcases on the multicolored patchwork quilt covering the bed and edged her way around to the table. Quilt tops. Dozens of them, all folded and stacked like a tower of pancakes.

She turned an astounded look on Griselda Ann. "You made these?"

Pride glimmered in the woman's tawny-brown eyes. "Indeed, I did." She crossed the threshold but remained just inside the door. "Folks from my church, and some others in town who want to be helpful, bring clothes that are too worn to wear. I cut the clothes into pieces, then sew the pieces together again. About once a month, I take the tops to church, and a group of women put batting between pairs of them, bind them, and tie them together. Then we hand them out to people in need."

Addie ran her hand down the stack of tops, silently counting. "You made all of these in a month?"

"I did."

Addie would never ask, but she couldn't help wondering how someone who moved so slowly at work had accomplished such a feat. Her expression must have communicated her confusion, though.

A grin lifted the corners of Griselda Ann's thin lips. "I live alone, Addie. Nobody needs my attention, so I spend nearly every waking minute that I'm not at the library sitting right there" — she pointed at the round stool in front of the sewing machine — "putting pieces together."

Addie gaped at the stack. Griselda Ann must stay awake most of the night. Suddenly, the woman's sloth-like behavior at the library made sense.

Griselda Ann sighed. "Oh, none of these quilts are works of art, not like the pretty one on the bed here that my mama made before I was born, but a person who needs a blanket to ward off the winter chill doesn't much care what it looks like."

"But they are pretty." Addie lifted the top one, unfolded it, and held it in front of her, admiring the perfectly matched squares of various fabrics. "They remind me of Joseph's coat of many colors."

"Why, that's probably the nicest thing anyone's ever said to me." Tears winked in Griselda Ann's eyes.

If she'd never heard anything kinder than Addie's simple comment, this woman truly needed encouragement. Addie impulsively scurried across the narrow slice of open floor and gave her hostess a hug. A worry tiptoed through her heart, and she pulled back. "Will my being here interfere with your blanket making?"

"Well, it might. Because I won't intrude

70

upon your privacy." Griselda Ann sucked in her lips, brow furrowing. She peered in the direction of the sewing machine, and Addie believed she witnessed longing in the woman's expression.

"Maybe . . ." Should she offer? Addie had never used a sewing machine nor done any kind of stitchwork. She might do more harm than good. But perhaps Griselda Ann could teach her. Daddy always said the wise person grasped opportunities for learning. She touched the woman's arm. "If you show me how, I could cut the clothes into pieces for you. I could . . . help."

Griselda Ann's face lit. "Oh, if I had fabric squares ready to go, I could double the number of tops produced in a week." She grabbed Addie in a hug so tight it stole her breath. "Thank you."

Addie laughed, wriggling. Griselda Ann released her hold, and Addie smiled. "It's the least I can do to repay you for your kindness. Truly, I don't know what I'd do if you hadn't offered me a place to stay." What a wonderful feeling, to know she was secure. For now. But Mother always advised against overstaying one's welcome. "I want you to know, I won't take advantage of your kindness. I intend to keep seeking employment, and as soon as I have a job, I will find a room to let."

Would her wages be enough to cover rent, meals, and the outstanding bill at the college? Daddy didn't have money to pay the remaining balance, which left the debt up to her. An ache formed in her belly.

Griselda Ann chuckled softly. "You might tire of me before I tire of you. I haven't had anyone else living under this roof since my mama graduated to Glory seven years ago. I've become rather set in my ways."

"You tell me right away if I do something that disturbs you."

Griselda Ann glanced at Addie's suitcases. A slight frown creased her face. "Perhaps you'd like to put your clothing in the closet? There are shelves and hooks available. Then tuck your cases under the bed. I'll start our supper, and you can assist with that when you have the room tidy again."

Addie could hardly call this room tidy, given its mountains of clothes and cluttered appearance. But her suitcases didn't belong on the quilt pieced by Griselda Ann's mother. She reached for the smaller suitcase. "I'll be out quick as a wink."

Griselda Ann nodded. "And after supper, I'll show you how to cut usable squares from the clothes. You can cut some more tomorrow when your shift at the library is done."

Mrs. Hunt had granted Addie permission to attend the college graduation ceremony instead of coming to the library for her final Saturday shift, but Addie declined. She needed those wages. Addie smiled. "I'll cut patches clear past bedtime if you'd like me to."

Griselda Ann's eyes widened. "Oh, we mustn't stay up late tomorrow. We will attend church service Sunday morning, and yawning during a sermon is most certainly a sin."

Emmett

Was he really graduating? The week of final examinations had gone so fast that Emmett still couldn't believe it was over. He'd prepared well and performed his best on every exam. Spence had poked fun at his undivided focus, but he'd been given money by the college to take these classes. He owed the scholarship committee members his best efforts. Between examinations, he visited each of the businesses in town that had posted job openings and talked to the hiring agents. Some were blunt, some acted sheepish, and others seemed flat-out bored, but every one of them sent him away with a

73

"No thanks." The reason? His degree.

"Sorry, young man," the agent at the chicken-processing plant, the kindest of the men, had told him, "but there ain't even a ghost of a chance we'll hire you. Somebody with your education ain't gonna be happy yankin' feathers from a chicken carcass. No, you need to hire on at a bank or big department store or even with one o' the minin' outfits — they got office jobs, too, y'know. But we can't use ya here. Nope, not here."

The man's dismal statements rolled in the back of Emmett's mind when he should have been listening to the guest speaker at the graduation ceremony. Maybe he shouldn't have come for the ceremony. But he'd worked so hard for his diploma. It seemed as if he'd earned the right to cross the stage and shake the college president's hand like the others. So he lined up with everyone else and waited his turn. Since they went in alphabetical order, he waited a pretty long time while the sun scorched through his robe and the wind tried to yank the cardboard hat from his head.

"Emmett Emil Tharp."

Emmett watched the toes of his shoes poking out from the hem of his gown — how did ladies make walking in gowns look so graceful? — and climbed the three wobbly steps to the stage set up in the middle of the football field. There wasn't anybody in the audience celebrating his accomplishments. Nobody who clapped extra hard or let out whoops of joy for him, as happened for many of his fellow graduates. The half-hearted applause given to be polite tried to dull some of the shine of receiving his rolled-up sheepskin from President McVey, but he told himself to be proud, the way Maw would be proud. He could imagine what she'd say to him right then: "Son, you're the first college graduate to hail from Boone's Holler, Kentucky. Just 'cause nobody else knows you done somethin' extra special don't mean it ain't special."

Planting Maw's voice in his head helped, and he left the stage with a smile and a firm grip on his diploma.

When the last student received his diploma, the dean of the College of Law stepped up to the podium and delivered a lengthy prayer of blessing over the graduating class of 1936. At his somber "amen," as they'd planned before marching in procession onto the field, the male graduates snatched off their caps and threw them in the air with shouts of glee. Emmett threw his cap, but he didn't holler. A lump seemed stuck in his throat, and a shout couldn't escape.

Students milled in a mob, some of the girls hugging one another and most of the boys slapping one another on the back. Emmett worked his way to the edge of the group, holding his diploma against his chest. He wanted to keep it nice until he got home and showed it to Maw and Mr. Halcomb. After they'd taken their fill of gawking at it, he'd put it away in his trunk, and it could get smashed flat in there.

Spence trotted up to him, grinning big. He'd already gotten rid of his gown somewhere and rolled up the sleeves of his shirt. He looked a lot more comfortable than Emmett felt. Spence gave Emmett's shoulder a whack. "Well, ol' bloke, I reckon this is it, time to say goodbye."

Emmett couldn't honestly say he and Spence had been good friends. Not like he'd been with his longtime buddy from back home, Shay Leeson. But after four years of rooming together, he'd gotten used to the freckle-faced man. He might even miss seeing him every day.

He bounced his fist on Spence's shoulder. "Reckon we'll see each other in our room later on. Still have to pack up. No need to say goodbye yet."

76

Spence shook his head. "I'm headin' home with my folks now. Dad'll send somebody next week for my stuff. 'Course" — he put his hands on his hips and gave a mock scowl — "that means I'm trusting you not to take my clothes back to Boone's Hollow with you."

Emmett laughed. Spence was six inches shorter and probably forty pounds lighter. Not even Maw, who was clever with a needle, would be able to stretch the fabric and make Spence's clothes fit Emmett. But maybe she could shrink them down for his little brother. The eight-year-old was closer to Spence's size than Emmett was. Emmett couldn't imagine Dusty wearing such fancy duds, though. "Your stuff's safe, Spence. You can trust me on that."

"Aw, I know it. Just joshin' you. Well . . ." He walked backward and gave a salute. "Nice knowin' you, Emmett Tharp. Take good care now."

Emmett waved, then turned toward Bradley Hall. He worked his way between groups of chattering, celebrating students and families, feeling more alone with every step. He'd hoped for a job here in Lexington, but the kind of job he wanted — the kind for which people would hire a man with a BS in commerce — probably wouldn't exist

77

until the country got on its feet again. That might be years from now. So there really wasn't any other choice except to do what Spence said and go back to Boone's Hollow.

He reached the men's dormitory and slung off his robe, careful not to catch his diploma in the fabric. He flopped the robe over his arm and climbed the stairs. Slow. Plodding. Putting things off. Because once he packed up, what would he do? Go home, for sure. He wanted to see Maw, Paw, and Dusty. But after that . . . what?

Like the wind yanking at his hat, a remembrance breezed through him. What had the hiring agent at the chicken plant told him he should do? Try hiring on with a mining outfit because they had office jobs. He came to a halt midstep, letting out a huff. Why hadn't he thought of it himself? Of course the mining companies needed office workers. And what better mining company to work for than the US Coal & Coke Company in Lynch, where Paw had worked for the last fifteen years?

Hope lifted his spirits. He jogged the rest of the way to his room and dragged his old carpetbag from under his bed. He'd pack, head to the station, and catch the first train to Lynch.

Six

Boone's Hollow
Bettina Webber

Bettina tapped her fingertip on the big black number in the middle of the square on the calendar page. She nudged her friend with her elbow. "This here's the day, Glory. Emmett's graduation-from-college day. He's all done with his schoolin' now, so he'll be comin' home."

Glory squinted at the calendar. "How do ya know for sure today's his" — she scrunched her face the way they used to do when biting into persimmons — "gradjee-a-shun? It ain't wrote on there."

Bettina rolled her eyes. "Like I'd scribble up my Christmas present." Pap had ordered the calendar from the Sears 'n' Roebuck catalog, and he'd even let Bettina hang it in her bedroom instead of putting it out in the main room of their cabin, so it was *hers.* She loved admiring its photo of the Dionne

79

quintuplets from Canada all lined up in pretty little ruffled gowns. Bettina'd never seen fancier gowns on babies, nor on nobody else for that matter.

She leaned against the chinked log wall and slid her hands into the pockets of her baggy overalls. "I know for sure 'cause way back in January his maw told me his graduatin' day was the fourth Saturday in May, an' I tucked it way inside my head. Been countin' the days off one by one. An' now it's here. An' he'll be comin' home for good this time, not just for a short spell."

A smile pulled on the corners of Bettina's lips. When Emmett was home for good, they could really get to sparking. Seemed like she'd waited forever, but wouldn't be long now and she'd be putting on a fine gown. Not as fine as the ones those little babies were wearing, but finer than any of the folks from around here had seen before. She'd already used some of her WPA money and bought one at the company store in Lynch — a creamy ivory crepe with real lace at the collar and a pale blue silk ribbon bow floating over the bodice like a waterfall down a hill. Pap had bellowed like a mad bull when he found out about it, but what did she care? She'd be a married-up woman soon, so she didn't have to answer to Pap no more.

Should she show the dress to Glory and watch her turn green with envy? Might be fun, but even better was saving it, letting Emmett be the first one to see her in it. She closed her eyes, imagining herself in that pretty dress with her brown hair done up in curls. Emmett'd wear a black suit, and the two of them would stand so proud in front of the preacher. Everybody in the church would cry tears of pure joy when she pledged herself to Emmett for the rest of her earthly days. Her whole frame gave a little shiver, and she popped her eyes open.

Glory was grinning. "Soon as he's home, reckon I know what you'll be doin'."

"You're right about that." Bettina hunched her shoulders and giggled. "An' high time, too."

"You're so lucky, Bettina." Glory plopped onto the edge of Bettina's bed. The ropes squeaked like a mouse with its tail caught in a trap.

Bettina hated them traps. And she hated that sound. She sat next to Glory, real careful so the ropes wouldn't squawk. "Don't I know it? When me an' Emmett get our house, we'll buy a real bed frame an' one o' those sets with a box spring an' a cotton-filled mattress to put on top, like they got at the store in Lynch. No more straw-filled sack laid out over a tangle of ropes." She slapped the patchwork quilt hiding the offending bed from view. "No sirree, me an' Emmett'll live fine as frog's hair. Now that he's got goodly educated, he'll be takin' a high-payin' job."

Glory's jaw dropped open. "You figure on movin' to the city?"

Bettina shrugged. She rose and sashayed to the corner of the small room, swaying her hips the way the movie starlets from the picture shows at the Lynch theater did. She spun and faced Glory, giving her head a toss. The starlets did that, too, and it looked real sassy. "Don't see how we can avoid it. Ain't no work around here worth havin'." If it wasn't for President Roosevelt wanting the folks living up in the hills to have books to read, she wouldn't have a job at all. She didn't much like making that long trek up into the mountains every day, hauling a heavy leather satchel full of books, but she sure liked having her own money to spend. What of her pay Pap let her keep, that is. But she'd give up the whole pay in the flash of sunlight on a large mouth bass's belly to be Mrs. Emmett Tharp.

Glory bounced up and caught Bettina in a hug. The smell from her family's last dinner — sauerkraut, baked apples, and smoked beans — filled Bettina's nostrils, and she angled her face as far from Glory's tangled hair as possible. She wouldn't never cook sauerkraut nor beans for Emmett when they was wed.

"I'm gonna miss you somethin' fierce." Glory held Bettina so tight she near cut off Bettina's breath. "You an' me been friends since we was hardly out o' the cradle."

Bettina gave Glory's pointy shoulder blades a quick pat, then wriggled loose. "No sense in carryin' on while I'm still here. Reckon me an' Emmett'll want a little time for courtin' before we take our nuptials. But when our weddin' day comes . . ." She took hold of Glory's hands and looked her friend straight in the eyes. "I'm gonna want you to stand up front with me."

Glory's brown eyes near popped out of her head. She squealed so loud that Bettina's ears rang.

She clamped her hand over Glory's mouth. "Hush that! My pap hears you, he'll wanna know why you're caterwaulin', an' I don't want him squashin' none o' my plans. You gonna be quiet?"

Glory nodded, and Bettina let go of her mouth. Glory clasped her hands under her chin. "I'm so excited, Bettina. I can't hardly wait for your weddin'."

83

"Me neither." Bettina scowled at her closed door. "If Pap has his way, I'll be here cookin' his meals an' washin' his clothes 'til I'm as old as Nanny Fay."

Glory laughed. "Won't nobody 'round here live as long as Nanny Fay. My maw says she's stirred up a special tonic for stayin' alive an' she's really over a hunnerd years old."

Bettina didn't care how old the herb lady was. She only cared about Emmett understanding how old Bettina was. When Emmett had left for that college in the city, she'd been nothing more than a little girl, still climbing trees and taking aim at squirrels with a slingshot. But that hadn't kept her from giving her heart to him. Now she was eighteen, a full-growed woman. And she needed him to see her as more than the bothersome little girl who'd tagged after him and his friends.

She folded her arms over her chest and tossed her head again. "Emmett'll likely be home tomorrow. Day after at the latest. I gotta be ready. Wanna help me wash my hair?"

Glory's blue eyes sparkled. "An' rinse it with your lily-o'-the-valley toilet water so it smells all good?"

Guilt tried to grab Bettina. In actuality,

84

the toilet water belonged to her maw, given to her by Pap their last Christmas together. But Maw was dead and buried. She didn't need it no more, and she'd want Bettina to use it for something as important as Emmett coming home again. She nodded. "Been savin' it up special, just for him."

Glory grabbed Bettina's hand. "Let's hurry. In case he gets home tonight already."

Bettina didn't figure he'd make it all the way from Lexington on the same day as his graduation, but she didn't mind hurrying. Maybe her hurrying would hurry him.

Lynch
Emmett

Thank goodness the Louisville and Nashville Railroad sent two passenger trains on a line through the coal-mining towns every day, including Sunday. Emmett caught the midmorning train and arrived at the red-painted Lynch depot a little after one o'clock, right on schedule. With it being Sunday, he hadn't expected a lot of activity in town. The coal miners were likely enjoying their single day off by relaxing. Not to mention the biblical admonition most folks honored about keeping the Lord's day holy. But after the constant bustle of activity on the college campus, the stillness was almost unsettling.

He fetched his battered carpetbag from the deck, nodded hello to an elderly woman sitting on a trunk, fanning herself, then set off on the main street, heading west. If he were a crow, he could fly straight north about a thousand feet and light in Boone's Hollow. But no way a man toting a heavy bag could walk that uphill climb through all the trees and undergrowth. Even without the encumbrance of a carpetbag, a fellow would be taxed by the climb. He'd take the mile-long dirt road that wound its way up Black Mountain to the little town where he'd been born and raised.

The sun beat down, making him drip sweat under his suit coat. He considered taking the jacket off, but then he'd have to carry it. Toting the bag that held his textbooks, diploma, and a few articles of clothing was enough. Besides, when he came walking into Boone's Hollow, he wanted to be dressed like a gentleman. Paw might say he was putting on airs, but he wanted Maw to be proud of him. He'd put up with the heat.

He left the main road and started up the mountain road carved out of the forest more than fifty years ago. Beech and hemlock trees grew thick on both sides and blocked

86

most of the sun. They couldn't block the humidity, though. Perspiration ran in rivulets down his face. He used his handkerchief to wipe it away and blinked hard against the sting in his eyes. He squinted at the trees — at their trunks and leaves — and calculated his distance by what was growing. The tall beech and shaggy hemlock gave way to birch, hickory, magnolias already showy with pink or white blooms, and an abundance of maple. Paw used to tease when they walked up this road that if they stumbled onto chestnut or oak trees, they'd know they'd gone too far. Emmett didn't intend to reach the oaks and chestnuts today. Getting to Boone's Hollow would be distance enough.

Dust rose with every step. When had it last rained in these parts? Reddish-brown powder coated his shoes and the hem of his britches. Maw could smack the dust out, but she might have a time getting the sweat stains from the underarms of his suit coat. His roommate's half of the closet had held three or four suits, plus stacks of button-up shirts, sweaters, vests, and trousers. Emmett had only the one suit, his present from Maw and Paw when he graduated from the local school. After four years of wear, it was getting some threadbare, but it was still the nicest set of clothes he owned. Had ever owned. And Maw'd been so proud to give it to him.

A flash of orange in the sea of green to his left caught his attention, and Maw's voice from ten years past spoke in his memory. "I'm lettin' ya have that slingshot your paw made for ya, 'cause somebody's gotta keep the crows out o' my garden patch. But, Emmett, if I catch ya takin' aim at one o' my pretty orioles, I'll use that slingshot for kindlin', an' you won't never be given another." He'd known back then that Maw meant what she said, and he only shot at the pesky black birds that tormented her beans and squash and tomatoes. To this day, when he saw the telltale orange belly of an oriole, he thought of Maw.

Thoughts of Maw always led to thoughts of home, and eagerness made his feet speed up, even though the muscles in his calves and the backs of his thighs burned almost as hot as the sun. The quicker steps jarred him, and the arm bearing the bag's weight felt like it could disconnect from his shoulder. He switched hands, not breaking stride. He set his lips in a grim line and ignored his aching muscles. He'd gotten soft walking only from building to building on mostly flat ground for the past four years.

He heaved mighty breaths and swiped at sweat and pushed himself upward, upward, upward. Finally, legs quivering like the limb on a hemlock bush in the breeze, he entered a narrow clearing lined with wooden structures. He paused in the break between the trees and set his bag beside his feet. Hands on his hips, he took in the familiar setting. Not a thing had changed since his last visit home a year ago, except somebody'd painted the Blevins' old smokehouse. White with blue trim, the same as his fraternity colors.

His college buddies would probably scoff at the uneven dirt streets, weathered buildings with rock foundations, and grassless yards in front of the houses. But it was a welcome sight to him. He'd reached Boone's Hollow. He was home.

"Emmett! Emmett Tharp!" a female voice blasted, its tone so full of joy that Emmett automatically smiled.

He turned in the direction of the call, expecting to see Maw running to greet him. Instead, Bettina Webber was coming at him. And she had her arms spread wide.

SEVEN

Boone's Hollow
Emmett

Emmett rubbed his eyes, not sure he was seeing right. But when he lowered his fists, the same image filled his vision — Bettina, coming so fast puffs of dust hung in the humid air behind her. Her blue-checked skirt flew up and exposed her dirty knees, and her freckled face wore the biggest smile he'd ever seen.

He scratched his temple. Why'd she have her arms open like that? She was fixing to hug somebody. He glanced over his shoulder. No one else was there. So that meant —

"Emmett! Oh, Emmett, you're home!" Without even a pause, she leaped.

He grunted, his arms closing around her in reflex, and staggered backward two steps. Good thing he'd put down his carpetbag or the two of them would probably be in a heap on the ground. He wouldn't have been

90

too pleased at getting his best clothes dusty from the suit collar to pant cuffs.

Between her stranglehold on him and some kind of flowery scent rising from her sweat-damp hair and filling his nostrils, he couldn't breathe. Weary from his long walk, damp head to toe with perspiration, and worried he'd faint dead away if he didn't draw a good breath soon, he leaned forward until her bare feet met the ground. Then he unwound her arms from his neck. With one wide sideways step, he put himself behind his luggage. From the safety of his barrier, he pulled in a full breath and then let it out, eyeing her close in case she decided to take another lunge in his direction.

She tilted her head, fluttering her eyelashes. "Hey, Emmett. I been watchin' for you so I could welcome you home."

He could've asked how she'd known when to expect him, but he was half-afraid to start a conversation. She was acting as if she didn't have good sense. Had she dipped into her pap's jug of moonshine? The still high on the mountain in the pine trees behind the Webbers' place was supposed to be a secret, but everybody in town knew why Burke Webber planted a patch of corn every year, and it wasn't to feed his daughter.

"That's —" His dry throat croaked the

word. He swallowed. "That's nice of you, Bettina." He grabbed his bag's handle and lifted the case, then moved in the direction of town. "I'm gonna head on home now, see my folks and brother."

"Ooh, law, they'll be so glad to see ya. Even gladder'n me, I reckon." She matched him step for step, grinning big. "You're all done with your schoolin' now, ain'tcha? That's what your maw told me."

Maw must've mentioned he'd be home today. Too bad Maw hadn't warned him about Bettina's welcome. He could've planned a response. He wasn't sure what to do with Bettina now any more than he'd been when he was fourteen and she was ten, trailing him like a puppy dog. Mercy, the girl could be a pest. But he'd be kind to her, the way Maw expected. "Yes, I graduated. I'm all done."

"Gonna getcha a job in the city?" She linked her hands behind her back and swung her hips as she walked. Her skirt swayed east to west, brushing his pant leg on the east swing.

He switched his carpetbag to the other hand so it hung between them and blocked her skirt's swish. "I'm not real sure yet."

"Ain't nothin' 'round here that'll let ya use a fancy degree." Her hazel eyes stayed locked on him, and the smile never left her lips. "Seems to me you got no choice 'cept to leave Boone's Holler for the city."

He'd already explored the city, but he didn't want to have this conversation with Bettina Webber. "Reckon time'll tell." He gave a start. How quickly he'd slid into the uncultured hills talk of his neighbors. His first year at college, he got poked fun at plenty of times for his speech patterns. By listening close to the city kids and studying the textbooks for more than the information they could give, he'd lost much of his backwoods dialect. But here it was, creeping in, and he hadn't even been in town half an hour yet.

"I've always wanted to live in a big city. Betcha now that you had all them years in Lexington, this ol' holler's gonna seem like nothin' more'n a mouse hole." She wrinkled her nose, a few freckles disappearing in the creases. "What's it like livin' in a place where there's fine restaurants an' hotels an' trolley cars?"

Hunger glimmered in her muddy-green eyes, but Burke Webber would have his hide if he filled Bettina's head with ideas about the city. Emmett cleared his throat. "Listen, Bettina, I'm kind of eager to see my folks. I do thank you for the welcome home. I didn't figure anybody'd watch for me with it being Sunday, so that was" — how could he phrase it so he wouldn't hurt her feelings? — "quite a surprise."

She beamed at him and swung her arms, making her skirt flare north and south. "Oh, you're welcome as welcome can be, Emmett. You gonna come to the singin' service at the low Baptist church tonight?"

Funny how the folks around here differentiated between the Baptist church in Boone's Hollow and the other in the little town a mile up the road, Tuckett's Pass, as low and high, based on their locations on the mountain. The same preacher delivered sermons every Sunday in both buildings, but no one from Boone's Hollow would go to the high, and no one from Tuckett's Pass would come to the low. All because way back when a Tuckett did something that irked some folks in Boone's Hollow and now they couldn't even worship together. Why didn't Preacher Darnell choose a building and make everybody come together?

Emmett shrugged. "You know my maw. She never misses a service unless she's ailing, and she'll want me with her. I'll be there."

"Glad o' that." Bettina gave him a look-

94

see from his head to his toes, then up again. "You're dressed fine enough for church, all right. Even good enough to go to a weddin'. Or be in one." She batted her lashes again.

Emmett gripped the carved wooden handle with both hands and hung the bag against his knees as a partial shield. She'd either sipped some moonshine or smoked some loco weed. She was acting, as Paw would say, like a blooming idiot. "Yes. Well. Good to see you, but I think I'll mosey on now, see my folks."

"Sure thing." Still smiling bright, she moved backward, bare toes drawing lines in the dirt. "Tell your maw howdy for me. I'll save you a seat at the singin'. Me an' Glory — you recall my best friend, Glory Ashcroft? — we always sit with Shay an' some of the other young folks. Reckon you'll wanna sit by Shay, since you ain't seen him for a spell."

He'd probably sit with Maw and Dusty, but it'd be good to catch up with Shay after the service. If Shay wanted to catch up, that is. He hadn't been overly friendly last summer during Emmett's school break. "We'll see. Bye now, Bettina." Emmett waved and hurried through the narrow gap between Belcher's General Store and the little building that served as both telephone office and

95

post office for Boone's Hollow and Tuckett's Pass.

A dirt path, packed as hard and smooth as marble from years of use, climbed a slight rise and ran along a row of three houses. He followed the path to the Belchers' clapboard bungalow, the fanciest house in the whole town, even nicer than Doc Faulkner's place. Ned and Swan Belcher sat on the front porch in matching rocking chairs, the runners squeaking against the tongue-in-groove floor.

Mrs. Belcher nodded a greeting, and Mr. Belcher lifted his hand in a lazy wave. "Emmett Tharp, that you?"

Emmett wanted to get on home, but he stopped and smiled politely at the general store's owner. "Yes, sir."

"You home for good now?"

Emmett chose a careful answer. "For a spell, at least." No sense in starting rumors.

Husband and wife nodded in unison and continued rocking.

Emmett bobbed his head and moved on. Next was the Shearers' cabin with its coating of dark-green moss climbing to the roof on its north side, then the Barrs' tumbledown shack set well back from the path against the sloping ground. Emmett always thought it looked as if the Barrs' house either grew out of or was trying to shrink into the hillside. All eight — or was it nine? — members of the family lived in the decrepit place. Paw didn't know a lot of Scripture, but he recited Proverbs 21:25 anytime Jasper Barr's name was mentioned. "The desire of the slothful killeth him; for his hands refuse to labour" ran through Emmett's mind as he slowed and took in the dwelling's sagging roof, cracked windows, and yard littered with rusty cans, soggy cardboard, and animal droppings. Two scrawny chickens pecked and a speckled pink pig rooted in the mess.

Emmett released a small huff, shaking his head. Nobody in Boone's Hollow lived like a king, especially these days, but from the looks of the Barr place, Jasper didn't even try to live as well as a pauper. The only thing Jasper Barr did well, according to Paw, was make new little Barrs. Noisy little Barrs, based on the shouts and wails escaping between the cracks in the shack's walls.

A battered boot with a hole where the toe used to be sat on the rock that served as a stoop below the warped front door. A cluster of drooping wildflowers spilled over the boot's shank. Probably placed there by Jennie Barr, Jasper's soft-spoken, long-suffering wife. Half the folks in town pitied

Jennie. The other half scorned her for staying with someone so work shy and slovenly. Maw'd taught Emmett not to cast stones, and he did his best to honor her, but looking at the sorry house in need of repairs made him side with those who thought Jennie could do a lot better. But if a man with a college degree couldn't find work, how would an uneducated woman provide for herself and her youngsters? Jennie was trapped. Emmett's feelings swung to the pity side.

He hurried beyond the ramshackle building and climbed the curving path leading to the little house Grandpaw Tharp built in 1882 for his new bride. Just a two-room cabin with a loft then, but Paw had built a shed-style addition on the west that held Maw's prized cookstove and the handmade table and chairs she'd brought with her when she married Paw. Nothing fancy, not even by Boone's Hollow standards. But when compared to the Barrs' place, it seemed like a palace. He left his bag at the foot of the walkway and hop-skipped over the flat rocks Grandpaw had laid down for paving stones. He leaped up onto the narrow porch and reached for the door's string latch. Before he gave it a pull, though, a familiar sound made him pause. He tilted his ear to the door, listening.

A smile tugged at the corners of his lips. Sure enough, he heard Maw's sweet voice and Dusty's chortles. He caught snatches of words — Striped Chipmunk, Purple Hills, Grandfather Frog . . . Maw was reading from *Old Mother West Wind,* the storybook she'd read to Emmett on Sunday afternoons when he was Dusty's age. Remembrances carried him backward in time, and longing for the simpler days of childhood struck hard. Sure, he was home now. But all grown up and armed with a college degree, he couldn't live in his parents' loft again. Not forever.

If the Coal & Coke Company hired him, they'd probably let him rent one of the company houses in Lynch, which had been built for the coal workers. If they did, he probably wouldn't make the trek to Boone's Hollow for Sunday services. He wouldn't eat suppers around the table with his folks and brother or clean Paw-caught catfish before dawn. He was home . . . but he wasn't home.

Sadness hit as hard as a tree trunk landing on his shoulders, and his hand fell away from the string. He'd gone to college to better himself, believing his schoolteacher's insistence that the degree would make his life richer and happier. But would it really?

Bettina

Bettina held her breath and tapped on Glory's bedroom window, praying Glory's nosy maw wouldn't poke her head out the front door of the cabin and ask who was disturbing their Sunday naps. She should've gone straight home. After lunch, Pap gave her permission to go for a walk while he took his usual Sunday afternoon snooze, but she'd waited under the tree by the church for almost two hours until Emmett finally showed up. By now Pap was probably awake again, shuffling around the cabin, wondering what'd happened to her and building up his temper. But she had to talk to somebody or she'd bust. And she sure couldn't tell Pap what was bubbling inside her.

Oh, where was that Glory, anyway? She gritted her teeth and tapped again.

The muslin curtains swished to the side, and Glory looked out the window. Her mouth fell open. Bettina gestured, and Glory nodded. Bettina scurried around to the back of the cabin. The Ashcrofts' back door always gave Bettina the shivers. Pap would not tolerate a back door. If a person

100

had two doors, he might accidentally go out one and come in another, and everybody knew bad luck would come to that fool person and everybody who lived in the house. She bounced on the balls of her feet until Glory stepped out and closed the door real careful behind her. Bettina darted over, grabbed Glory's arm, and dragged her to the Ashcrofts' animal lean-to.

Inside the shadowy space that smelled strong of earth, animals, and manure, Bettina took hold of Glory's hands. "Guess what."

"He's home."

Bettina held in the squeal she wanted to let out and squeezed Glory's hands hard. "Yep. An' guess what he done when he seen me?"

Glory's eyes blazed. "Can't guess."

Of course she couldn't. Glory didn't have so much as an ounce of imagination. Bettina sucked in a big breath, counted to three, then let the air whoosh out with her words. "Scooped me off the ground an' hugged me, that's what." She thought sure Glory's eyes would pop right out of her head. She laughed, then sashayed to the center post and leaned against the weathered wood. "Oh, Glory, you shoulda seen it. It was so romantic. Just like bein' in a movie."

Glory gaped at Bettina. Glory's fuzzy brown hair stood out like a lion's mane around her moon-shaped face. Glory wouldn't never keep a beau if she didn't learn how to tame that frizzy hair of hers. The picture-show heroes never went after girls who looked like they didn't know what a comb was for. "Tell me what all he done. Did he kiss you?"

"Well . . ." Bettina ground her toe into the soft dirt, giving Glory a sly sideways look. "He couldn't kiss me. Not right there in the middle o' the street."

"Was someone lookin'?"

"No, nobody was lookin'. Nobody was around 'cept for him an' me. That's what made it so romantic." She closed her eyes and filled her mind with the image of Emmett, his fine suit hugging his solid frame, the sound of a bird singing from a nearby bush, the warmth of sunshine pouring down on the two of them . . . and the heart-fluttering remembrance of Emmett's blue eyes aimed at her, as if he couldn't get enough of seeing her. Oh, what a pretty picture.

"What's so romantic if he didn't even kiss you?"

Bettina popped her eyes open. She stomped over and smacked Glory on the arm. "Ain't only kissin' that's romantic, Glory Ashcroft. You think he'd snatch me up an' kiss me out in the middle o' town? He was bein' a gentleman, treatin' me like a lady. That's romantic, too."

Glory rubbed her arm and scowled. "Don't seem to me it was all so special if all he did was hug you. Shootfire, anytime me an' Shay are alone, we always —"

"We ain't talkin' about you an' Shay. We're talkin' about me an' Emmett."

Glory hung her head. Her chin quivered.

Bettina sighed. She brushed Glory's shoulder with her fingertips. "Sorry I whacked you like I did." Although that little whop wasn't even close to what Pap'd do if she didn't get herself home soon. "Reckon I'm a little wrought up, seein' Emmett after bein' apart for so long an' then havin' to tell him goodbye so quick. He needed to get on home to see his folks."

Glory peeked at Bettina. Her eyes sparkled, and a little grin curved her lips. "I get some wrought up myself when I ain't had time alone with Shay for a while. I don't hold no grudge against you for bein' tetchy." She grabbed Bettina in a quick hug. "You wait 'til Emmett sees you next. He'll get to kissin' you right quick."

Bettina gave Glory a squeeze and stepped

free. "An' afterward, I'll come tell you all about it. Every little romantic bit."

Glory grinned.

"Glory? Glory, where are you, girl?" The warbling voice blasted from outside.

Glory aimed a frown in the direction of the lean-to's opening. "That's Maw. I gotta go."

"Go, then. But don't tell her I was here."

Glory nodded and scuttled out, calling, "Comin', Maw!"

"What're you doin' in with the donkey an' goats? Land's sake, girl, sometimes I —" The slam of a door cut off the rest of Mrs. Ashcroft's words.

Bettina waited a little, then skedaddled home. She hadn't realized Glory was doing so much kissing with Shay Leeson. Maybe she should've asked how Glory and Shay did it. The kissing she'd done so far sure hadn't felt the way it looked in the picture shows.

Up there on the screen, the hero and heroine stared all dreamy like into each other's eyes and held each other like they was made of fine porcelain. No boy had held her like she was made of porcelain. And no boy took the time to stare in her eyes, either. Just grabbed, puckered, and mashed his lips to hers. Sometimes she

104

wanted to push whoever it was away. Probably because she'd only kissed boys who didn't hold no piece of her heart. Emmett, though, he owned her whole heart. When they kissed for the first time, it'd be even better than anything in the movies.

Her heart danced in her chest, making her feel light as air. She'd see him at church tonight. Maybe he'd ask to walk her home. It'd be the gentlemanly thing to do, and Emmett was a gentleman. Maybe after tonight's singing service, she'd get her first romantic kiss. Then she'd tell Pap. And she could plan her wedding for real.

EIGHT

Emmett

" 'Bringin' in the sheaves, bringin' in the sheaves, we shall come rejoyyyycin', bringin' in the sheaves!' "

Emmett's doldrums got washed away midway through the third hymn. How could a fellow let sadness hold him captive while singing such rollicking songs? Especially when he was sitting next to Maw, who sang with such gusto the flowers on her hat jiggled. She'd donned her straw hat with the wide pink ribbon and cluster of pink silk roses sewn to the front brim — her "special day hat," she called it. This was a special day because Emmett was home again. Even if he wasn't home "fer good," as she'd put it during supper, having him with her gave her joy, and her joy was contagious. So he smiled while he sang, his bass a complement to her soprano.

On his other side, Dusty sang loud. For a

little fellow, he had some big lungs. He belted out every word, always about three notes off pitch. And that only made Emmett smile more. Because Dusty didn't care a bit about whether or not he matched the notes. Paw couldn't match the notes, so he never came to the singings. But Dusty made a joyful noise, the way the Bible said people should. His joy also rubbed off on Emmett. Even if he was only here for a short spell, he'd carry away good feelings when he went to . . . wherever he found a job.

From "Bringing in the Sheaves" to "When We All Get to Heaven," "When the Roll Is Called Up Yonder," and "There Is Power in the Blood," the folks who'd gathered in the low Baptist church sang powerfully enough to rattle the rafters. All through his college years, Emmett had attended Sunday services regularly at a Presbyterian church in Lexington. He'd promised Maw he wouldn't neglect gathering with believers, and he always kept his promises. But he hadn't enjoyed singing like this since the last time he'd been in Boone's Hollow for a Sunday evening sing. By the time they reached the fifth stanza of "Shall We Gather at the River?," Emmett's voice was getting hoarse, and Dusty'd lost his volume. The sing would be done soon, and he knew which hymn would end it. One that nobody'd call a toe tapper, but a perfect one to close an evening of singing God's praise.

" 'Gather with the saints at the river that flows by the throne of God.' " The song leader's voice carried over everyone else's with the final phrase. Then he swung his hands upward in an invitation to rise.

Benches groaned, floorboards squeaked, rustles broke out all over the small sanctuary. The organist struck a warbling chord, and as one they sang, " 'Amazing grace! How sweet the sound . . .' "

Tears rolled down Maw's cheeks, the same way they always did when she sang the old song about being saved from sin by God's grace. Emmett slipped his arm around her narrow shoulders, and she shot him a watery smile even while continuing to sing. They held the hymn's last word, "be-guuuuuuun," until the organ's bellows ran out of air. Then Preacher Darnell offered a closing prayer.

At his rumbling "amen," chatter broke all over the room, and someone — a female someone — called Emmett's name. Was it . . .

Maw's knowing grin confirmed his suspicion. "Bettina's beckonin' you."

"Bettina's hollering for me."

They spoke at the same time.

Maw laughed. She gave Emmett a light shove on his chest. "Best go see what she's wantin'. Prob'ly gonna ask ya to join up with her an' the other young folks for a spell o' talkin' an' such, like they do pret' near every Saturday an' Sunday evenin' around here."

Before he left for college, Emmett was always part of the gathering. Back then, Bettina was too young to join in. Some of the young folks his age, including his childhood best buddy, Shay, were still in the group. But on his former visits, a few of the fellows had made sure Emmett understood he didn't fit in as well as he used to.

He made a face. "I'd rather go on home with you an' Dusty."

Dusty tucked himself against Emmett's hip and held Emmett's arm the way Emmett used to hold vines for swinging on. He beamed, showing the gap where he'd lost his front teeth. "Sun ain't sleepin' yet. Wanna shoot marbles with me, Emmett?"

A perfect excuse. Emmett grinned. "Sounds good."

Maw clicked her tongue on her teeth and shook her finger at Dusty. "Now, listen here, your brother's too grown up for marble shootin'. He ain't seen his friends for a good long while. We can't be selfish with him." She caught Dusty's hand and pulled him to her side. "Besides, it's nigh on your bed-time."

Dusty folded his arms over his chest and poked out his lower lip.

Emmett started to defend his brother, but Bettina crowded close and spoke first. "Emmett, didn't ya hear me? I was callin' for ya."

Maw slipped her arm through Bettina's elbow. "He heard ya, honey. He was just tellin' me an' Dusty here good night." She tipped her head back and examined Bettina's uncovered head. "Why, Bettina, you look real purty with your bangs pulled back in a barrette like that. Brings out your eyes right nice. An' you smell good, too. Like I recall Rosie smellin', God rest her soul."

Bettina twirled a strand of her brown hair around her finger. "Rinsed my hair with my maw's lily-o'-the-valley water."

So that's what Emmett had smelled when she jumped him earlier. His nose twitched in remembrance.

Her fingers moved to the smooth piece of silver metal pinned at the crown of her head. "But the barrette's mine. Real sterlin' silver. I bought it at the company store in

110

Lynch with some o' my WPA money."

"I'm sure havin' that money come in is a blessin'." Maw kept hold of Bettina's arm but turned to Emmett. "Bettina an' a couple other girls work as lib'arians, takin' books up to the mountain folk every week. Been a real good job for them, an' it's helpful for the hills families, too, gettin' their youngsters some book learnin'."

Emmett knew about various Works Progress Administration programs instituted by the president of the United States, even knew there were WPA lumber cutting and road building outfits right here in Kentucky. But one about book reading implemented in his very own community surprised him. And Bettina serving as a kind of librarian? An unusual occupation for a person who had no use for reading. How many times had she sneaked up on him during recess and yanked the book he was reading from his hands or called him a sissy for wanting to read? But he didn't hold a grudge against her. He knew why she had no use for books.

He offered a slight nod and smile. "Good for you, Bettina."

"It's a heap o' work." She wrinkled her nose. "Takes the whole livelong day, near sunup to sundown, to visit all the houses on my route an' get back home again." She

111

pointed to a short, plump gray-haired woman visiting with the preacher's wife in the corner of the sanctuary. "That there's Miz West, from Louisville. She runs the lib'ary, an' she tells me an' Glory an' Alba what books to take where. She can't do none o' the actual deliverin' 'cause she's got some kind o' breathin' problem. So she stays at the lib'ary all day instead."

Emmett frowned. "What library?"

"The one here in Boone's Holler."

"Boone's Hollow has a library?"

"Why, sure we do. An' it smells like ham inside."

He must've heard wrong. "Did you say ham?"

Bettina and Maw laughed the way old friends sharing a joke do. Maw said, "Don't see as it can help it since it was the Blevins' smokehouse before it became our lib'ary. Now, I'm sure I wrote to you last November or so about some workers comin' in, paintin' up the Blevins' smokehouse so's the book lady the government sent would have a place to stay an' store the books an' such these gals cart all over the hills."

If she had, he'd forgotten. Wouldn't he have liked having a library to visit when he was a youngster? He rubbed Dusty's head, tousling his brother's thick dark hair. "What do you think about having a library? Do you check out books?"

"Nuh-uh."

"How come? I know you like books."

Dusty shrugged.

Bettina tossed her head, making her hair bounce. "It ain't that kind o' lib'ary. Folks don't come in an' check out books. The books get took to folks. But only certain folks."

Emmett arched one eyebrow. "That doesn't seem quite fair. Shouldn't everybody be able to access the library?"

Bettina rolled her eyes. "Like I said, it ain't that kind o' lib'ary. Now, you wanna come to Alba's place with me an' the others? Miz Gilkey baked brown-sugar cookies an' mixed up a pitcher o' sweet tea." She glanced toward the back of the sanctuary and grimaced. "Aw, shucks, ain't none of 'em here now. They've all gone on. Prob'ly got tired o' waitin' on me. But" — her grin turned sly — "you an' me can still go. I doubt Shay an' the other fellas've finished off all the cookies yet."

If Emmett escorted Bettina to Pat and Sophie Gilkey's place, folks would take one look at the two of them setting off together and make assumptions. Incorrect assumptions. "I appreciate the invitation, Bettina, but —"

Maw squeezed his upper arm. "Go on now, Emmett. You been so busy studyin' you ain't had time for fun. It'll do you good to cut up a bit. Besides, you ain't seen your friends in a good long while. You go." Then she winked. "But don't stay out too late, you hear? The wagon that takes the men from here an' Tuckett's Pass to the coal mine leaves for Lynch real early. Shay an' pret' near all the other young fellers from these parts'll need to be on it."

Bettina caught hold of Emmett's elbow with both hands. "Mr. an' Miz Gilkey'll shoo us all away no later'n half past nine. They're always ready to have us come over, but they're real particular about the hours Alba keeps."

"That sounds just fine." Maw cupped the back of Dusty's head with her hand and herded him toward the door. "You have fun, Emmett. I'll leave the string out so you can let yourself in."

Bettina giggled and fluttered her eyelashes. "C'mon, Emmett. You recall the way to the Gilkeys' place?"

The Gilkeys lived in a house east of Boone's Hollow, up the mountain a bit, but he'd never been to their place. He shook his head.

"Then I'll lead the way. C'mon."

What had Maw gotten him into? Emmett gritted his teeth and willed the next hour to pass quickly.

Lexington
Addie

Addie set the scissors aside and massaged her aching fingers. If only she had enough hands to massage her lower back at the same time. How could cutting up fabric tax a person so? The pendulum clock ticking on the dining room wall showed ten minutes past nine. Nearly bedtime. Addie was ready to tumble into bed. But the rhythmic thumps and hum of the sewing machine drifting up the hallway told her Griselda Ann wasn't ready to stop for the evening.

She sank onto a dining room chair and sighed. At home and even at the college, she'd spent Sundays resting or reading, and the day had seemed to pass more quickly than she wished. Never had a Sunday stretched so long as this one. Tomorrow's work at the library and the fresh job search would be a reprieve after her hours of standing at the dining room table, snipping six-and-a-half-inch squares from shirts and skirts and britches. Then she'd taken the leftover pieces and cut three-and-a-half-inch squares because four smaller squares could be pieced together to create a six-and-a-half-inch square.

Griselda Ann had cautioned her about using every bit of available fabric, saying, "My mama advised, 'Waste not, want not.' Doesn't it sound like something Benjamin Franklin would say? The folks who gave these items gave with the assurance that their contribution would be fully utilized. Besides, the more squares we have, the more blankets we can make." Apparently, Franklin was a hero of sorts to either Griselda Ann or her mother, because an intricately stitched sampler with a Franklin quote — "The noblest question in the world is, what good may I do in it?" — hung on the parlor wall.

With the words from the framed admonition and Griselda Ann's spoken instruction rolling in Addie's brain, she was compelled to keep cutting, even though her fingers ached and a blister was rising on the inside of her thumb. She searched through the basket of discarded shreds in case she'd missed a piece large enough to create another small square. She located a scrap of yellow-flowered calico from a child's well-worn dress and laid it flat on the table. Griselda Ann had told her to never cut against the grain or the pieces wouldn't stay square when sewn. She aligned the edge of the smaller cardboard square with the threads' direction, then slid the square up and down the scrap until she'd assured herself it was too small to cut a full square.

With a flick of her fingers, she sent the scrap sailing into the basket. As it landed, something touched her shoulder, and she released a squeak of surprise. A chuckle rumbled. Addie whirled in the chair and peered up into Griselda Ann's amused face.

"Goodness, you were quite engrossed. Didn't you hear me say your name?"

Addie's ears still rang with the hum of the sewing machine. She shook her head and stood, stifling a groan when her back muscles pinched. "No, ma'am. I'm sorry. Did you need something?"

"Yes. I needed to apologize for losing track of time. I should have let you retire to your room a half hour ago at least." Remorse glimmered in the woman's pale brown eyes. "To be honest, I forgot you were here."

Considering the short time Addie had resided under Griselda Ann's roof, she couldn't be offended by the oversight. She offered a weary smile. "It's all right. I made

117

good use of the time." She held her hand to the stacks of fabric squares, arranged by size and color. "I don't know how many squares it takes to make one blanket, but I hope there are enough here for at least one side."

Griselda Ann shifted her attention to the cluttered tabletop, and her jaw dropped. "Oh, Addie, you have been busy." She touched the stacks by turn, running her thumb along the edges as if silently counting. "And it appears you were very diligent in both sizing and cutting on the grain. These will go together smoothly into a new blanket. Having them cut and so neatly organized will be very helpful to me. Thank you."

Her sincere appreciation made the aches in Addie's hands and back worth it. "I'm glad to have helped."

Griselda Ann patted Addie's arm, then released a huge sigh. "There are so many needs in this world of ours, Addie. So much suffering. Sometimes I wonder why I'm so blessed."

Addie tilted her head. Griselda Ann had lived all her adult life with her mother, and she had no husband or children or, it seemed, friends. She spent her time either at work or at a sewing machine. Wouldn't loneliness be her constant companion?

Addie saw few blessings in the woman's single, monotonous state.

"I have this house." Griselda Ann spoke softly, her gaze aimed beyond Addie's shoulder as if she'd drifted away somewhere. "I have a job that meets my needs. I've always had enough food to eat, and I've never gone without adequate clothing. I've been given much."

"Look for the blessings, Addie." Mother's sweet voice played in Addie's memory. Tears threatened. Her lips quivered as she formed a smile. "As have I. Including being invited to stay here with you."

Griselda Ann zipped her focus to Addie. Affection bloomed on her round face. "I believe you're going to prove to be a blessing to me, Addie. I'm only sorry your parents' misfortune led to my receiving the blessing of your help and companionship."

"My mother would say your taking me in is God's way of providing for me." Addie glanced at the fabric squares stacked on the table, then at the growing blister on her thumb. The oddest thought trailed through her mind, that the blister would one day be viewed as a blessing in her life.

"Well, let's put these squares in the ready-to-sew basket, and then we should ready ourselves for bed." Griselda Ann scooped up an armful of squares and headed for the hallway.

Addie filled her arms and followed, inwardly laughing. She must be overly tired to think a blister could ever be a blessing.

NINE

Boone's Hollow
Emmett

Maybe he should walk instead. It'd seemed like a good idea to get up with Paw before the sun rose and ride the company wagon into Lynch with the twenty or so men and older boys from Tuckett's Pass and Boone's Hollow who worked in the mine, but now Emmett wasn't so sure.

No one seemed too keen to have his company. Paw had snorted when Emmett came down from the loft dressed in his suit. Then he'd hurried ahead on the path, as if he didn't want to be seen with his son. Those who were waiting, including Shay and some others who'd been at the Gilkey place last night, held their distance from him. A couple of the older men, ones who claimed Paw as a friend, spoke a greeting to Emmett and asked what he was doing out so early, but after he told them he was going to try to get a job in the offices at the Coal & Coke Company, they turned away, too.

Emmett tried not to take offense. The folks from the hills didn't cozy up to strangers — they never had — and he'd been gone long enough to become a stranger to most of them. But couldn't Paw or Shay talk to him? Paw was joshing with the older men, and Shay was cutting up with the younger ones, and Emmett felt as out of place as he had his first weeks on the college campus his freshman year.

Nervousness made his belly quiver. He shifted from foot to foot, adjusting his tie and the collar of his suit coat. "Fancy duds," he heard one of the younger men mutter. He pushed his hands into his pockets and forced himself to stand still. No sense in calling attention to himself. He already stuck out like a daisy in a patch of thistles. But what else could he wear? His professors at the university stressed the importance of appropriate attire. One paraphrased Mark Twain's quote about clothes making the man by adding that society has no place for those in sloppy clothing. He'd gotten to where he didn't feel like himself unless he wore trousers and a button-down shirt.

The crunch of wagon wheels against dirt

rumbled, and a pair of small brown birds shot from a bush near the road. "Here it comes," someone said.

Emmett looked to the north entrance of town. A pair of white-nosed mules, heads bobbing, came through the gap in the trees. They pulled a green-painted wagon driven by a wiry little man who looked to be at least ninety years old. Everyone shuffled to the side of the road, lunch buckets clanking. The driver stopped the wagon in front of Belcher's General Store. Paw and one of his buddies, Wiley Landrum, pulled themselves up onto the wagon seat next to the driver. The five or six men from Tuckett's Pass already in the bed shifted to the front, and the others who'd been waiting climbed over the sides.

Emmett crossed to the wagon and looked up at the driver. "Good morning, sir."

The man, his face as wrinkled as a dried plum, squinted at Emmett. "Mornin', young feller."

"Do you mind if I ride along into Lynch?"

"Ain't no never mind to me. 'Course, it'll depend on if you c'n squeeze in. Purty tight fit back there."

Muffled laughter rolled from the wagon bed.

Emmett pretended not to hear and tipped

123

his hat. "Thank you." He moved to the bed and planted his foot on an iron step screwed to the wagon's side. He pulled himself up and started to step in, but there wasn't even space for him to plant his foot in the bed. He froze in place, one foot on the step, the other on the edge of the wagon's warped side, hoping someone would shift enough to let him in. No one moved.

"We need to git, young feller." The driver's gravelly voice seemed loud and gruff in the silence of the morning. "Climb on in if you're goin'."

"Well, I . . ." Why hadn't he walked to Lynch instead of waiting for the wagon? He could have saved himself this embarrassment.

Shay, wedged in the back corner, nudged the man closest to him. "Git your big feet out o' the way, Delmas."

Delmas snorted, but he pulled his heels tight against his buttocks, and Emmett placed his foot on the floor of the bed. He wriggled his other foot in, but there wasn't enough space to sit. So he perched on the edge, holding back a grimace when the threads of his trousers caught on the rough wood. He gave Delmas a nod. "Thanks."

The man smirked. "Best hold tight. This thing bounces worse'n a rubber ball on a brick floor." The others laughed.

Emmett clamped his hands over the warped length of wood. His rear end would probably be full of splinters by the time they made it to the coal mine. The wagon lurched forward. His body jerked backward, and his hat slipped. He started to straighten it, but a mighty bump threatened to throw him. Which would be worse, losing his hat or losing his seat? He chose to keep his seat, and to his relief his hat remained in place. He gritted his teeth against the bumps and jars and prayed he'd be able to hold on until they reached Lynch.

The men joked and bantered with one another, but none of them involved Emmett in their talk. He caught Shay glancing at him a time or two, but his old pal didn't say a word to him. Same as he'd done last night. The twenty-minute ride down the mountain while the sky changed from gray to dusky pink seemed to take hours. Frustration built in Emmett's chest, and stiffness attacked every muscle in his body.

Tomorrow he would definitely walk.

The driver guided the mules to the cave-like opening of the mine. The men leaped over the edge on both sides of Emmett's perch, reminding him of trout escaping a net. He waited until they'd cleared the bed before straightening his stiff limbs and climbing to the ground. He reached up and straightened his hat, and a muscle in his back twinged. He groaned.

A wry chuckle rumbled. Emmett turned his head and met the driver's grin. The man pointed at him. "Next time ya hitch a ride, don't be so shy about it. Jest get in. Then you won't hafta ride the edge like you was sittin' on a fence rail." His face scrunched into a frown, and he scratched his head, making his few tufts of gray hair stand straight up. "You ain't goin' into the tunnels in your funeral suit, is ya? It'll get all mucked up."

Emmett brushed the seat of his trousers with his palms. "No, sir. I'm going to talk to the mine directors about a job in the office."

"Ah." The old man nodded wisely. "Well, then, you should oughta be able to stay clean. Them offices don't open 'til eight, though, so you're a mite early."

"I know. I don't mind waiting."

The seven o'clock whistle blasted. Emmett clapped his hands over his ears. The pair of mules pranced in their traces, and the driver double-gripped the reins and scowled, hunching up his skinny shoulders. The whistle rang for a full ten seconds, then took another half minute or so to fade to a raspy whispering note. Even after it died, it continued to ring in Emmett's ears. The mules snorted and wagged their heads, as if trying to shake loose the memory of the shrill attack. Emmett battled the urge to try the same tactic.

"Hoo boy, ain't never gonna get used to that thing. Pret' near splits a feller's eardrums, an' that's a fact." The driver twisted in his seat and peered down at Emmett. "Gotta switch out the wagon so's these two ol' beasts can be put to work haulin' coal, but it'll be a while before any o' the carts come out, so I don't gotta do it right away. You want me to ride ya over to the office buildin'? You can sit up here on the seat with me 'stead o' ridin' in the back."

"Thank you, but I think I'll walk." Walking would eat up some of the time, and it would let him work some of the kinks from his stiff muscles.

"Suit yerself." The old man snapped the reins down on the mules' backs. The wagon groaned forward.

Emmett followed slowly, staying out of reach of the small dust clouds swirling behind the wagon's wheels. Even though he'd come through Lynch traveling between home and Lexington several times over the

127

past four years, he still found himself a little awed by the town. Sure, it was small compared to Lexington, and its main street sported gaps between buildings, but it spread out a full mile's distance, and its rock buildings were every bit as tall and showy as some on Lexington's Main Street. He passed the two-story bathhouse, where Paw did his best to scrub himself clean before going home to Maw every evening. The US Steel Corporation must've invested a heap of money building this town around the mine. Everybody said the coal company intended to stay, that Lynch would become a permanent dot on Kentucky's map. And that was good for him because he needed a job that would last through his lifetime.

Beyond the bathhouse, a square, squat building with a shiny tin roof and a front window the size of a bed mattress sat well off the road. A pair of spindly butterfly bushes not yet in bloom guarded the front double doors. Arched gold letters as tall and broad as Emmett's hand spelled out US Coal & Coke Company on the glass. A nervous flutter went through his stomach. This was the place.

Emmett followed the poured concrete sidewalk to the low stoop. No lights were on inside, so he didn't bother trying the door. He hitched up his pant legs and sat on the stoop to wait. He'd hardly had a chance to get comfortable before a tall man wearing a three-piece suit and a gray fedora, as stylish as any businessman from Lexington, came up the street. He made a crisp turn at the sidewalk and headed for the US Coal & Coke building without slowing his pace.

Emmett quickly stood and removed his hat. The man reached the stoop, and Emmett stuck out his hand. "Good morning, sir."

"Good morning to you, young man." The fellow gave Emmett a firm handshake, then reached in his trouser pocket. He withdrew a key and stepped past Emmett, aiming the key for the door lock. "What can I do for you?"

"Well, sir, I'm here to apply for a job."

The man clicked the lock and pocketed the key again. Hand remaining in his pocket, he faced Emmett. "The supervisor at the coal mine hires workers. You'll want to talk to —"

"I'm interested in an office job, sir." Emmett cringed. He shouldn't have interrupted, but impatience to get a job, earn money, and make use of his hard-earned degree stole his manners. He swallowed and forced a calmer tone. "That is, I'm qualified for an office job. I'm a 1936 graduate from the University of Kentucky with a bachelor of science in commerce."

"Did you graduate from the high school here in Lynch?"

"No, sir. I attended the Boone's Hollow and Tuckett's Pass mountain school."

The man shook his head. "Can't use you."

"There aren't any office jobs available?"

"I didn't say that."

Emmett squeezed his hat, flattening the wool crown. "But I have a —"

"Degree. Yes, I heard you." The man gripped the brass door handle. "We give college scholarships to any young man who graduates from Lynch High School and agrees to come back here to use his knowledge in our company. We reserve our office openings for them."

The flutters changed to a stone weighting his gut. "You won't consider hiring me?"

The man's salt-and-pepper eyebrows descended. "As I just said, our openings are for our graduates. You aren't one of our graduates, so . . ."

He didn't need to finish the sentence. Emmett's hope sputtered and died. He smacked his hat on his head and jammed his hands into his suit pockets. "What about in the mine? Do you reckon the supervisor would give me a job in the mine?"

The man stared hard at Emmett for several silent seconds. Then he huffed. "Son, let me ask you the questions the supervisor will ask. First, do you have any experience in coal mining?"

"Not firsthand, no."

"Do you intend to make coal mining a longtime occupation, or would you see working there as biding time until something better comes along?"

Emmett cringed. He wished he could tell a fib, because telling the truth would surely earn him another rejection, but his conscience wouldn't let him so much as bend the truth. "I'd rather not work the mines for the rest of my life, if that's what you're asking."

"That's what I'm asking. We train our miners not only how to extract the coal but also how to keep themselves and everyone around them safe. If we hire a fellow, we make an investment in teaching him, and we want to know our time and effort isn't going to waste. Unless you're fixing to stay on, to be loyal to the US Steel Corporation, we —"

Emmett stepped off the stoop. "I understand." He understood, but he sure didn't like it. "Thank you for your time."

"You're welcome. Good luck to you." The man entered the building.

Emmett stayed at the edge of the stoop and stared at the closed door. Another closed door. Another lost opportunity. *"Good luck to you,"* the man had said. Luck? This economic decline had stolen so much from people. Luck no longer existed.

He stepped onto the sidewalk and sent his gaze up the street. There were other businesses. Maybe one of them would hire him. Maybe he should spend the day here, visit all the places in town, then catch a ride back to Boone's Hollow on the company wagon. His chest went tight. He didn't want to be ignored by the miners during another uncomfortable ride. And he didn't want to hear another "No, thanks," either. A fellow could take only so much rejection in one day.

With a sigh, he turned to the road. Might as well start the long walk home.

Lexington
Addie

Addie set off for work at a quarter past nine. Her shift began at ten, and Griselda Ann — or rather Miss Collins, as Addie needed to remember to call her while on duty — said the walk from her little house to the library would take thirty minutes. Since the route wasn't yet familiar, Addie gave herself extra time in case she got turned around somehow. Mother always said it was better to arrive early than late to social events. Addie presumed the rule applied even more stringently to places of employment. Even if her time as a library employee was quickly drawing to an end, she wanted to leave with a good recommendation, so early was better.

She'd donned one of her most flamboyant outfits — a spring-green flared skirt that fell a modest four inches below her knees and a green-polka-dotted white blouse. Sometimes she wore the blouse tucked in, but today she'd opted to leave it out and buckled a wide black belt around her waist. Her black patent pumps, bearing a fresh coat of polish, finished the look. Felicity had once told her she looked sophisticated in the outfit, which gave Addie confidence, and she needed all the confidence she could muster. After she finished her shift at the library, she planned to revisit some of the places where she'd already been turned down for jobs. Mother's letter claimed Daddy wasn't giving up on finding a job, so Addie wouldn't give up, either. Maybe they'd be more inclined to hire a girl who possessed sophistication.

She could hope, right?

By following the directions Griselda Ann had recited before she left the house at seven thirty that morning, Addie arrived at the library within the predicted half-hour span of time. She pattered up the front steps, crossed through the building's vestibule, and started for the little room where the time-punch machine for employees was kept.

"Pssssst, Addie." Griselda Ann waved her over to the main checkout desk.

Addie changed directions and stopped on the opposite side of the desk. She smiled. "I made it just fine using your directions. Thank you."

Griselda Ann's brows pinched. "I presumed you would. I have a message for you from Mrs. Hunt. She needs to see you."

"All right. Do you know what she wants?"

"Yes, I do."

Addie waited for a few seconds as Griselda Ann sat with tightly sealed lips. Addie held her hands outward. "Well?"

The woman laughed softly. "Oh, no. She specifically said to send you to her. She'll have to tell you herself."

Curiosity twined through Addie's middle.

"But —"

"Go, Addie."

"Shouldn't I clock in first?"

Griselda Ann flicked her fingers. "Go."

Addie hurried toward the staircase leading to the second floor and climbed the steps. What did Mrs. Hunt want with her? Being invited to Mrs. Hunt's office wasn't an unusual request. The head librarian stayed involved in all aspects of the library's operation and often delivered personal instructions or accolades or, according to some other employees, an occasional reprimand. Addie didn't expect a reprimand. However, the last time she'd been summoned to an office, she received unexpected, distressing news. The remembrance stirred hints of apprehension, and her hand trembled slightly as she raised it and tapped on the doorframe.

"Come in, Addie."

Addie entered the room and crossed to the director's desk. The smile on the woman's face diminished the uncertainty that had gripped Addie. She smiled in response. "Grisel— Miss Collins said you wanted to speak to me."

"Indeed, I do. Please sit down."

The straight-backed chair from the corner now sat facing Mrs. Hunt's desk. Addie's apprehension flickered to life again. Apparently, Mrs. Hunt planned a lengthy conversation if she wanted Addie to sit. Addie's knees went weak. She sank into the chair and folded her hands in her lap.

"Have you been accepted at any of the places of employment at which you've applied for positions?"

Addie shook her head, hoping her negative response wouldn't discourage her boss. After all, the woman had penned a very kind letter of reference for her. "I plan to revisit some of them after work today, though." Oh, please let her sophisticated appearance garner fresh attention.

Mrs. Hunt lifted a folded sheet of paper from a box on the corner of her desk. She waved it slightly. "Before you decide to revisit those places of business, let me tell you about an opportunity of which I became aware over the weekend. Have you heard of the Works Progress Administration?"

"Isn't it a program established by the president to give people jobs?"

"It is." Mrs. Hunt unfolded the sheet, then laid it on her desk and linked her hands on top of it. "My mother's cousin Lydia West received a WPA job as director of a very small library in a town nestled on the side of Black Mountain. It's an impoverished area with many uneducated families living in the hills. Lydia organizes the library's books and various reading materials. These books are distributed among the hills people so they, especially the children in the families, are exposed to reading and literature."

Recalling the joy of checking out books from the library when she was a child, Addie couldn't resist smiling. "What a wonderful idea."

"I quite agree. The books are carried to the families by employees who ride horses up into the hills. Lydia calls them" — she glanced at the paper under her hands — "packhorse librarians."

Such a quaint title. Addie imagined it as a book title, and at once a story formed in her mind.

"According to Lydia, the three young women serving as packhorse librarians are overtaxed by the many stops they must make. She petitioned and received approval to add a fourth rider. And, of course, I thought of you."

Still contemplating the delightful story that could grow from sending out librarians on horseback, Addie almost missed Mrs. Hunt's final comment. The woman's meaning sank in, and she gave a little jolt. "Me?"

The woman chuckled. "Why not? You

need a job, and the WPA pays a fair wage. You're familiar with the inner workings of a library system, and I know you're a proponent of reading." Her lips curved upward and her eyes sparkled. "What do you think, Addie? Are you interested in becoming a packhorse librarian?"

TEN

Addie

Addie stared at Mrs. Hunt while searching for an appropriate reply. Of course she wanted a job. She needed a job. But as a packhorse librarian in a little town so far away? She'd imagined herself working in Lexington, only a short train ride from Georgetown where Mother and Daddy and all things familiar were found. Kentucky's Black Mountain was three hours away in what amounted to the opposite direction of home. Did she want to go to Black Mountain?

"Addie, what are your thoughts?"

Mrs. Hunt would think she was addle-brained if she didn't say something. "I . . . I'm . . ."

Mrs. Hunt laughed. "I'm sure you're full of questions. Let me provide a little more information, hmm? First of all, the position pays twenty-nine dollars a month."

139

Addie's mouth fell open. She'd earned six dollars and fifty cents a month working at the Lexington Public Library. The prospect of earning twenty-nine dollars a month felt like a windfall.

"And, of course, you must be able to ride a horse. Are you familiar with riding a horse?"

On the way home from the orphans' asylum after Daddy and Mother adopted her, they'd taken her to a little fair. She'd eaten cotton candy, won a rag doll by knocking over milk bottles with small bean-filled bags, and ridden a pony named Gert on a circular track. A photo of her sitting astride Gert's back had been displayed for years on a table in the parlor, and she surmised Mother and Daddy now had it in their room at the boardinghouse. Of course, riding a full-sized horse on mountain trails would differ from her brief ride on Gert's back, but at least she wasn't completely inexperienced. "Yes, ma'am, I've ridden before."

"The town where Lydia's library is stationed is called Boone's Hollow, not far from the mining town of Lynch. There are no boardinghouses or hotels in Boone's Hollow — it's much too small for that — but Lydia stays in the library building itself.

Given the difficulties of the times, someone should be willing to board you for a small stipend each month, or perhaps you could take a room at one of the boardinghouses in Lynch. Lydia says rooms are available to let for two dollars and fifty cents a week, and Boone's Hollow is only a mile from Lynch."

The distance between Boone's Hollow and Lynch didn't alarm Addie nearly as much as the distance between Boone's Hollow and her parents. But how could she turn down the opportunity to earn almost thirty dollars a month? Even after paying for boarding, she'd have plenty left over. She could send some to the college and still be able to help Mother and Daddy. Fear drummed a wild beat within her breast. She held her breath, willing her erratic pulse to calm, and bit the inside of her lip.

Mrs. Hunt set the letter aside and folded her hands on the desk, brows low. "Addie, if you aren't interested in the position, you will not offend me by saying so."

Addie's breath eased out. She swallowed. "I'm sorry, ma'am. I was thinking. Deciding." A nervous giggle escaped. "I've never made such a big decision on my own. It's a little overwhelming."

Understanding bloomed on the library director's face. "Of course it is. Would you like to call your parents and seek their counsel before answering?"

As much as Addie wanted to talk to her parents, she shouldn't waste money on a telephone call. She could almost hear Mother's voice in her head. "We've been praying for provision, and God has provided." Daddy's deep yet tender voice followed. "Working beneath the direction of a woman who is known and recommended by someone you trust gives me full confidence you will be well cared for."

Addie held her hands outward. "Mrs. Hunt, I know how my parents would counsel me. They would say God has opened a door and I should walk through it."

Mrs. Hunt smiled. She reached for the telephone sitting on the corner of her desk. "Shall I let Lydia know a new packhorse librarian has been located?"

Addie's heart thudded in both apprehension and anticipation as she nodded.

Mrs. Hunt picked up the receiver and dialed the 0. "Operator? Please connect me with Boone's Hollow, Kentucky."

Boone's Hollow
Bettina

Bettina flung the saddlebag-like pouch over her shoulder. The weight smacked down on

142

her back, and she winced. It must've hit right where Pap'd landed a blow last night at supper. Her own fault. She shouldn't have fed him beans without no salt pork in them. She'd hoped he'd be too pickled to notice, but . . .

She shifted the pouch and glared across the beat-up old table and stacks of books at the city-lady librarian. "How many books've you loaded me with this time, Miz West? Feels like a hunnerd at least."

The woman sent Bettina the kind of look Alba Gilkey gave bugs that landed on her hand. "Now, Bettina, you know we have a strict rule about limiting the weight of the packs to twenty-five pounds." Then she let out a little airy sigh. Bettina'd never been around anybody who sighed more'n Miz West. Glory thought she did it because she had breathing problems. Bettina wasn't so sure. "Of course, the scale I use might not be one hundred percent accurate. But I do try not to overburden you."

Alba Gilkey gave Miz West a pat on her rounded shoulder. "Don't worry none about it, ma'am. Bettina ain't happy unless she's got somethin' to fuss about. She's always been that way."

Alba smiled while she talked, like she was telling a joke, but Bettina bristled anyway.

143

That Alba was always trying to cozy up to folks and make herself look so good and perfect, but Bettina knew better. And Bettina had lots of reasons for fussing. Losing her maw before she was fully growed, having to duck away from Pap's swinging fists whenever his temper got hold of him, not being smart enough to —

"Well, I have some good news for you girls."

Bettina slammed the door on her inner grumblings and gave Miz West her full attention. Seeing as how she hadn't gotten even a peek at Emmett yesterday and got smacked by Pap last night, she could use some good news.

"I got a telephone call from Lexington yesterday afternoon." Miz West beamed, proud as a jaybird. "Another rider will soon join us."

Glory gasped, eyes wide. "She's gonna carry books, too?"

"Indeed, she will. We'll divide the book-drop locations between the four of you, which means you'll each have fewer stops on your routes."

Glory and Alba squealed. Bettina didn't squeal. Squealing hurt Pap's ears, so she'd long ago trained herself not to make the happy noise. But she couldn't help smiling.

Fewer stops meant not so many hours in the hills. Not so many hours in the hills meant more hours free in the evenings. She wouldn't spend those evenings at home, either. She'd be courting.

Hooking her thumbs in her overall straps, she leaned forward some to better balance the pack. "When's she gonna get here? Today?"

"No, not today. Most likely not until next week."

Glory and Alba groaned, and Bettina huffed. "How come it's gonna take so long?"

Alba nudged Glory. "There she goes, fussin' again."

Like her and Glory hadn't complained, too? Bettina glared hard at Alba. The girl's cheeks went all pink, and she looked to the side. Bettina gave a little *humph* and turned to Miz West. "What I'm meanin' is trains go between Lynch an' Lexington twice every day. She could get here this very afternoon if she wanted to."

"That's true." Miz West handed Glory her pouch. It didn't look near as fat as Bettina's. "But there's paperwork and such I need to complete, and she's committed to another job until the end of the month. So it will be a little while yet." As she talked, she slid books into the third pouch. Now she fastened it and gave it to Alba, who almost dropped it.

Bettina held back a snort. Alba was so spindly she couldn't hardly carry a cup of buttermilk.

Miz West bounced her smile on Glory, Alba, and Bettina. She left it aimed at Bettina. "But help is coming. It's good news, yes?"

The three of them nodded, but a sudden worry smacked Bettina as hard as Pap's fist ever had. "If we ain't gonna have as many stops, are we gonna make less money?" Now that Pap'd got used to her turning over all but nine dollars of her pay every month, he'd have a conniption fit if she brung him less. He'd probably think she was holding out on him. She shivered, considering what he'd do.

Miz West held up her plump hands. "No, no, your salary won't drop by even a penny."

Bettina grinned. Well, now, that was better-'n-good news. "Thank you, ma'am. We best be goin'. Still got all our stops to make today." She headed for the door.

"Be safe, girls."

"Yes, ma'am," they chorused.

Bettina stepped from the dark smokehouse-turned-library to the street. Morning sunlight attacked her eyes, and she

146

squinted at Glory and Alba, who trailed after her same as they'd done since they was little bitty girls. She went straight to the trio of animals waiting with their reins draped over the straggly limbs of bushes at the edge of the woods. "Wonder how she'll divvy things up."

Glory double-stepped up next to Bettina. "Reckon she'll take some o' yours an' some o' mine an' Alba's, an' make a fresh route for her."

"Nah." Alba huffed and puffed, acting like she was carrying a whole ton of coal instead of a little ol' pouch of books. Bettina just knew Alba's pack weighed less than hers. Probably all magazines and no books at all. "Can't do it that way or she'll be zigzaggin' like a rabbit all over the mountain. Miz West'll likely make all new routes for each of us."

Glory's mouth fell open. "All new? I ain't hardly got used to the one I got now."

Alba shrugged. She braced herself, then heaved her bag over her horse's rump. She swiped her forehead with the back of her hand, making her curly pale blond hair fluff up. "Won't bother me none to learn a new route. 'Specially if it'll keep me from havin' to cross Tuckett's Creek. Neither me nor Biscuit" — she rubbed her horse's white

147

nose — "are fond o' that rushin' water."

"You think you got it bad?" Glory put her fist on her hip, acting all sassy, the way movie starlets did when they were fixing to let loose on somebody, most often on the rival for their man. "My route near goes straight up to get to the Pascals' place. Have to do it on foot. Poor Posey here can't climb such steep slopes. Don't know why the Pascals is on the list anyhow. Don't reckon there's a one of 'em in that cabin who even knows their ABCs. All they want is picture books."

Alba snickered.

Bettina's face burned hot. She real quick took the two paper-wrapped salt-pork-on-biscuit sandwiches she'd made for her lunch out of her pocket and slid them into the book pouch. Then she flopped the bag across her mule's back and swung herself on after it. "Ain't gonna know what'll change until the new gal comes, so we might as well get to deliverin'."

Glory made a sling with her hands and helped Alba onto her horse. That Alba was helpless as a newborn in some ways. Then Glory climbed onto her horse's back. She grabbed the reins and sent a smirk at Bettina and Alba. "Be safe."

This time Bettina snickered along with

the other girls. Every morning, Miz West told them the same thing when they left for their routes. The comment always made her want to laugh. City lady . . . scared of the dark, most likely. There wasn't one solitary thing out on the mountain that scared Bettina. Her scary thing lived under her very own roof. But soon as she and Emmett married up, she'd be able to leave Pap and be safe and happy. Emmett was so big, so strong. He'd never let Pap hurt her again.

That new girl couldn't get to Boone's Holler quick enough to suit Bettina.

Alba set off through the trees to the west, Glory went southeast, and Bettina guided her mule in a northeasterly direction. Her first stop was right close — Nanny Fay's cabin, set at the edge of what folks considered the border of Boone's Holler. She slid her hand into the bulky side of the pack while passing between the low branches of close-growing maples. Miz West made things easy by arranging the books so's they were in the order of her stops. Her fingers closed around the top one, which felt as thick as a stack of flapjacks, and she pulled it out. A colored picture on the cover showed two boys fishing on what must be a riverbank because a boat of some sort floated on the water. There probably wasn't no pictures inside, though. Only skinny books had pictures on their insides.

"Don't reckon there's a one of 'em in that cabin who even knows their ABCs. All they want is picture books." Glory's snide voice rang in Bettina's memory.

Bettina gritted her teeth. She wouldn't never be caught looking inside the skinny books, no matter how much the pictures enticed her. She held the book chosen for Nanny Fay out in front of her and scowled at the big letters printed at the top of the cover. She knew *t, a,* and *e* because her name had those same letters in it. But the whole words? She growled under her breath. "Fat as this thing is, it's gonna have lotsa words in it." And she couldn't even make sense of the two on the cover.

Mule broke through the trees into a small clearing. Nanny Fay's cabin sat a little off center in the open spot. A garden stretched all the way to the trees on one side, and a woodpile the size of a beaver's dam lurked on the other. The old lady herself waited on a bench on the little porch, the same way she always did on book-delivering day. She stood and walked to the railing, carrying a book in her gnarled hands the way Bettina'd seen some mamas hold their babies during Sunday service. The same way Emmett used

150

to hold books. He always was one for studying. So handsome, and so smart, too.

Bettina was proud of Emmett for his fine-working brain, but it kinda irked her that some old lady who'd married herself to a Tuckett could read the hundreds — no, more like thousands — of words in these fat books. Didn't seem right that she could and Bettina couldn't.

"Mornin', Bettina."

Nanny Fay talked real kindly to everybody. Bettina wanted to say "Mornin' " back, but she didn't. Pap'd told Bettina a long time ago not to get friendly with the old woman. Pap said they couldn't trust no Tucketts because they'd mingled their blood with Cherokees. Nanny Fay didn't start out a Tuckett. She'd married one. And the one she married was way down the line. Couldn't hardly be any Cherokee blood left in him. But it didn't matter to Pap. Same as most folks in Boone's Holler, he didn't like the Tucketts, and he thought Nanny Fay was a witch. He'd told Bettina, "She's a witch, all right. Only thing that makes sense, her bein' older'n dirt an' always mixin' herbs an' such."

Truth be told, the woman probably wasn't a witch. Would a witch come to services at a Baptist church? Would a witch sit on her

151

front porch in the daylight hours? Bettina didn't know a lot about witches, but Nanny Fay sure didn't look nor act like a witch. But Bettina could be wrong. Pap said Bettina didn't have the sense God gave a turkey, and turkeys were so dumb they'd stand in the rain and drown. So she kept her thinking to herself. If she spoke up, folks might stay shy of her the way they shied away from Nanny Fay and she'd be lonelier'n lonely then.

She drew the mule within arm's length of the railing and held out the fishing-boys book.

The old woman's face lit up like candles on a Christmas tree. "Oh, a Mark Twain story."

Bettina recalled Miz West calling Mark Twain a famous author. She imagined repeating the comment. She'd say it real casual, like it was common to her. But wouldn't she sound important, talking about authors, making people think she knew things others didn't? She'd say it sometime. Maybe to Emmett. But not to Nanny Fay.

Nanny Fay traded the Mark Twain book for one with a plain blue cloth cover and some gold letters stamped on its spine. Bettina dropped the blue book in the empty side of the pouch and gave the reins a little tug.

"Bye, Bettina. Have a good day now, y'hear?"

Bettina poked Mule with her bare heels and made him trot out of the clearing. She couldn't stick around here and chat. Pap'd have her hide, maybe even make her quit taking books around to folks if he found out. If she didn't have this job, how would she get money to buy pretty things to wear or be able to stay away from her cabin for hours at a time? No, she couldn't risk it. But it seemed sad to leave the old woman standing on her porch with nothing more'n a book keeping her company.

ELEVEN

Emmett

Emmett walked Dusty to school Tuesday morning. His brother had pouted all through supper the night before because Emmett went into Lynch instead of going with him to the one-room schoolhouse yesterday morning. "There's only four days left 'til we're all done for the year. You wanna miss 'em all?" he'd said with his lower lip poked out. All the explaining in the world hadn't made a bit of difference to the eight-year-old. Dusty considered himself more important than any old job, and that was that. So even though Emmett wanted to visit every place of business in the low-lying communities near Black Mountain, he carved out time to walk his little brother to the schoolhouse where Emmett had spent so many hours in his younger years. He even carried Dusty's lunch pail.

Dusty jabbered nonstop, pausing now and

then to pick up a stone and throw it into the trees or pluck a fresh green leaf and twirl it. Time slid backward as Emmett walked the familiar path, swinging a battered cracker tin and squinting against the morning sun. For more than forty years, kids from Tuckett's Pass and Boone's Hollow had come together at the one-room mountain school, but for only a few months of the year. Then when Emmett was eight or nine years old, Mr. Halcomb came and insisted the school should be open a full nine months, same as in the big cities. It took three years before everybody in Boone's Hollow and Tuckett's Pass sent their kids for all nine months. These folks resisted change the way a criminal resists arrest, but Mr. Halcomb had won, finally. But there was one battle he was still fighting. Tuckett's Pass parents continued to insist that their kids sit apart from Boone's Hollow kids. How many generations would be taught to follow the old feud?

Emmett had asked Dusty if he'd made friends with Tuckett's Pass kids, and Dusty stared at him as if he'd said something foul. Funny how the old rivalry between the two little towns, so close in proximity but so far apart in friendliness, stayed strong generation after generation. Maw and Paw said it'd been that way their whole lives and their folks' lives and before them, but they couldn't honestly say what had started the conflict. All Emmett knew was if a fellow came from Boone's Hollow, he snubbed the folks from Tuckett's Pass. Pretty silly.

The sound of children's hoots and laughter carried from ahead, and Dusty gave a little hop. "They're playin' dodge-the-ball!"

Emmett chuckled. "Now, how can you know that when you can't see —"

Smack!

"Ouch! Hey, that hurt!"

Laughter rolled.

The sounds carrying from the other side of the trees proved Dusty's theory and brought a rush of memories. Emmett winced, recalling how much it'd stung when the large rubber ball connected with his side or legs.

Dusty grabbed his wrist. "C'mon, Emmett, hurry or I won't get to play!"

Emmett jogged the remaining distance with Dusty but then passed the rings of children — a smaller group on one side of the yard and a larger group, to which Dusty ran, on the other — and entered the unpainted clapboard building. He set Dusty's pail with others cluttering the long bench in the narrow cloakroom, then entered the classroom. The same desks and benches, cloudy slate boards, and smell of coal oil greeted him. A strange sensation gripped him, something his college professors would probably call déjà vu. He crossed the creaky floorboards slowly, observing the teacher, who sat behind his desk with his head low, his hand moving rhythmically between an inkpot and a sheet of paper. The *scritch-scritch* of his pen seemed loud in the otherwise quiet room.

Even though things hadn't worked out the way Emmett expected after earning a college degree, affection rolled through him. He'd never known, and might not ever know, a more dedicated person than Mr. Halcomb. He stopped midway across the floor and slid his hands into his trouser pockets, watching, waiting, remembering.

Mr. Halcomb set the pen aside, sat up, and met Emmett's gaze. A smile broke over his face. He stood and rounded his desk, hand already reaching. "Why, Emmett Tharp . . ."

Emmett shook his teacher's hand. The man looked a little older but no less scholarly than Emmett recalled. With Mr Halcomb's neat goatee, short-cropped gray hair, black suit, and string tie, he'd blend right in with the college teachers. "Hello,

Mr. Halcomb. Good to see you."

"Please, call me Ralph."

Emmett smiled. He'd never be able to call his teacher anything but Mr. Halcomb.

"Dusty said you were back, but I thought he might be makin' up a story."

Emmett raised his eyebrows. "Making up stories?"

The teacher chuckled. "He has an active imagination. I suspect when he got to missin' you too much, he'd pretend you were home, and his pretendin' got carried away. He's never a spiteful liar."

Even so, Maw would have a conniption fit if she knew Dusty'd been spewing falsehoods. He'd have a talk with Dusty after school.

Mr. Halcomb gave Emmett's hand a squeeze, then let go. "I reckon you're only home for a visit, though. Unless you're plannin' to start your own business here on the mountain."

He'd need more imagination than Dusty possessed to come up with a business that would sustain him in the small town. "After being away so long, I wanted some time with my family. But I plan to find a job in a city somewhere. I'm still . . ." How could he speak the truth without disappointing the man who'd held such high hopes for

158

him? "Exploring."

Mr. Halcomb clapped Emmett on the shoulder. "Someone with your intellect and drive will be successful wherever you land. I'm proud of you, Emmett, and I'm sure your folks are, too."

Emmett wasn't so sure about Paw. He seemed to have trouble looking Emmett straight in the face. But Maw was proud, so Emmett could nod without being untruthful.

Shrill, angry shouts exploded from the play yard. Mr. Halcomb leaned sideways and peered past Emmett, frowning. "I need to bring the children in." He gave Emmett a rueful grin and started for the door. "I'd like to talk more, though. Get caught up with you. How long will you be in Boone's Hollow?"

Emmett fell in step with his teacher. "I don't honestly know. But I'm pretty sure Maw won't mind if you come to dinner one night. I'll check with her and have Dusty let you know which evening she says."

"That sounds fine, Emmett, real fine. We'll talk at length then." He yanked the frayed rope attached to the small brass bell hanging in the cupola on top of the building, and the bell clanged its call to study.

The children swarmed the porch. Emmett

worked his way down the stairs, getting bumped from every angle. Dusty flung himself against Emmett's middle for a quick hug before darting around him and disappearing inside. Emmett retraced his steps from the schoolyard to the road. As he rounded the trees, a mule emerged from the brush. Bettina Webber straddled the animal.

Her freckled face lit. When she smiled, she really was pretty, even while wearing a pair of men's overalls over a long-sleeved pink flowered blouse and with no shoes on her dirty feet. But in a flash, her smile turned flirtatious, and just as quickly, unease attacked Emmett.

She rode up close to him, then reined in. "Hey, Emmett. What're you doin' out here?"

The mule snuffled his shoulder, and he scratched its prickly chin. "Dusty wanted me to walk him to school. I'm heading back home now."

She wrinkled her nose. "Betcha you're awful glad to be done with that place. I couldn't hardly wait 'til Pap said I could quit."

Emmett had noticed Bettina's struggles. Pretty hard to miss when students of all ages shared a single room. The same sympathy he'd often experienced during their school days tiptoed through him again. He stepped free of the mule's probing nose. "Did you graduate?"

"Nah." She tossed her head. "I stopped goin' halfway through my ninth year. Maw died that winter, an' Pap said he needed me at home. An' since I —" She looked sharply aside and clamped her lips so tight they turned white. She sat that way for several seconds, then faced Emmett again. Her self-assured smile returned. "I got as much book learnin' as I need to be a good wife an' maw. Don't see no reason to be sittin' in that classroom anymore."

Maybe she was right. His mother had gone through only five years of school, and she did fine. But Maw didn't have the struggles Bettina did.

She sighed and patted the leather bag draped over the mule's neck. "Well, it's real good to see you, an' much as I'd like to stay an' talk, I got books to deliver. Bye for now, Emmett." She waggled her fingers at him, then kicked the mule into motion.

He watched her disappear into the brush, and then he set off for home. Why had Bettina not been able to absorb what she called book learnin'? The girl wasn't dim witted. Even Emmett could tell that. So why did learning come so hard for her? The

161

question still plagued him when he reached his family's cabin, and he asked it of Maw when he stepped through the open doorway.

She paused at the washstand, hands in sudsy water, and gave him a thoughtful look. "Do you recall Bettina's maw?"

An image of a quiet, sweet-faced woman formed in Emmett's memory. He nodded.

"Me an' Rosie growed up together. A kinder, gentler soul was never born." She took up the soapy rag and used it on a plate while she talked. "Handy with a needle? Oh, law, that girl made the prettiest hankies you ever did see, with cutwork an' fine stitches on the hems or little flowers embroidered on all the corners. Still have the one she give me to carry on the day I married your paw. But she never did no samplers."

Emmett took a cup from the drainboard and put it on the shelf. "Samplers?"

Maw grinned. "Why, with all your learnin', you don't know what a sampler is?"

He chuckled. "I reckon they didn't teach that at the university."

She laughed, the sound merry. "All little girls learned their ABCs by stitchin' them in a row on cloth." She dipped the plate in a pan of filmy water, her brows pinching into a V. "Rosie's letters . . . they were

162

always every which way."

Emmett took the plate and placed it on the drainboard. "Don't most kids turn letters every which way when they're first learning?"

Maw nodded. "When they're first learnin', sure. But poor Rosie never learned how to turn 'em the right way. They stayed all mixed up until her dyin' day." Tears swam in her eyes. "How her maw used to switch her . . . left welts on her little legs that lasted for days. But none o' that whippin' ever made a ounce o' difference. Rosie never did learn to read."

Her hands stilled in the water, and she stared out the window, as if drifting off somewhere. "I often ponder if that's why she married Burke when she was so young. She said she loved him, but she was only fourteen when she pledged herself to him. Still a little girl. I think it's more likely she wanted to get away from her maw an' not hafta go to school no more, an' Burke was her escape."

"But Rosie was . . . bright?"

Maw jerked her attention to Emmett. Indignation burned in her eyes. "Bright as a new penny." Then she slumped her shoulders, sadness clouding her face. "Not that she ever saw herself that way. I reckon whatever kept Rosie from understandin' letters an' such got passed on to Bettina. But what is it that keeps 'em from learnin'? I wish I knew. I'd try to fix it. Too late for Rosie, but Bettina's got lots of livin' left to do. An' it's a downright shame she has to go through life feelin' as disgraceful as Rosie always did."

Emmett leaned down and kissed his mother's cheek. "You're a kind soul, too, Maw."

She blushed and flicked soap suds at him. "Oh . . ."

He grinned. "But I don't think you need to worry about Bettina. She seems pretty sure of herself. Even told me she knows enough to be a good wife and mother."

Maw's eyebrows shot up. "She told you that? When?"

"On the road by the school this morning."

"That girl . . ." She clicked her tongue on her teeth and shook her head. "She's droppin' hints, Emmett. She's wantin' out o' her pap's house, same as Rosie wanted out. 'Less I miss my guess, she's set her sights on you."

Heat attacked his face. "Well, she'd better look in another direction. I don't intend to marry Bettina Webber. I'll come right out and tell her so if I need to."

Worry pinched Maw's forehead. "Be careful. And be kind. She ain't nearly as sure of herself as she acts." She returned to washing dishes. She kept talking, but Emmett got the feeling she was speaking to herself more than to him. "I'm glad she got one of them WPA jobs. I keep prayin' she'll squirrel away the money she makes an' use it to get herself out o' Boone's Holler, away from Burke. Rosie deserved better. An' so does her daughter."

TWELVE

Emmett

Emmett changed from the shirt and dungarees he'd worn for his walk with Dusty into his suit. He grimaced at the slight fraying on the cuff of his right sleeve. As soon as he got a paycheck, he needed to buy a new suit. This one had about worn out its use. Of course, it depended on what kind of job he got. He might not need a suit if he ended up being a shelf stocker or a cashier or a janitor. Whatever job was open, he intended to apply for it. Or beg for it.

With his hat covering his getting-too-long hair and determination squaring his shoulders, he walked to Gilliam's Livery and asked to rent a horse from the livery owner.

Kermit Gilliam smiled big, showing a wad of chewing tobacco where his bottom teeth used to be. "Sure thing, Emmett. Where you headin'?"

"Lynch first. Then I might ride to Ben-

166

ham. Kind of depends on how things go in Lynch."

The man sauntered to a stall and slid the gate open. "I'll give ya Red, then. He ain't one to dawdle, an' he can keep goin' fer a piece without wearin' out. Yessir, he's a fine one."

Emmett fingered the coins in his pocket. He'd earned pocket money by tutoring other students in mathematics, but he'd spent most of it on train fare to get home. If he didn't find a job soon and start earning a wage, he'd have to ask Paw for help. He hoped he wouldn't have to stoop so low. A man with a college degree shouldn't need to borrow money from his paw. "How much?"

"For the whole day? Two bits."

Emmett counted out two dimes and a nickel and dropped the coins into Kermit's grubby hand.

The man pocketed the money quick and thrust the horse's reins at Emmett. "If you come back before noon, I'll give ya ten cents o' that back."

Emmett didn't expect to be back before noon. Maybe not even by suppertime. "That's fine, Kermit. Do you have a saddle?"

"Sure do."

"Is it extra?"

"Sure ain't." He spit into the straw at his feet. "But you gotta saddle him up your own self. Saddles an' blankets in the tack room. Take your pick."

Emmett chose the least mouse-chewed blanket and saddle from the smelly, windowless room in the back corner of the barn. He hadn't saddled a horse in at least four years, but he managed it fine and couldn't deny a sense of satisfaction at having remembered how to cinch the girth so the knot was tight and lay flat against the horse's belly. He figured Red would appreciate his know-how, too.

He stuck his foot in a stirrup and swung himself onto the leather seat, then tugged Red's reins. "All right, big fella, let's go."

Red carried Emmett from the shadowy barn into the shaded street. Emmett aimed the horse for the road, his mind running ahead to Lynch's business district and the possible places he could find a job. The door to the Blevins' old smokehouse was propped open with a brick, and a lantern burned behind one of the newly added windows.

An idle thought trickled through his mind. The government had hired a librarian, and she'd hired some book deliverers. Maybe she needed another person to help keep the library functioning. There was no harm in asking.

"Whoa there, Red." The horse obediently halted. Emmett slid from the saddle and led the horse to the smokehouse. He peeked inside. The older woman Bettina had pointed out the night of the singing sat at a large table in front of the window, applying blue cloth tape to the binding of a book. "Morning, ma'am."

She shifted her attention to him. "Good morning to you, young man. May I help you?"

Emmett looped Red's reins around a branch on the closest bush and stepped over the threshold, removing his hat. Bettina'd been right — the place smelled like ham. "Maybe. I'm Emmett Tharp. My family lives here in Boone's Hollow."

She angled her head and seemed to examine him. "Are you Emil and Damaris's older boy?"

It didn't surprise him a bit that she'd know about him. There was no such thing as a secret in Boone's Hollow. "Yes, ma'am."

She set the tape aside, rose, and extended her hand to him. "I'm Miss Lydia West." She drew in a breath and sighed it out. "It's nice to meet you."

Emmett shook the woman's hand. "It's

nice to meet you, too."

"Your mother told me all about your winning a scholarship to attend the University of Kentucky. She's very proud of you. I confess, I'm also quite impressed." She sighed again.

"Thank you, ma'am. I graduated this year with a bachelor of science in commerce."

"Congratulations." She returned to the chair and sat.

"Thank you. So now I'm looking for work."

"Oh, my." Her lips puckered. "I imagine that's been challenging, given these difficult times."

"Yes." He lightly bounced his hat against his thigh. "Do you need any more help here? I could take books to folks in the hills or . . ." He glanced around the small space. A curtain made from blankets hung on a wire and hid whatever was in the back half of the smokehouse. In the front part, short shelves lined the opposite walls, three on each side. All held a few books and tattered magazines. He pointed to the closest shelf with his hat. "I could organize books, keep records of what goes out and comes in, whatever you needed done."

"I wish you'd come in a week or two earlier, Mr. Tharp. If I'd known you were interested in working here, I wouldn't have contacted my cousin in Lexington about a new rider. But the job's already been granted to" — another sigh — "someone else. She's due to arrive this coming weekend."

Emmett wanted to sigh, too. He nodded and slipped his hat onto his head. "I understand. I appreciate your time." He started toward the door.

"If something changes and the young lady from Lexington decides not to come, I'll let you know."

Emmett smiled his thanks and left the building. He didn't expect to hear from Miss West. Only a fool would turn down a steady job these days. He grabbed Red's reins and pulled himself onto the saddle. "C'mon, Red, let's get ourselves to Lynch."

Over the remainder of the week, Emmett gave every last penny of his tutoring money to Kermit Gilliam for the privilege of riding Red down the mountain. By Friday, he'd visited every department store, bank, grocery store, factory, and office in Lynch, Benham, and Cumberland. Everywhere he went, he received a variation of the same reply — "I'm sorry, young man, but we're not hirin'."

In desperation, he even went to Tuckett's

Pass and asked the man operating a little mill if he could use an extra hand. The man glared at him through narrowed eyes. "Ain't you from Boone's Holler, boy?" At Emmett's nod, he added, "Then you'd best skeedaddle."

Emmett returned Red to the livery early Friday afternoon. As Kermit poured oats into a bucket for Red, Emmett asked if he needed any help at the livery.

Kermit burst out laughing. "Hooeey, boy, you ain't gonna leave nary a stone unturned, are you?" He slapped Emmett's shoulder, his laughter fading. "I wish I could say yes. My ol' bones, they're gettin' weary o' tendin' these beasts, an' I know you'd be a real good worker, comin' from such good stock an' all. Yessir, I'd be hard pressed to find finer folks'n your maw an' paw. But I ain't got money to pay nobody. Barely got money to pay for oats. I'm sorry."

Emmett was sorry, too, but like Paw sometimes said, sorry didn't change anything. He left the livery and headed home, his steps slow and his heart heavy. This evening his family planned to attend the Boone's Hollow and Tuckett's Pass mountain school graduation ceremony. Everybody in town went to school events, whether programs or baseball games or spelling bees or graduations. Maw would expect him to go with her, Paw, and Dusty, but he hoped he'd be able to talk his way out of it. He'd had a long visit with Mr. Halcomb after supper at his folks' place Wednesday evening, so he didn't feel the need to see his old teacher. After his frustrating, fruitless days of job searching, he needed some time alone. To think. To plan. And, as Maw would encourage, to pray.

Emmett passed the Barrs' shack. Mrs. Barr was in the yard hacking at weeds with a hoe while a runny-nosed toddler wearing a shirt but no pants hung on her skirt. Emmett waved hello, the polite thing to do, and the woman bobbed her head in reply. The sorrowful, resigned look aging the woman's face pained Emmett in ways he couldn't understand, and he hurried to the rise leading to his folks' cabin.

The cabin door stood open in silent invitation, and Emmett stepped in. To his surprise, Paw sat at the kitchen table with his work boot propped on his knee and a can of polish open in front of him.

Emmett glanced at the clock on the fireplace mantel, then turned to Paw. "How come you're home so early?" He could remember only two times that Paw came home midday, and both times somebody'd gotten hurt in the mine. "Was there an accident?"

Paw dipped the rag in the polish and rubbed it on the toe of his boot. "Nothin' like that. Boss let any of us from Boone's Holler or Tuckett's Pass off early today since it's graduatin' day for the youngsters."

Relief sagged Emmett's bones.

"Three of 'em gettin' diplomas this year. All girls, two of 'em from Boone's Holler."

He dropped into the chair across from Paw. Strange how Paw's voice didn't take on a hard edge when speaking of other folks' children earning diplomas. He saved his disdain for his own son. Emmett pushed the wry thought aside. "It's nice they let you go."

Paw shrugged. "Started it last year. The big boss figures it's good for . . ." He scrunched his face. "Forget what they call it."

"Morale?"

"Yeah. Morale." Paw snorted. "Whatever that is."

Emmett could define the word but decided not to. "Where's Maw?"

"Went to Belcher's. She's wantin' to bake an almond cream cake for the after-graduation party, an' she was out o' almond flavorin'. Hope Belcher's has what she's

174

needin'. There ain't time to get all the way to the company store in Lynch, an' she's sure got me hankerin' for a slice o' her cake."

Emmett watched his father shine up his old work boot. He couldn't help staring at the coal dust ground under Paw's fingernails and lining his cuticles. No matter how much he scrubbed, the black never came completely off. But Paw wasn't bothered by dirty hands. He said working in the coal mine let him care for his family. There was no shame in honest work.

"Paw?"

Paw didn't look up. "Huh?"

"Would you teach me everything you know about coal mining?"

Paw's fingers stilled. He kept his head low but lifted his eyes. "Why?"

"I need to know. When I talked to an administrator about working in the mine, he said they didn't have time to train me. I figure if you teach me, they'll be able to take me on."

Slowly Paw's head raised, and he looked Emmett square in the face. "You wanna be a miner?"

He didn't, but beggars couldn't be choosers. He'd run out of options. "It's honest work. It's been a good job for you."

Paw stared at Emmett for several seconds, expression blank. Then a smile twitched at the corners of his lips. "Yeah. Yeah, it's been good for us. We ain't never gone hungry or without clothes on our backs. It'd sure please your maw to have you stickin' around close to home instead o' settlin' in a big city somewhere."

"So, you'll help me?"

Paw dropped the stained rag on the table and placed his hand over Emmett's. "I'll teach you everything I know." He patted Emmett's hand, then returned to polishing.

Emmett looked at his hand. Folks always said he looked more like Maw with his straw-colored hair and blue eyes, that he was tall and broad shouldered like her father and grandfather. They called him more a McCallister than a Tharp, unlike Dusty, whose dark hair, dark eyes, and wiry build branded him a Tharp. Emmett had always wondered if his looks added to the distance between him and Paw. But the polish from Paw's fingers had left smears on his fingers. Black smears. The color of coal.

Finally, there was something about him that resembled his father.

Mrs. Hunt placed the pay envelope in Addie's palm, then sandwiched Addie's hand between hers. "Here you are, my dear. Pay for a job well done."

Addie swallowed an unexpected knot of emotion. "Thank you, ma'am. I've enjoyed working here. I . . ." She swallowed again. "I'm going to miss all of you."

"And we will miss you." Mrs. Hunt squeezed Addie's hand and then stepped back. "I trust you'll drop Miss Collins or me a line now and then to let us know how you're doing. We will want to know all about Boone's Hollow."

"I will." Addie slipped the envelope into her purse.

The library director folded her arms over her chest. "When do you leave?"

"I leave for Boone's Hollow on Sunday afternoon, but I'm taking a train to Georgetown tomorrow morning. I want to see my folks before I go."

"And I'm sure they want to see you."

"Yes, ma'am." Addie was already dreading the coming goodbye, but at the same time, she eagerly anticipated starting the job that would allow her to help her parents.

Mrs. Hunt leaned forward and wrapped

Addie in a quick hug. "You take good care of yourself, Miss Adelaide Cowherd. I suspect you're going to be a real blessing to the people of Boone's Hollow."

Addie blinked rapidly and hurried from the room. She hadn't realized how fond she'd become of Mrs. Hunt and the other employees at the library until it was time to bid them farewell. She would miss them as much as she missed Felicity.

She stopped at the front desk and told Griselda Ann in a whisper that she planned to cash her check at the bank and then go to the house. "I'll make supper tonight as a thank-you for hosting me."

Griselda Ann shook her head so adamantly her short brown curls bounced. "No, I will make supper. Tuna-and-noodle casserole with potato chips on top. And sugar dumplings for dessert."

Addie's mouth watered. "You don't need to go to so much trouble."

"I owe you more than just a special supper for all the help you've given with the quilts for the downtrodden."

Addie absently rubbed the callous on the inside of her thumb. "Cutting out fabric wasn't so much. You did more for me than I did for you."

"We don't have time to argue." Griselda

Ann scurried from behind the desk and gave Addie a little push toward the door. "The bank will close before you get there. Now go. I'll see you later."

Addie obeyed, mostly because she didn't want to miss getting her check cashed. She followed Mill Street to downtown Lexington and reached the bank with a half hour to spare. She tucked the bills and coins into a secret pocket of her purse, then set off for Griselda Ann's at a leisurely pace. While she walked, she admired the storefronts and peeked into windows.

Mrs. Hunt had said Boone's Hollow was a small town. Would it have a sweets shop or a drugstore with a soda fountain? Perhaps a little café where she could get together in the evenings with the friends she was sure to make? A dress shop, even if it had only a few offerings, would make a fine meeting place as well. She and Felicity had spent many cheerful hours browsing the racks at Appel's department store and trying on hats and scarves and gloves until the salesladies' disapproving frowns sent them out to the sidewalk, where they broke into bouts of giggles.

At least she knew for sure Boone's Hollow had a library, albeit a small one. She mustn't get her hopes up that it would be as large as Lexington's Carnegie Library or even have as many books as she'd found in the stately brick building that served as the Scott County Library in Georgetown. But a town with a library was a good town. She'd be happy there. In time, she'd feel right at home.

THIRTEEN

Georgetown
Addie

Addie stepped from the train car onto the wooden boardwalk and scuttled away from the other disembarking passengers, who blocked her view. The midmorning sun, beaming from a cloudless sky, almost blinded her after her being in the enclosed car. She cupped her hand above her eyes and searched the length of the wooden walkway, heart thrumming in eagerness.

"Addie! Addie, honey!"

She spun in the direction of the call, and a little gasp of joy left her throat. She was a mature young lady of twenty-one wearing a dress and heels instead of a seven-year-old in a romper with sturdy Mary Janes on her feet, but she broke into a run toward the couple waiting beneath the depot's over-hang. Daddy moved forward a step, and she threw herself into his arms with the same

181

enthusiasm she had when she was a child and he'd returned home from a day at the bank. His arms closed around her, and she breathed in his familiar scents — peppermint, cherry tobacco, and bay rum. The scents that represented security.

He kissed her cheek and delivered her to Mother's embrace. Mother didn't hug as tightly as Daddy, but she rocked Addie gently side to side, her warm, soft cheek pressed to Addie's. While Mother hugged her, Daddy rubbed her back and said, "Welcome home, sugar dumplin'."

Addie laughed and pulled loose. "Funny you should call me that. The lady who boarded me this past week fixed sugar dumplings for supper last night. But she used raisins instead of pecans and store-bought syrup, so they weren't as good as yours, Mother."

Mother laughed and cupped Addie's face in her hands. "Honey, if I had my own kitchen, I'd fix you a pan of your favorite treat." She kissed Addie's forehead and released her. "I can't make them for you this visit, but you wait. When we're in a house again, I'll bake so many sugar dumplin's you'll make yourself sick eating them."

How could her independent, self-sufficient parents bear to live in a single room under someone else's roof, eating someone else's cooking? Linking elbows with them, Addie secretly vowed to save every penny possible and send it to her parents. They walked to the baggage dock, where Addie's suitcases waited at the edge. Temptation struck hard to pop the larger one open and show Mother what Griselda Ann had given her yesterday after supper, but the many people milling around didn't need to receive a glimpse of her personal belongings. She'd have to wait until they reached the boardinghouse.

Daddy grabbed the handle on the big suitcase, and Addie took the small one. Mother pointed to a black coupe with a leather bonnet parked nearby. "Preacher Finley loaned us his Plymouth."

Addie had expected to walk to the boardinghouse. Riding in Preacher Finley's coupe, even though it was much smaller than Daddy's Model A, would be a treat compared to carrying her suitcases so far. Daddy loaded her cases in the rumble seat, and then they climbed into the cab, with Addie in the center. Three abreast was crowded now that Addie was all grown up, but she loved sitting between Mother and Daddy, as she'd done on so many Sunday afternoon drives through the country in Daddy's now-sold Model A.

A lump filled her throat. So many experiences, so dear in heart, would forever reside only in memory unless their financial position drastically changed. She sent up a quick, silent prayer of thanks for her job waiting in Boone's Hollow. Twenty-nine dollars . . . If she paid ten for boarding and five each month to the college, she could send the remaining fourteen dollars to Mother and Daddy. By Christmastime, would they have enough saved up to be able to rent a little home? If Daddy found a job, too, they might be able to leave the awful boardinghouse even sooner. Her heart fluttered with hope.

Daddy turned off Depot Street onto Douglas Avenue. The tune of rubber tires on brick pavement carried through the open windows. Mother placed her hand on Addie's knee. "Preacher Finley and his wife have opened their home to you for tonight, since there isn't a place for you to sleep at the boardinghouse. They've been so kind to us in this time of trial."

"A true blessing." Addie grinned at Mother, repeating the phrase she'd heard so often from her mother's lips.

Mother squeezed Addie's knee, then linked her hands in her lap. "Indeed, it is. Mrs. Finley will take you to the train station in the morning, before church service."

The vehicle picked up speed, and the breeze streaming through the open side windows tossed Addie's hair over her eyes. She captured the long strands and drew them over her left shoulder, then clamped the thick tail to her collarbone with her fist. "But I wanted to attend service with you before I leave. Isn't there an afternoon train I could take instead?"

Mother tsk-tsked. "Your daddy checked. There are four stops between Georgetown and Lynch."

"Lexington, Mount Vernon, Pittsburg, and Cumberland." His hands on the steering wheel, Daddy raised a finger for each location. He sent a sideways glance at her, then faced the street again. "As it is, leaving here at nine in the morning won't get you to Lynch until late afternoon. And then you still have to travel to Boone's Hollow."

Addie folded her arms and bit her lip.

Daddy nudged her with his elbow — a silent message she'd received in childhood when her behavior displeased him. She automatically mimicked Mother's pose, hands in her lap.

Daddy bumped her again, but this was a friendly bump. "Who is picking you up from the depot in Lynch?"

185

Addie addressed Daddy's profile. "Mrs. Hunt's cousin Miss West — the one who directs the library in Boone's Hollow — made arrangements for someone named Kermit Gilliam to meet me with a wagon."

"Not a car?"

Addie turned at Mother's question. "No, she said a wagon."

"The roads in the mountains are steep." Daddy drew Addie's attention again. "Most people up in the mountain communities still use horses and wagons instead of motor vehicles."

Addie'd seen a few wagons on the streets of Georgetown. Mostly farmers hauling vegetables or small livestock to the markets. But she hadn't contemplated horses and wagons being the main means of transportation anywhere in Kentucky. Perhaps she should have, given that she'd be riding a horse to make her book deliveries.

She shrugged. "Mrs. Hunt said a person could walk from Lynch to Boone's Hollow but since I'll have luggage with me, I need a ride. I'm glad Miss West arranged it for me."

Daddy turned into the residential area where Preacher and Mrs. Finley lived in a bungalow with their school-age daughters. "Did she arrange boarding for you, too?"

Nervousness wriggled through Addie's

186

belly. "She said I would share her lodging until I could find a place to stay. I might need to take a room in Lynch." She hoped to find something in Boone's Hollow, though. Even a room in someone's private house would be preferable to making the trip from Lynch each day. And maybe a room in a house would cost less than ten dollars a month.

Daddy pulled up to the preacher's house and turned off the coupe's engine. The vehicle sputtered a bit before coughing and falling silent. "Before we go in, let's pray together." He slid his arm around her shoulders and held his other hand to Mother.

She placed one hand on Addie's shoulder and took hold of Daddy's hand. Their arms formed a circle around Addie. A knot filled her throat. When she'd left for each school year, she'd known she would see them again on breaks or the occasional weekend visits. This leave-taking was so different, with much uncertainty surrounding it.

The longing to be their little girl again, cosseted and protected, rolled through her with such force it brought the sting of tears. But she wasn't a little girl. She was grown up, and now it was her turn to take care of them. She sniffed hard and placed her hands over their joined hands. "May I pray?"

Surprise registered on Daddy's face, but he nodded.

Addie closed her eyes. "Dear God, thank You for my mother and daddy. They taught me that You love me, and they taught me to love You and Jesus, too. They taught me that You're always there for me, no matter where I am." The reality of their teaching reached deep into Addie's soul. She nodded, smiling. "Even in Boone's Hollow. Please be with us while we're far apart. Keep us safe and well. Provide for our needs, and let us be a blessing to those we encounter. May Your peace, which passes all understanding, keep our hearts and minds on Your beloved Son. Amen." She opened her eyes.

Tears formed moist tracks down Mother's cheek, and Daddy's eyes were watery. He briefly touched his forehead to hers, then straightened. "To be honest, Addie, I wasn't sure you were ready to go off on your own. In here" — he touched his chest — "you're still my little girl. But with things being the way they are, we didn't have a choice." He sighed, and the scent of peppermint filled the small space. "Your mother, who's nearly as wise as Solomon, told me I'd never be ready to let you go and that these difficult circumstances could very well be God's way of seeing His plans for you fulfilled."

The circumstances Daddy referenced — his losing his job, their losing their house, her having to leave school and take a job far from home — paraded through her mind. Addie searched Mother's eyes for signs of uncertainty. "Do you really believe God orchestrated all these changes?"

"He could have. But even if He didn't, He can use them for our betterment. The Bible tells us all things work for good for the believer." Mother's calm, sure voice soothed the frayed edges of Addie's heart. "Yes, it's hard right now, but should we doubt Him when He's been so faithful to us in the past?"

She'd never seen her parents flounder in their faithfulness. Not to God, not to each other. And not to her. She wouldn't disappoint them now. She shook her head.

Mother smiled, and Daddy said, "That's our girl." They enfolded her in a hug so tight it stole her breath, but she didn't mind. She memorized the feeling of being wrapped in their arms, wrapped in their love, so she could carry it away with her and relive it in lonely moments that were sure to plague her before she found her place of belonging in her new town.

FOURTEEN

Lynch
Emmett

Paw jammed a wad of chewing tobacco in his lip, tucked the pouch in his back pocket, and rested his elbow on the edge of an empty, black-stained coal car. "Now, before you do any blastin', you gotta have a dummy ready to stem the hole."

Emmett nodded, but he wasn't altogether sure what Paw was talking about. Dummy? Stem the hole? The words joined other nonsensical terms — *brow, hogsback, dip* — that were muddled in his mind. How did Paw keep everything straight? When the administrator had said there wasn't time to train him, he'd been a little perturbed. How much time could it take? To his way of thinking, all a fellow needed to do was swing a pickax and shovel out what fell loose. But now he wondered if he had enough years to learn it all. He'd never realized there was

190

such a science to bringing up coal from deep in the earth.

He and Paw had walked down the mountain to Lynch after lunch. Paw said it would be easier for him to teach Emmett on a Sunday, when things were quiet — no workers bustling here and there and no machines running. "A mine's a noisy place. Hard for a feller to think," he'd said. For the past two hours, he'd led Emmett around the area that made up Mine Thirty-One, but Emmett had learned more about his father than he had about mining.

The way Paw spoke held Emmett's attention. Such pride showed in his father's stance and filled his voice as he named each piece of equipment and explained its purpose. Twice Paw had clapped him on the shoulder and told him how good it would be to work together, father and son, side by side. Paw was proud of his work, sure, but more than that, he was proud to share it with his son.

"Come on over here." Paw guided Emmett to the opening of the mine. "Lookee there."

Emmett peered into the dark shaft.

"What do you see?"

Emmett couldn't see anything except the entrance of a big, dark tunnel. He shrugged.

Paw snorted. He gestured, the movements broad and impatient. "See that openin'? Bigger'n a stack o' elephants. I had a hand in carvin' that openin'. I've had a hand in bringin' out to the light o' day chunks o' rock that've laid under the ground for hunnerds of years. Think of it. What we call coal was grass an' flowers an' livin' critters more'n a thousand years ago. An' sometimes when you're followin' a drift, you can almost hear the breath o' those critters sighin' from the past." He stretched one hand toward the mine and slowly closed his fingers into a fist. "When I'm touchin' that black rock, I'm touchin' pieces o' yesteryear."

Sweat broke out on Emmett's back. An odd, almost hollow sound that wasn't really a sound at all seemed to echo from the tunnel's depth. Was he hearing it with his ears or with his imagination?

"Under the ground, where it's all dark an' cool, sometimes you get an idea of what it feels like to be dead."

Emmett shot his father a sharp look. Was he trying to scare Emmett now?

Paw stared into the shaft with a faraway look in his eyes. "An' then you come out, an' you breathe the clean air an' feel the sun an' wind on your face, an' you know

192

you're alive. An' bein' alive means more to you than it did before." Paw's body jerked, as if someone had pinched him, and his expression turned sheepish. "Reckon I sound pretty foolish talkin' that way."

Emmett shook his head. "No, Paw. Not foolish at all. I . . . I like what you said. I feel like I know you better than I did before."

Paw scuffed his toe against the ground, head low. "Well, now, I ain't never talked this way to nobody before. Not even your maw." He aimed a grin at Emmett. "But if you're gonna be a miner, like me, it's good for you to understand a miner's heart. For you to know this ain't just a job. It's takin' what the Lord made an' puttin' it to good use. It's bein' what the Bible calls a good steward. Do you understand, Son?"

A lump filled Emmett's throat. He couldn't talk, so he nodded.

Paw blew out a big breath. He smacked Emmett's shoulder and set off toward the road. "I reckon that's enough for today."

Emmett walked alongside Paw, matching his stride.

"Come tomorrow mornin', you can ride the work wagon down with me, an' I'll have a talk with the boss about bringin' you on. He knows me good — knows I ain't no greenhorn. If I tell him I been teachin' you an' I'm willin' to be responsible for you 'til you learn it all, he'll likely hire you on the spot." Paw's saunter became a strut. "Yessir, gonna be good havin' my boy work with me. Gonna be real good."

Addie

No one else disembarked in Lynch, so Addie waited alone on a boardwalk that stretched the full length of the red-painted depot. She judged its length at perhaps twenty-four feet, hardly a real boardwalk at all, though the boards were still white, smooth, and new looking. The L&N engine sent up puffs of smoke and shuddered in place, making the boards beneath her feet quiver. Or maybe it was her own nervousness rattling through her. She couldn't be sure.

She hid a yawn behind her hand. She'd stayed up far too late last night visiting with Mother and Daddy, then slept the distance between Mount Vernon and Lynch, not even awakening at the stops between. If the conductor hadn't shaken her shoulder, she might have missed her stop entirely. She stared past the train at a tree-covered incline that seemed to stretch all the way to the clouds. Apparently, she'd been deposited at the back of the depot. At least, she hoped she had. Otherwise, the city of Lynch was hiding somewhere in that thick growth of trees and brush.

A short, pimple-faced young man in a rumpled blue uniform scuttled to her and thumped her suitcases near her feet.

She smiled. "Thank you, sir."

He tipped his little cap. "You're welcome, miss. You needin' help gettin' your things to the Lynch Hotel? I can carry 'em for you."

"No, thank you. I'm not staying at the hotel."

"Your folks comin' for you, then?"

"No." Although she hoped someone was coming. There didn't seem to be anyone around other than this depot employee.

He scratched his head. "Then what'm I s'posed to do with you?"

She stifled a chortle. This fellow took his job seriously. Or maybe he was seeking a sizable tip. He'd be disappointed. After paying for her train ticket and an egg salad sandwich in Mount Vernon, she carried less than three dollars in her purse. She needed it to cover her expenses until her first WPA wages arrived.

With a smile, she picked up her suitcases and turned for the corner of the building. "I'll be fine. Thank you for your concern."

He made a face that expressed doubt, but he ambled to the door of the building and stepped inside. As he closed the door, the train's whistle blew. Its wheels squealed against the track, and the locomotive rolled beyond the depot.

The vibration of the boards made Addie feel unsteady, and she hurried from the boardwalk to a concrete sidewalk. She followed it to the opposite side of the depot building, which, as she'd presumed, was the front. She paused for a moment, startled by the size of the town spread out haphazardly along a winding parcel of gently sloping ground. To her delight, a bank building constructed of carved stone matched the grandeur of those in Georgetown and Lexington. She spotted a three-story brick building with signs indicating it housed a restaurant and a movie theater. According to a poster hung on the side of the building, *Mutiny on the Bounty,* starring Clark Gable and Charles Laughton, was the featured film. She'd seen it last year with Felicity and her "guys," but she wouldn't mind watching it again. Felicity had declared that Charles Laughton's accent was enough to make a girl swoon.

A smile tugged at her lips, images of excursions with the other packhorse librarians and young people from Boone's Hollow forming in her head. But first she needed to get to Boone's Hollow. The sun was already sneaking behind the mountaintops, and shadows fell heavy over the valley. She preferred to get settled before full night arrived. Where was the driver Mrs. Hunt had promised would come for her?

A wagon pulled by a white horse with black speckles on its rump rolled toward the depot. A man and a woman sat at opposite ends of the driver's seat. The woman held on to the seat's edge with one hand and raised the other in a wave.

Addie set down her suitcases and waved in reply.

The man drew the wagon within a few feet of Addie, set the brake, and squinted down at her from beneath the brim of a floppy, stained leather hat. "You there, young lady — is you Adelaide . . . Adelaide . . ." He scowled at the woman. "What did you call her back name?"

"Cowherd." The woman pushed the word through gritted teeth. She reached her hand to Addie. "Are you Miss Cowherd?"

Addie took hold of the woman's hand. "Yes, ma'am. Please call me Addie. Are you Miss West?"

"I am. Please excuse our tardy arrival. Mr.

Gilliam's, er, pulling horse had a loose shoe, to which he needed to attend before we set out."

"It's all right. The train only left a few minutes ago."

"As long as you weren't concerned you'd been forgotten."

The thought had crossed her mind, but she wouldn't distress her new boss by saying so. The older woman seemed uptight enough. "No, ma'am, not at all."

An airy sigh left Miss West's throat. She released Addie's hand and turned to the driver. "Please put Miss Cowherd's belongings in the wagon bed. I believe she and I will sit in the back for the drive to Boone's Hollow."

"Dunno why you'd wanna do that. Can put the girl up here betwixt us." He grinned, and Addie tried not to squirm. He was nearly toothless and had a moist wad of something grimy caught in his lower lip. She'd been taught not to stare at folks, but she found it challenging not to. "This bench sits three fellers. It'll sit the three of us just fine." He waggled his eyebrows.

Miss West blew out a dainty breath. "I believe it will be less dusty for us in the back." She brushed fine bits of grit from the lap and ruffled bodice of her pink floral dress. Her chest rose and fell as if she'd recently run a race. "I don't wish to be on that mountain road in the dark, Mr. Gilliam. Let's hurry, shall we?"

The man shrugged and hopped over the edge of the wagon. He stomped around to Addie and grabbed her smaller case's handle. He tossed it into the back, then with a grunt sent the larger one sailing over the edge. Addie gasped, and he grinned at her. "Stronger'n I look, ain't I? That was no trouble at all. Want me to help you in?"

Would he give her the same treatment her suitcases had received? She moved to the rear of the wagon. "That's kind of you, but if you'll remove the hatch, I should be able to get in on my own."

"You might snag your stockin's."

How would Mother respond to a comment like that? "Um . . . thank you for your concern. But as I said, I'll be fine."

"All righty, then. Here you go." He lifted the hatch out of the way, and while she clumsily climbed in from the rear under Mr. Gilliam's unwavering attention, Miss West stepped cautiously over the driver's backless bench into the bed.

She pointed to Addie's larger suitcase. "May I use this as a seat, Addie?"

Addie couldn't expect the older woman to

sit on the floor of the bed. She nodded. Miss West sat gingerly on the larger case, and Addie sat on the smaller one. Mother's fine leather cases would bear scuffs and dents from this day forward, but there wasn't anything she could do about it now.

Mr. Gilliam dropped the hatch into place and then heaved himself onto the seat again. He sent a grin over his shoulder. "You ladies ready?"

Miss West clamped her hand over the edge of the wagon's high side and nodded.

The wagon jolted forward, and Addie slid several inches across her suitcase. A little yelp escaped before she could stop it. She shifted to the floor. Resting her elbow on the suitcase, she bent her legs to the side, as ladylike a position as she could manage. As Mr. Gilliam had warned, her stockings caught on the rough wood. She'd be as snagged as if she'd walked through a patch of rosebushes, but she felt more secure on the floor.

The high sides on the bed hid her view of anything except the mountaintop and sky, but she surmised they weren't traveling on a paved roadway. The wagon bumped and rocked, squeaked and moaned. Addie was tempted to moan, too.

Instead, she forced a smile and aimed it at

her new boss. "Thank you for giving me the chance to work with you. Mrs. Hunt spoke highly of you, and my parents held no apprehension about allowing me to come because of her recommendation."

Miss West's tense expression relaxed. "That's kind of you to say, Addie. My cousin Carrie spoke well of you, too. I'm sure you'll do a fine job." Her thin, graying brows tipped low. "It's a bit unnerving making a trek to an unknown place, where everyone is a stranger."

Addie wondered if she was talking about her own feelings or Addie's. "Yes, but it's exciting, too. My first foray into true independence." She laughed lightly.

Miss West remained stoic. "When Carrie told me you'd accepted the position, I asked Brother Darnell, the minister of the Baptist church, to make inquiries about lodging for you. He's familiar with everyone in the community, so I trusted him to know best. This morning after the service, he told me two people have expressed a willingness to board you. One is a widower whose daughter is also a packhorse librarian" —

Mr. Gilliam chortled loudly enough to be heard over the wagon's clamor.

— "and the other is an elderly woman who lives by herself."

Mr. Gilliam jerked his head and gaped at Miss West. "You talkin' about Nanny Fay?"

Miss West frowned at the man, and he snapped his attention forward. "You will discover very quickly, Addie, that people in these mountain communities hold to a host of superstitions and unfounded grudges."

Another snort burst from the wagon's driver.

"I, personally, prefer to judge a person on his or her own merits." Miss West raised her voice, aiming a scowl in Mr. Gilliam's direction. "I also have a term to define superstitions as a whole. *Hogwash.*"

Mr. Gilliam harrumphed and smacked the reins on the horse's rump. The beast broke into a trot.

Addie sucked in her lips and held back a snicker. Miss West's graying bun and genteel appearance didn't match the fire snapping in her grayish-blue eyes.

"If you're interested in my opinion, I will tell you whose offer I believe you should accept."

Addie cleared her throat, erasing any humor from her tone, before answering. "I would welcome your opinion, ma'am."

"I would choose Nanny Fay Tuckett. If you were my daughter, I would feel more assured about your staying with a single, older woman than a middle-aged, unmarried man, even if there is a chaperone residing under his roof."

Daddy and Mother would agree with Miss West. "Then I'll make arrangements with Mrs. Tuckett when we reach Boone's Hollow."

"The arrangements can wait until tomorrow. I've prepared a pallet for you in my living quarters for tonight. As for Mrs. Tuckett" — Miss West produced a handkerchief from her sleeve and patted her throat with it, sighing — "I'm sure she'll prefer you call her Nanny Fay, the same as everyone else in town does. The people of Boone's Hollow don't stand on many city conventions." She returned the handkerchief to the cuff of her sleeve. "If it proves too difficult for you to board with her, you can always take a room at the hotel or in one of the boardinghouses in Lynch."

Something in the woman's expression sent a prickle of unease across Addie's scalp. "Is there a reason why staying with her would be difficult?"

Miss West gripped her hands in her lap. She gazed over the edge of the wagon's side. "I'm not a talebearer, Addie. I'll allow you to draw your own conclusions."

FIFTEEN

Boone's Hollow
Addie

"An' here you are, Addel-ade Cow-herd. Welcome to Boone's Holler."

Why had Mr. Gilliam's attitude taken such a turn? Midway up the mountain, he had seemed to cloak himself in derision. His tone now dripped with ridicule. The way he spoke her name — in choppy syllables, as if trying to flay her — made her cringe.

"If people are unkind, kill them with kindness." Mother's directions to her when she suffered bullying on the schoolyard played in Addie's memory. She injected warm appreciation into her voice. "Thank you, Mr. Gilliam."

He snorted.

Addie shifted to her knees and peered over the wagon's edge. The rattly conveyance rolled slowly along an uneven dirt street.

204

She blinked several times, certain the heavy shadows were hiding the actual town. But no matter how many times she cleared her vision, the sight remained the same. A wide dirt road with thick bushes and trees lining both sides spread in front of her. A spattering of wooden buildings were tucked beneath the branches overhanging either side of the road. She counted three places of business on the right — a tiny wooden building marked Post Office-Telephone Office, a rambling log structure with Belcher's Genral Merchendice painted on its false front, and a huge barn. On the left were an equal number of houses, constructed of logs or planked wood. The first house's door bore a doctor's shingle. She searched both sides again. Where was the library?

Mr. Gilliam drew the wagon to a stop in front of the barn, set the brake, and hopped down. He stomped to the rear of the wagon and yanked the back gate free. He leaned the gate against the wagon wheel and scowled at her. "End o' the road. Come on outta there now."

Addie glanced at Miss West, who was glowering at Mr. Gilliam the way a schoolteacher disciplined an unruly student. Apparently, she was bothered by the man's unpleasant demeanor, too, which told Addie it was out of the ordinary. She must have done something to bring it about. But what?

She unfolded her stiff legs and rose. The wagon rocked slightly, making her feel unstable. Using the wagon's side as a handrail, she moved to the end and then sat on the edge of the bed. Mr. Gilliam stood a few feet away, hands on overall-clad hips, observing her. She waited for a few seconds, hoping he would offer a hand of assistance, but he didn't. She slid out, grimacing when her skirt caught on the rough wood.

Addie helped Miss West alight, then turned to Mr. Gilliam. His stormy expression warned her to keep her distance, but she needed his help. "Sir, would you please retrieve my suitcases?"

He blew out a breath that spoke unquestioningly of aggravation and climbed into the wagon's bed. He handed her the cases one by one with much more gentleness than he'd used putting them into the wagon. She smiled, aware of her quivering lips, and thanked him. Without replying, he hopped down and made a wide berth around her. He grabbed the gate, took the same path on his way back to the wagon, and smacked the gate into its frame. She gripped the handles of her suitcases. Why was the man who'd offered to let her sit on the driver's seat beside him now acting as if she had leprosy? She bit the inside of her lip, heart aching.

Mr. Gilliam gave a brusque yank on his hat's brim, which she interpreted as a farewell, then clomped to the front of the wagon. Without a word, he began removing the horse's traces.

Miss West took the smaller case from Addie's hand. "Come along, Addie. I'll show you to the library."

Addie eagerly trailed Miss West away from the wagon and Mr. Gilliam's dark countenance. She needed a library's sweet sanctuary to soothe her hurt feelings. She considered asking her new boss what she'd done to upset the driver, but the woman's breath emerged in laborious huffs. Perhaps Addie shouldn't tax her by expecting her to answer questions.

A chorus of crickets serenaded them as Miss West led her through lengthy gray shadows to the opposite side of the street and then away from the livery barn. Addie's gaze swept her surroundings, her heart sinking a bit more with each step. Had she really imagined buying a soda in a drugstore or browsing a dress shop? How could they even call this gathering of mismatched structures a town? Although the appearance disheartened her, a sweet smell that reminded her of the flowering vine on the fence at her childhood home permeated the entire area. She inhaled the scent, and it eased some of her apprehension.

They rounded a cluster of thick bushes growing beneath a huge tulip tree near the road, and Miss West stopped in front of a log building approximately twice the length of its width. Addie hadn't noticed it when they entered Boone's Hollow. Shielded by the tree's branches and fronted by the bushes, it was half-hidden from sight. A door constructed from upright planks held together with rusty iron bands created a dark rectangle against the building's coat of white paint.

"Here we are, Addie."

Addie gave Miss West a startled look. "Here we are . . . where?"

"The library."

Addie's jaw dropped. Library? Why, this was nothing more than a . . . than a . . . She couldn't find a suitable description.

Miss West crossed to the door and pulled a leather string that emerged from a small hole. A scraping noise intruded against the crickets' singing, and the door swung open on creaky hinges. She glanced at Addie, a slight frown creasing her forehead. She

208

released a heavy sigh. "Come along now."

Addie gave a little jerk that set her feet in motion. Yellow light flickered behind the small front window and then flowed out the doorway and across the sandstone block serving as a stoop. She stepped inside as Miss West lit a second lamp and blew out the match. Oil lamps, not electric. But their glow sufficiently lit the small space, giving her a full view of the building's — the library's — contents. Such as they were. Dismay flooded her belly. How could anyone call this place a library? To do so was an insult to every other library she'd visited. She'd find no soothing sanctuary here. Except . . .

A savory aroma, very different from the one permeating the town's street, filled her nostrils, and her stomach growled. She pressed her hand to her belly. "Oh, I'm so sorry."

The woman chuckled. "I suppose the smell of smoked meats, particularly ham, has that effect on most people."

Addie sniffed, and memories of Sunday breakfasts and Easter dinners rolled in her mind. "Yes, that's exactly what I'm smelling. Ham." Miss West must have had ham for lunch earlier.

"I had the same reaction each time I

entered this building for the first few weeks. The scent saturates the interior surfaces due to the building's previous service as a smokehouse, but eventually you'll adjust to it and won't smell it at all."

Addie looked up. Thick, smoke-blackened beams, one still holding an iron hook, formed an evenly spaced row beneath the peaked ceiling. A library in a former smoke-house. Even her active imagination couldn't have conjured such a thing.

"You're likely tired after your day of travel. Let's get you settled." Miss West picked up one of the lamps and carried Addie's suit-case to a wall of blankets. She used her elbow and pushed one flap aside. "It will be quite crowded with both of us in here, but for one night we should manage fine."

Addie moved to the opening between the blankets and peeked in. A little squeak left her throat. "This . . . You . . ." She gaped at the librarian.

A sad smile curved the woman's lips. She placed Addie's suitcase in a tiny slice of open floor between a round iron stove and a full woodbox. "You must remember, Addie, you're not in the city anymore." She set the lamp on top of a rickety little bedside table next to a knee-high cot covered by a red-and-white patchwork quilt, then turned to face Addie. "As dreary as this may seem to you, it's nicer than many of the cabins or shacks the hills people call home. You'll discover that truth as you travel your delivery route." She withdrew her handkerchief and patted her throat and chin, sighing. "And I must tell you, despite their lack of education and their seemingly backward way of living, they are proud people. You'll need to school your expression."

Addie gulped. "What do you mean?"

Miss West dropped the rumpled handkerchief on the stand next to the lamp. "Distaste and sympathy are warring on your face right now. Neither will endear you to the folks you encounter in and around Boone's Hollow and Tuckett's Pass. You'll find it challenging enough to fit in here without them thinking you're either looking down your nose at them or viewing them with pity."

Had something in her expression turned Mr. Gilliam against her? Mother and Daddy had taught her to treat others the way she wanted to be treated. Her status as an orphan had earned her pitying looks from some, while others treated her with contempt, as if her parentless status made her unworthy of their attention.

She gripped her hands together and shook

her head, sending the remembrances away. "I'd never want to shame anyone."

Miss West's expression turned tender. She reached out and took hold of Addie's hand. "I don't mean to scold you. In some ways, you may feel as if you've stepped into a foreign land. But I can see you're an intelligent, compassionate young woman. Perhaps even a little self-reliant? I sensed it when you refused Mr. Gilliam's offer to help you into the wagon."

Addie laughed, hanging her head. How many times had Mother thrown her hands up in defeat at Addie's insistence to do things her own way? A leftover habit from being in the orphanage, where everyone over the age of three took care of him or herself. "Maybe."

Miss West squeezed her hand and let go. "Each of those characteristics will serve you well here. Be patient with yourself as you adjust to living more simply, and be patient with the folks of the communities as they get to know you." She sighed again, this time even deeper and longer than any before. "All will be well."

She gestured to a narrow pallet lying on the floor in front of a four-drawer bureau and stretching almost to the edge of her cot. "I hope you'll be comfortable tonight. I'll go to the library side and give you some privacy while you change into your night-clothes. I have biscuits, hard cheese, and dried apples in tins, so while you're changing, I'll make a plate for you." She moved through the gap in the blankets and swished them together, sealing Addie in the tiny living space.

Addie gazed down at the stack of folded blankets. A pallet on the floor. A cold supper. A library in a smokehouse. So different from what she'd expected. But she'd adjust. Mother's and Daddy's well-being was worth any amount of discomfort she had to endure.

Bettina

Bettina plopped the tin plate of grits, biscuits, and fried eggs in front of Pap, then sat across from him with her bowl of grits. Pap dug right in to his breakfast, not even looking at her. Back when Maw was alive, Pap prayed before they ate. Bettina suggested it once about a year ago, and Pap told her to mind her own business if she knew what was good for her. She knew, so she didn't ask again. But she missed the days when Maw was there and Pap prayed, before life got so ugly.

Pap jammed a chunk of biscuit in his

mouth, then pointed at Bettina with his fork. "You be sure an' tell that new book gal two dollars a week for stayin' here." He talked with a mouthful, and little pieces of bread sprayed out.

Bettina stirred butter into her grits and tried not to think about where that chewed food might've landed. "I will."

"Tell her nobody else'll put her up an' feed her for less'n that." He slurped from his coffee cup, dark eyes glaring at Bettina over its rim.

"I'll tell 'er, Pap. Two dollars for a room an' meals." She wished she had the courage to ask why she had to give up her room to the new book gal. Pap could sleep in the barn as easy as Bettina could. Easier maybe. He ended up out there some nights when he got himself too pickled to find his way to the house anyway. Didn't seem fair, having to hand over so much of her pay and now not even get to sleep in her own bed.

Bettina filled her spoon and blew on it. She hated burning her mouth on the first bite. "Since you ain't askin' a lot o' pay, me-bbe she can help some with cookin' an' cleanin', too. Earn some of her keep."

Pap's fist came down on the table so hard the coffee cups bounced and Bettina tossed her spoonful of grits down the front of her overalls. She hissed through her teeth.

Pap jammed his finger at her. "Don't you say nothin' to that gal except what I told you to say."

She dabbed at her front with the rag she'd used to wipe the table before they sat to eat. "All right, all right, I just thought —"

"You don't do the thinkin' in this house. You ain't got brains enough to do the thinkin'."

She clenched her teeth so tight her jaw ached. She flicked every bit of grits from her clothes, not caring at all that it landed on the floor, where it'd get stepped on and ground into the dirt.

Pap shoved his plate aside and stood. "I gotta go or I'll miss the wagon. Make sure you get these dishes washed an' your room spiffed up before you leave. Don't want that gal thinkin' we ain't clean people."

Bettina bit back a laugh. Clean? Pap could shower every day at the Lynch bathhouse if he wanted, but he only went in on Fridays. At least Bettina used a bucket and cloth every night before she went to bed. She couldn't hardly stand feeling all sweat itchy. She put a little dab of Maw's lily-o'-the-valley water under her armpits every morning, too, to cover up the body odor.

It'd be a heap harder to keep herself

halfway clean once she was sleeping in the barn every night. But Emmett shouldn't wait too much longer to start courting her. When she and Emmett got married, they'd have a real bathroom in their house, with a flush toilet — no more stinky outhouse — and a genuine tub, and she'd sit in bubbles up to her chin every night so she'd be sweet smelling for him when she crawled under the covers.

"Girl, are you listenin' to me?"

Bettina jumped. Was Pap still here? Her face blazed hot, and she nodded. "I'm listenin'."

"You best be. An' you best do as I said."

Had he said something more? She didn't dare ask. "I will, Pap."

He grabbed the bucket lunch Bettina had packed for him and walked out, slamming the door.

She picked up her bowl, no longer hungry, and scraped the food into the slop pail. She scrubbed the dishes and put them away, made her bed, and changed into a blouse and dungarees. She tossed the mucked-up overalls into her clothes basket, then picked it up, intending to carry it out to the barn. But she froze in place, a worry holding her captive. If the new girl took over Bettina's room, that girl would bring in her own clothes. All of Bettina's clothes — what few she owned — had to go out. Including the beautiful dress she'd bought from the company store.

"I can't keep my weddin' dress in the barn!"

Bettina hung her head and moaned. What was she gonna do?

Sixteen

Addie

Unfamiliar sounds — thumps and scrapes — woke Addie from a restless sleep. She sat up, then blinked in confusion, pulse racing. Strange shadows surrounded her, and the smell of ham hung heavy. Where was she? Ah, yes. She hugged herself, willing the panicky feeling to ease. She was in the Boone's Hollow library . . . which wasn't really a library at all.

She squinted across the narrow space, her eyes adjusting. Miss West's cot was empty. All the noises coming from the other side of the blanket barrier must be the librarian preparing for the day. Addie should rise and help. She was on the payroll now, so she needed to earn her wages.

She flopped aside the colorful quilt Griselda Ann had given her as a going-away gift and dug through her suitcase for clean underclothes and a dress. She put them on,

218

then ran her brush through her hair, bemoaning the absence of a mirror. She'd looked for one last night, but Miss West told her the person who set up the living quarters hadn't provided one. Some of the hills people thought a mirror's reflection could steal the reflected one's soul, so mirrors were in short supply. Addie found a ribbon in her suitcase and tied her hair into a tail at the base of her skull. She hoped she looked somewhat presentable since she'd be meeting many Boone's Hollow residents today. First impressions were important, Mother always said. Not that Mr. Gilliam had been terribly concerned about the impression he'd made last night.

She threw her hairbrush into her suitcase and closed the lid. Even if she was living in a community of what Miss West had called backward people, she could maintain the morals and values she'd learned in the city. That included being kind to people, even if they weren't kind to her. She slipped her bare feet into a pair of brown leather pumps and stepped beyond the blankets.

Three windows, one on the front and one on each side, should have given the room plenty of light. No sunlight came through any of them. Was it too early for sunshine, or did the trees outside block it from entering? A lamp, shining from the center of the large table pushed into the front corner of the room, gave the space a cheery glow. Tablets and stacks of books sat on the table, evidence that Miss West had been busy already, but the woman was gone.

The front door stood open, held in place by a red brick. Addie moved to the doorway and peeked outside. It must be early. Not even a hint of pink softened the dove-gray sky, and a foggy mist clung to bushes and the tops of trees. She looked first left and then right. "Miss West?"

No one answered, although blasts of laughter and muttering male voices carried from somewhere up the road. Wariness tingled up Addie's spine.

What were those men doing out before daylight? And where was Miss West?

She took a hesitant step out onto the stoop, hand curled around the rough-hewn doorjamb. "Miss West?"

"I'm here, Addie."

Addie jumped. Miss West seemed to materialize from the morning mist. Addie moved aside and allowed the librarian's entrance.

Miss West went to the table and pulled out her chair, then sat heavily, chest rising and falling with great intakes of breath. She placed her hand on her bodice and gazed at Addie, brows low. "You're up very early. Do you want breakfast?"

The savory aroma clinging to the log walls tormented her and stirred her appetite, but more than food, Addie needed the outhouse. Should she go out, though, with who knew how many men lurking outside somewhere? "Um . . ."

"You remember where to find the necessary?"

Addie nodded. Miss West had taken her to it last night before bed, and it wasn't far behind the smokehouse, between a pair of sapling maple trees.

"Go on out, then." She flicked her fingers at the door and rose. "I'll light a fire in the stove and heat water for coffee and oatmeal. Would you like chopped dried apples added to your oatmeal?"

"Yes, please." Addie peeked out the door. The men's chatter and laughter continued, but she couldn't see anyone. The thick patch of trees and bushes hid them from view. What if the men were between her and the outhouse? What kind of impression would she give if the first sighting of the newcomer to town was of her running for the toilet?

"Addie?"

Addie looked over her shoulder. Miss West

was gazing at her, confusion pinching her face.

"Are you sure you don't need me to show you to the outhouse?"

Addie gestured to the open doorway. "I hear people out there."

Understanding dawned in the woman's expression. "It's the coal workers. They're waiting in front of Belcher's for the wagon that takes them to the mine in Lynch."

"Oh." What a goose, frightened by voices of men who had every reason to be awake so early. Not to mention they were clear up the road near the general merchandise store. They wouldn't be able to see her beyond the barrier of trees. "Well, then . . ." She hurried out the door and around the corner, hoping the morning air would cool the heat of embarrassment burning her cheeks.

Bettina

By the time Bettina left her cabin, she'd already put in two hours of work. She grumbled as she led Mule over the footbridge across Boone's Creek and to the path leading to the Blevins' place. If she cut through the trees between the Ashcroft and Landrum cabins, the shortcut would take her straight to the main road and would be easy walking to the library. But she'd likely

222

run across Glory, and Glory'd want to jabber the whole way to work. Bettina needed some quiet to shake off the irksome feelings resting heavy on her toward Pap for booting her out of her own house to take in some city gal they didn't even know. She'd take the back path instead. The back path . . . her peaceful place.

When Maw was alive, she and Bettina took this path a lot. Maw liked walking in the shade under the trees. She spied out birds or baby bunnies or butterflies. She said this path by the woods was tranquil — a highfalutin word that meant calm. Maw favored the calm. Said the Good Lord Almighty Hisself built the woods, with its big trees that sang lullabies and flowers that showed off their colors and bushes that made homes for wiggly-nosed bunnies and toads and such. Bettina didn't care all that much about trees and toads, but she loved that Maw took her along to her place of calm.

Maw could name just about every growing thing, from Sweet William to lupine and Cumberland spurge. She never said where she learned 'em, but she sure knew 'em. Maw particularly liked the yellow toadflax. When she spotted one in full bloom, she'd stop and pinch one of the blossoms, making it bite the air like a little dragon. And she'd laugh and laugh. She made up a story once about the snapping flowers, but it was too long ago, and Bettina couldn't recall it no more. But she recollected walking this path, coming out of the trees at the main road, and then heading on to Lynch for shopping at the company store. Bettina missed those days. Missed her maw.

She kicked at a clump of wild grass at the edge of the narrow path. Why'd Maw have to up and die? Pap'd hollered when Maw was alive. Hollered a lot. But he'd never once raised a hand to Bettina when Maw was there. Nowadays, though, seemed like she couldn't even make it through a full week without him whopping her for something. With warm weather coming on, she wanted to wear blouses with short sleeves, but she couldn't if she had marks on her arms. Folks'd point and whisper. She hated when folks pointed and whispered.

Nope, Pap hadn't swung at her when Maw was with them. Having Maw there sure made a difference. Maybe having that new girl living in the house would — She came to a stop, and Mule bumped her with his nose. She yanked the reins and shot the animal a glare. "Be careful. Can't you see I'm needin' to think?"

Mule snorted and tried to pull free, but she held tight. She'd been plain mad about moving to the barn, giving up her room. Her pretty calendar looked silly nailed to one of the stall posts. And if the chickens pooped on the blankets she'd spread out in the straw for sleeping on, she'd cook 'em up in a stewpot no matter if it meant no more fresh eggs. But if that new book gal was living in the house, Pap would have to behave himself. He wouldn't be taking swings at Bettina no more.

She laughed and danced a little jig. Mule snorted, but she grabbed him by his prickly jaw and planted a kiss on his nose. "I was lookin' at it all backward, Mule. Her livin' in the house — it's gonna be a good thing after all. She'll keep Pap calm, an' he won't be pickin' at me. An' livin' in the barn'll make it easier for me to come an' go without him knowin'. Me an' Emmett'll be able to see each other every night if we want. Yessir, Pap says I'm the dumb one, but who's the dummy now?"

Still grinning big, she hurried Mule down the path and through the break in the trees. Glory's and Alba's horses were already at the library, munching the tender grass close to the bushes. Bettina gave Mule's reins a toss over a mountain holly and darted inside the building. Alba had a full pack draped over her shoulder, and Miz West was sitting at the table, poking books inside Glory's pack. Bettina cringed. She'd dawdled too much.

She stepped close to the table and turned what she hoped was a remorseful look on the librarian. "I'm sorry I'm late, ma'am. Pap set me to some extra chores this mornin', an' —" A girl with eyes as brown as a wet walnut shell and wavy goldish-brown hair pulled into a loose tail sat in the second chair.

The girl stood up and took a step toward Bettina with her hand reaching out. "You must be Bettina. Glory and Alba were telling me about you."

A flutter went through Bettina's middle. What'd they say?

"I'm Adelaide Cowherd. But everyone calls me Addie."

Bettina hadn't ever shook hands with another girl. She didn't want to do it now. Not after hanging on to Mule's sticky reins. But she didn't know what else to do. So she gave the girl's fingers a quick squeeze and then jammed her hands into her dungaree pockets. "Howdy."

She looked Addie up and down. They must grow girls taller in the city, because

Addie stood at least two inches higher than Glory, who was maybe three inches taller than Bettina. She wore a yellow-and-white-striped dress, with short puffed sleeves and real lace around the cuffs and collar. Her shoes were brown, with heels and a little strap that buttoned on the side. Bettina couldn't help but stare. How would she get on a horse's back in that fancy outfit? But boy, oh boy, what Bettina would give to have a dress and shoes like hers.

Glory nudged Bettina on the shoulder. "Miss West said Addie's gonna stay here today instead o' goin' on a route."

That explained the outfit. Bettina turned to Miz West. "How come?"

Miz West's lips puckered up the way Maw's had when Pap came in pickled. "She requires a day to settle in, Bettina. She doesn't yet have a horse to take on a route, and she needs to arrange lodging."

Bettina rocked on her heels. "Lodgin' is all settled." She whisked her smile back and forth between the new girl and Miz West. "That's part o' why I was so late. I was makin' up her room. My pap says she can stay with us for two dollars a week."

Addie puckered her lips, too. She reached for Bettina again and brushed her fingertips on Bettina's checkered sleeve. "That's very kind of you, Bettina, but I'm going to stay with a lady."

"What lady?"

Alba snickered. "She's fixin' to stay with Nanny Fay."

Bettina's mouth dropped open. "What?" She had it all worked out in her head. This new book gal couldn't go and ruin it now. "Why're you stayin' with her? I got everything ready for you."

Addie's face went pink. "I'm so sorry you went to so much trouble. Maybe if I'd known . . ."

She would've known if she'd asked. Bettina stomped her bare foot. "Only a fool would take up with Nanny Fay. She's a witch. She —"

"Bettina, Bettina." Miz West took hold of Bettina's wrist and gave it a gentle shake. "We shouldn't speak so unkindly of someone."

Bettina yanked loose. "Even if it's the truth?"

The librarian stood and looked Bettina straight in the face. "It isn't the truth. There are no witches in Boone's Hollow."

The mad she thought she'd got rid of came back stronger than ever. Bettina huffed. "But Nanny Fay ain't from Boone's Holler. Not a livin' soul in these parts knows where she come from. My pap says she —"

"I already know what your father and too many others in this town say." Miz West gave Bettina such a glower that Bettina looked aside. "And I don't believe one word of it. Nanny Fay is a kind old woman who has opened her home to Addie. It's up to Addie to choose where she wants to stay, and she's chosen Nanny Fay's place. Now, that's the end of it."

Bettina gritted her teeth for a few seconds, thinking hard. Then she swung her attention to Addie. "How much you payin' her? Me an' Pap, we'll take less. Dollar an' a half a week." Bettina'd have to make up the other fifty cents out of her pay, but it would be worth the sacrifice to keep from getting whopped and being able to see Emmett more. She leaned closer to the new girl. "Dollar fifty for room an' meals. You ain't gonna get a better price'n that."

Addie looked from Bettina to Alba, to Glory, and finally to Miz West. With her lips all clenched up tight, she kept looking at the librarian.

Miz West let out a big sigh. She put her hand on Bettina's shoulder. "Bettina, please thank your father for his kind offer, but the decision has been made." She turned and picked up Bettina's pouch. "You girls have your packs. You should get going. Be safe."

Bettina wouldn't be safe. As soon as she told Pap this new book gal wasn't coming, he'd beat her black and blue. She snatched the pack and stormed to the door, then scowled at the new book gal over her shoulder. "You be safe, too, Addie. You're gonna need them good wishes if you put yourself under Nanny Fay's roof. Wait an' see."

SEVENTEEN

Lynch
Emmett

Emmett plopped a battered metal hat onto his head, grabbed a shovel from the half dozen leaning against the wall right inside the mine shaft opening, and followed Paw. Lit lanterns hung from the thick beams lining the tunnel and made it easy for him to keep track of his father, even though dozens of men swarmed the underground space.

Every man Paw passed got a bop on the shoulder, followed by a variation of the same proud statement. "My boy's signed on. Startin' work today. That's him behind me — Emmett."

Emmett received more smiles, nods, and greetings in the first fifteen minutes of his official employment at Mine Thirty-One than he'd gotten in his first several months at college. They were a friendly lot, for certain. Paw had said every kind of man —

231

Italian, German, Hungarian, Irish, descendants of former slaves, and more — worked together in the mine, but Emmett had secretly questioned how well they got along. Now he saw for himself.

Their backgrounds didn't seem to matter much. Not the way his hills heritage had been received by some of the students from the city or the way his education put off folks at home, including Paw. Shoveling coal into wagons for transport out of the mine might not have been his first choice for a job, but he felt at ease with the men. Accepted. He belonged. And he liked the feeling. He especially liked how proud Paw was of him.

The tunnel curved slightly, and they reached a hill formed by chunks of coal. Two men jammed shovels into the pile and dumped the shovelfuls into wooden carts with steel wheels. Coal dust hung in the air like a cloud, and Emmett fought back a sneeze. A third man, heavyset with a thick black beard, stood close by with a clipboard in his hand. Paw gave Emmett a little nudge toward the clipboard-holding man. Up close, Emmett realized the man's beard itself wasn't black, but it looked black from a coating of dust.

"Stead, this is my son Emmett. He's

gonna be one o' your shovel men."

The man named Stead stuck out his stained hand, and Emmett shook it. "Good to have you. Did they give you some coal checks?"

Emmett patted his pocket where a dozen round brass pieces stamped with the number twenty-seven clinked together. "Yes, sir."

"Well, then, you're set. Ain't a complicated job. Scoop up what's on the floor an' put it in the cart. When the cart's full and heaped, hang a coal check on the little hook at the front of the cart. Yank that rope good" — he pointed to a frayed rope attached to a tarnished brass bell — "an' some fellers'll come push this cart out o' the way."

Emmett touched his finger on the little hook and glanced at the bell. "Then what?"

"You fill the next one."

Emmett glanced up the tunnel. He counted six carts, but the curve of the shaft probably hid more from view. He turned to Stead. "How many do we fill in a day?"

Stead grinned, his teeth exceptionally white against the blackness of his beard. "Seein' as how you get paid per ton, as many as you're able."

Paw put his hand on Emmett's shoulder. " 'Member what I said about keepin' your hat on. Fellers'll be dynamitin' on up the line. You don't gotta get rattled by the booms or how the ground'll shake, but if you hear a whistle give two short blasts followed by a third long one, hightail it for the openin'. You got that?"

Emmett nodded. "I understand, Paw. Keep working unless I hear two short whistle blasts and one long one. Then run." He wrung his hands on the shovel handle the way someone might wring a chicken's neck. Sweat broke out across his back underneath his shirt. "How often does the warning whistle blast?"

Stead's expression turned grim. "Even once is too often." He shrugged and gave Emmett a light tap on the arm with the clipboard. "But we've gone comin' up on three months now with no cave-ins, an' nobody's been serious hurt for longer'n that, so don't fret."

The man's statement removed some of Emmett's worry. "Thank you, sir. I'll try not to."

Paw scuffed backward, lifting his hand in a farewell. "I'll see you at lunch break. Have a good mornin'."

"You, too, Paw."

Paw spun on his heel and trotted off. The tunnel and its cloud of dust swallowed him up. Emmett took a good grip on his shovel.

If he got paid by the ton, he'd better get busy.

Boone's Hollow
Addie

While Miss West recorded information in a notebook, her careful application of pen to paper reminding Addie of Griselda Ann's slow motions at the library desk in Lexington, Addie put away the books and magazines the packhorse librarians had brought back last Friday. She'd become so familiar with the shelving system in Lexington that she could put things away in her sleep. Although much smaller and with limited resources, the Boone's Hollow library was organized just as well. Addie easily located where every item should go.

As she placed things on the shelves, she took note of tattered pages, bent covers, water stains, and other signs of age or damage. She stayed quiet, but inwardly she seethed. Had the people who received these items treated them poorly? Such a disrespectful thing to do, especially considering the effort being made to deliver the books directly to the families. When she made her first delivery, she would give a short lecture about the treatment of precious books.

She carried a particularly tattered copy of

Ladies' Home Journal to the table and waited quietly for Miss West to acknowledge her. When the woman looked up, Addie held out the magazine. "Ma'am, this is falling apart."

Miss West took the periodical and thumbed through it, grimacing. "Yes, this one is in particularly poor shape. It's been popular, though, because of the recipe section. Any of the magazines with recipes are sought after by the women here." She laid it aside and turned sideways in her chair, her gaze drifting across the shelves. "When I arrived a year ago, I brought four crates of books and magazines with me, all donated by various charity groups. Unfortunately, none of the groups donated new items. Being bounced around on horseback and passed through so many eager hands . . . well, they simply can't hold up."

Guilt tickled Addie. She'd jumped to a conclusion. An unfair one. She fingered the torn cover of the magazine. "If you have some stiff paper and glue, I could cut out the articles and such and paste them onto pages. They could be put together again into something sturdier and more usable."

Miss West jerked her attention to Addie, wonder blooming on her face. "What a fine idea, Addie. Instead of discarding the magazines, we could make scrapbooks.

Perhaps with themes, such as recipes or short stories or subjects like birds or insects. Yes, I like the idea very much." Then her expression faded, and she seemed to forget Addie stood in the room. "But it would take a great deal of time. The girls already spend eight to ten hours on their delivery routes. It wouldn't be fair to ask them to work on scrapbooks when they have responsibilities in their homes, as well."

Addie waited several moments, but when Miss West didn't speak again, she cleared her throat. "I won't be living with a family, so I could use my evening hours to make scrapbooks, if you'd like." As soon as the idea left her mouth, she realized she'd offered the only time she would have to work on her writing projects. The notebooks and pens in the bottom of her suitcase begged to come out, to record the ideas that filled her imagination and tell the stories residing in her heart. But she wouldn't retract her offer.

Miss West turned to Addie, brows pinching into a thoughtful frown. "I appreciate your willingness. It's a fine idea. Truly. I wish I'd thought of it myself. And I will give it more thought and seek a means of implementing it." She rose and slipped her hand through the bend of Addie's elbow. "But right now, let me escort you to Nanny Fay's cabin. If you're going to accept her offer of lodging, we should get you settled. Then we'll see about finding you a horse, and" — she sighed — "tomorrow we'll send you out with books."

A prickle of apprehension attacked Addie's spine. "Miss West, should I lodge at Bettina's house instead? The things she said about Nanny Fay . . . And Mr. Gilliam didn't seem to think highly of her, either."

The woman's lips turned down into a stern scowl. She shook her finger at Addie. "Bunk and nonsense. I want you to put those words and opinions out of your mind. You're old enough to form your own conclusions. If, after meeting her yourself, you believe you would not be able to live comfortably under her roof, then you can change your mind. But I will be sorely disappointed if you refuse this woman based on the prejudicial yapping of superstitious fools."

Addie gaped at her.

Miss West clapped her hand over her mouth. She grabbed Addie by the shoulders. "Please forgive my outburst. My own bias shouldn't influence you, either." She released Addie and sank into the chair, a sigh wheezing from her throat. "It's best if I don't accompany you to Nanny Fay's. You should have time alone with her if you want to form your own opinion. I'll take you as far as the path to her cabin, then send you on your way. Visit with her for as long as you need to make an informed decision. Whatever you choose, I will support you in it."

Nanny Fay

Nanny Fay knelt in the dirt and used her fingers to carve a little moat around each cabbage start. She chuckled. "Whose hands is that a-workin' the soil?" Would she ever get used to seeing the wrinkles and age spots? Must've been there for years already, and they still didn't seem to belong. Her hands showed proof of time passing by. "I wasn't s'posed to get so old, Eagle."

A pair of red birds kept a steady trill from a bush at the edge of the woods. With them a-chattering, she shouldn't need to add to the noise. But the birds were talking to each other, not paying her a bit of mind. Sometimes she hungered for another human voice. So she talked to herself.

"Hello?"

Nanny Fay shot a confused look toward the bushes. The birds took off, the male's bright feathers easier to follow than its mate's brownish-red ones as they disappeared into the trees. She scratched her head. "I'm hearin' things. Really am gettin' old. An' mebbe even tetched."

"Excuse me . . . Ma'am?"

Now, that wasn't inside her head. Came from behind her. Nanny Fay shifted herself around. A pretty young girl in a sunshine-striped dress stood at the edge of the turned soil no more'n a few feet away. How'd she got so close without being heard? "I was lost in thought, an' that's a fact."

The girl tilted her head. "Pardon me?"

Nanny Fay shook her head. "Don't matter." She folded back the brim of her bonnet to better see the girl. This must be the one Preacher Darnell had said was coming to Boone's Holler and might need a place to stay. She'd said of course she'd be pleased to host the new packhorse librarian, but she sure hadn't figured the girl would actually show up here. Nobody in town had got to her yet, it seemed. Might as well enjoy her company before it got took away.

She pushed herself to her feet, grunting a little when the catch in her spine twinged, and brushed her palms on her apron skirt. "You the new book gal?"

The girl nodded. A strand of hair come loose from her ponytail and drifted across her cheek. She pushed it behind her ear. "Yes, ma'am. Miss West, the librarian, sent me over to meet you. I'm Adelaide Cowherd, from Georgetown."

Nanny Fay didn't have no fancy introduction to give. "I'm Nanny Fay, but I reckon you already know that if Miss West told you to come."

"Yes, ma'am."

"Well . . ." Nanny Fay took one toddling step and paused. My, but her joints stiffened up quick these days. She waddled out of the garden, stepping careful around the little green shoots that'd grow into beans and peas. "How 'bout you an' me go to the porch there? Got a nice bench settin' in the shade. We can rest a spell an' get acquainted."

Adelaide Cowherd smiled. "That sounds fine, ma'am."

They headed across the grass. The girl was long legged, could've reached the porch in three, maybe four good steps on her own, but she stayed slow and matched her steps to Nanny Fay's. Sure looked funny, her fancy shoes up close to Nanny Fay's lumpy, wrinkled bare feet. But if Adelaide thought so, she did a good job hiding it.

Nanny Fay grabbed the porch post and pulled herself up on the warped floorboards.

Adelaide hopped up behind her, spry as a colt. Nanny Fay sat at one end of the thick length of smooth, weathered wood held up by four sturdy legs and patted the spot beside her. "There's room for both of us. My Eagle, when he built somethin', he made it to last. Bench has been here over twenty years, but it still sits as solid as the day he set it under the window. Come ahead. Set yourself down."

Adelaide tucked her skirt underneath her and sat. She sure was a graceful thing. Reminded Nanny Fay of a swan. Or maybe a lily a-swaying in a light breeze. The girl put her hands in her lap and angled her face toward Nanny Fay. Her pink lips formed a little upward curve, and her eyes, brown as Eagle's had been, didn't hold nary a bit of fear. Curiosity, sure. Couldn't blame her for that. But after being looked at with mistrust for so many years, having this sweet-faced girl sit right next to her made Nanny Fay want to laugh and dance with delight. Now wouldn't that be a sight? Best get to business.

"So, you're needin' a place to stay, is that right?"

"Yes, ma'am." The girl pushed that wavy curl of hair behind her ear again. "Miss West said you had a room I could rent, but she didn't say how much it would cost."

Nanny Fay fiddled with the brim of her bonnet. "I don't rightly know. Never had a boarder before. I reckon meals an' such is to come with it? Mebbe doin' up your sheets when I do mine?"

"I'm happy to do my own laundry. I can even help with cooking. Well, with breakfast and supper at least. I'll be on a route at noontime."

The eagerness in her voice made joy sprout in Nanny Fay's chest. Seemed as if this girl wanted to stay with her. Was even willing to bargain for the privilege. "Well, now, if you're willin' to put a hand to some o' those chores, I wouldn't feel right askin' a heap o' money from you. Would" — she licked her lips, thinking hard — "four bits a week be fair?"

Adelaide's mouth fell open. "No, ma'am!"

Nanny Fay hung her head. She shouldn't ought to be greedy. "All right. Two bits, then."

The girl popped up off the bench like a striped chippy coming out of its hole. "I won't take advantage of your hospitality. If you're providing me with meals and a place to sleep, then I need to pay you at least two dollars a week. Anything less wouldn't be fair to you."

Tears burned Nanny Fay's eyes. This girl was worried about being fair to her? She stood. "Honey, I'd be — how'd you say it? — takin' advantage of you if I accepted all that money before you even seen where you'd be sleepin'. Mebbe we should go inside. Let you see what you're gettin' yourself in for. Would that be fair?"

Adelaide nodded.

Nanny Fay opened the door and left it wide for the girl to follow. She came on in, went as far as the braided rug in the middle of the sitting and cooking room, and stopped. Her brown eyes wide, she looked from one corner to another until she'd almost turned a circle. Seemed as if she was biting on her lip. Girl from the city probably lived in a big house with fancy furniture and lots of rooms. This old cabin was home, but it surely mustn't seem like much to somebody from as far away as Georgetown.

Nanny Fay pointed to a door on the right. "That there's the room you'd stay in."

The girl lifted the crossbar and pushed the door open. She stepped inside, and the little sleeping room got the same going-over she'd gave the front room. Nanny Fay stayed in the doorway and watched her move from the iron bed to the rocking chair in the corner to the row of pegs pounded into the log wall to hold clothes. She dragged her finger over the top of the four-drawer chest next to the rocking chair, and Nanny Fay cringed.

"Things in here ain't been touched with so much as a feather duster for quite a while." She hadn't figured this girl would come. She wished now she'd figured different. Already thoughts of sitting in front of the fireplace in the evening, sipping sassafras or catnip tea, and talking the way she and Eagle used to do when day was done were filling her mind. It'd hurt worse'n stubbing a toe to lose the company now. She took a hopeful step into the room. "But it won't take long for me to tidy it for you."

Real slow, Adelaide turned until she was looking full into Nanny Fay's eyes. "It's a fine room, ma'am. Real fine. I'd like to stay here, but I won't pay a penny less than two dollars. And I'll do the tidying myself."

My, this girl had pride. Stubborn pride, same as Eagle. Nanny Fay chuckled. "I reckon I'd be wastin' my breath to argue with you."

"May I move in today?"

She could move in that very hour if she wanted to. "You sure can."

"Thank you."

Tears clouded up her vision. Wouldn't take

long and the girl would move out. The folks in town, they'd make it so hard on her she wouldn't have no other choice, and Nanny Fay wouldn't hold a grudge against her for it. But for a little while at least, Nanny Fay would have someone besides herself, the birds, and the Good Lord to talk to, the way it'd been when the gal of her heart was still alive.

She sniffed hard and swished her eyes with her apron. "Adelaide Cowherd . . . thank *you*."

EIGHTEEN

Addie

Addie whisked a peek over her shoulder. Kermit Gilliam still stood outside the wide doorway of his livery stable, fists on his hips, scowling after her and Miss West. Thank goodness Miss West hadn't sent her to the livery on her own. Mr. Gilliam proved himself the opposite of Nanny Fay when it came to making business deals. He demanded two dollars a week for the privilege of using one of his horses for a book delivery route. Miss West bargained him down to seventy-five cents, but he wasn't happy about it. Mostly because Addie had "joined herself with that ol' herb lady," as he put it.

They reached the little post office-telephone office, which seemed far enough from the livery that Addie felt confident she could speak without being overheard. After this morning, when she'd experienced the men's voices carrying all the way up the road, she wondered whether the mountain air had some ability to transport sounds.

"Can you explain something to me, Miss West?"

"What's that?" The librarian huffed like a steam engine and repeatedly wiped her cheeks and throat with a handkerchief as they walked.

"Nanny Fay was very nice to me." She envisioned the woman's round face and pink cheeks, her snow-white hair peeping from the brim of her old-fashioned poke bonnet, her faded blue eyes gazing at Addie the way a child admired a new toy. "And her cabin was as neat as a pin. Why do the people around here dislike her so?"

Miss West gestured Addie through the open library door, then followed her in. She sank into a chair. "For the same reason they aren't terribly fond of me. Because we don't hail from Boone's Hollow."

Addie sat on the second chair and rested her chin in her hand. Something didn't quite make sense. "But when you and Mr. Gilliam came for me yesterday, he was friendly at first. He even wanted me to sit on the wagon seat beside him."

"Of course he did. He's a man, and you're a comely young girl. He wanted to impress you."

Recalling his unexpected sullenness, Addie released a little huff. "He sure changed his mind about that."

Miss West opened her record book and picked up her pen. "Which shows how closed minded he is. You expressed an interest in residing with Nanny Fay over one of his cohorts, Burke Webber. He couldn't see, from our point of view, the sensibility of staying with a single woman instead of a single man. Add to that his irrational belief that the old woman is, as Bettina so crassly put it this morning, a witch, and he became downright childish in his actions. His overcharging you for the use of a horse is further proof of his childishness. I suspect if you'd decided to lodge at the Webbers', he would have let you use one of his horses for twenty-five cents a week."

To what kind of community had she come? When Miss West referred to the people as backward, she'd been right. "Is everyone here so closed minded?"

Miss West tsk-tsked. "As a general rule, the people here are resistant to outsiders and staunchly attached to the superstitious beliefs passed down from previous generations. But there are exceptions to the rule, too. The Baptist preacher and his wife, although both grew up on the mountain, don't hold with the prejudicial attitudes. Nor do a handful of local residents, although they're less likely to speak up against them since they live here and desire to keep peace with their neighbors." She sighed. "Education is key to changing the old mindsets and opening the people here to rational discourse. Which is why I believe so strongly in this program." She paused and stared at Addie for several seconds. "Addie, may I be blunt?"

Given the woman's serious bearing, Addie was half-afraid to assent, but curiosity rose above concern. "Yes, ma'am."

"The other girls who take books to the hills families do it because it's a job. It's a means of earning an honest wage, something that's never been easy to come by for young women in this area. But I see the delivery of these books as something deeper, more important than a mere job. A book takes one into another person's thoughts and emotions. Books open up worlds beyond the view from one's own window. Stories can stir compassion, can inspire integrity, can show different lifestyles and problem-solving skills. Books, Addie, have the power to change people for the better."

Her breathing became heavy and labored, her cheeks mottled with pink, but she continued with fervency. "If we can inspire the hills people to read, we have the opportunity to eliminate the long-held, fear-based superstitions that keep them mired in petty feuds and foolish prejudices. We can impact this community and its future generations by placing books in their hands and encouraging them to read."

Addie gazed at the librarian, captured not only by her words but also by the conviction behind them. Somehow, she'd encapsulated why Addie had always liked to read and why she wanted to write. To inspire and educate and, yes, even change hearts for the better. Her fingers itched to take out her notebook and pen and record every word she'd just heard so she could reflect on it later. She started to ask permission, but Miss West began speaking again.

"I tell you all this because you're an outsider, the same as I am. There are some who will snub you the way they've snubbed me. But, Addie" — Miss West gripped her wrist — "don't give up. Don't let their actions dictate your reactions. You know what books can do. You know what words can do. Don't give up. Will you promise me? Don't you dare let them make you give up."

"Don't give up, boy." Paw growled the command into Emmett's ear while massaging his shoulders.

The pressure of Paw's fingers sent ripples of pain up Emmett's neck and all the way down his arms. The sunshine felt good after being in the dark mine for hours, and the air tasted fresh after breathing the acrid smell of dust all morning. He wanted to stay out here in the sun and never go into the mine again. "I don't want to give up, Paw, but . . ." He groaned.

A couple of men sitting on a patch of gravel with lunch boxes in their laps glanced his way and then smirked at each other.

He shrugged free of his father's touch and held out both hands. Bleeding blisters dotted his palms. "Paw, look. How am I going to make it to the end of the day?"

Paw plopped down next to Emmett and reached for his metal lunch box. "Same way every other feller who works here does — take it one hour at a time."

Emmett touched one particularly large blister and winced. "I'm not sure I've got another hour in me."

Paw glared at him. "A man keeps goin' even when it's tough." He nudged Emmett

252

with his elbow. "Eat your lunch. It'll bolster you for the afternoon."

Paw's lack of sympathy pained Emmett more than his aching muscles. He opened the peanut butter tin Maw had used to pack his lunch and pulled out a wax paper–wrapped sandwich. He wasn't hungry. The weariness seemed to have reached all the way into his bones and stolen his hunger. But he'd eat anyway. If he took the lunch home untouched, Maw would worry. Besides, Paw was right. He needed strength to face the afternoon.

While he ate his sandwich, pickled beets, and cookies, those around him chatted and laughed, much the way the workers from Tuckett's Pass and Boone's Hollow did on their morning drive to the mine. But Emmett didn't join in. Talking took energy he didn't have. He swallowed the last bite of cookie, then checked the big round clock on the side of the firehouse. He stifled another groan. Five more minutes of the lunch break, and then he'd have to go in and pick up his shovel.

Paw got to his feet. "Gonna get me a drink an' visit the outhouse. Prob'ly won't see you again until end o' the day." He pointed at him. "Stay strong."

"Yes, sir." Emmett rested his elbows on

253

his knees and let his head dangle, stretching the tight muscles in his back. A shadow fell across him, and then a hand clamped over his shoulder. He looked up.

One of the men who'd seemed to poke fun at him earlier grinned down at him. "You Tharp's son?"

Emmett nodded.

"They put you on the shovel crew?"

He nodded again.

"Thought so when I seen him tendin' to you an' then got a look at your blisters. Them're shovel blisters, for sure. Why didn't you buy your equipment before you started?"

Emmett stood and folded his arms over his chest. He was too worn out to fight anybody, but he wasn't in the mood to be ridiculed, either, not even by a man twenty pounds heavier and probably as old as Paw. "I only got hired this morning. No one told me to buy equipment."

The fellow pulled a pair of leather gloves from his belt. "Common sense says you oughta wear gloves if you're usin' a shovel." He smacked his palm with the gloves in rhythmic whacks. Dust rose with every whack.

"Yeah, well, I guess I didn't take the course on mining common sense at the

University of Kentucky." He hadn't intended to be snide. Maw would gasp in disapproval, and even Paw would give Emmett a foul look if he heard Emmett talk so disrespectfully to one of his elders. He braced himself for backlash, but the man burst out laughing.

"Lemme educate you a little bit here, college boy. Pushin' a shovel causes friction. Friction causes blisters. Blisters can get infected. Infections keep you from workin'. So, it all comes down to needin' gloves." He flicked the gloves against Emmett's middle.

Emmett automatically took hold of them.

"Put 'em on. But not 'til you've seen the mine physician an' had him clean an' bandage those sores. After work, get yourself to the company store an' buy your own."

Emmett fingered the worn gloves. "I don't have money."

The man snorted. "You're a mine employee now, aren't you? They'll put it against your comin' pay. Get at least two pairs." He dropped his attention to Emmett's feet. "Get some boots, too. Them shoes you're wearin' might be fine for Sunday mornin' church, but they won't hold up over time in the mine."

The whistle blared, and everyone started toward the mine opening. The man drew

Emmett away from the flow and pointed in the direction of the physician's shack. He hollered, "Go see the doc. I'll let Stead know where you are. If you don't see me at the end o' the day, give him my gloves. He'll make sure I get 'em back." The whistle faded down to a shrill hiss.

Emmett waved the gloves. "I sure appreciate this, Mister . . . Mister . . ."

The man grinned. "Just call me Teach." He took off at a trot and joined the others returning to the shafts.

With his hands bandaged and the borrowed gloves in place, Emmett made it through the day. His afternoon productivity didn't match the morning, though. The gloves were a little big, making it harder to grip the shovel, so he couldn't scoop as much. But remembering Paw's admonition that a man keeps going and Maw's penchant for quoting Philippians 4:13 about doing all with Jesus's strength, he lasted the full day.

Paw and the others went to the bathhouse when the quitting whistle sang, but Emmett looked for Teach. In the crowd of milling dust-covered men, the fellow didn't stand out, so Emmett handed off the gloves to Stead and made his way to the company store. It'd been a few years since he'd been in the store owned by US Steel. Like the last time he'd been there, the shelves were stocked with choices. Lots of shoppers browsed the different areas. All the sales personnel were busy with other customers, so Emmett wandered the store and waited his turn.

They'd added electric appliances to the household goods section, and he couldn't resist opening the door on a refrigerator. A light came on, illuminating the shelves inside, and cool air flowed out. Wouldn't Maw like to have one of those in place of her old icebox? But they'd need electricity run to the house to operate it. Paw'd been saving for years to have the electric company bring a line to their cabin. Emmett glanced at the refrigerator's price tag and whistled through his teeth. If a fellow put one of those big items on his tab, he'd never have the money to run electric wires to his house.

He moved on and found a display of leather work gloves. He tried on several pairs until he found some that fit tight without cutting off his circulation. Teach had said to get two, and he seemed to know what he was talking about, so Emmett followed his advice. Then he headed for the area where boxes of shoes and boots formed towers. He examined the drawings on the ends of the boxes, looking for boots similar to the ones Paw had worn for as far back as Emmett could remember.

A clerk hurried over. "Sorry it took so long. Been busy in here all day. Usually is, the first Monday after payday. How can I help you?"

Emmett glanced at the beanpole-thin, sweaty-faced youth. "I need some boots for working in the mine."

The clerk stepped past him and gestured to a stack at the end of the rows. "This here style is what most o' the miners wear. Tall shank, double-thick sole, and a steel toe. What size you need?"

Emmett shrugged. "Eleven, I think."

The clerk squinted at the boxes, then slid one free from the middle of the stack. He handed it to Emmett. "Most of the men put good thick socks on, too, so they don't rub blisters."

Emmett didn't want any more blisters. "Better get me some, then."

"Sit down over there an' try on them boots." The clerk flapped his hand at a low bench nearby. "I'll fetch some socks. Three pairs or four?"

"Four, I guess."

"Four it is." The fellow scurried off.

Emmett gritted his teeth and clomped stiffly to the bench. He'd spend half of his first paycheck before he even got it. But he supposed he could call the purchases an investment in his future as a miner. The thought didn't do much to cheer him. He sat and pulled off his shoe. Black dust filtered down to the white tile floor. Emmett rubbed it away real quick with his sock, hoping nobody noticed. The boot fit a little loose over his stocking, but a thick sock would fill the gap. This pair would do.

He put the boots in the box, closed the lid, and slid his feet back into his shoes. At the counter, he signed his first ticket as an official employee of US Coal & Coke's Mine Thirty-One, then tucked his purchases under his arm and left the store. He stood at the edge of the boardwalk and looked up the street. Where was the wagon that took the Boone's Hollow workers home? He shifted his gaze to the firehouse clock, and his heart sank. The shift had ended almost an hour ago. The wagon had probably already gone on. Without him.

He leaned against a porch pillar, his entire frame sagging. A tiredness beyond anything he'd known before strained every muscle in his body. And now he had to walk that mile-long road up the mountain. Maybe he should take a hotel room instead. Didn't the Miner's Hotel let workers sign receipts?

Temptation to travel the short walk to the hotel pulled hard, but in the end he couldn't make himself do it. If he didn't get home, Maw would worry.

"A man keeps goin' even when it's tough." He pushed off from the post and aimed his aching feet for the road.

NINETEEN

Boone's Hollow
Bettina

Mule plodded down Boone's Holler's main street, and Bettina didn't give him so much as a nudge to hurry him along. Dawdling was fine. She'd dawdled all day. Done it on purpose. But now dusk was falling and she'd delivered her last books, and Miz West'd be wondering why she hadn't turned up yet. There wasn't no choice but to drop her pack off at the library and go on home to Pap's wrath.

Her stomach hurt.

At the other end of town, a man, toting packages and wearing coal dust from head to toe, trudged up the street. His head bobbed like he was falling asleep on his feet, and his shoulders hung as sloped as rain-soaked branches. He sure looked beat. More beat than Mule after a full day of carting her over her mountain route. Fool feller must've missed the wagon. She swallowed a little chortle. Reckon he wouldn't do that again.

"C'mon, Mule, let's go see who it is there that got left behind." She tapped her heels. Mule snorted, but he clopped a little faster. Bettina kept her squinty gaze pinned on the feller, and all of a sudden his predicament didn't seem funny anymore. She ordered Mule to stop, slid to the ground, and hollered, "Emmett!"

His head came up, and his gaze lit on hers. He stopped dead in his tracks.

She dropped Mule's reins and hurried to him. Up close, he surely was a sight, his hands wrapped with strips of blood-stained cloth and his face so filthy she couldn't hardly tell it was him. She took the boxes that dangled from his fingers by strings and gawked at him. "Since when're you workin' in the mine? An' how come you're walkin'? The wagon shoulda brung you back two hours ago."

He scrunched his face. Coal dust formed whiskers in the creases. "I had to buy gloves and boots, and I guess I took too long at the store, because the wagon went on without me." He lifted his arm real slow and swiped his face with his sleeve. The whiskers got lost under a smear of black dust. "So I walked."

Bettina shook her head, swinging his boxes. "If I'd known you was stranded, I'da brung Mule down the mountain to carry you home." She would've got up behind him and wrapped her arms around his middle to keep 'em both on the mule's back. Wouldn't that've been fine?

"That's nice of you, Bettina, but I think your old mule works hard enough taking you on your book route."

She plunked her fist on her hip, bopping her thigh with the smaller box. "You sayin' I'm a heavisome burden for Mule all by own self?"

He drew back. "No. I meant —" He blew out a big breath. "I'm too tired to think."

She should oughta let him go home, rinse off the layer of dust, and drop into bed, but she needed the pleasure of talking to him to reflect on later, when she was home and Pap was bellowing at her because the new book gal wasn't staying with them. "Pap didn't tell me you was workin' at Mine Thirty-One."

"He didn't know. I didn't know myself until this morning. I had to get a job, so . . ." He reached for the boxes. "Listen, Bettina, my maw's probably worrying about me. I better go."

She flopped the boxes behind her back. "You're plumb wore out. Lemme carry these for you."

"That's real nice, but —"

"You're near to drop. Here." She put the boxes on the ground and curled her hands around his arm. His muscles felt tight and quivery, and it made her insides shiver. Yessir, he was strong. Stronger'n Pap, for sure. She guided him toward the library. "You sit there on the lib'ary stoop, an' I'll fetch ol' Mule. After I turn in my pack, you an' me'll ride Mule to your place. Don't that sound better'n climbin' the path when you're so tuckered you can't hardly put one foot in the front o' the other?"

His feet dragged like he was wearing concrete shoes, but he made it to the library and sank down on the stoop. He let out a low groan. "This is a mistake. Now that I'm sitting, I might not be able to get up again."

She patted his shoulder, raising a little puff of dust. "Don't you worry none about that. I'll help you up."

Miz West stepped into the doorway. She looked at Bettina, then Emmett, then Bettina again. "Is everything all right?"

"Yes'm." Bettina beamed at the woman. Oh, how she liked taking care of Emmett. She felt sorry for him, but now he'd get a little peek at how good she'd be to him when they was married. "This here's my friend. He needs to sit for a minute an' catch his breath. Soon as I get my pack for you, we'll be on our way. Shouldn't take no longer'n two shakes of a lamb's tail."

Emmett put his elbows on his knees and sagged forward.

Miz West stared at him for a few seconds, then gave Bettina one of her pinched-lips scowls. "Please hurry. I'd like to get your returns cataloged. Addie and I are late to supper."

Bettina scampered off, though she didn't care one bit about that new book gal going hungry. If she'd agreed to stay with Pap and her, then Bettina wouldn't have took so much time on her route and they could be sitting down to a meal right now. 'Course, then she would've missed seeing Emmett come up the road. Maybe the new book gal had done her a little bit of a favor. Maybe.

She grabbed Mule's reins and pulled him close to the library. She yanked the pack from his back, eased past Emmett into the building, and flopped the pack onto the table.

The new book gal opened the pack and smiled. "Thank you, Bettina."

Bettina grunted and hurried back outside.

"Lemme get your boxes, Emmett, an' then I'll help you up on Mule's back."

He pushed his hand against the rock stoop and stood. "It's all right, Bettina. I'm so tired I'd probably fall off his back. But if you don't mind, I'll let you carry those boxes for me." He looked at his bandaged hands. "I hate to admit how much these hurt."

A gasp came from the library's doorway.

Bettina looked up, and Emmett half turned, too.

The new book gal stared at Emmett's hands the way Bettina might stare at Pap's raised fist. She looked straight into Emmett's face. "What happened to you?"

Emmett's whole body jerked, like somebody'd sneaked up behind him and poked him with a stick. He leaned toward the new girl, wobbling a little bit, and his mouth fell open. "Addie Cowherd?"

Addie

Addie moved onto the stoop, gaze locked on the blue eyes of the young man who wore stained bandages on his hands and splotches of black dust on every inch of his skin and clothes. Between the fading sunlight and the smears marring his face, she couldn't make out his features. But his voice

266

seemed slightly familiar. "Do I know you?"

A lopsided smile formed on his lips. "I think that's what I asked you at the UK bonfire."

She drew in a breath and reared back. "Now I remember. You're Emmett. Emmett . . ." She couldn't recall his surname.

"Tharp." He bobbed his hands. "I'd offer to shake hands, but . . ."

"It's all right." She cringed at the dark stains on the cloth. "Were you in an accident?"

"No, these are from ignorance."

She shot him a puzzled look.

"I shoveled coal for four hours without first putting on gloves."

Addie gripped her throat. "Oh, my . . . Four hours is a long time to shovel coal."

"Actually, I shoveled closer to nine hours in total, but I used gloves in the afternoon." He turned a rueful grimace on his hands. "Of course, it was too late by then."

Bettina had stood to the side, her attention shifting between Emmett and Addie the way spectators watched a tennis match. She scuttled close to Emmett and curled her hands around his upper arm. "C'mon, Emmett. I'll getcha home now."

Addie stepped to the ground. "Just a moment, Bettina." She'd come out to deliver a message, but Emmett's pathetic appearance had distracted her. She shouldn't let Bettina leave without fulfilling her duty to the librarian. "Miss West said your pack is short a book, a copy of Tolstoy's *Anna Karenina.* Her records indicate it was loaned to the Tool family."

Bettina clung to Emmett's arm and scowled. "I brung back everything the folks give me. Mebbe Miz Tool wasn't done with it yet an' kept it."

"That's possible. It is a lengthy novel."

Emmett set his head at a proud angle. " 'All the diversity, all the charm, and all the beauty of life are made up of light and shade.' "

Addie laughed. How peculiar to hear the beautiful words recited by someone who appeared to have recently rolled in an ash pile. "You've read it?"

He shrugged, and his body seemed to deflate. "Yes, but don't ask me anything more about it. Right now I'd have trouble spelling my own name."

Bettina yanked on his arm. "Let's go."

He stood firm, staring at Addie. "What are you doing here?"

She linked her hands and let them fall against her skirt front. "I'm the newest packhorse librarian. I arrived yesterday evening. I wasn't able to deliver books today since I didn't yet have a horse, so I stayed here and helped Miss West. But Mr. Gilliam is lending me one of his horses. Tomorrow I'll go out with one of the other girls and learn my way around here."

A short, disbelieving chuckle left his throat. "So . . . you're the one who took my job."

"Excuse me?"

"Huh?"

Addie and Bettina spoke at the same time. Emmett glanced at Bettina, then turned a weary smile on Addie that made her heart ache. "I asked Miss West about working for the WPA, taking books to families the way the girls do, but she'd already hired you."

Bettina pressed her cheek to Emmett's bicep, her narrowed gaze spitting fire at Addie. "Aw, I'm sorry, Emmett. It'd be so perfect for you an' me to get to work side by side every day, seein' as how we know each other so good."

Addie knew when she'd been warned off. She stepped up on the stoop. "It's very nice to see you again, Emmett. I'd better let Miss West know about that book." She hurried inside.

Miss West waited at the table. She tapped the pen on the edge of the inkpot. "Well?"

269

"Bettina said she brought back everything the families gave her. She suggested the woman who borrowed *Anna Karenina* might need more time to finish the novel."

Miss West sighed. "That seems a reasonable explanation, but this is the second time she's neglected to retrieve all the loaned books. The previous book has never found its way back here. When we have so few resources to begin with, a loss is —" She pursed her lips and closed her eyes. When she opened them, remorse glimmered in her expression. "Forgive me. I shouldn't voice my concerns to you."

Sympathy rolled through Addie's middle. Miss West carried a large burden, and she lived far away from family and friends in a community that, as she'd stated earlier, held no fondness for her. She must be lonely. Same as Nanny Fay. Addie moved close to the table and offered an encouraging smile. "It's all right. You're a responsible person, and you care about the people in Boone's Hollow. It makes sense that you'd worry about books not coming back."

The woman patted Addie's hand. "You're very kind and understanding. Thank you." She sighed. "Here it is, close to nine o'clock. The sun has nearly disappeared, and you've not yet had your supper. It's time you depart for the evening."

Addie looked outside. Heavy shadows shrouded the entire town. Earlier, with fingers of sunlight sneaking through the trees, the walk to Nanny Fay's cabin hadn't bothered her. But could she find it in the dark?

Miss West stacked the paperwork and set it aside, then rose. "You aren't yet familiar enough with the area to walk to Nanny Fay's alone in the dark. I'll escort you."

Addie nearly collapsed in relief. "Thank you, ma'am."

The librarian picked up the lamp from the table. "Fetch your suitcases and we'll go."

The trek took longer with Addie carrying her suitcases on the upward-climbing path. Miss West's breathing seemed labored, so even though an idea rolled in Addie's mind and she longed to ask her boss's permission, she held it inside. Besides, she hated to desecrate the beauty of the night with talk.

Locusts and crickets sang an off-key chorus. Lightning bugs flashed in the darkness of the forest like stars twinkling against a black sky. The scent she'd noticed on her arrival to Boone's Hollow yesterday was even heavier deep in the trees. Earlier on this trek, she'd discovered its source — wisteria growing wild. The purple blossoms hung like clusters of grapes from bushes and tree branches. Its heady aroma pleased her senses, and she drank in the scent as she followed Miss West and the bobbing lamplight.

They broke through the brush into the clearing where Nanny Fay's cabin waited with yellow light glowing behind the windows. The woman sat on her bench in front of a window, a book in her hands and a serene smile on her face.

She rose and moved to the edge of the porch as Miss West and Addie approached. "There you are. I wondered if you mighta decided to stay elsewhere."

Not even a hint of condemnation came through in the old woman's tone, but Addie still experienced a prick of remorse. "I'm sorry."

Miss West stopped beside the porch, holding the lamp in such a way that all three of their faces were illuminated. "It's all my fault. The day got away from me. I should have sent her much earlier. Tomorrow she'll be here by suppertime."

Nanny Fay chuckled. She hugged the book to her middle and smiled. "Got a shepherd's pie tucked on the back o' the stove, keepin' warm for you. Miss West, you come in an' have some, too, if you ain't et."

"I haven't, and I will not refuse a bowl of your shepherd's pie." Miss West handed the lamp to Nanny Fay and then grabbed the railing and pulled herself up on the porch.

Addie managed the single step with suitcases in hand and followed Nanny Fay and Miss West into the cabin.

Nanny Fay laid the book on a little stand near a rocking chair and gestured to the door of the bedroom she'd indicated would be Addie's. "You can take them bags to your room after you've et. Leave 'em there by the door for now." She waddled toward the rear of the cabin.

Addie followed the woman's directions, then trailed Miss West to a square table covered by an oil cloth. She'd thought the cabin quaint earlier, but somehow the glow of lamplight enhanced its simple beauty. Nanny Fay's furniture was all obviously handcrafted from rough-hewn lumber, but every chair or bench wore a bright-colored throw or patterned pillow. Woven tapestries and a variety of wreaths made of dried flowers and leaves hung on the log walls.

Mother and Daddy's parlor at home had nearly been overtaken by photographs — Mother loved displaying images of family members, especially Addie. But only one photo graced Nanny Fay's cabin, and it held a place of honor on the thick length of wood serving as a mantel above her rock-lined fireplace. As she slid onto one of the stools at the table, Addie stared at the grainy image portraying a young girl with long dark braids and a winsome expression. Was the girl Nanny Fay's daughter? If so, where was she now?

Nanny Fay turned from the stove with two crockery bowls. She placed the bowls in front of Addie and Miss West, then pulled spoons from her apron pockets. "There you are. Now, I ain't got milk to offer, but I got water boilin' so I can steep you some tea."

Miss West's eyes lit. "Birch tea?"

The old woman's face pursed into a sympathetic pout. "Your bones achin' again?" She reached up to a shelf lined with small glass jars, all filled with what looked like ground dried leaves, and lifted one down. "I was hopin' with warm weather here, them aches'd ease for you. But a cup o' birch tea'll take the edge off your hurtin'." She twisted the lid on the jar, turning to Addie. "Mebbe strawberry- or raspberry-leaf tea for you? 'Less you got achy bones, too."

Addie shook her head. "My bones aren't

achy." In her mind's eye, an image of Emmett's bandaged hands intruded. She tipped her head. "But would birch tea ease the pain of open wounds?"

Nanny Fay frowned. "You got open wounds?"

"No, ma'am." Addie told her about Emmett's blisters and the blood-soaked bandages. "I'm sure he's hurting, and he'll have to shovel coal again tomorrow."

"I'm afraid I can't do nothin' about that."

"Oh." Addie fiddled with her spoon, head low. "It's a shame there isn't something that could help."

"Oh, there is somethin' that could help. Lavender oil to soothe an' ground yarrow root tea to speed the healin'."

Addie sat up. "Wonderful! He'll be so relieved." She could hardly wait to tell him about Nanny Fay's cures.

Miss West sighed, but not one of her usual catching-her-breath sighs. This one seemed laden with woe. "Addie, Nanny Fay could help Emmett's wounds. But she won't."

The woman who'd so graciously offered a room in her house for twenty-five cents a week to a total stranger wouldn't help someone from her very own community? "But why?"

"Because Emmett's father wouldn't allow it."

TWENTY

Bettina

Bettina slept in the barn Monday night, even though she moved all her things back into her room after supper. Pap was madder'n a wet hen about losing the boarding money from the new book gal, and she felt safer with some distance between them.

Come morning, he was still grumbling and blaming her for scaring off Addie, but she kept quiet and fixed him his favorite breakfast. So she didn't get swung at. No new bruises to worry about. A few more days, and the old ones would be faded enough she could wear a short-sleeved blouse. It was June already. People would start thinking she was wrong in the head if she kept wearing winter shirts. She might faint dead away from sweating, too. The sun wasn't even full up, but already the air was heavy and hot.

Pap left for the wagon, and she enjoyed a

peaceful hour alone in the house before she saddled Mule, grabbed his reins, and took the short path across the creek and between the Ashcroft and Landrum cabins to the main street. Across the way, at the other end of the street, the new book gal came out of the trees behind the post office. All at once, Bettina's stomach went tight and trembly. She heard Emmett's voice in her head. *"Addie Cowherd?"*

He'd sounded surprised and happy at the same time. Tired and sore as he'd been, him finding that much pleasure in seeing someone sent up all kinds of warnings in Bettina's mind. She tugged Mule behind a stand of trees and peeked out at Addie Cowherd. At her dress — a dress again! And shoes. Flat ones today, kind of like ballet slippers. She walked with her head high and shoulders straight, like she knowed she was somebody special. The girl was smart, Bettina'd already figured that, but her knowing the lines Emmett said from the Anna Carryin'-nina book rubbed it in. Bettina needed to get rid of this girl.

Addie disappeared inside the livery, and Bettina pulled Mule from their hiding spot. "C'mon, let's go." She hurried the animal past the livery and Belcher's. She'd almost reached the library when somebody called her name. She looked back. Glory was coming, leading her horse and scowling like she'd ate a rotten egg. Bettina stopped and waited for her to catch up.

Glory ambled up alongside Bettina. "Saw you pass my window. How come you didn't wait an' walk with me?"

"Sorry. Guess I wasn't thinkin'."

Addie came out of the livery. She led one of Gilliam's horses, a filly named Russet for its shiny red-brown coat. Bettina'd always admired that horse. She'd asked Pap about renting her for her routes, but Pap said Mule was good enough. Now Addie'd be riding her. That tight feeling grabbed hold of her gut again.

Glory pointed. "Lookee there. Guess Addie's found herself a horse, so she'll be takin' books now."

"Uh-huh."

"That's good for us." Glory ran her fingers through Posey's white mane. "Don't see how she's gonna sit in the saddle, though, with a dress on. I read a book one time . . . It was set in England, but I can't recall the title. When the ladies went ridin', they sat in somethin' called a sidesaddle so they didn't have to sit astride." She giggled. "I don't reckon Gilliam's got anything so fancy in his livery."

"Reckon not." Just a plain old everyday saddle was cinched on Russet's back. If Addie tried to sit sidesaddle on it, she'd probably slide right off. The thought put the first smile of the day on Bettina's face. She flopped Mule's reins over a bush and grabbed Glory's arm. "Let's get inside, find out who's gonna take the new book gal around to meet folks today."

Glory twisted Posey's reins around a low-hanging branch and trotted after Bettina to the lib'ary's open doorway. The girls stepped inside, and Glory let out a squeal. Bettina slapped her hand over her mouth to keep from doing the same.

Miz West was lying flat on the floor, gripping her dress bodice with both hands and gasping like a fish on a creek bank.

Addie

Addie stopped in the middle of the street and cocked her head. Had someone screamed? The horse's nostrils flared, and it bounced its powerful head up and down. "You heard it, too, didn't you?"

Glory burst out of the library, waving her hands in the air. "Help! Help! Somebody help! Miss West is dyin'!" She took off up the street.

Addie let go of the horse's reins and ran

to the library. She darted inside. Miss West lay on the floor. Bettina bent over her, holding the woman's hand.

Addie hurried to Miss West's other side and crouched down. "Miss West, what is it?"

The woman's wide eyes met Addie's. "Cuh-can't . . . b-b-breathe . . ." Her chest rose and fell in quick little bursts.

Bettina patted Miss West's hand, the pats as fast and frantic as Miss West's puffs of breath. "What's wrong with her? She was right as rain yesterday."

"I'm not sure. She was fine last night at Nanny Fay's, too."

Bettina gaped at Addie. "She went to Nanny Fay's?"

Addie scowled at the girl. Bettina's freckles stood out like pennies tossed on a snowbank. She seemed as frightened as if she'd seen a ghost, but for such a ridiculous reason. "Yes. She had supper there last night."

"She ate Nanny Fay's food?" Bettina let go of Miss West's hand and scuttled backward like a crab. "Did she drink somethin', too?"

"Some tea. For her aching joints."

Bettina clapped her hands to her cheeks. "Nanny Fay poisoned her."

Addie huffed. "For heaven's sake, if she'd been poisoned, she wouldn't be breathing at all." She slipped her hand under Miss West's shoulders and tried to lift her. The woman was heavier than she looked. Addie needed help. "Bettina, come over here and help me sit her up."

Bettina didn't move.

"Bettina, she can't breathe well lying flat like this! Help me!"

Bettina shifted to her knees but stayed a few feet away, her fear-filled gaze locked on Miss West's face. Addie started to holler at her again, but a tall gray-haired man rushed into the library and pushed Bettina aside.

He dropped a black bag on the floor and knelt beside it, barely glancing at Addie. "Get some pillows."

Addie scrambled to her feet, tossed the blanket curtain aside, and grabbed the feather pillow from Miss West's cot. She came back out. Alba had arrived, and she huddled in the doorway with Glory and Bettina. The girls all gaped at Miss West, reminding Addie of a trio of owls with their round eyes. The man wore a stethoscope and held the little bell-shaped listening device against Miss West's chest, his bushy brows scrunched together like a caterpillar crawling across his forehead. Addie hugged the pillow and waited for instruction.

He glanced at the pillow. "Only one?"

"That's all she has."

"Fold it in half an' put it underneath her when I pick her up." He grabbed her in a hug and lifted.

Addie did as he'd said, her hands trembling. He laid her on the pillow, then sat up, staring hard at her face. Miss West's chest wasn't heaving so fast anymore, but the doctor's grim expression did little to calm Addie's racing pulse. She stroked Miss West's coarse gray hair, praying wordlessly.

Bettina crept close, wringing her hands. "Doc Faulkner, is she dyin'?"

"She's havin' an asthmatic attack."

"What's that?" Glory's voice quavered.

"A spasm of the bronchial tubes."

Bettina peeked over the doctor's shoulder. "Did Nanny Fay do it to her?"

The doctor sat back on his heels. He sent Bettina a fierce look. "What?"

"She was at Nanny Fay's last night. Had supper there an' drank a potion."

Addie gasped. "It wasn't a potion! She drank a cup of birch tea. She asked for it because she said it helped her joints not ache."

The doctor shooed Bettina with a wave of his hand, and she scuttled back to Glory and Alba. Then he put his hand on Miss West's shoulder. "Miss West, are you rested enough to talk?"

She nodded.

"All right. I need to know . . . have you had an attack like this before?"

"Yes." She licked her lips and closed her eyes. "Have had them . . . off and on . . . since I was a child. But lately . . . lately . . ."

"They been worse?"

Another nod.

The doctor stood and leaned over, hands on his knees. "All right. I'm gonna get you up on your feet. We'll put you in a chair there at the table, an' then we'll have us a talk." He straightened. "Bettina, pull out one o' those chairs."

Bettina screeched the chair across the floor and stood behind it, hands on its high back.

"Glory an' Alba?"

The two girls jolted to attention. "Yes, sir?" they chorused.

"Go to Belcher's. He's not open yet, but bang on the door until he answers. Tell him I need a copper bowl — at least two-quart size — an' a good thick cotton towel. The biggest one he's got."

The two scampered out, holding hands.

He looked at Addie. "You stay close in

case she's woozy. We don't want her to fall."

"Yes, sir."

The doctor took hold of Miss West's arms and pulled her to her feet. Addie slid her arm around the woman's waist, and she and the doctor eased her into the waiting chair. Doc Faulkner resumed his hands-on-knees position and peered into Miss West's face. "You okay?"

"I'm fine, Doctor. Thank you." She put her fingers under her sleeve cuff, but there wasn't a handkerchief. "Oh . . ."

Addie spotted the square of cloth on the floor. She snatched it up and placed it in Miss West's hand.

Miss West offered a wobbly smile. "Thank you, dear." She patted her throat.

Bettina took several sideways steps from the table and then hurried out the door.

Addie suddenly realized she'd left Mr. Gilliam's horse standing in the middle of the street. She should check on Russet and let Miss West and the doctor talk privately. "Excuse me, please."

To her relief, Russet had joined the other horses at the trees near the library. Bettina stood in their midst, rubbing their noses by turn. The girl's face had returned to its normal color, but her hands still trembled. Addie's heart went out to her. She'd worked for Miss West for a year already. Finding her lying on the floor must have frightened her badly.

She moved close and touched Bettina's arm. "I'm sorry you received such a shock this morning."

Bettina jerked away from her. "I'm fine."

Addie laughed softly and folded her arms. "I wouldn't be fine if I'd come in and found someone lying on the floor. I would've screamed, too."

"That was Glory, not me. She's such a fraidy-cat." Bettina shifted her attention to Alba's horse. "Only thing worries me is if we'll be able to go out today. We don't deliver an' pick up books, I might not get paid, an' I need the money comin' in."

Addie suspected Bettina's brave front was only that — a front. But she wouldn't shame the girl by calling her on it. She imitated Bettina's ministrations and rubbed Russet's nose. The horse snuffled her neck, and Addie smiled. "Are you saving up for something special?"

A huge smile burst over Bettina's face. "I sure am. My weddin'."

"Oh? You're engaged?"

"Mm-hmm." She nodded big, pressing her cheek to Glory's horse's jaw. "Me an' my beau, we're in the courtin' stage, but

286

won't be long now an' we'll set us a date."

Addie wasn't surprised. A lot of girls married young. According to the records the orphanage had given Mother and Daddy, her birth mother was only seventeen years old when Addie was born. Bettina was probably seventeen or eighteen, a marriageable age. But she didn't wear a ring or other piece of jewelry. Did girls in the hills receive some symbol of betrothal? Maybe Bettina had one but didn't wear it on her rides.

"That's wonderful. What's your beau's name?"

Bettina's smile turned cunning. "Why, Addie, you already know. It's Emmett."

Addie drew back. "Emmett? You mean Emmett Tharp?"

"Mm-hmm. We go way back, him an' me."

"But —"

Glory and Alba appeared, bare feet pounding. The horses milled, and Addie automatically ran her hand down Russet's nose. Glory held up a large yellowware bowl. "We got the stuff Doc wanted. Well, sorta. Belcher's didn't have no copper bowls, so I got this instead."

Alba patted the folded towel draped over her arm. "Least he had good cotton towels. This'uns big enough for Miss West to wrap herself up in if she wants to." Alba looked

287

from Addie to Bettina. Her fine, pale brows pulled low. "What'sa matter with you two? You're all red faced an' twitchy."

Addie hadn't realized the shock of Bettina's announcement showed. She forced a smile. "We're fine. Just worried about Miss West is all."

Bettina's lips formed a wry grin. "Yeah. Worried about Miz West. That's all." She nuzzled her mule's cheek.

"Girls?" The doctor beckoned them from the stoop. "C'mon in here. Miss West needs to talk to you."

TWENTY-ONE

Bettina

"Comin', Doc." Bettina darted toward the library building. She sent a sly glance over her shoulder. Yessir, she'd got the new book gal's attention. That oughta keep her from getting all chummy with Emmett. Finding out they'd been at that college together kinda shook Bettina's confidence, but see how it'd worked out? She'd just keep the two of them apart, and she'd have Emmett all to herself.

Miz West sat at the table in her usual spot. She held her handkerchief in her fist and her fist against her chest, like she was fixing to take a vow. Bettina took the other chair, and Alba, Glory, and Addie crowded close, too.

Doc Faulkner went down on one knee beside Miz West's chair, almost like a man asking a woman to marry up. Bettina couldn't wait for Emmett to kneel in front of her that way. Her heart fluttered, and she released a soft, airy giggle.

"The bowl from Belcher's won't hold heat like a copper one would," the doctor said to Miz West, talking as if the girls weren't even in the room, "so you'll have to keep water boilin' an' ready to go. But do like I told you — lean over the steamy water with the towel makin' a tent for you an' the bowl, and breathe in that steam at least ten minutes every hour for the rest o' the day."

"Yes, Doctor, I will, as soon as I've finished speaking to the girls. Thank you."

He stood and picked up his bag off the table. "I'm right next door if you need me."

Bettina leaned sideways on the chair and watched the doctor leave. He didn't so much as pause and look back. When he'd come to their house to see to Maw's bad hurting in her belly, he'd stopped in her doorway and stared at her in her bed for a long time before taking his leave. Bettina'd never forgot it. If the doc left so easy now, he must not be too worried about Miz West.

Bettina's worry faded fast away, and she turned to the librarian. "Who's gonna take Addie around today? We're late settin' out. Folks'll be lookin' for us."

Miz West gave Bettina a stern look. She was real good at those stern looks. But this one seemed a little sad around the edges. "You'll set out when I send you." She sighed one of her usual sighs and put her head down. "I'm afraid I have some unsettling news."

Addie moved in closer and put her hand on the librarian's shoulder. "Are you dreadfully ill, Miss West?"

Bettina almost rolled her eyes. Doc had left, hadn't he? Sure, Miz West had a spell that morning, but she was fine now.

"I'm afraid I'm more ill than I'd realized."

Bettina sat up.

"Apparently, the pollens in the mountains are different from those in the city. I've always had a few attacks during the fall, especially when the goldenrod is blooming, but managed fairly well the other seasons of the year. That hasn't been the case since I arrived in Boone's Hollow, though. Doctor Faulkner believes tree pollen is to blame for today's attack, which was particularly severe."

Glory nodded so hard her frizzy hair bounced. "Like to scared the stuffin' out o' me to see you all laid out that way. I thought you was a goner, for certain sure."

Miz West squeezed Glory's hand. "I'm sorry to have frightened you. To be honest, it frightened me, too. I feared I might die then and there."

The girls gasped. Alba wrung her hands, leaning in. "That ain't gonna happen again, is it? Now that the doc seen you an' told you what to do, you'll be all right, won't you?"

"I'm afraid not."

Bettina nodded, her chest pinching like somebody had wrapped a rope around it and pulled. The doc coming didn't mean things got fixed. Maw being in the ground proved it.

"Doctor Faulkner has advised me to leave the mountain for the sake of my health. I told him I would make arrangements. I should be gone by the end of the week."

Glory and Alba grabbed each other in a hug, and Addie blinked fast, the way folks did when they were trying not to cry. Bettina gritted her teeth real hard. If Miz West left, there'd be no more book routes. Bettina was losing her job, losing the money. Pap would have a conniption fit when he found out. But at least this book gal who'd gone to college with Emmett would get herself out of Boone's Holler. Bettina didn't wish ill on Miz West, but she wouldn't be sad to see Addie Cowherd go away.

The gloves helped. Emmett scooped another shovelful of coal and flung it into the cart. Without his hands slipping up and down the length of wood, he developed a steady rhythm of scoop, fling, scoop, fling.

After his supper last night, Maw had dropped a handful of wintergreen leaves into a tub of hot water and made him soak for a good long while. Then this morning, she rubbed wintergreen oil all over his shoulders and back. Emmett had massaged the oil into his leg and arm muscles, too. Maw claimed it would help ease the pain and stiffness. When he asked where she'd gotten the medicine, she put her finger on her lips and shook her head. That told him all he needed to know.

Every muscle in his body still ached like a stubbed toe, but maybe the oil had helped more than he realized because he could swing the shovel in spite of the pain. And he sure smelled good. When he'd gotten on the wagon that morning, the other fellows asked if he was going courting. Even Shay joked with him about it, and Emmett had begun his day laughing. A good start.

Scoop, fling, scoop, fling . . .

The dust was awful, so thick it blurred his

vision and made him sneeze. But if he kept his pace and held his position, he rarely let so much as a single chunk of coal bounce over the edge.

Stead ambled up and watched Emmett for several seconds, tapping his leg with his ever-present clipboard. "You got a good aim, Tharp. Keep goin' like you're doin' now, an' you'll have a full cart by midmornin'."

One of the other shovel men, nicknamed Pumpkin Pete for his curly orange-red hair, lobbed a grin in their direction, his shovel still swinging. "Sure, an' he's doin' fine fer someone who smells like he's been rollin' in pine needles."

Emmett waved away dust and barked a laugh. "If you can smell my wintergreen oil with all this coal dust being sucked up your nose, you should rent yourself out as a bloodhound."

Pumpkin Pete roared with laughter, and Emmett couldn't stop grinning. It had taken three years in his fraternity to feel comfortable enough to josh with his fellow Delta Sigma Phi brothers. Only his second day here, and already he was one of the boys. An unexpected benefit.

Stead smacked Emmett's shoulder, gave a nod, then headed on up the tunnel. Emmett returned to his steady scoop, fling, scoop, fling. His muscles screamed in protest at every motion, but he was finding out how tough he was. He grinned and kept going. He could hardly wait to clang the bell and let everyone up the line know he'd filled another cart.

Boone's Hollow
Addie

Addie skittered backward several feet, then caught her balance. She stomped her foot and huffed. "Why is this so hard? I was able to mount the pony at the fair without a bit of trouble."

Bettina leaned on her saddle's horn and smirked. "An' just how big was that pony?"

Looking through six-year-old eyes, it had seemed enormous. But when she remembered the photo in the parlor, it was probably more the size of a Great Dane. She groaned. "Less than half the size of Russet."

"Try again. Poke your foot in the stirrup, grab hold o' the horn, an' pull." Bettina punctuated her instructions with sharp jabs of her finger.

Addie gritted her teeth, took a firm grip on the horn, and tried once more to slide her foot into the dangling stirrup. Russet shifted sideways a few inches, and Addie's foot went all the way through the opening. She lost her grip on the horn, flailed for another hold, found none, and landed hard on her bottom, her foot still caught in the stirrup. Russet snorted and pawed the ground.

Bettina swung down as quickly as a snapping turtle lunged. She grabbed Russet's reins and looked at Addie, eyebrows high. "That's a good way to get yourself dragged."

Addie shook her fists in the air, wishing she could shake Russet instead. The animal would not cooperate. "Maybe I need a different horse."

"What you need is differ'nt shoes. Them little things with no heel ain't gonna stay put in a stirrup."

Addie twisted around and freed her foot, certain she was showing off everything she'd put on under her dress that morning. Thank goodness the other girls had already left for their routes and she and Bettina were still half-hidden by the trees outside the library. She'd rather not have even Bettina as an audience, but at least the entire town wasn't observing her ineptitude.

She stood and brushed dirt and grass from her skirt. "You're barefoot — no shoes at all! — and you don't slide out of the stirrup."

Bettina scowled. "Never mind about my feet. Ain't we lost enough of our day with Miss West's troubles? Stop yammerin' an' try again."

Addie stared at Russet's regal profile. "I don't know, Bettina. It's already awkward enough thinking about straddling the horse when I'm wearing . . ." She batted at her rumpled dress. "I must, at the very least, have secure footing or I won't be able to . . . to . . . remain proper." She gave Bettina's overalls a quick examination. "Does Belcher's sell britches like you're wearing? Maybe I should buy some."

A gleam entered Bettina's hazel eyes. "Why, sure, Belcher's sells britches. We can go over there right now an' find you some. Prob'ly should fix you up with a pair o' boots, too — some with a heel that'll catch on the stirrup an' keep you from slidin' through an' fallin' flat on your rump again." She snickered. " 'Less you wanna be like me an' go barefoot."

Addie had gotten a peek at the bottoms of Bettina's feet before she hopped down from her horse. Her soles appeared as thick as leather. She could probably walk through sticker patches and come out unscathed. Addie's feet, always appropriately clad at Mother's insistence, needed protection. "I'd like to look at both overalls and boots."

"Well, c'mon, then." Bettina slung herself into her saddle, still holding Russet's reins. She urged her mule into motion and led the sorrel.

Addie hobbled after the pair of animals, face flaming. If Miss West hadn't promised the girls another director would be assigned to the Boone's Hollow post, she wouldn't waste her money on clothes and shoes she'd likely never wear outside this community.

But Miss West had said, "President Roosevelt is determined that the hills people are given every opportunity to better themselves, so the council in charge of the packhorse librarians program will hire a replacement for me. While you wait for the new director to arrive, you girls must continue your routes with all due diligence."

Miss West's insistence inspired Addie to do the job for which she'd been hired. As soon as she could get up on Russet's back.

Bettina hopped down, looped the animals' reins around a porch post, then gave a little leap onto the long covered porch in front of Belcher's store and sauntered to the door. Addie stepped up with less grace. Her backside still hurt from her thump on the hard ground. Bettina waited at the screen door, snickering, but she didn't say anything as Addie limped into the store.

Whirring ceiling fans and light bulbs at the end of twisted brown wire hung from the high beamed ceiling. She'd presumed Boone's Hollow was without electrical service since the library had none. The touch of civilization gave her an unexpected lift. As did the variety of goods available for sale. Units of unpainted freestanding shelves stood in rows from one end of the interior to the other. Handwritten signs tacked to the shelves advertised sales on canned peas, yard goods, Dreft detergent, and Post Toasties.

"This way." Bettina led Addie toward the rear of the store. "Clothes're back here. Belcher's don't keep dresses an' such — ladies sew their own or order from the Sears an' Roebuck catalog. A few of 'em go into Lynch to the minin' store. But you ain't needin' any more dresses." She humphed and turned a corner, then pointed to folded stacks of blue, tan, or railroad-striped overalls. "Reckon you need a shirt, too. Unless you wanna stuff that skirt into your britches."

Addie had no intention of stuffing her dress inside a pair of britches. She ran her finger down the stack of tan bibbed overalls. "What size do you wear, Bettina?"

299

The other girl folded her arms over the bib of her faded blue overalls. "Why you wanna know?"

Why was she always so defensive? Addie drew in a slow breath, praying for patience. "Because it will help me know what size to buy. I'm a little taller —"

"An' wider." Bettina looked Addie up and down, one eyebrow higher than the other.

What an impolite thing to say, even though it was true. Bettina was as slender as a willow branch. Addie sighed. "Yes. I thought if I knew your size, I'd just go up a size or two and we could save the time of my trying them on."

Bettina smacked her finger down on the tag attached by a string to a pair of blue overalls. "That there's what I wear."

Addie added two more numbers, slid the tan overalls from the stack, and tucked them into the crook of her arm. "Now, boots."

"Them are in a bin near the front counter." Bettina headed off, and Addie followed. A woman and a little boy were at the bin, pawing through the boots, and Bettina hurried over to them. "Miz Tharp! An' Dusty. Hey, how you doin'?"

The woman turned and wrapped Bettina in a hug. "Why, Bettina, what are you doin' in here? Shouldn't you be on your delivery route?"

"You're right, I should be." Bettina laughed and pulled free. She poked her thumb in Addie's direction. "But our new book gal here needs some horseback-wearin' clothes."

The woman finger-combed the little boy's dark hair and aimed a shy smile at Addie. "Howdy. Been hearin' about the new gal in town. It's right nice to meet you. I'm Damaris Tharp, an' this here is my boy Dusty." Friendliness seemed to exude from the woman.

Addie eagerly stepped forward. "It's nice to meet you, Mrs. Tharp. I'm Addie Cowherd. Did you say your name is Damaris? I've never heard it before, but it's lovely."

"Why, that's real kind o' you." She dipped her head in a humble gesture. "My maw took it from the Bible. I've always been right fond of it."

Tharp . . . In a town this small, would there be more than one Tharp family? "Ma'am, are you any relation to Emmett Tharp?"

Surprise registered on the woman's face. "He's my oldest boy. You met Emmett?"

Addie nodded. "In Lexington at the university. We —"

Bettina pushed between the women. "Guess you heard about Miz West havin' a breathin' fit this mornin' an' needin' Doc Faulkner."

Mrs. Tharp's eyes widened. "Oh, my . . ."

"Yep. Turns out she's got some kinda sickness, an' she ain't gonna be able to keep livin' here on the mountain. Said she'll be gone by Friday, Saturday for sure, 'cause if she stays, she might keel over dead."

Miss West hadn't given the girls permission to share her personal information with others. Addie touched Bettina's sleeve. "Bettina? I —"

Bettina wriggled her arm, not even bothering to look Addie's way. "I was scared at first they'd shut the place down an' I wouldn't have a job no more. But she's callin' President Roosevelt hisself, she said, about findin' somebody else to run the lib'ary."

Addie tapped Bettina's arm again. "Bettina, she said she'd talk to —"

"Me an' the other riders" — Bettina's voice rose in volume — "is s'posed to keep doin' our deliveries like always. An' I will, just as soon as we get Addie here outfitted with britches an' boots." She rolled her eyes. "She can't get on her horse in the getup she's wearin'. City gal . . . Don't reckon she knows no better." She turned to Addie and frowned. "Well, you gonna pick out some boots or not? We're gonna lose the whole day if you don't hurry up."

The little boy hunched his shoulders and giggled, and Addie couldn't resist winking at him. "Yes, I'll find some boots." She and Dusty both reached into the bin at the same time, his impish grin aimed at her.

Mrs. Tharp pinched her chin, gazing at Bettina. "Bettina, has Miss West made that telephone call you were talkin' about yet?"

Bettina shrugged. "I dunno. She was sittin' at the table, writin' on some papers when me an' the others left to go on our routes."

The woman took hold of Dusty's arm and turned him to face her. "Dusty, you keep lookin' for boots. Remember, they gotta be good an' loose so they'll last awhile."

The little boy nodded. "For church now an' school later. I know, Maw."

She ruffled his hair. "Good boy. I'll be right back."

The boy crinkled his nose. "Where you goin'?"

"Over to talk to Miss West." She smiled at Bettina. "There's a feller right here in Boone's Holler who'd be fit as a fiddle for runnin' that book program."

303

Addie followed the woman's thoughts. "Are you thinking of Emmett?"

Mrs. Tharp nodded, a happy little laugh trickling out. "I sure am."

TWENTY-TWO

Emmett

"So . . . Miss West made a telephone call to Washington, DC!" Maw's eyes shone as bright as they had the day Emmett received the scholarship letter from the university in Lexington. She'd started talking the moment after Paw finished blessing their supper, and she still hadn't taken a bite of the bean-and-hotdog casserole. "I stood right next to her in the telephone office while she told the feller at the other end about you havin' a college diploma, an' how you live here in Boone's Holler, an' how you'd come in lookin' for a job."

Paw paused with his spoon halfway between his plate and his mouth. "What's wrong with the job he's got now?"

Maw made a face. "Now, Emil, ain't nothin' wrong with workin' in the coal mine. It's honest work. I'm grateful for how your job there keeps this family fed. But look at him." She gestured to Emmett's hands. Strips of fresh gauze, splotched with the healing oil Maw'd rubbed on his wounds when he got home that evening, hid the healing blisters. "Emmett ain't used to such labor. He's a . . ." She tipped her head and seemed to search the ceiling beams, then bounced a satisfied smile at Paw. "Intellectual. Ain't that what Mr. Halcomb called him? It means —"

Paw scowled. "I know what it means."

Dusty stabbed a slice of hotdog on his plate and poked it in his mouth. "What's it mean, Paw?"

"Somebody who uses his head to work."

"Oh." Dusty sat straight up. "I wanna be a coal miner instead of a . . . a . . . what Emmett is."

Emmett swallowed a bite. "The word is *intellectual,* Dusty, but I'm not sure that really fits me."

Maw lightly smacked his arm. "It does, too, an' you need to be proud of it." She turned to Dusty. "Why don't you wanna be like your big brother?"

" 'Cause if I use my head for workin', I might get blisters on it."

Maw and Emmett laughed, and even Paw grinned a little. He took a piece of bread from the plate in the middle of the table and mopped at the tomatoey juice on his plate. "A feller don't get blisters from too much thinkin', or your maw would have a whole headful."

Maw slumped in her chair and sighed. "Emil, I'm sorry. Maybe I should've talked to you first."

"Sure should've."

"But it seemed so perfect, me runnin' into Bettina in Belcher's an' findin' out about the job at the lib'ary so quick, havin' Emmett home here an' needin' to make use of his degree . . ." Tears glittered in Maw's eyes. "Seemed like God was makin' a way."

Emmett contemplated what Maw'd said. His mind trailed through the series of rejections he'd received from business owners in Lexington, Cumberland, Benham, and Lynch. Sure, he'd finally been hired at Mine Thirty-One, but only after Paw spoke up for him. And the job he had now didn't require much thinking.

He looked at his bandages and considered his seeping sores and aching muscles. If he worked as director of the library, he wouldn't come home hurting from head to toe. But then, when these blisters finally healed and his body adjusted to the hard labor of swinging his shovel, he probably wouldn't hurt like this either.

At the library, he'd be mostly alone. At the coal mine, he had a whole community of fellow miners who'd welcomed him into their ranks. If he got the job at the library, Maw'd be so proud. But working at the mine had awakened in Paw a pride for his son that Emmett had never seen before. Had never expected to see.

He glanced at Paw, who'd laid off eating but dabbed the folded piece of bread against his plate, lips set in a stern downward turn. Gaze fixed on his father's profile, Emmett said, "Maw, did Miss West say the man in Washington wanted to hire me?"

"No, she said he'd talk it over with his committee an' call her back."

"Did she say when?"

"By the end o' the week."

Paw's eyes met Emmett's. He sat rigid, eyelids narrowed, for several seconds. Then he jerked his focus to his plate and started eating again.

Emmett gave Maw's hand a squeeze. "Thanks for looking out for me. Reckon we'll wait and see what the man in Washington wants." He wasn't sure what he wanted.

Bettina

Why'd she gone and opened her big mouth? Bettina clanked the last clean plate on the shelf and tossed the dish towel over the nail by the window. All through cooking, serving, and cleaning up supper, she'd gone over her talk with Emmett's maw and thought up a dozen different things she could have said instead.

She plopped into Maw's rocking chair and reached for the top item in the mending basket — Pap's church shirt. He'd ripped a seam loose near the right elbow. Probably happened when he took a swing at her. She dug a needle and thread from the cigar box Maw'd used as a sewing kit and set to work closing the seam so he could wear it to service next Sunday.

Although she'd rather do most any chore besides stitching, she liked having the house to herself. Peaceful. Pap hadn't been happy about her coming in so late, but when she explained what'd happened with Miz West an' her late start getting on her route, he calmed down and ate his cold supper without no more complaints. Then he went out right after eating. He didn't tell her where he was going, but she knew anyway. His jug in the barn needed refilling.

She rested her head against the chair's rolled back and closed her eyes, sighing deep. If Emmett started working at the library, everything would fall apart. Him working at the mine in Lynch, even though it wasn't a fancy city job like she wanted for him, was perfect. Wouldn't take him long to get tired of sleeping in his folks' loft. He'd rent himself one of the company houses in Lynch, and then he'd need somebody to do his cooking and cleaning and such, and he'd for sure ask her to be his somebody. Wasn't nobody else who'd take care of him better.

And with him working in Lynch, he'd be far away from Addie Cowherd.

She snorted. "Addie Cowherd. More like Addie Coward."

Dumb girl was scared to get on a horse. Then she was scared to stay on it for the uphill climbs. Whether on or off, she'd kept looking this way and that, thinking snakes or bobcats or bears would get her. Of course, she might not've been looking so hard if Bettina hadn't warned her about mountain critters and how they liked to surprise folks. But Miz West had said to train Addie, and there was plenty of critters in the mountains that wouldn't mind taking a bite out of a person, so Bettina had to tell her.

A little snicker found its way from Bettina's mouth. She wove the needle in and out, in and out, lips twitching. Too bad Emmett hadn't seen Addie in those overalls and boots. The men's clothes sure took the fancy out of her. 'Course, she didn't look so citi-fied and proper flat on her back in the dirt with her foot stuck in a stirrup and her frilly underclothes on display, either. Bettina put her head back and laughed long and loud. My, but that'd been funny. She couldn't wait to tell Glory and Alba about it. She'd be sure and tell them how she'd saved Addie by keeping Russet from running off with her, too.

Maybe she should've let it be. Addie'd be all the way to Cumberland by now. Wouldn't it be a fine thing if Addie disappeared? Emmett hadn't showed no interest in any gal from Boone's Hollow until Addie came along. Bettina couldn't rightly blame him for looking. Addie's pretty clothes, the way she talked, even the way she walked — like the movie starlets did, all straight and proud — made her stick out. But if he had lots of chances to look, then he might start think-ing Addie was a better pick than her, and she couldn't let that happen.

She made a knot in the thread and bit it off. She folded Pap's shirt real careful, then carried it to his room and put it on his bureau, where he'd be sure to notice she'd fixed it. Not that he'd thank her. But he wouldn't pester her about it, and that'd be good enough. Would Emmett thank her if she stitched up a tear in one of his shirts? She reckoned he would.

She left the room and closed Pap's door behind her. There was more mending waiting, and she should oughta get to it. She reached her hand to the basket, but she didn't pick anything up. Pap wasn't there to scold or call her lazy, so she'd enjoy a few minutes of sitting. Thinking. She'd always been good at painting pictures in her head. She did it in the classroom when the other kids was reading. She did it in her bed at night when she was trying to forget something hurtful Pap'd said to her. Wasn't many things she was good at, but pretending was one of 'em, so she closed her eyes and let herself slip off. Pretty pictures took shape and flowed like a movie on a screen in her head.

Emmett asking her to carry his boxes for him, then giving her a thank-you and a sleepy half smile.

Miz Tharp smiling and pulling Bettina into a hug that felt so good.

Addie on the ground with her foot caught, then wearing those too-big overalls, then sitting all white faced and nervous in the saddle. Bettina's whole body shook in silent laughter. She searched for another Addie picture.

Addie staring, all surprised about Emmett being Bettina's beau.

Her eyes popped open. She'd said too much to Miz Tharp, and she'd said too much to Addie. Sure, it'd seemed smart at the time. If Addie thought Emmett was engaged to be wed, she wouldn't be friendly with him. No decent girl went after another girl's beau, and even if Addie was from the city, she'd know the rules. But what if Addie told Emmett "Congratulations" or asked him about wedding dates? Bettina'd be caught in a lie.

Or was it a lie? Emmett would court her. Sure, he would. He was just settling in. Hadn't he gave her that big hug when he came back from school after his graduation? Hadn't he walked her to the Ashcrofts' place after the Sunday sing? Hadn't he asked her to carry his boxes home and then thanked her real sweet at his door before going inside?

Still, he might not be happy about her talking about it to somebody before he made it all official-like. Men were funny that way. They liked to be the one in the lead, same as Mule did anytime there was a horse traveling alongside him. 'Course, the bit in

313

Mule's mouth gave her some control over his leading. Once she had a ring on her finger, she'd have some control over Emmett. Until then, she'd have to keep Addie and Emmett apart.

Which would be a whole lot easier if he kept working the coal mine.

TWENTY-THREE

Addie

"Dearest Mother and Daddy . . ."

Addie yawned and then gave herself a good shake, trying to chase away the tiredness that gripped her as tightly as nettles held to the cuffs of her britches. Of all the difficult tasks she'd encountered over the past four days, removing the little hairs from the coarse fabric had proved the least enjoyable. Even holding the pen now stung her fingers, but she had to write this letter. Almost a full week had passed since she'd spent the afternoon and evening with her parents.

A few feet away, Nanny Fay stirred something on the stove. The concoction smelled horrible, but the woman hummed as she stirred, seemingly unbothered by the pungent aroma. The time Addie had actually spent in the elderly woman's presence had taught Addie that Nanny Fay let very little upset her.

Rabbits nibbled down her cabbage starts — "They gotta eat, too."

The jar of dried black snakeroot fell from the shelf when she moved another jar, scattering the precious herb all over the floor — "Reckon the Good Lord decided I could use another traipsin' trip to the upper reaches o' Black Mountain."

People moved to the opposite side of Belcher's when she and Addie met there to buy flour and sugar after Addie had gotten done at the library — "They ain't bein' hateful. They just don't know no better."

The past days of riding — or leading — Russet through narrow mountain passes and over steep rises and shallow streams had taxed Addie's physical stamina. But Nanny Fay's comment about people's lack of knowledge, coupled with Miss West's fervent declaration about the power of reading to change people, strengthened Addie's resolve. She would put books into these people's hands, and they would learn to know better!

Ignoring the sting in her fingertips, Addie filled two pages with descriptions of her new town and home and humorous or touching anecdotes about the people she'd encountered. She focused on the positive, seeking

316

the blessings, as her mother had taught her. She shared about how Miss West sent her out on routes with the other girls her whole first week so she could become familiar with the area before setting out alone and about her eagerness to discover the people's interests and meet them with appropriate reading materials.

Then she penned a request.

There are very few books on the shelves of the little library, and the magazines are so tattered they aren't even fully intact. I had the idea of pasting magazine pages into scrapbooks, and Miss West fully supported the idea, but of course we don't have blank scrapbooks available here. Mother, your church ladies' group is always searching for a charitable project. Might they consider sending several scrapbooks for our use? I promise the materials would be very appreciated and used for the benefit of people who desperately need connections to and information from the world outside this tiny glen.

She bit the inside of her lip, gathering courage. After they'd lost so many belongings, she resisted asking her parents to make yet another sacrifice. But she couldn't seem to set aside the thought. Didn't a persistent nudge usually mean God was trying to gain one's attention? Daddy had told her so years ago, and she'd answered a nudge when deciding to become an author. Both Mother and Daddy would tell her to obey a nudge from God.

Drawing in a deep breath, she placed the pen nib against the page and continued.

I appreciate your saving the books from the shelf in my bedroom and all of Daddy's collection. I love you so much for knowing how important the books are to me. But I wonder if they might serve a better purpose by being shared with the folks in Boone's Hollow and Tuckett's Pass? As I mentioned, the selection in our little library is woefully inadequate — not even a hundred books! I won't fuss if you choose to keep them, but I haven't been able to set aside the idea that these people need them more than I do, so I decided to ask.

Miss West said the books we have now arrived in crates on the railroad, so I am sure the same means could be used to transport the scrapbooks and, if you decide to let them go, the books from our house.

"Adelaide, you about done?"

Addie jolted and looked up. For reasons Addie didn't understand, Nanny Fay preferred to call her by her given name instead of her familiar nickname. Nanny Fay waited next to the table, a cup cradled between her palms and her ruffled nightcap covering her snow-white hair. Addie glanced at the mantel clock and grimaced. "Oh, my goodness. Nine o'clock already? You want to turn in, don't you?"

"I do." The soft smile Addie had come to expect curved her pink lips. "Got lots of gardenin' to finish, an' my woodpile's gettin' low. I'm gonna need my strength for the morrow." She glanced at the pages. "You writin' a book?"

Addie grinned. How wonderful that Nanny Fay loved books. The older woman took three breaks a day for the sole purpose of reading. She was currently reading Twain's *Adventures of Tom Sawyer*. When Addie told her there was a book all about Tom's friend Huck, her face had lit up and she declared she had to read it, too. Addie hadn't seen it at the library, but she had a copy in her personal collection. If Mother and Daddy sent her books, she would make

319

sure Nanny Fay got to read about Huckleberry Finn's adventures before anybody else in Boone's Hollow.

"Not right now. Only a letter to my folks."

"Well, now, I reckon they're right eager to hear from you." She took a little sip from her cup. "If you don't mind stayin' up by your own self, I'll trust you to put out the lamp when you're done, an' I'll go on off to bed."

Addie glanced at her letter. If she kept writing, she would need to add a third page, which would probably require another stamp. She should bring the missive to a close. "I won't be much longer, but please don't let me keep you up. I'm glad to put out the lamp." Would she have ever thought she'd become so comfortable lighting and extinguishing coal oil lamps? At first she'd been nervous, certain she'd start a fire, but after only a week of using the lamps in place of electric lights in both the library and Nanny Fay's cabin, the primitive lighting didn't worry her at all.

"All right, then. You sleep well." Nanny Fay turned toward her bedroom door but paused. "Do the lib'ary girls go out on Saturdays?"

Addie shook her head. "Only Monday through Friday, but Miss West leaves for

Louisville tomorrow around noon, so the other girls and I are meeting her at the library midmorning for a little send-off." Would Miss West tell them the name of the next director? She hoped they wouldn't be left handling things on their own for too long. Bettina, Glory, and Alba didn't seem terribly concerned about the record-keeping part of the program, but Miss West had been adamant that the WPA council needed to know to whom the books were going.

Nanny Fay pursed her lips. "Mm-hmm . . . I'm gonna miss that lady. Would you tell her so when you see her tomorrow?"

"Why don't you come with me? She would appreciate being able to give you a proper farewell."

The old woman's smile turned sad. "Aw, honey, this send-off's for you lib'ary girls. I wouldn't belong there."

Addie understood what Nanny Fay meant. The other girls wouldn't welcome the herb lady's presence. She tried to smile, but her lips refused to cooperate. "I'll give her your message."

"Thank you, Adelaide. G'night now."

Addie bit the end of the pen and watched Nanny Fay cross the wide-planked floor to her bedroom. She closed the door behind her, and still Addie gazed in that direction.

She hadn't intended to share anything of a negative nature with her parents. They were far away, and they'd only needlessly worry. But the prodding she'd experienced concerning the books now attacked for another reason.

She bent over the page.

Mother and Daddy, I know you both pray for me every day. Would you also pray for the kind lady who has taken me in? She's old, and she has no family and not even any friends. She has a very lonely existence. Please pray that God would

Addie paused, pen frozen in place. Would what? Give peace? Comfort? Despite Nanny Fay's solitary existence, she seemed content. She held no grudges against the people who spoke unkindly of her or ignored her. As odd as it seemed, given the woman's simple surroundings, hardscrabble life, and ostracism, she didn't really seem to need a thing.

All at once, Addie knew what to write.

soften the hearts of those in the community so they might reach out to her and learn from her. She really is a remarkable woman.

> With love forever and always,
> Your Adeladybug

Addie arrived at the library a little past nine on Saturday morning. She carried a small calico pouch of dried birch leaves, a farewell gift from Nanny Fay, along with a handwritten note of appreciation for giving her not only a job but a charge to fulfill. She hoped Miss West would appreciate Addie's solemn promise to not give up. Three cents and the letter she'd written to Mother and Daddy rested in her dress pocket. She intended to mail the letter after she'd said goodbye to her library director.

As usual, the library door stood open, so Addie walked in. A suitcase and two crates waited inside the door. Scraping noises filtered from the other side of the blanket wall. Was Miss West trying to drag out another crate? Given her health condition, she shouldn't do such difficult tasks on her own.

Addie set the pouch and note on one of the crates and crossed to the blankets. "Miss West?"

A hand — larger, broader, and more masculine than Miss West's, with black rimming the fingernails — caught the edge of one of the blankets and pushed it aside. Emmett Tharp appeared in the opening.

Addie took a backward step. "What are you doing in there? Where's Miss West?"

He brushed his palms together. The bandages he'd worn the last time she'd seen him were gone. "Rearranging. She's at the post office, using the telephone. She'll be back shortly."

Addie peeked past him into the small area portioned off as sleeping quarters. The pieces of furniture remained, although arranged differently, and Miss West's personal items were gone. The space seemed empty and sad. "Oh. Did Miss West ask you to ready the room for the next director?"

An odd smile briefly tipped the corners of his lips. "Sort of."

Another thought struck, and she beamed at him. "You're the new director, aren't you?"

"Yeah. I am."

Why didn't he seem happier about it? "That's wonderful, Emmett. Congratulations."

"Thanks." He moved past her to the table. She hadn't noticed the stacks of bedding and articles of clothing on its top when she came in. He picked up the bedding stack and clomped through the opening. The sheets, blankets, and pillows hit the cot, and then he turned and closed the gap in the blanket wall, blocking Addie's view.

She stared at the mouse-eaten edges of the blankets for several seconds, hands on her hips, then huffed and marched out of the library. A horse-drawn wagon entered town from her right, and she waited for it to pass before darting across the street to the little building that served as both post office and telephone office. Its screen door stood open, as seemed to be customary in every place of business in town, so she entered and nearly collided with the counter that divided the tiny building into two uneven portions.

Miss West was on the other side in the corner with her back to the wall, talking on the wall telephone. She gave Addie a little wave, then turned her back to the door.

A slender, gray-haired man Addie presumed was the postmaster unfolded himself from a little desk chair and placed his hands on the counter. "Can I help you?" His eyebrows descended, some of the wiry hairs catching behind his spectacles. "Don't b'lieve we've met."

Addie extended her hand. "I'm Adelaide Cowherd. I'm new in town."

He squeezed her fingers and let go. "Bay-

325

lus Landrum. I'm old in town." He chuckled. "You the new book gal I been hearin'
about?"

Addie nodded. "Yes, sir." She pulled the
letter and coins from her pocket. "I'd like
to send this."

"Well, you've come to the right place for
it." He slid the pennies across the counter
into a drawer and took out a stamp and glue
bottle. "You plannin' to stay in Boone's
Holler fer a while? 'Cause if you is, we
should oughta set you up with a box." He
pointed with his bony chin toward a set of
small wooden cubbies standing at the end
of the counter. "With Miss West leavin', her
box is open. You can have box six if you
want it."

Mail was delivered free of charge to
houses in Georgetown, but people who used
a post office box paid a small fee each
month. After already paying for lodging and
a horse, she needed to make sure she could
afford a mailbox. Every expense took away
from what she would be able to send home
to Mother and Daddy or to the college.
"How much does it cost?"

"Fifteen cents a month."

Addie wouldn't deem fifteen cents an
exorbitant amount, but wouldn't avoiding
the cost be best? "Um . . . what if I share

326

someone else's box? I'm lodging with Nanny Fay Tuckett. Does she have a box?"

The man slid backward as if someone had grabbed his suspenders and dragged him. "I'd heard the new book gal had taken a room with that ol' herb lady, but I didn't believe it. So, it's true?"

"They just don't know no better." Nanny Fay's voice in Addie's ear stifled the sharp comment forming on her tongue. She nodded. "Yes, it is. She's given me the use of a very nice room and is treating me as if I were family. So . . ." She smiled. "Am I able to share a box with her?"

He snorted something unintelligible under his breath and returned to the counter. "If that's what you wanna do, fine. You can take it up with her on how to divide the cost."

"Thank you."

He glued her stamp to the envelope and dropped it in a wooden tray at the opposite end of the counter from the cubbies, all without looking at her. Then he returned to his chair. As he did, Miss West hung up.

She scurried to Addie and linked arms with her. "Now that my train transport is verified, let's go to the library." Tears brightened her eyes. "My, it's going to be harder for me to say goodbye than I realized." She urged Addie toward the door.

327

"One moment, please." Addie half turned toward the counter. "Mr. Landrum?" She waited for him to acknowledge her and maintained her smile in the face of his frown. "I wondered . . . are you on the library's book route?"

He shook his head.

"Well, then, I'd be happy to add your name to the list. You and your family would have reading material delivered to your house every week." She whisked a grin at Miss West. "Books offer such enjoyment, and you can learn new skills, such as woodworking, or explore subjects from mathematics to outer space. Would you like to receive books, completely free of charge, on a weekly basis?"

A flicker of interest showed behind the lenses of his spectacles. "Who'd be bringin' them books to me?"

Addie shrugged. "One of the four book girls — Bettina Webber is one, and then there's Glory Ashcroft and Alba Gilkey." She inwardly commended herself for remembering their names. "And me, of course."

"I'd like to know about takin' care o' critters. Or maybe growin' flowers. My wife would like that." A scowl marred his brow. "If it's one o' them others bringin' the books, then you can put down my name."

Although his deliberate rebuff stung a bit, Addie offered a nod. "Yes, sir. Animal care or gardening. I'll write it down. Good day, now."

Miss West ushered Addie across the street, lips pressed into a firm line. As soon as they reached the library, she threw her arms around Addie and hugged her tight. "I'm so proud of you! You refused to be cowed by him, you gained his interest, and you did it all with a kind spirit." She pulled loose and sighed. "You followed the biblical admonition 'Do good to them that hate you.' "

Addie swallowed. "Do you really think the people of Boone's Hollow hate me?"

Miss West hugged her again. "No. No, I don't." She kept hold of Addie's upper arms and gazed fervently into her face. "But even if you begin to believe they do, if you continue to treat them as you did Mr. Landrum, you'll win them over in time." She sighed. "I only wish I could be here to see it happen."

TWENTY-FOUR

Emmett
Lord, am I making a mistake?

On the other side of the curtain, Miss West and the book delivery girls chatted and laughed and occasionally sniffled. Thank goodness he hadn't been invited to the farewell party. Girls . . . What did he know about working with girls?

Emmett arranged his shaving gear on top of the dinged-up waterfall bureau. He laid his razor next to his comb and recalled the Christmas he'd received it. Paw had grinned and winked, saying, "Reckon you're growin' into a man if you've got enough chin whiskers to carve off every mornin'." Emmett's chest had swelled with pride, being called a man by his father.

Paw hadn't said one word to him over breakfast this morning. Hadn't even looked at him. Pretty much the way he'd acted the day Emmett announced he'd be using his college scholarship and working for a degree. The past week, going to the mine every morning with Paw, eating lunch with him, coming home together, and talking at the dinner table had made his strained muscles, blisters, and bone-deep weariness worth it. Having Paw's approval . . . Was there anything better? And now it was gone again.

But he couldn't shake Maw's notion about things falling too neatly into place for it to be anything except God lining up the dominoes. When Miss West had come by yesterday evening, showed him the record-keeping books, and gone through the list of duties, he'd known right off he'd be able to do what was required as the library director. Her belief in the importance of putting books into the hands of the hills people inspired him and set his pulse galloping as much as when he'd cheered for the UK Wildcats at a home football game. Then she told him the salary the WPA job paid, five dollars more a month than he'd make at the mine. He wouldn't have to worry about that bill he had at the company store in Lynch. Plus, he could live right there in the library. Earning more money? Not having to share a loft with his eight-year-old brother? No other answer except yes formed in his mind. So he said it.

Then he'd seen Paw's face, and a part of him had wanted to take it back. Except Maw'd jumped up and hugged his neck, so happy for him, and Miss West had seemed so confident to entrust "her" library to his keeping. Then, most hard to resist, the feeling in the center of his soul that God had made it all happen . . . What else could he do?

"God, could You help Paw understand I'm not going against him?" He whispered the prayer to his reflection in the razor's silver casing. "Could You let him be proud of me, even if I don't follow in his footsteps?"

He suddenly realized it was quiet on the other side of the blanket wall. He crossed to the overlap and pushed one flap aside. The library side of the old smokehouse was empty of the girls and Miss West's stack of belongings. The driver must've come for her. He'd have the rest of the day here to himself — time to familiarize himself with the materials on the shelves, see which books were in the hands of which families, and review the process for sending records to the committee in Washington, DC, every month.

A shiver went down his spine, and he shook his head in wonderment. He, Emmett Tharp of Boone's Hollow, Kentucky, got to communicate with people who worked for the president of the United States. Would he have ever imagined such a thing? Even if this job was temporary — the economy would improve again, wouldn't it? — he couldn't deny feeling special for having been chosen to be a part of something that could result in so much good.

If only Paw could see it that way.

Nanny Fay

Nanny Fay sat on the porch step, fanning herself with her apron skirt and watching Adelaide carry another armload of firewood to the pile next to the cabin. My, the shock on the girl's pretty face when she'd come back from Miss West's send-off and seen how much chopped wood lay all over the side yard. She'd said for Nanny Fay to sit and let her stack it. Nanny Fay didn't voice nary an objection. Her arms were plumb wore out from bringing down that ax.

Truth be known, this might be the last year she chopped her own wood. Her sixty-ninth birthing day'd passed three weeks back. Shouldn't a body ought to be able to rest after living for seven full decades? But, of course, her not chopping her own wood depended on finding somebody else to do it for her. She'd set to praying on that now, and the Lord would provide. He always did.

Hadn't He provided help in the form of a comely, tall city gal who didn't look strong enough to carry so much as a basket of kindling? Look at her now, all red faced and puffing but picking up those chunks of wood and stacking 'em as nice and neat as if she'd been doing such chores her whole life long. Determination, that's what she had. And a hardworking spirit. Add in her tenderness, and the Lord done real good when He crafted Miss Adelaide Cowherd. And now Nanny Fay got to count her a friend. Yes, the Lord sure did rain down blessings.

"Honey, why don'tcha stop for a minute an' rest yourself?" Nanny Fay patted the spot beside her. "That wood ain't goin' no place. Your face gets any redder, you're likely to bust a blood vessel."

Adelaide grinned at Nanny Fay over her armload of wood. "If I do, is there something in one of your jars to fix it?"

Oh, law, listen to her making jokes about them herbs instead of being scared of 'em. Nanny Fay laughed. "I reckon there is, but wouldn't you ruther not hafta to make use o' one? Come. Set for a spell."

Adelaide emptied her armload onto the pile, swiped her forehead with the back of her hand, then ambled over. She sank down next to Nanny Fay and stuck her legs straight out, same way Nanny Fay was sitting. Her legs stretched farther — gracious, she was as leggy as a young colt — but she'd kicked off her shoes so they was both with bare feet and toes pointed to the sky. Seeing their uncovered feet there, side by side, made Nanny Fay's heart smile.

"Nanny Fay, since I'm living here" —

Her heart smiled bigger.

— "would you mind if I shared your mail cubby?"

Nanny Fay chuckled. "I don't mind a bit. Can't even recall the last time somethin' showed up in that cubby. Don't got nobody to write to me. But I reckon your folks an' friends'll be sendin' you letters an' such fairly regular."

The girl's eyebrows pinched together, and it sure looked like she was biting on the inside of her lip. A sorrowful face if Nanny Fay had ever seen one. Adelaide touched Nanny Fay's arm. "Don't you have any family at all?"

"None I know of. Not livin', anyways." In her mind's eye, Nanny Fay traveled through the trees, up the mountain, to a small clearing and a row of wooden crosses. "But I got kin in heaven. My man, o' course, an' our

335

young'uns."

Now Adelaide's eyebrows shot up. "You had children?"

The mix of joy and agony that always came when she thought about her babies swooped through her like a hawk swooping under the wind currents. "Can't call 'em children since not a one of 'em ever took a breath here on earth. But their little souls are well an' happy with Jesus. Along with their pappy's. I'll be with 'em again, by an' by."

Adelaide blinked real hard. "I'm sorry. Is that why you stay here in Boone's Hollow — because your husband and children are buried close by?"

Nanny Fay spread her apron neat across her knees and smoothed the faded fabric. "Honey, I stay here 'cause I ain't never had any other home. Me an' my man, we was here before anybody else come along. Boone's Holler sort of growed up beside us." She chuckled, recalling Eagle proclaiming those folks coming along and settling meant her and him were right smart to choose this place. 'Course, it was his people who'd settled the area before any of the white folks come this way.

"But if you were here first, then they" — she waved her dirty hand in the direction of the town — "are the outsiders, not you. Why do they treat you as if you don't belong here?"

"Well, now, I s'pose it's 'cause I was married to a part-Cherokee man. They see me as differ'nt from theyselves."

"But you aren't Cherokee. Not even a little bit."

Nanny Fay narrowed her eyes and peered at Adelaide. "Would you be friendly to me if I was?"

"I . . . I . . ." The girl bit on her lip again, uncertainty showing as plain as the dirt smudges on her face. "I've never encountered any Cherokees, nor anyone who'd married a Cherokee. To the other people living in Boone's Hollow, it must make a great deal of difference, but I don't think it would matter to Mother and Daddy. Penrose and Fern Cowherd are friendly to everyone, no matter their origin of birth or the color of their skin, even when it means being snubbed by others who hold a different opinion."

Nanny Fay smiled. "Sounds like your folks read an' follow the teachin' in the Good Book about how to treat folks."

She offered a slow nod. "You're right. They do. Even if you were Cherokee, they'd be friendly to you, and I would be, too."

Tears stung Nanny Fay's eyes, but she couldn't stop smiling. "That's good. That's real good." She plucked a long grass stem from next to the rock and picked off the seeds from its head one by one, dropping them onto her lap.

Adelaide pulled a stalk free and imitated Nanny Fay. "May I ask you a question?"

"Seems to me you just did."

The girl grinned. "I meant may I ask how you came to marry a Cherokee? I thought all the Cherokees were gone from Kentucky a long time ago."

Such pain attacked that Nanny Fay cringed.

Adelaide tossed the stalk of grass and took hold of Nanny Fay's wrinkled hand. The sadness crinkling her sweet face pained Nanny Fay more. "Please forgive me. I shouldn't have —"

"No. No." A warm tear rolled down Nanny Fay's cheek and landed on her lip. She licked its saltiness and shook her head. "It's good for someone to know. 'Cause I'll leave this earth, same as my Eagle did, an' I got no child to carry on our story. Tellin' you . . . that means somebody'll know." Her lips trembled, and another tear ran down. "Then Eagle, his folks, an' his granny, they won't be forgot. If I tell you, will you write it down on paper? Like a real story?"

"Of course I will. I'll write it all out for you."

"No, child." Nanny Fay cupped Adelaide's cheeks. Her rough palms were probably chafing her flesh, but she needed to connect with the girl. "Will you write it out for you? To remember?"

"Yes."

Nanny Fay lowered her hands, almost collapsing with joy and relief. "Good. Good."

Adelaide shifted to the grass and folded her legs to the side. She fixed her focus on Nanny Fay's face. "I'm listening."

Nanny Fay closed her eyes. Gathered her thoughts. Then she aimed her sight on the tips of the waving trees branches. "Eagle's story starts over a hunnerd years ago, with a young Cherokee maiden named White Fawn. She an' her tribe lived right here on the mountain. They hunted some, an' they farmed some, an' they lived in peace on this land." Even without trying, her voice turned almost singsong, the same way Eagle's had when he talked of times long ago. "White Fawn was promised to a man from her tribe, a brave man named Wohali." They was gonna marry late in the spring of her seventeenth year, after Wohali built their house. But he didn't get the chance to build it.

"Soldiers came, sent by the president named Jackson." Pictures formed in Nanny Fay's head, and while she talked, the words played out in her mind's eye. "They forced White Fawn's tribe to leave their homes. The Cherokee was marched off this mountain, allowed to take nothin' with 'em except what they could carry. But White Fawn had a crippled leg from a bad fall when she was still a itty-bitty girl. She couldn't keep up with the march. She fell behind, an' the soldiers left her to die. So many of her people died on that long march to Oklahoma Territory. But White Fawn, she was stronger'n them soldiers knew. She didn't die. She found her way to a cabin, where a Scottish man an' woman an' their son took pity on her. She stayed with them all that summer, an' when fall came, the son — a man named Ben Tuckett — made her his bride."

"Is that who Tuckett's Pass was named after?"

Nanny Fay jumped. She'd almost forgot Adelaide was there. She nodded and looked at her to tell the rest of the story. "After Samuel Tuckett. He was Ben's daddy. Now, three boys was born to Ben an' White Fawn, but only one growed to manhood. That one was named Chetan, which means 'hawk.' In the year 1858, he married up with a red-haired girl named Sarah McKee, who come from Ireland as what they call an indentured servant. She birthed a boy they named Wohali in 1860."

"Wohali . . . After White Fawn's first love?"

Nanny Fay nodded, pleased. "You're rememberin' real good. Sarah caught a fever only two years after that little boy was born, an' Chetan buried her up in the mountain a piece, right close to where White Fawn's tribe had lived. White Fawn and Ben are laid to rest up there, too."

A frown sagged Adelaide's pretty face. "That's so sad."

Nanny Fay shrugged. "Maybe. But that's the way o' things, with people bein' born an' people dyin'. We ain't made to live forever. Our bodies gotta die afore our souls can go on to heaven."

"That might be true, but I don't like it." The girl's eyes spit fire. "Too many people die too soon. My birth parents" —

Nanny Fay gave a little jolt. The girl was took in by folks who didn't birth her?

— "and the Cherokees who were forced off the mountain. Sarah McKee. Your husband, and the babies you birthed . . . You

341

didn't even get to nurse them."

Nanny Fay hung her head, pain stabbing anew.

"I think everybody ought to be able to live as long as they want to. It isn't right for mothers to die when their children are so young or for babies to die before they've even had a chance to take a breath."

Head low, Nanny Fay sniffled. "That ain't our choice to make. Only the Good Lord knows the number of our days, an' He's the only one wise enough to make the decision, so we'd best leave that to Him."

Adelaide sighed. "I suppose you're right. Please finish telling me the story."

Nanny Fay lifted her face and shrugged. "It's all done."

Adelaide frowned. "No, it's not. You haven't told me about Eagle yet."

Nanny Fay held back a grin. My, but the girl looked arguesome. "Yes, I did. Chetan and Sarah McKee's little boy, Wohali — he's my Eagle. Wohali means 'eagle' in English."

Adelaide's mouth fell open. "Ohhhhh . . ." Then she shook her head. "Something's still missing. You didn't tell me how you met Eagle. How you came to be his bride."

Nanny Fay ducked her head, remembrances rushing in and bringing with them a shame she'd carry to her dying day. The squirrels ceased their chatter, like they, too, sensed her worthlessness in the eyes of those who'd birthed her. But it was part of the story, and she should tell it all. "I was sold to him, in exchange for two goats an' a barrel o' gun powder."

Adelaide gasped.

With as much effort as it took to force her ax blade through a chunk of wood, Nanny Fay shoved the shame aside and looked into Adelaide's shocked brown eyes. "An' he said it was the best trade any man ever made."

TWENTY-FIVE

Addie

She should extinguish the lamp and go to bed, but her mind refused to shut down. These words must be given release to the page. Nanny Fay's confession about being sold by her very own parents to a man they didn't even know horrified her. Oh, such a deep, moving story existed in the woman's life! At the tender age of thirteen, she was purchased by and wed to a complete stranger, not knowing he'd only done it to protect her. Then she grew to love the man and became his wife in every way three years later.

Addie had been stunned to learn that the photograph on the mantel of the young girl in a simple muslin dress, her hair in braids, was of Nanny Fay on her wedding day. Addie's eyes were opened to a world beyond anything she could have imagined. She'd never encountered a more tender love story than the one she heard from Nanny Fay's lips. Not even her own Mother and Daddy's story of meeting by chance on an April evening and marrying a mere four months later topped it. She would record every word of it not only for herself, as the old woman had requested, but for others.

If the folks of Boone's Hollow knew the truth of Nanny Fay's difficult childhood, of how she learned to gather herbs and roots for medicinal cures from an old Cherokee woman named White Fawn, of how she used her knowledge and treatments to cure fevers, heal wounds, and ease women's pain during childbirth, would they still view her as a witch, as someone to distrust and ostracize?

Addie prayed that putting Nanny Fay's story into a fictional account of a little girl named Lydia — in honor of Miss West, who'd assured her of the power of words — would help the people in Boone's Hollow realize their fears were misguided. She prayed Nanny Fay would find a place of acceptance before her body gave out and she joined Eagle and her stillborn babies in the little burial plot up the mountain.

Lamplight flickered, casting dancing shadows across the page. Addie paused and adjusted the wick. The light brightened, reflecting off the room's glass windowpanes. She applied pencil to paper again, writing as quickly as her aching fingers allowed, aware that outside, night creatures went about their business of hunting and stars winked behind a sheer curtain of clouds. Folks in the hollow were asleep, as was Nanny Fay, evidenced by the steady snore carrying from the other side of Addie's bedroom wall. But Addie couldn't sleep. Not until the entire story had been released from deep in her soul.

It was *wrong* to sell a child.

It was *wrong* to brand someone a witch.

It was *wrong* to reject someone simply because the person's heritage differed from one's own.

The injustices burned as hot in Addie's chest as the flame did in the lamp, but she didn't state the truths. She showed them in the terror and helplessness of a little girl, in the heartache of a young woman who desired friends and acceptance, in the pride and determination of a tribe of people who carved a life on the mountainside.

"Books, Addie, have the power to change people for the better."

If she was going to live and work and worship in this community, then she would do her best to leave the town of Boone's Hollow better than she'd found it. Just as Miss West had tried to do.

Bettina

Bettina fastened the silver barrette in her hair, then gave herself a quick look-see in the round cracked mirror hanging on her wall. She'd cracked that mirror herself so her soul could escape if the mirror captured it, but she didn't want to take no chances by looking at herself too long. Still, she wanted to know. Miz Tharp had said she looked pretty with her bangs clipped away from her face — said it brought out her eyes. But maybe that wasn't such a good thing.

Why couldn't she have green eyes like Alba or brown like Glory? Instead, she got a muddy mix of the two. Hazel, her maw had called it. Not even a real color name. She yanked out the barrette, losing a few brown hairs with it, and let her bangs flop over her forehead. She grunted. No better.

She sank onto her bed and fiddled with the barrette. She didn't have no other way to make herself look nice for Emmett. She couldn't change into a dress. Mule would buck her right off if she tried climbing on his back while wearing a skirt. That ol' mule, he was plain peculiar about flapping fabric. Of course, the other girls'd all be in their overalls or dungarees, too, including Addie Coward, so wearing her overalls didn't trouble her near so much as having something that would set her apart from the others in a good way.

All her playing with the barrette had left fingerprints behind. She rubbed it shiny again on her pant leg and returned to the mirror. She sucked in her breath to keep hold of her soul and stared at her reflection, trying to see herself the way Miz Tharp had. Now, Damaris Tharp, she was a kind lady. Maw and her had been the best of friends, and that's what put Bettina and Emmett together so much. Seemed to Bettina it meant they was s'posed to always be together. Miz Tharp thought her eyes was pretty, even if they didn't have a real color name. Did Emmett maybe think the same as his maw?

She ducked away from the mirror and let her breath whoosh out. Standing here staring at herself wouldn't change her looks. It'd only make her late to work, and she wanted to be the first one through the door on Emmett's first day of directing the library.

On her way across the dewy grass to the barn, she slicked her bangs away from her

348

forehead and clipped them into place. The morning mist was already fading away from the treetops, looking more like spiderwebs than clouds. She'd piddled too much, messing with her hair. Now she'd be late. She growled under her breath, thinking hard. If she didn't saddle Mule, she could get going a lot faster. Staying on his back on some of those steep climbs wouldn't be easy without a saddle, but if she held real tight with her heels, she could do it.

She put his harness on him and led him from their lean-to barn. The carrots she'd put in her pocket for lunch, along with a brown-sugar-and-butter sandwich, made a fine bribe to keep him moving. She kept them right out of his reach until she got to the library. At the smokehouse, she tossed his reins over a holly bush and gave him one of the carrots as a reward. Then she darted for the open doorway, setting her face in a smile.

The mumble of voices brought her to a skidding halt. She tilted her ear to the opening, then let out a huff. Oh, that Addie! She'd got there first! Bettina stomped to the stoop, then jerked backward. Addie stood on the other side of the threshold.

The girl smiled big, like she knew she'd bested Bettina. "Good morning, Bettina.

Please excuse me. I need to go get Russet."

Bettina eyed Addie up and down. She'd rolled the cuffs of her overalls and fixed the straps so the bib didn't hang so low. How could she look so respectable, even without a silver barrette holding her wavy hair away from her brown eyes? Probably 'cause she was tall.

Bettina stretched out her chin. "How come you didn't fetch her already?"

"I tried, but the livery wasn't open yet. So I came here instead."

She must've got up before the sun even peeked over the mountains to reach the library so early. Tomorrow Bettina would leave at the same time as Pap. Then she'd be waiting on the stoop when Emmett opened the door.

Addie eased past Bettina, still smiling all cheerful-like, and headed up the street, walking high headed and straight shouldered. If that girl didn't think she belonged in the movies, Bettina would put ketchup on her barrette and eat it for dinner.

But now Emmett was in there all by hisself, so it was her turn to get his attention. She sashayed through the doorway like she didn't have a care in the world. Emmett was at the table in Miz West's chair. Giving her head a toss to show off her silver barrette,

350

she crossed to the table and rested her palms on its top. "Howdy, Emmett. You already workin'? My, ain't you as busy as a bee."

He took off his wire spectacles and laid them next to the lamp. "I'm not working yet, just glancing over what Addie gave me."

Bettina's heart jumped a little in her chest. "Since when's she doing reports?"

He laughed real soft, like she'd said something funny. "It's not a report. It's a story."

Bettina glared at the pages all covered over with Addie's writing. Those letters might as well be marks left by a cricket that jumped in an inkwell and then on the paper, for all the sense they made. " 'Bout what?"

Emmett stacked the papers and moved them to the corner of the desk. "I'm not sure she wants me to tell anyone about it yet, Bettina."

Now he and Addie were keeping secrets? She put her hand on her hip. "Well, la-di-da. If she don't want nobody to know, how come she showed you?"

"I guess she trusts me. Now . . ." He pulled Miz West's notepad close, put his spectacles on, and picked up a pencil. He tapped the pencil on the notepad. "According to Miss West's notes, there are seven

351

stops on your Monday route — the Cissells, the Days, the Fromans, the McCashes, the Neelys, the Toons, and Nanny Fay Tuckett. Is that right?"

Bettina wanted to talk more about that story Addie'd wrote and was keeping secret, but she couldn't be all testy with Emmett. She made herself use her sweet voice, the one she pulled out when Pap needed gentling. "Yes, Emmett, that's sure right."

He glanced at her, the corners of his lips twitching.

She tossed her head again. "But you got the order all mixed up. First I go to —"

"They're listed alphabetically. I realize you visit them according to their location."

If he didn't sound just like Miz West, all highfalutin. Bettina scrunched her lips tight so she'd stay quiet.

"Because the Cissells and the McCashes take you pretty far north of the other cabins, I'm going to give those two stops to Addie instead."

Bettina scrapped her vow to stay quiet. Or to be sweet. "But I like goin' to the Cissells. Miz Cissell always gives me a cup o' apple cider." Sweetest cider on the whole mountain. Her mouth watered thinking about it. "Why not give Nanny Fay Tuckett to Addie instead? Not like she don't see the ol' herb woman anyway."

Emmett put down the pencil and turned in his chair. No more sideways glances. He looked full in Bettina's face. And he didn't smile.

"Hey, good mornin'!" Alba and Glory came in, and Addie followed them. They all crowded close to the table, but Emmett didn't say howdy to them or even act like he knew they was there. He kept looking right at Bettina. With those spectacles over his blue eyes, he seemed a heap older. And stern. A stern stranger.

"Bettina, Miss West left me her notes and recommendations, and I'm using them to get started. I might stick with what she suggested, and I might deviate from her suggestions over time. But either way, I'm not going to give you a lengthy explanation. The fact is I've been hired to direct this program. That means you and the other girls" — his eyes flicked toward them and came back — "will have to trust me to do what I think is best."

Bettina folded her arms right over her chest. He didn't talk mean. Not like Pap did. But she still wanted to shrink into the floorboards, being spoke to that way by Emmett in front of Addie, Glory, and Alba. Worst, she didn't know what *deviate* meant, but Addie probably did.

"So, with that being said . . ." He flipped a page on the notebook and shifted himself in front of the book again. "Let me share what changes to today's schedule have been made to make three routes into four."

Emmett took away one stop from Glory and two from Alba and gave them to Addie. Glory asked how come she'd only lost one stop. He told her it had to do with distance and that the number of stops would all balance out by the end of the week. He didn't scold her for asking a question, and Bettina came close to reminding him he wasn't gonna give no explanations. But then he handed out their packs, and when Bettina took hers, their fingers brushed. Did he do that on purpose? She gave him a little smile. He didn't seem to notice, and her spirits sank to her stomach like a rock to the bottom of a well.

He stood and pushed his hands into his pockets. "All right, ladies, you're set."

Ladies? Miz West always called them girls. Bettina kinda liked being called a lady instead.

"I'll see you all back here around five, if my calculations are correct."

"Five?" Glory near shouted the word. She sent a big smile at Addie. "I ain't been home before six, not one single time since we started these routes. This's gonna be great havin' you out there takin' books, too."

Bettina made a sour face and hoped Glory saw it. She wouldn't even mind if Emmett saw it. She stomped out the door. First Emmett kept secrets with Addie, then Glory acted like Addie was their new hero. Bettina wouldn't complain, because she wanted her evenings free so her and Emmett could get to courting, but he was gonna have to get off his high horse when they was at work together. And she was gonna have to find out what Addie'd wrote on them papers.

TWENTY-SIX

Black Mountain
Addie

"Who're you?"

Addie clung to Russet's reins and stared down the barrel of the rifle. She swallowed hard. "I'm Addie Cowherd, Mrs. Cissell."

The tip of the rifle lowered slightly, but the woman didn't remove her finger from the trigger. "I don't know nobody named Cowherd." Three children clung to her skirts and peered at Addie over the edge of the porch railing. The fear in their eyes made Addie's heart ache.

"I came with Bettina Webber last week when she brought you your books. Remember?"

"Nope."

"She brought . . ." Addie consulted the list Emmett had given her. "A copy of *Life* magazine, two children's picture books — *The Little Red Hen* and *Jolly Pets* — and *A*

356

Farewell to Arms by Ernest Hemingway." She patted her bag. "I have some new books to exchange with you. If I may —"

The rifle barrel bounced up, and the woman squinted one eye shut. " 'Less you want a new part in your hair, you stay right there." The smallest child began to whimper. "I recollect Bettina comin', same as she always does, an' I recall some girl a-standin' in the trees."

Which was where Bettina had instructed her to remain. "Yes, ma'am. That was me. Bettina brought me here because she won't be delivering books to your house anymore. You're on my route now. If you'd let me come up close, I'll take last week's books and give you these new ones." She braved a smile at the round-eyed, dirty-faced children. "I bet your children would enjoy reading *The Cowardly Lion and the Hungry Tiger.* The pictures are delightful." She reached inside her pack, intending to hold up the book.

"Do you have rocks for ears? I said you ain't welcome on my land. Whatever you got in your bag, you keep it an' move on."

Addie tugged Russet's reins and encouraged the animal to carry her into the brush, where she'd be out of sight. Then she stopped and rearranged the books in her pack in readiness for the next stop. How she hated leaving without handing these books to those little children. Their wide, frightened eyes haunted her. Certainly some strangers were to be feared — those who came with ill intent. But to teach children to distrust every new face they encountered wasn't healthy. Somehow she needed to find a way to communicate that truth.

Sighing, she set aside thoughts of the Cissell children and examined her schedule. According to her list, the Donohoo cabin was next. The Donohoos lived about a half mile northeast, across a creek and beyond a boulder covered in moss. There were no street signs or numbers to direct a person on the mountain — only landmarks. But Addie's good memory served her well. She found the Donohoo cabin, which had been built on such a sharp rise that its front half stood on stilts. If a person fell from the porch, he or she would certainly suffer broken bones.

She slipped from Russet's back and walked the horse the final uphill yards. At the base of the rise, she cupped her hands around her mouth. "Hello in the cabin!"

A tattered white curtain shielded the single window, and the front door stood open. No one came to the doorway, but

Addie was sure she saw someone lift the curtain aside, peek out, and drop it back into place.

She rose up on tiptoes for a better glimpse. "Hello? Mrs. Donohoo? It's Addie, from the library. I've brought you some books."

What sounded like a child's wail came from somewhere in the cabin, followed by a harsh "Hush, you!" and a door slamming. Silence fell.

Addie waited a few more seconds, watching the doorway. But no one came. "Mrs. Donohoo?" She'd heard a child. What were the names of the Donohoo children? She checked the information Emmett had given her. "Darlene? Margie? I'm here with books."

No response.

The silence unnerved her. People were inside the cabin. Why wouldn't they come out? She thought about putting the books she'd brought on the porch, assuming she could climb up there. But she wasn't supposed to leave more unless the previous ones were returned. And according to her paper, the Donohoos already had five books on loan.

"Git outta here or I'll sic the hounds on you!"

Addie jolted so violently she almost lost

her footing on the steep incline. The male voice had blasted from somewhere nearby, and a dog's fierce yaps followed it. She sent startled looks right and left. She couldn't see the person giving the threat, but she decided to take it seriously. She put her foot in the stirrup and tried to pull herself onto the saddle, but Russet turned a slow circle. Addie hopped beside her while maniacal laughter rang from the bushes.

She jerked her foot free and snagged the horse's reins. "You dumb beast!" She started down the rise, her face flaming, embarrassment giving way to anger. Such rudeness, to holler and cackle but not let her see who menaced her. These people didn't deserve to be on the list to receive books.

Then she remembered the child's plaintive cry. Had it been Margie or Darlene crying for a new book? Sympathy replaced her fury.

She drew Russet to a stop and turned backward. "If you change your mind and want to swap books, please come by the library in town. I'll make sure they're waiting for you there."

"You just git!" No humor graced the man's tone.

Addie reached the creek. Several large stones lined a portion of the bank. She eyed the largest rock. If she climbed on it, she might be able to swing herself into the saddle again. But what if the awful person with the dog was following her? She'd waste less time and get to her next stop, the Mc-Cash cabin, faster by walking. With a firm grip on Russet's reins, she sent a furtive glance over her shoulder and splashed into the creek. Frigid water soaked the bottom inches of her pant legs and filled her boots, and she sucked in a gasp. Her feet sank into the soft creek bed, and she fought for every forward step as if walking through clay. When she reached the opposite bank, her whole body was shivering.

She paused for a few minutes, panting hard and gathering her bearings. The Mc-Cashes lived in a quaint cabin in the center of a small clearing beyond a thick stand of pines, maples, and pokeberry bushes. If she remembered correctly, a split-rail fence circled their yard. The fence would make a fine ladder for getting up on Russet's back again. If they allowed her to use it.

"Come along, Russet. A brisk walk should get me dry again."

Russet snorted and trailed her like a faithful hound dog. While she walked, she ate the strawberry jam sandwiches Nanny Fay had sent along. The sweetness of the jam took the sour taste of rejection from her tongue, and by the time she reached the McCashes' fence, she'd set aside her irritation.

As she'd done previously, Addie called from the edge of what she considered the yard.

A slump-shouldered woman with brown hair straggling in her face stayed in the doorway. She shook her head sadly. "My man don't allow no strangers around here. He'll be comin' in most any minute now for vittles, so you best get on outta here."

"Ma'am, I'd like to trade these books from the li—"

"Not today."

Addie held back a grunt of aggravation and pointed to the fence. "May I use your fence to get on my horse?"

"You best move on." The woman disappeared inside the cabin.

Addie moved on toward the next stop, consoling herself that at least no one aimed a rifle at her or threatened to sic a dog on her here. Mother would probably call that a blessing, albeit a minuscule one. But she'd used up half the day, seen three families, and hadn't delivered even one book. Or collected one. How would she face Emmett and the other riders after failing so dismally?

Boone's Hollow
Emmett

As Emmett had predicted, the first rider, Glory, returned well before five o'clock. She handed in her books, smiling big, and told him Alba was right behind her. Alba came in as jubilant to have the evening free as Glory was. The girls left together, jabbering and giggling. It heartened him to know they were leaving happy. He and Miss West had done well in organizing their new routes.

He'd just finished recording Glory's returns when Bettina sauntered in. Recalling their unpleasant exchange that morning, his stomach tightened, but she flopped her pack onto the corner of the table and then offered him an eyelash-batting smile, as if their disagreement hadn't taken place.

She patted the stack of books Alba had brought back. "Looks like everybody's gettin' in early. Tell you what . . ." She fluttered her eyelashes again and rested her weight on one leg, hip jutted out. "When you've got the returns marked in the book the way Miz West always done, why don'tcha come to my place? Got some cream I need to use up, so I'll be makin' creamed peas an' chicken over biscuits for supper. Don't mean to brag or nothin', but I'm a pretty fair cook. My biscuits are light as an angel's wings."

He rubbed his stomach. "That sounds good, Bettina, but Maw's expecting me for supper."

She shrugged. "Come over after supper, then. Mebbe we could play dominoes. Or slapjack. Pap's got a deck o' cards just sittin' around waitin' for somebody to use 'em."

Maw would skin him alive if he played card games. She didn't hold with games of chance — said they were of the devil. He didn't share her view, but he respected her too much to partake behind her back. "I better not. I've still got quite a bit of work to do here. I might have to finish up after supper."

Bettina flicked the pages on the closest magazine. "Ain't fair for you to have to work clear into the evenin' if all us girls got the hours free."

"Well, so far you, Alba, and Glory have the evening free. Addie isn't back yet." He pulled out his timepiece and checked it. Only a quarter after five. He shouldn't worry yet. He lifted his head and found Bettina examining him through slitted eyes.

"Are you makin' excuses so's you can stay

here this evenin' an' read that story Addie wrote up?"

Emmett had already finished it during his lunch break. Addie's ability to weave pictures with words had impressed him. She wrote well. Maybe as well as some published authors he'd read. But more than that, she'd stirred his emotions. He wouldn't share his thoughts with Bettina, though. She didn't need any more fuel for her jealousy fire.

He forced a smile. "I've got too much work to do to think about reading for pleasure. It'll take me a while to learn every part of this new job."

Bettina whirled, giving her head a toss. "Well, then, I reckon I better leave you to it. But if you change your mind, just mosey on over." One more eyelash flutter and she slipped around the corner.

Emmett sagged into his chair. Mercy, that girl was unpredictable. One minute all smiles and charm, the next flinging daggers with her eyes. But as he recalled from their growing up together, she flitted from one interest to another much like a butterfly moving from flower to flower. She'd turn her attention to something — or someone — else soon enough. In the meantime, he had work to do.

He cataloged the returned books, put

them in their proper places on the shelves, and organized materials to send out tomorrow. In between, he checked his timepiece. The supper hour came and went, and Addie hadn't returned. He pulled out the paper where he'd drawn a rough map of her route and traced it with his finger. It would have probably taken her an hour to reach the Cissells'. Then on to the Donohoos' was roughly thirty minutes on horseback. He paused, scowling out the window. She had been on horseback, hadn't she? Yes, he'd seen her depart, and she'd been in the saddle.

She should have reached the McCash cabin by noon. Mrs. McCash might have invited her in to visit during lunch. Addie would certainly have accepted. If she stayed for an hour, she should have reached the Clinkenheards' by half past two. She'd pick up the Watkinses' place on the way back to town. By his estimation, she should have come in by four thirty at the latest. So where was she?

The evening shadows were getting heavier. He lit the lamp on the desk, then crossed to the door and looked up and down the street. His gaze reached Gilliam's Livery, and an unpleasant idea filled his head. He took off at a trot and burst into the barn.

Kermit was stabbing up clumps of hay with a pitchfork. He spun around and aimed the tines at Emmett, his expression fierce. Then he let the fork fall. "What're you doin', comin' in here like a posse's on your tail? You near about got speared."

"Sorry to startle you, Kermit, but one of my riders, Addie Cowherd, hasn't come back. She rents Russet." Emmett peeked in Russet's stall. "I wondered if maybe the horse came back on her own."

"Ain't seen mane nor tail o' Russet since this mornin'." He shook the hay loose from the fork into a stall, then moved to the next one. "I can send one o' my boys over to let you know when she's back, if you like."

Emmett nodded and shifted out of Kermit's way. "That'd be nice of you."

Kermit sent a scowl over his shoulder. "Although I gotta tell you, I'd ruther that new book gal wasn't borrowin' one o' my horses. Once her pay runs out, I might tell her I ain't gonna rent to her no more."

Unexpectedly, defensiveness rose in Emmett's chest. He slid his hands in his pockets and forced himself to speak amiably. "Oh? Why's that?"

Kermit gawked as if he thought Emmett had lost all sense. " 'Cause she spends nights at Nanny Fay's cabin, that's why. All the brews an' such that woman stirs up, the new book gal prob'ly carries the smell of 'em on her. Might not be healthy for Russet to breathe it in, if you catch my meanin'."

Emmett coughed a disbelieving snort. "Aw, c'mon, Kermit, you don't really think that old woman's soups and herbal cures could do any harm, do you?" His hands were a lot better after Maw applied the oil she got from Nanny Fay. Not that he was supposed to tell anyone. Paw didn't like it when Maw visited the herb lady. Not for the first time, Emmett questioned Paw's attitude.

Kermit planted the tines of the fork in the ground at his feet and turned on Emmett. "I sure do. An' I ain't the only one. There's somethin' tetched in that ol' lady's head, the way she walks through town a-smilin' like she knows things the rest of us don't. An' always prowlin' in the woods, diggin' up this an' that. She ain't —"

A scuffle at the barn's opening brought Kermit's words to a close. Emmett turned around as Addie came in, pulling Russet by her reins. His knees went quivery. He hadn't realized how worried he was until the concern was put to rest. He released a sigh of pure relief. "There you are."

Kermit let go of the pitchfork and grabbed

the horse's reins. He glowered at Addie. "Almost dark again. Didn't I tell you last week to get her back here before the sun goes to bed? I'm gonna charge you extra if you can't bring her in at a decent hour."

Like the other girls, Addie had flopped the book satchel over the horse's neck just above the pommel. She slid the satchel free and draped it over her arm. "I'm sorry, Mr. Gilliam. I would've been here earlier if she would have let me get back in the saddle."

Kermit rubbed Russet's neck, sending Emmett a knowing frown. "Like I said, she prob'ly smells somethin' she don't like." He led the horse to its stall, murmuring to the animal.

Emmett guided Addie onto the street. "What do you mean the horse wouldn't let you in the saddle?"

Addie flung the satchel over her shoulder and held one hand toward the barn. "She wouldn't hold still for me. I got down at the Donohoo place because of the steep rise, and I never got on again."

Emmett drew back, his jaw going slack. "You mean to tell me you walked your route from the Donohoo place on?"

She nodded. "And when you look in my pack, you'll see I didn't distribute a single book. No one would take them from me.

369

Mrs. Cissell pointed a gun at me, someone at the Donohoos threatened to send the hounds after me, and" —

Emmett shook his head, certain he was hearing incorrectly.

— "Mrs. Clinkenheard said to tell you if you send me again, she won't ever take another book from the library."

He wasn't unfamiliar with the community's distrust of newcomers, but Addie had gone on routes with the other girls, who'd been instructed to introduce her to the hills folks. Even after introductions, they might still be standoffish. That was common. But outright threatening? "Did she tell you why?"

"No friend of Nanny Fay is welcome on her property." Addie spoke flatly, but the hurt flickering in her eyes spoke volumes.

Emmett gripped Addie's upper arms. "I'm so sorry. I wish I knew what to say."

Tears winked in her eyes, and she blinked them away. "There's nothing you can say. I've never encountered such a narrow-minded group of people in my life." She slipped free of his grasp and balled her hands on her hips. "But if they think I won't come back, they need to think again." She shoved the pack at him, whirled on her heel, and stomped off.

Emmett watched her go. He appreciated her determination to return to the hills folks' homes and try again. But she might never be allowed onto their land if she didn't find a different place to lodge. With Addie's satchel on his shoulder, he returned to the library, weighted by concern more than by the books in the pack. He flopped the satchel onto the table, and his stomach rumbled.

"Yeah, yeah, I know it's suppertime." He opened the satchel, and the books slid out across the tabletop. He reached to gather them. "I'll get fed when I'm done with —"

He stared at the table, at the spot next to the burning lamp. That spot hadn't been empty when he'd left the library. What was missing? Chills attacked his scalp. The story Addie had written was gone.

TWENTY-SEVEN

Addie

Friday evening, after a full two weeks of being turned away from one cabin after another and not delivering even a single book, Addie needed her mother. She trudged into the post office-telephone office and asked Mr. Landrum if she could use the telephone.

"Twenty-five cents," he said.

She dug the coin from her pocket and handed it over. Then she eased past the counter to the corner. She took down the earpiece, jiggled the cradle up and down, and waited. An operator's voice crackled through the line, requesting the number.

Addie recited the number for the Georgetown boardinghouse, then waited.

"Fee boardinghouse." The woman on the other end sounded aggravated. The same way every person Addie had encountered over the past weeks had sounded. Were it not for Mother's instruction to treat others the way she wanted to be treated, she might grouse at this unknown person. But she wouldn't dishonor her dear mother in that way.

"Hello. This is Adelaide Cowherd. May I speak to Fern Cowherd, please?"

"Everybody's sittin' at the dinner table right now, young lady. Call back later."

Panic gripped Addie. "I can't call later. The telephone office here will close. Please . . . I'm sure she won't mind leaving the table."

No reply came, but a dull thump followed by mutters indicated the person had placed the receiver on a hard surface instead of hanging up.

Addie held the earpiece tight against her head and counted the seconds until —

"Adeladybug?"

Tears filled Addie's eyes. She leaned against the wall and cradled the earpiece with both hands, wishing she could reach through the line and hug Mother. "Hi, Mama."

A trickle of affectionate laughter came through the phone. "You sound like my little girl again, calling me Mama."

Addie wished she could be a little girl again. To curl in her mother's lap and be rocked and sung to. She forced a strangled laugh from her dry throat. "I miss you."

"Your daddy and I miss you, too, honey. He's standing right here if you want to say hello."

Addie's heart turned a little cartwheel. "Oh, I do!"

Muffled whispers, unintelligible, met her ear, and then, "Hey, sugar dumplin'."

A smile automatically pulled on her lips. "Hi, Daddy. How are you?"

"I'm doing fine. How are you? Mother says you sound a little sad."

"I guess I'm homesick. Missing everybody. And . . ." She'd intended to tell her parents about her difficult weeks, but was it fair to dump her problems on them when they had their own burdens to bear? She cleared her throat. "I wanted to hear your voice."

Daddy's soft chuckle, so comforting in its delivery, soothed Addie's bruised heart. "It's good to hear yours, too, honey. But I'm sorry you're feeling sad. Maybe this news'll cheer you up a little bit."

Addie jolted. "Did you find a job?"

"I did. At Kennedy's marble and granite company."

Addie cringed. Kennedy's made headstones. A necessary item, certainly, but so unpleasant to consider needing one. "Are

374

you their bookkeeper?"

"No, I'll be sweeping up in the workshop."

She almost dropped the earpiece. "Sweeping up? You mean you'll be a . . . a janitor?"

"Is there something wrong with being a janitor?"

"Well, no, of course not. Janitors are important. But, Daddy, you're . . ."

"I'm . . . what?"

She gulped. "Old."

His laughter rang in her ear.

Addie hung her head.

"Honey, I'm grateful to Mr. Kennedy for hiring me when he could have hired a younger, stronger man."

She knew she should be thankful. Daddy was drawing a wage. With both of them saving up money, her parents would be able to leave Fee's boardinghouse in no time at all. That is, if she didn't lose this job due to her ineptitude. But more than anything else, sadness weighted her. She bit the inside of her lip, imagining her gentle daddy, who'd never done physical labor, cleaning up after younger workers who might make sport of him. "Are you sure it won't be too hard for you?"

"I managed the first two days without a wrinkle. I work seven to ten every night after the stone masons have gone on home, so

I'm not in their way."

Addie found a small blessing in his words. At least the others wouldn't be able to poke fun at him if he was too slow or had trouble scooping up the chipped remnants of stone. "I'll keep praying for an office job for you. I know you'd be happier with a pen than a broom in your hand."

"I won't argue with you there. Now, I'm going to give you to your mother. She's standing here, all wiggly and impatient."

Fern Cowherd was never wiggly and impatient, but the thought made Addie smile. "Bye, Daddy. I love you."

"I love you, sugar dumplin'."

A brief pause, then Mother's voice came on again. "All right, Addie, tell me all about delivering books. I want to know every detail."

"Oh, Mama . . ." All thoughts of withholding her heartaches whisked away like a flower petal tossed on a breeze. She told her mother about being ordered from properties, threatened with guns and dogs, and flayed with ugly words. "They treat me like I carry the plague. All because I lodge with Nanny Fay."

"The feelings against the woman are that strong?"

Addie sighed. "I'm afraid so."

"But why?"

"For ridiculous reasons, really. It has to do with the person she married over fifty years ago and the herbal medicine cures she learned from her husband's Cherokee grandmother."

"What?"

Addie nodded at Mother's aghast tone. "Rather senseless, isn't it? Emmett told me I might have a better chance of being accepted by the community if I find someplace else to lodge. He even offered me the little room at the back of the library, where he's staying. He said he'd move into his folks' cabin again. But —"

"Who's Emmett?"

Addie inwardly groaned. She hadn't told her parents about Miss West's departure and Emmett's taking over the director's position. She offered a quick explanation. "He's doing a fine job with the library side of things, but I think he's having some trouble with . . . er . . ." How could she define his seeming inability to mold the four female riders into a cooperative team? Were it not for Bettina, he might find success, but the girl seemed bent on stirring conflict. "Human relations."

A soft grunt sounded from behind her. She glanced over her shoulder. Mr. Landrum sat with his back to her, but his head was cocked in her direction. No doubt trying to catch every word. How much had he already overheard?

Addie cupped her hand around the mouthpiece. "I'll tell you all about it in a letter, Mother."

"I must confess, Addie, I'm less confident about you remaining there under the direction of a young man. And I'm not at all comfortable with the thought of people threatening you."

Addie closed her eyes. She shouldn't have said so much. "Please don't worry. Emmett is a perfect gentleman, and I hardly see him at all. A few minutes in the morning and again in the evening." Odd how much it stung to admit how little time they had together. Besides Nanny Fay, he was the only person she saw on a regular basis who was kind to her. "The rest of the time, I'm either trying to deliver books or at Nanny Fay's. As for being threatened, Emmett's mother — her name is Damaris, and she's one of the kindest people I've ever met — talked to me at church Sunday and assured me the hills folks would never follow through on any of the threats. There's an honor system that prohibits them from physically hurting a woman. They only hurt my feelings."

And Nanny Fay's.

She sucked in a breath. "Mother, what do you think about Emmett's offer for me to stay in the library building instead? Should I consider it?"

"Absolutely not." Her firm tone lifted Addie's spirits. "If you're certain the threats are idle, then these people need to see someone standing up for Nanny Fay. Perhaps it will inspire them to change their ways."

Addie's story was supposed to inspire them. But now it was gone. After searching for days, Emmett remorsefully admitted he'd probably discarded it by accident. He apologized, and she forgave him, but she couldn't help but mourn the loss. She'd sat down every evening since it disappeared and attempted to re-create it, but so far, the words had emerged flat and emotionless. Tonight she would start a new story, and perhaps she would regain her passion.

"Then I'll do as you suggest and stay where I am." Addie sighed. "Oh, Mother, I wish you and Daddy could meet Nanny Fay. She's such a remarkable woman." Other faces flashed in her mind's eye — Emmett, Damaris, little Dusty, Brother Darnell, even Jennie Barr, who'd hesitantly accepted a copy of *Ladies' Home Journal* from Addie on the street and then scuttled off, hugging the periodical the way a child hugged a teddy bear. "There really are some fine people here."

"Ahem!"

Addie gave a start and looked at Mr. Landrum. Scowling, he pointed to the clock on the wall. She grimaced and faced the phone again. "Mother, the telephone office needs to close, so I have to go."

"One more thing, and then I will hang up. My church ladies and I have gathered up a veritable mountain of scrapbooking items, novels, picture books, cookbooks, and magazines. Mrs. Fee is quite eager to have them out of her parlor, so Daddy and another man who lives here will crate them and deliver them to the railroad tomorrow morning. Will someone be able to retrieve them from the Lynch depot?"

Excitement roared through Addie's chest. She gave a little hop of joy. "Oh, yes, I'll make sure of it! Thank you so much, Mother!"

"You're welcome, my Adeladybug. We're happy to contribute to your ministry."

Her ministry? She'd never considered her job in such a light. A lovely shiver coiled through Addie's frame.

"I will pray you'll find the strength to show Jesus's love to those who are unkind to you."

"I need those prayers, Mother, because some of the people here" — she risked a glance at Mr. Landrum, who scowled at her with his arms folded tight across his skinny chest — "are very hard to love."

"All the more reason they need it. Now, let's say goodbye, and you call again next week, all right? I love you."

"I love you, too." Addie hung the little earpiece on its hook and scurried to the other side of the counter. Remembering her mother's words, Addie aimed a smile at the glowering postmaster. "I'm sorry to hold you up, Mr. Landrum. It was so good to hear my mama's voice that I didn't want to say goodbye."

His expression didn't clear, but he lowered his arms. "Reckon I can't fault you for that. Get your mail now" —

She had mail? She darted to the cubbies and peeked in Nanny Fay's box. Two envelopes waited.

— "an' skedaddle. My missus has got supper waitin', an' I'm not keen on cold suppers."

Addie removed the envelopes from the box and stepped outside. The door slammed behind her. Boone's Hollow didn't have a single lamppost to light the street, and the evening shadows made reading the dark writing on the envelopes difficult to decipher, but she recognized the handwriting. Both were from Felicity, and they would certainly cheer her as much as her chat with Mother and Daddy had. Across the street, lamplight glowed behind the library's windows and flowed from the open doorway.

She gave a little skip that set her feet in motion toward the smokehouse building. Emmett needed to be made aware of the coming delivery.

TWENTY-EIGHT

Emmett

What was he going to do about Addie? Emmett stared at the log of her deliveries and pickups. Except there were none. In ten days of heading out, she delivered only one item — a magazine to Jennie Barr, who wasn't even on the route. So, of the twenty-one families to whom she'd been assigned, she didn't deliver a book. She didn't retrieve a book.

Every business class he'd taken had taught if an employee didn't perform her job to expectation, she should be fired for the betterment of the organization. He rubbed his throbbing temples. Could he really fire Addie? Maybe he wasn't cut out to be a business director after all. Which would prove Paw right. He might even start talking to Emmett again if he resigned from his position as library director.

Someone tapped on the doorjamb.

He slapped the log closed and looked toward the door. "Who is it?"

Addie peeked around the corner, her face alight. She hadn't smiled much over the past two weeks. Not that he could blame her. Between being chased from people's yards and facing Bettina's criticism at every turn, she didn't have many reasons to smile. And if he fired her, he'd wipe off the one she now wore. He prayed he wouldn't have to do that to her.

He waved his hand. "C'mon in."

She entered and half walked, half pranced to the table. Something had sure put a bounce in her step. "Am I disturbing you?"

"Working on some record keeping." Her inactivity made part of it easy. He glanced at the letters she held. Maybe they were the cause of her good mood. From a beau, possibly? A beau who wanted her to return to Lexington? That'd simplify things for him. But it wouldn't make him happy. He shook his head and dispelled the strange thought. "What've you got there?"

She slid the envelopes into the patch pocket of her overall bib. "Letters from a friend. But I came over to tell you some news I think you'll like."

He could use good news. He gestured to the second chair. "Have a seat."

With a grin, she yanked out the chair and perched on its edge. "Miss West and I had an idea about how to make use of the magazines that are too tattered to lend. If we cut out the articles, recipes, and pictures, we could paste them into themed scrapbooks for people to check out like they do the books."

He rested his chin in his hand, envisioning the idea. "That's smarter than throwing them away." He grimaced. He'd never forgive himself for losing the story she'd written. If he hadn't thrown away the stack of worn-out magazines, she might still have it.

Addie nodded. "That's what Miss West thought. The problem was we didn't have any scrapbooks and Miss West said there were no funds to purchase some. So I wrote to my mother, and she and her church ladies organized a drive, and" — she flung her arms wide, triumph igniting her face — "tomorrow afternoon a crate of scrapbook materials and books will arrive at the Lynch depot."

Emmett sat up. "It will?"

She laughed. "There might be more than one. Mother said she and her ladies collected a veritable mountain of scrapbooking items and books of all varieties. Do you

385

think you'll be able to borrow a wagon and go after them?"

"Kermit Gilliam has a wagon I could probably use."

"Oh." She wrinkled her nose. "I should probably go, too, since my name will be on the boxes."

He chuckled. He'd never seen her so lighthearted. Not even at the bonfire at the university. He liked this side of her. "That seems fair."

"Wonderful!" With a bright smile, she rose and headed for the door. "What time should I meet you here tomorrow afternoon?"

He scratched his temple. The thudding pain had departed. "Well . . . the afternoon train arrives at three thirty on Saturdays. So, by one? That'll give us plenty of time to make it down the mountain. And before we pick up the crates, I'll treat you to a soda at the drugstore to celebrate this wonderful windfall."

"Perfect." She grinned, waved, and bounded out the door.

He gazed after her, plans taking shape in his mind. If he assigned her the task of putting the scrapbooks together, she wouldn't face another rifle barrel or be subjected to threats. And he wouldn't have to fire her if she had a viable job to do for the library.

Relief flooded him. He hadn't wanted to fire someone who tried so hard. The stubborn folks who couldn't see past the ends of their superstitious noses were to blame for her failure. Didn't his business professors advise placing people where they could best use their skills? Even though he still believed someone with Addie's passion for the written word should have the privilege of placing books into needy hands, her excitement about the coming materials told him she'd apply the same enthusiasm and determination to putting the scrapbooks together as she'd shown for delivering books. And she'd be successful with it.

Of course, with her pulled from a route, he'd have to divide all the families between three riders again. He inwardly groaned, imagining the girls' reactions. They'd sure enjoyed having their workdays trimmed down. But if he didn't fix this mess, the report the committee in Washington expected every month — which would show how twenty-one families didn't receive books over a two-week period during his first month of directorship — might mean the end of the program altogether. No program, no wages. The girls would have to understand and be supportive.

A snide snort formed in his throat. Bettina, supportive? He'd better start praying now. Despite these worries, he could go to bed happy about one thing. He wouldn't have to fire Addie.

Bettina

Bettina hunkered behind the bushes under the open library window. Ooh, that Addie. Getting her rich maw to send a bunch of books so she could make points with Emmett.

When Bettina'd seen Addie skipping across the street from the telephone office straight for the library, she'd come real close to throwing the whole plate of cookies she'd brung for Emmett at her. That girl turned up all the time, like a bad penny. But she was gone now, so Bettina could go in. Still, she stayed put, balancing the plate of cookies on her knees. She'd wait a little longer. Make it seem like she'd only just got there. She couldn't let Emmett know she'd heard every word. Including taking Addie into Lynch tomorrow so they could get a soda.

A soda! If he was gonna take anybody for a soda, it should oughta be Bettina. Addie knew Emmett'd been spoke for. She should've said no. And why was she even still in Boone's Holler? By now, any sensible girl would've packed her bags and gone home.

Bettina's knees were starting to cramp. She stood real slow, holding the plate steady. She didn't want even one of these cookies to slide off into the dirt. When she was all the way upright, she wriggled a little bit to shake the wrinkles out of her skirt. She'd put on the blue-checked dress she wore the day Emmett came home. Addie'd still been in her overalls. Bettina's dress would look like a breath of fresh air compared to them clay-colored overalls.

Real quiet, she slipped around the bushes and onto the street. Then she set her feet hard, giving Emmett good warning that somebody was coming, and walked up to the door.

"Knock, knock!" She made her voice singsong and cheerful. Emmett wouldn't ever know how much mad burned inside her chest. A shadow fell across her — Emmett in the doorway. She smiled big and held up the plate. "Brung you some fresh-baked oatmeal-raisin cookies. From my maw's recipe. I recollect how much you liked 'em when you was a little feller. Figured you still might."

He took the plate and gave her a soft smile that made her knees go wobbly. "Why, thank you, Bettina. That's real nice of you. I'll enjoy these." He turned and walked beyond the doorjamb.

She followed him, swinging her hips so her skirt would sway. He put the plate on the table and sat down. She looked real close at the papers scattered all over the table. Didn't none of them look like Addie'd been writing on them. She'd spent plenty of hours studying Addie's writing on the story pages, so she'd know the girl's hand if she saw it again. Took some doing, snatching them while Emmett was over at the livery. He hardly left the library, except for meals and visiting the outhouse. But she'd been clever enough to not get caught. "You still workin'?"

"I've got lots of reports to fill out, Bettina." He unscrewed the lid on a fat little inkpot.

"Ain't you gonna have a cookie?" She pushed the plate a little closer to him. "I put chopped walnuts an' cinnamon in 'em. Them walnuts come from a tree growin' up the mountain some behind our place." Pap was out wandering, but he could smell Maw's cookies from a mile away. If Emmett didn't get these ate fast, Pap might bust in and take them.

"I'll have one before I turn in. It'll be my

reward for finishing these reports."

If Pap didn't get to 'em first. She roamed up and down the shelves, searching for anything with Addie's writing on it. "Too bad you ain't got a cookie jar." She'd ask to take Maw's when she married and moved out. Pap'd probably let it go. "You should ought to put 'em in somethin', keep bugs off. Pests'll find a way in every time if you ain't careful."

"Mm-hmm." He *scritch-scritch*ed his pen against the page. "I've experienced that myself."

He was busy with his notebooks, not even looking her way, so she peeked behind the blankets hiding the living quarters from view. She'd never snooped when Miss West lived in the library, but since this might end up being where she lived with Emmett for a while until they found a decent place, she needed to know what all was there. A narrow cot, a bureau with four drawers, and a chair. Not even a rug on the floor. She huffed out a little breath. Not much. This place needed some fixing, but she could see to it, if he'd let her.

She'd put a rug on the floor, the quilt Maw'd made on the cot, some framed pictures or a little ceramic figurine on the bureau, and her Dionne quintuplets calendar on the wall. Those things would make a heap of difference.

She walked back to the table. She turned her hands backward and leaned on the edge. She'd figured out holding her arms that way pushed her shoulders back and made her chest seem a little bigger. She hoped he noticed. "What you thinkin' on doin' tomorrow? Now that you don't gotta go to the mine on Saturdays, you should oughta plan somethin' fun."

He glanced at her. Did a little bit of guilt show behind them spectacles? "I'm going to Lynch tomorrow, to the depot. I need to pick up a delivery for the library."

A prickle made its way up Bettina's back. He'd spoke the truth, but he was leaving an awful lot out. "That right? I ain't been to Lynch in a good long while. I hear they got two movie houses now. Me an' Glory, we've visited the Lyric Theater four, maybe five times. Her an' me went with Shay one time."

Would her having gone to the picture show with his friend make him jealous? She wanted it to. If he said he was jealous, then she could tell him what was good for the goose was good for the gander — let him know how she felt about him taking Addie to get a soda.

He kept writing.

She gritted her teeth and forced a little giggle. "Sure is somethin', watchin' them actors up on that big screen. You get to hear 'em talkin', too, just like they was in the room with you. Yessir, it's somethin'."

He blew on the ink, flipped a page, and wrote some more.

She leaned closer. "You ever been to the picture shows, Emmett?"

He ran his finger down the page and started writing in a little square. "Went to some in Lexington."

Jealousy struck as hard as Pap's fist. "Oh, yeah? You go with a friend, like I did with Shay?" She nudged his shoulder with her elbow. "Didja?"

He laid the pen down. "Bettina, I'm really sorry if I seem unfriendly, but if I'm going to catalog new books tomorrow, I need to finish this paperwork tonight."

"That's all you'll be doin'? Fetchin' an' catalogin' books?" She waited for him to spill the other part of his plans. If he'd come out and tell her, she'd know he wasn't trying to hide things from her. She'd feel a whole lot better about it if he'd say all his plans.

He stood and took a real light hold on her elbow. "I appreciate the cookies. It was real nice of you to remember I liked them and

393

bring some over." He ushered her to the door. "I'm sure I'll enjoy them if they came from your maw's recipe. But right now, I have to work. I'll see you Sunday, all right?"

She perked up. "Sunday?"

"At church."

Oh. He didn't mean nothing special.

"Good night, Bettina."

He left her on the stoop. She curled her bare toes over the edge of the rock and scowled across the gray-shrouded street. She wished she didn't know what he was gonna do with Addie tomorrow. She'd never get to sleep with all this mad rolling around inside her. She stacked her fists and pressed them to her mouth to hold back all the words she wanted to yell.

She wanted Addie out of Boone's Holler. She'd never met a more stubborn girl. Folks had done exactly what Bettina expected after she told them how Addie had took up with Nanny Fay. She figured two days of getting shooed away from folks' yards and Addie would turn tail and run for home, but nope. Ten days she'd took books and headed on the routes. Ten days she'd carried every book back. She must be dumber'n a rock if she thought them folks would change their minds about her.

Bettina hopped off the stoop and started

for home, dragging her heels. Addie was s'posed to meet Emmett at one o'clock to leave for Lynch. That give Bettina — she scrunched her face, thinking hard — around seventeen hours to figure out how to muddle their plans. She doubted she could keep Kermit Gilliam from renting Emmett a wagon. That feller was so money hungry he'd rent out one of his sons if somebody offered him a nickel. She doubted she could keep Emmett from going. He took to his job as library director like a duckling took to water. If there was a shipment waiting for him, he'd go get it. She might be able to keep Addie from meeting up with Emmett, though. Or, if nothing else, keep him from taking her to Lynch all by himself.

The corners of her lips tugged, wanting to smile. She changed direction and broke into a trot.

Twenty-Nine

Addie

Felicity's letters were full of sass and drama, and Addie heard her roommate's voice in her head while she read, which made her smile. And made her lonesome. She'd hoped to find friends here in Boone's Hollow, but so far none of the young people had taken much of a shine to her. Emmett was polite, but she really wanted a friend like Felicity. Someone to laugh, talk, and share secrets with.

She glanced across the sitting room at Nanny Fay, who sat in her rocking chair reading Mark Twain's *The Prince and the Pauper* by lamplight. At least she could call the old woman a friend. Every evening over supper they enjoyed long conversations. They had much in common — a sad early childhood, a love for reading, and a desire to please Jesus with the way they treated others.

Nanny Fay was a better friend to Addie than Addie was in return, though. Addie leaned heavily on Nanny Fay for support. The woman always had an encouraging word when she felt discouraged, advice when she was unsure, and a hug and a prayer when she was sad. On whom had Nanny Fay leaned since her husband died? Her loneliness must have been overwhelming at times, yet she remained content and cheerful. The way Mother was even now, without her home and fine belongings. Addie sent a slow look around the cabin. Although holding a simple beauty, these were primitive surroundings. She missed running water and electric lights, but she was learning to be content where she was. Perhaps she wasn't as different from Mother and Nanny Fay as she'd thought.

Nanny Fay sighed and set her book aside. "This story is good, but it can't top the one about Tom Sawyer. Oh, but that boy was a scamp! He worked harder tryin' to get others to do his chores than if he'd just done 'em hisself. I reckon there's a lesson in there."

Addie nodded. She'd thought the same thing when Mother read her the story years ago.

Nanny Fay yawned, a little squeak emerging, then sent a sheepish grin in Addie's direction. "Almost wish I hadn't come upon them blueberry bushes this mornin' when I went huntin' mushrooms. I plumb wore myself out pickin' the bushes clean. Tomorrow'll get all used up makin' syrup an' jam out o' the berries. But it'll be worth it come winter. Nothin' better'n wild blueberry jam on biscuits or blueberry syrup on hotcakes. Wait an' see."

Addie loved being included in Nanny Fay's winter plans. "I don't have to meet Emmett until one tomorrow, so I can help you in the morning." Over supper, she'd told Nanny Fay about the coming crates, and the old woman expressed such excitement that Addie had almost been moved to tears.

"Oh, honey, this batch ain't so much I can't do it myself. Now, way back, that was a differ'nt tale. 'Cause back then I went pickin' with Rosie. The two of us would gather so many berries one person couldn't take care of 'em all. We'd work at the stove together, talkin' an' laughin'. I recall stirrin' up berries while her little bitty gal slept in a basket on the floor or toddled around under our feet. Then we'd split the bounty, her carryin' away for her family an' me keepin' what I needed for myself. Oh, lawsy." A sigh left her throat, accompanied by a drowsy smile. "Those was good days."

Addie tipped her head, searching her memory. Had Nanny Fay ever mentioned Rosie before? "Who is Rosie?"

Nanny Fay sent a confused look at Addie. "Rosie?"

Had the woman already forgotten what she'd been talking about? "You said you and Rosie —"

She waved her hand. "Took me by surprise, hearin' her name on somebody else's lips after so many years o' not seein' her. She was a gal who grew up here in the holler. Her maw was a mean-hearted lady, had a whole passel of young'uns, an' for a reason Rosie couldn't help no matter what, the woman just never cottoned to her. I kinda took her under my wing. Did my best to love on her 'cause she sure needed it."

Addie's heart rolled over. She could imagine Nanny Fay loving on a sad, neglected little girl. "How come I haven't met her?"

Sadness pinched the old woman's features. "Rosie died some years back. Catched a bad sickness in her belly. But her an' me had drifted apart before that. When her little gal got big enough to do some talkin' about where she spent her days, Rosie couldn't risk her tellin' her pap they was with me. It would've caused trouble. So she stayed away, 'cept for now an' then when her little gal was at school an' her man was away." She chuckled softly, and her familiar soft smile returned. "But I hold my memories of her. All good ones."

Maybe Addie should stay here tomorrow and help Nanny Fay with the berries. Let her relive the days when Rosie came and helped. "Nanny Fay, about your jam making . . . I'll —"

"No, no, I'll see to it. You got plans to go into Lynch, get them books an' things, an' you'll prob'ly wanna take your Saturday night bath in the mornin' before you go. Make yourself all fresh an' purty for the trip to town." She winked.

For reasons Addie couldn't explain, heat filled her face. "Well, maybe . . ."

Nanny Fay chuckled. Then she yawned again and pushed herself out of her rocking chair. "I reckon you'll wanna write to your friend, so I'll let you have some time to yourself." She moved toward her room, pausing beside Addie long enough to squeeze her shoulder. "You sleep good tonight, Addie, you hear?"

"Yes, ma'am. You, too."

Nanny Fay closed herself in her room, and

Addie retrieved her writing paper and pencil from the little stand in her room. She placed the items on the fresh-scrubbed dining table, took the lamp from Nanny Fay's reading spot, and set it near her paper. Then she sat and picked up her pencil.

With Felicity's letters laid out in front of her, she answered her friend's many questions, then shared about her new life on Black Mountain. The open windows allowed in the night breeze, and a chorus of crickets accompanied a hoot owl's call. The sweetly scented air and pleasant melody kept her company. Peace settled gently on her shoulders. Little wonder Nanny Fay stayed here by herself. But Addie couldn't help smiling while she wrote, imagining Felicity's shock when she discovered that Addie lived in a cabin with no electricity or indoor plumbing. Felicity probably wouldn't find these surroundings peaceful, but —

The owl ceased its *whoo-whoo,* and the crickets fell silent. The sudden calm startled her as much as if someone had fired a rifle outside the cabin. Addie spun around, heart pounding. She rose and tiptoed toward the window that looked out over the garden, her gaze shifting back and forth from it to the square pane giving a view of the woods behind the house. With the lamp shining so bright inside and heavy shadows outside, she saw little more than a gray patch of nothing, and her heart pounded like the hooves of a galloping horse. She made it to the window, and after sending up a quick prayer for courage, she stuck her head out. She searched left and right, then scanned the tree line as far as she could see.

"There isn't anything here." She spoke aloud to assure herself. But it didn't work. Despite the hot, muggy air, she shivered. Her peace had shattered. She no longer felt safe sitting at the table in the open room. The security of her bedroom called. But first, she should make sure the cabin was locked tight. She closed the windows and put sturdy sticks in place that prevented anyone from opening the panes from outside. Then she hurried to the door as quickly as her trembling legs allowed. The string meant to lift the heavy crossbar was already in. No one would be able to open the door. Now to extinguish the lamp and lock herself in her room.

She lifted the globe and bent forward, but she held in her breath. Should she awaken Nanny Fay and tell her she feared someone might have been skulking outside the cabin? As soon as the thought formed, she dismissed it. The old woman was exhausted, and it might have been nothing more than a raccoon or possum scrounging for food. Why interrupt her sleep over a childish whim?

Addie blew out the lamp. The room plunged into darkness, discombobulating her senses. After a moment or two, her eyes adjusted and she made her way to her bedroom door. As her fingers closed on the little crossbar that held her door closed, the crickets began to sing and the owl added harmony with its *whoo-whoo.*

Her breath wheezed out, and she rested her forehead against the door. All was well. She'd gotten herself worked up for nothing. Somehow, though, even when she'd tucked herself under her pretty patchwork quilt and lay nestled in her comfortable feather bed, the earlier peacefulness of the evening refused to return.

Birds sang from the bushes outside, waking Addie. She swung out of bed and scurried to the window. Soft morning light touched the heavy mist hanging over the mountain, making the cloud-looking puffs glow like Chinese lanterns. A self-deprecating laugh found its way from her throat. Such a restless night she'd spent after her scare, but look at this glorious morning scene. So serene. So picturesque. How silly she'd been to let fear take hold of her.

She opened her window as far it would go and smiled at the grayish-pink sky. *I'm sorry for being such a ninny, Lord. I forgot what You told the children of Israel — "Fear thou not; for I am with thee." But I see Your fingerprints everywhere this morning, and I'll remember to take Your hand the next time I feel afraid.*

She chose a clean dress from a hook, clothed herself all the way down to her feet, then went out the door — the front door, since the cabin had no back door — for the trek to the outhouse. A lengthy walk, which Addie had bemoaned a time or two. But this morning, with the sun still hiding behind the mountain and the scented breeze holding a slight coolness, Addie savored it. Within an hour, the day would be sticky and hot. She took her time returning from the little necessary building, enjoying the moist dew collecting on her shoes, the choir of birdsong, and the fingers of sunlight creating a fan in the cloud-dotted sky.

Nanny Fay came out as Addie stepped up on the porch. She smiled, her gaze drifting toward the sky. "Mornin', Adelaide. Ain't it a purty start to a new day?"

Addie laughed. "Exactly my thoughts." An idea struck. "Since I'm leaving you to take care of the blueberries all by yourself, how about I make breakfast this morning?"

Nanny Fay cupped Addie's cheek with her warm, calloused hand. "That's real kind o' you, honey, but I already got a pot o' oatmeal started. Figgered we could toss in some o' them fresh berries."

Addie's mouth watered. "That sounds good."

"But if you wanna set bowls an' such on the table, that'd be helpful."

"That seems fair enough, since I left it kind of a mess last night." Addie headed inside and across the wide-planked floor. The room was still pretty dark, but by the time they ate, there would be sufficient sunlight coming through the windows. No need for the lamp. She lifted it by its glass base and carried it to the table beside Nanny Fay's rocker, the woman's favorite reading spot. She returned to the table and gathered up the letters from Felicity and her pencil and pad of paper. She frowned, scanning the items in her hands. Where was the letter she'd written?

Addie flipped through the pad, but the pages were all blank. She closed her eyes, trying to recall every detail of the previous evening. She'd been startled by the abrupt silence and had stopped writing, so she hadn't completed the letter, but she couldn't remember if she'd written directly on the pad or removed the pages from the pad first. If she'd torn them out, a breeze might have disturbed them.

She searched the floor under the table and examined every other surface in the dining area. She was on her way to her bedroom in case she'd carried them to her room, when Nanny Fay came in.

Nanny Fay looked across the room toward the dining area and chuckled. "You forget what you was s'posed to do? I saw you scuttlin' around like you was tryin' to find your sense."

Addie bit the inside of her lip, gripping Nanny Fay's hands. "Nanny Fay, before you went to the outhouse, did you pick up any papers from the table?"

The woman scuffed to the stove, shaking her head. "Nope. Didn't touch nothin' on the table."

Addie followed her and watched her add cinnamon and ground chicory root, her version of sugar, to the burbling oats. "This is very odd. I wrote a letter to Felicity last night. My paper and pencil are on the table where I left them, but the letter itself is gone."

Nanny Fay stirred the oatmeal with a long

wooden spoon, the motions slow and deliberate. "Well, honey, if you wrote one, it's gotta be here somewhere. I betcha if you set your mind to somethin' else, all o' sudden it'll come to you." She tapped the spoon on the edge of the pot. "This is right at the thickness I like it. Get out them bowls, will you? I'll help you look for the written pages after we eat."

True to her word, she searched with Addie after breakfast, but neither of them found the letter Addie had written. Addie finally sighed and held out her hands in defeat. "Maybe I only wrote it in my head."

Nanny Fay laughed. "Many words as you got floatin' around in your head, that wouldn't surprise me at all." She patted Addie's shoulder. "Tell you what, while I got the stove hot, I'll put some water to heatin' for your bath. Meantime, set yourself at the table an' get it all writ out. You can send it off at the post office before you leave for Lynch. Then you'll know for sure your friend is gettin' it."

Addie wrote — or rewrote? — the letter to Felicity. After her bath, while Nanny Fay hummed over a kettle of sweet smelling blueberries, she wrote one to Griselda Ann and Mrs. Hunt. She'd promised to let them know how she was doing, but in her busyness to learn the routes and write her story, she'd neglected it. She chose her words carefully, unwilling to cause her former boss angst. After all, her position as a book deliverer had gone very differently than either of them had envisioned. Mrs. Hunt might feel guilty for sending Addie to a place where the people were so opposed to outsiders. So, as she'd done in her letter to Mother and Daddy, she focused on the positive aspects. And by the time she finished, she'd managed to restore her own attitude.

"Look for the blessings," Mother always said. And there were blessings to be found here. Such as the still-warm wild blueberry jam on fresh-baked biscuits she enjoyed with Nanny Fay for lunch.

After she ate and cleaned up all her writing items, she braided her hair, tied the end with a bit of green ribbon, and headed to the post office. Mr. Landrum pasted on the stamps for her without speaking a word, but she chose not to let his taciturn behavior spoil her day. In another few hours, she'd enjoy her first soda since leaving Lexington, and then she'd have the joy of discovering what Mother and her church friends had sent for the library.

She exited the post office. Sunlight

smacked her eyes, and she winced. Most of the time, Boone's Hollow lay under a cloak of shadows from the mountains rising around it and all the trees surrounding it, but when the sun was high, the wide main street received unfettered sunshine. She cupped her hand above her eyes. A wagon with the same speckled horse that had brought her to Boone's Hollow three weeks ago waited outside the library. And someone was already on the driver's seat. Apparently Emmett was ready to go.

Squinting, she jogged straight for the wagon. Halfway across the street, though, she stopped. That wasn't Emmett sitting up high on the seat. Was Bettina Webber going, too? If she was, maybe it would give them a chance to talk, to find a way around the boulder of resentment seeming to always loom between them. It would be so much nicer at work if she and the other girls were friends.

Hope fluttering in her chest, she hurried across the street.

THIRTY

Bettina

The brake was set, so there wasn't no need to hold on to the reins, but Bettina held 'em anyway and watched Addie out of the corner of her eye. She hid a smirk. Yessir, Addie was for sure and certain jealous to see Bettina ready to go, too.

Addie bustled right up next to the wagon and looked at her all squinty eyed, the way Glory did when Bettina said something that set her teeth on edge. "Hello, Bettina. Are you going with us to Lynch to get the new library books?"

The word *us* sure rankled. There wasn't no *us* except Emmett and Bettina. Why, even their names fit together good. "I can't. Got chores to tend to." Pap'd be madder'n hops if he came home from work and didn't find a hot supper on the table. "But Emmett an' me bein' so close an' all, I couldn't let the Saturday go by without spendin' a little time with him for, you know" — she raised her shoulder and giggled all embarrassed-like, the way movie starlets did when they was talking of their fellers — "spoonin'. He's just so hard to resist first thing in the mornin', with his shirt undone an' his cheeks all red from shavin'."

Pink stained Addie's cheeks. My, but that flush said a lot. Addie leaned a little sideways and looked toward the library building. "Where is Emmett?"

"Oh, he ran on to his folks' house. He's fetchin' Dusty. Guess his pap stayed home from the mine today — ailin' in his belly, Emmett said — an' his maw don't want Dusty to catch whatever it is, so she asked if Dusty could go along to Lynch."

Bettina wanted to shout a cheer. But if she did, she'd scare the horse, so she didn't. Things couldn't have turned out better. She'd snuck into Nanny Fay's house through the cellar door and took the story Addie'd started writing last night, thinking maybe that'd keep her home writing it again. 'Course, her standing next to the wagon let Bettina know it hadn't worked. But it didn't matter none 'cause Emmett had told her he'd be toting Dusty along to Lynch. There wouldn't be no *us*, not with Dusty sitting between 'em and jabbering

411

like a magpie the whole time. He was a cute little feller, but he didn't never stop talking.

If she had her druthers, though, she'd go along. She wanted to get a soda with Emmett. She wanted to sit next to him on the seat all the way to Lynch and back again. She wanted Addie left behind instead of her. But if she couldn't have all that, then she'd be happy about Dusty going.

She fluffed her hair with her hand and grinned at Addie. "You don't mind havin' Dusty along, do you?"

"Of course not. I like Dusty."

And Dusty liked Addie. Leastwise, he'd sure seemed to take a shine to her. Why, he'd run right up to her at church last Sunday. Church, yet! Couldn't Addie stay away from anyplace Bettina went? Yep, Dusty'd pranced right over to her, giggling like he'd swallowed bubbly spring water, and showed off the boots he found in Belcher's the day Addie bought her overalls. Bettina ground her teeth. She didn't much care about Dusty liking Addie. But Emmett liking her? That was a different story.

Addie moved closer to the wagon and touched Bettina on the elbow. "I'm sorry you can't go."

Bettina snorted. Sure she was. She pulled her elbow out of Addie's reach and frowned fierce. "Well, lemme tell you somethin', an' you best hear me good."

Addie's eyes got big, and she backed up a few feet.

Bettina gave a satisfied nod. "The next time it'll be me an' Emmett goin', an' we won't take nobody else with us. You best remember —"

"Howdy, Addie!" Dusty galloped up and threw his arms around Addie's middle, a big toothless grin on his face. "Maw gimme two nickels. One to buy Paw some seltzer tablets an' one for licorice whips! I ain't had licorice whips since last Christmas. Mr. Belcher don't carry licorice in his store 'cause he says it stinks. But I don't think it stinks. It's the most best candy. So Maw says since I'm pickin' up Paw's medicine, I can get me some licorice at the drugstore in Lynch. I wish Paw got sick every Saturday."

Addie laughed.

Bettina did, too, but underneath she seethed. Dusty'd kept her from warning Addie off. But maybe she didn't need to say all the words. Addie was smart enough to figure things out. Especially if she got an eyeful of how much Bettina meant to Emmett. Emmett was coming now, so she wrapped the reins around the brake handle and stood. "Help me down, Emmett,

413

wouldja?"

Emmett's forehead puckered, like he wondered how come she needed help, but he reached for her hands. Quick as a cat could pounce, she put her hands on his shoulders and hopped, near colliding chest to chest. His hands clamped on her waist. Her feet hit the ground, but she didn't let go of his shoulders. She smiled up into his face and batted her eyelashes. "You all have a good drive to Lynch now, you hear?"

Emmett

Emmett let go of Bettina's waist and took a step backward. What was she doing leaping into his arms that way? Hadn't it been bad enough to have her burst into the library that morning before he'd finished shaving? She hadn't even seemed embarrassed to catch him with his shirt unbuttoned and his suspenders hanging by his knees. He'd been embarrassed, though — embarrassed enough to ask her to leave. And she had. But only long enough for him to button up and clean his razor.

Then she was in the library again, telling him how long it'd been since she'd taken a drive to Lynch, how her favorite soda was strawberry, how she was real good at cleaning and such . . . He'd pretended not to

414

understand her hints, and finally she'd come right out and said, "Why don'tcha take me along with you? You an' me, we can do whatever needs doin'." In desperation, he'd flat out told her Addie had to go to sign for the boxes. Plus, he was taking Dusty because Paw was sick. To his relief, she'd flounced to the door and declared she'd go home then. So why hadn't she?

One way or another, he had to find a way to work with her without always worrying about what she'd do next. Or one of them would have to leave the packhorse librarian program.

"Bettina, I —"

"Bye, now." She waved and darted up the road, flinging grins over her shoulder as she went.

Dusty tugged Emmett's sleeve. "Can we go? Huh?"

Emmett gave himself a mental shake. He'd worry about Bettina later. "Yeah, let's go, buddy." He lifted Dusty onto the seat, then turned to Addie. She stood several feet away, hands linked behind her back. Her brown eyes held a great deal of apprehension. Who could blame her? Bettina put everyone on edge. He gave what he hoped was a natural smile and bobbed his head toward the seat. "You coming?"

She glanced up the road to where Bettina had disappeared. "Um . . ."

Emmett sighed. "Look, Addie, I'm sorry Bettina does . . . well, what she does. She's always been a little unpredictable, but since I got home, she . . ." How could he explain something he didn't fully understand himself?

Dusty swung his legs, bumping the footboard with the balls of his bare feet on every forward swing. "She's loony as a rabid coon."

Addie gasped and clapped her hand over her mouth.

Emmett aimed a scowl at his brother. "What did you say?"

"What Paw said. She's loony as a —"

Addie scurried to the edge of the wagon. "Don't say that."

Dusty kept swinging his feet. "How come?"

"Because it isn't kind."

Dusty shrugged.

Addie took hold of Dusty's hand and held it between hers. "Dusty, do you believe in God?"

"Sure I do."

"Well, the Bible, which is God's holy Word, tells us, 'Be ye kind one to another.' "

Dusty scrunched his nose. His legs stilled.

"In another place, Jesus Himself told people, 'Inasmuch as ye have done it unto one of the least of these my brethren, ye have done it unto me.' He was talking about doing good things, but I think we can apply the rule to unkind things, too. That whatever we do to others, it's the same as if we've done it to Jesus." She tilted her head a bit and peered directly into Dusty's face. "Would you say Jesus is as loony as a rabid coon?"

Dusty's lower lip poked out. "No. But Jesus don't deserve it, 'cause He don't do dumb things like peekin' in people's windows or —"

"The Bible doesn't say we should be kind only to people we think deserve it. It says, 'Be ye kind,' so that's what we must do." Addie patted the back of Dusty's hand and let go. "We aren't going to talk in mean ways about Bettina or anyone else for that matter, agreed?"

Dusty hung his head. "Aw, all right." Then he sat up and held his head at a defiant angle. "But I ain't the one who said it first. Paw did. So you need to tell him to be kind."

Addie laughed. "Maybe I will." She turned to Emmett. Her lips quirked into a remorseful grimace. "I hope I didn't offend you by speaking so frankly to Dusty."

Emmett ambled forward, awed by her kindness even when offering correction. She'd be an amazing teacher. Or mother. "No, not at all. I was going to swat his behind. I think you handled it better."

She smiled. "I lived in an orphanage when I was a little girl, and people often spoke unkindly of me and to me. I retaliated with the same treatment. Even after I was adopted, I sometimes called people names or said mean things, probably trying to make myself feel more important. But my new mother and daddy assured me that I was loved very much by them and even more by God, and they taught me with patience and kindness to treat others the way I wanted to be treated. I truly have never regretted being kind to someone, but I have regretted doing the opposite."

Suddenly he understood her tenacity in reaching out to the hills people and her willingness to continue living with Nanny Fay, even though it made her a social outcast. "You have very wise parents."

"Indeed I do, and I can't wait to see what they sent us. So can we go?"

The impish gleam in her eyes made him laugh. "Yes, by all means, let's go."

He assisted her onto the wagon seat. She'd braided her long hair, which was pretty smart, considering how wind tossed it'd likely get during the ride to Lynch and back, and she wore a dress — green with white dots scattered here and there and a crisp white collar. He'd gotten so accustomed to seeing her in the pair of men's overalls that she seemed especially feminine and attractive. And he needed to shut those thoughts down.

"Interbusiness relationships wreak havoc with morale and productivity." Professor Downing's droning voice could lull a person to sleep, but Emmett recalled the stringent warning. He was doing his best to avoid any kind of relationship with Bettina. He'd be wise to apply the same effort with Addie.

Lynch
Addie

Three crates! Addie almost danced with glee right there on the loading dock at the Lynch depot. She'd expected one, possibly two . . . but three? And large ones at that. Large enough that Dusty's feet dangled a good six inches from the ground when he sat on one.

Addie stood beside Dusty's throne and waited for Emmett to locate someone to help him load the crates into the back of the wagon. She'd tried, but they proved too heavy for her. She rubbed Dusty's back, and

419

he rubbed his tummy.

"I feel real bad, Addie." His mournful expression pierced Addie's heart, even while the black ring around his mouth tempted her to snicker. "I think I catched Paw's sickness."

The culprit was more likely the black licorice he'd consumed after drinking a tall chocolate soda. Emmett had advised him to save some of the candy for later, but he'd cheerfully chomped through all five strings. Her stomach felt a little queasy thinking about digesting so much sugar. "Maybe you could chew one of the seltzer tablets you bought at the drugstore."

"Nuh-uh. Them are Paw's. He'll have my hide if I eat any of 'em." He rested his forehead against her rib cage and moaned.

Emmett trotted from behind the depot building, trailed by the skinny youth who'd worried about her the day she arrived from Georgetown and a portly man with a sour expression. Perhaps the gentleman would benefit from a seltzer tablet, too. She helped Dusty off the crate and led him to the shade under the depot's eaves. After a lot of grunting and maybe a few muffled oaths, the men slid all three crates into the wagon's bed. Emmett shook their hands and thanked them, and they returned to the depot, both holding their lower backs and walking stiff legged.

Addie offered them sympathetic smiles as they passed her, then hurried to Emmett. "I'm sorry the crates are so heavy."

He laughed. "I think it's great. That weight tells me there are lots of books in these things." He helped her up onto the wagon seat and then waved his hand at Dusty. "C'mon, buddy, let's go."

Dusty clutched his stomach and stayed put.

Addie leaned down slightly. "His stomach is hurting pretty badly."

Emmett rolled his eyes. "I told him not to eat that whole bag of candy at once." He strode to the depot, arms swinging, and scooped his brother up the way a groom carried his bride over a threshold. At the wagon, he laid Dusty in the bed. Then he shrugged out of his jacket. "Here, bud, roll this up and use it for a pillow. But if you think you're going to throw up, hang your head over the edge of the wagon. Don't get vomit on my jacket or the boxes."

Addie gasped at his nonchalant tone and uncaring directions.

"Okay, Emmett." Dusty wadded the jacket and shoved it under his head. He closed his eyes.

Addie couldn't stop gazing at the child, battling a wave of pity. Even if he had foolishly caused his discomfort, he looked so small and helpless lying beside the oversized crates.

Emmett pulled himself up onto the seat and released the brake. He glanced at her and grinned. "He'll be all right. He's a tough guy. Right, Dusty?"

Dusty's eyelids twitched, but he didn't open his eyes. "Right, Emmett."

Emmett whispered, "He'll be asleep before we're out of Lynch. Don't worry." He slapped the reins down on the horse's rump, and the wagon groaned forward.

As he'd predicted, by the time they reached the road leading up the mountain to Boone's Hollow, Dusty's mouth hung open and he snored softly. Convinced he was fine, Addie faced forward. One of the wheels hit a rut, and the wagon rocked sideways. Addie's shoulder connected with Emmett's. She scooted over a few inches, then kept her hands curled around the rough front edge of the seat. It wouldn't do for them to roll into Boone's Hollow and have people see her sitting so close to Bettina's beau.

Whether it was the privacy of the quiet road or the aftermath of spending such a pleasant afternoon with the Tharp brothers, Addie found herself asking a personal question. "Emmett, Dusty said your father called Bettina 'loony as a rabid coon.' Was he joking, or he is not particularly fond of her?"

Emmett snorted under his breath. "He wasn't joking. Paw doesn't think much of Burke Webber, Bettina's pap. He isn't fond of Jasper Barr — you met his wife, Jennie, and gave her a magazine, remember? — for the same reason. He thinks they're lazy and don't take good care of their families. In Paw's eyes, that makes them useless as men."

Addie cringed. She didn't know Burke Webber or Jasper Barr, but for some men, the country's economic depression got in the way of their seeing to their families' needs. Would Emmett's father think Daddy was lazy because he worked only a few hours every day at a menial job? "Is that why he doesn't like Bettina, too? If you don't like one person in the family, you dislike them all?"

Mouth set in a rueful grimace, Emmett glanced at her. "Sad to say, that's the code of the hills. You're caught up in the middle of it, with people not liking you because you like Nanny Fay. They don't like Nanny Fay because they didn't like her husband, and

423

they didn't like him because he was a Tuckett. It probably seems petty and childish to you, but to these people, it's an honor to hold on to generations-long grudges. And it's pretty hard to change a mindset that's been handed down from a beloved great-grandpappy."

She shifted a bit so she could talk to his profile. "Your mother doesn't honor the code, though. She's been kind to me, and I know she likes Bettina."

A half smile pulled up the corners of his lips. "Maw's got a good heart. A tender heart, kind of like you."

Addie's pulse skittered at the compliment.

"Maw and Bettina's mother were good friends from childhood. She refuses to get caught up in Paw's scorn toward Burke and Bettina, even though she wishes Burke was a better husband and father. I think when Maw looks at Bettina, she sees Rosie, and that makes her more accepting and patient."

Rosie . . . . Could Bettina's mother be the same woman who went berry picking with Nanny Fay? But that Rosie was dead, and Emmett said his mother wanted Burke Webber to be a better husband, so it was probably a different woman. "I'm glad your maw accepts Bettina. That should help. But won't it be hard to be married to her if your father

424

thinks so poorly of her and her pap?"

"Married to whom?"

"To Bettina."

Emmett's frame jerked. "To Bettina?" His tone rose a full octave. Dusty mumbled in his sleep, and the horse's ears twitched. He gaped at her, his spectacles reflecting the sunlight. "Why do you think I want to marry Bettina?"

Addie drew back and gawked at him. How ridiculous they must look, sitting on opposite sides of the bench, staring at each other with astounded expressions. "Because . . . She . . . I thought . . ."

Emmett shook his head so hard his spectacles bounced on the bridge of his nose. "I'm not marrying Bettina, Addie. She's like a pesky little sister. It'd be downright awkward. And it has nothing to do with how my paw feels about her or Burke. I just . . . couldn't."

"Then why does she think you are?"

"How should I know?" His voice rose again, and he swung one arm. "I haven't done anything to encourage her, I can tell you that. Especially not since Maw told me she's unhappy at home and looking for an escape. That's a pretty poor reason to marry somebody, don't you think?"

Addie didn't know what to say. How could

two people hold such different views of the same relationship? Sympathy for Bettina rolled through her. Even if her motivation was selfish, she seemed to love Emmett. Embarrassment at having opened such an uncomfortable conversation and uncertainty of what to talk about next kept Addie silent the remainder of the drive to Boone's Hollow.

Emmett drew the wagon to a stop outside the library and set the brake. He cleared his throat, his gaze aimed ahead. "Listen, Addie, I'm sorry I got so upset. I'm not sure why it bothered me so much that you thought I was . . . er . . . betrothed to Bettina. But I shouldn't have hollered like I did. I hope you'll forgive me."

Addie toyed with a fresh snag on her skirt, probably from brushing against the crate when she helped Dusty down. "There's nothing to forgive, Emmett, truly. It was a misunderstanding, and I shouldn't have been so nosy. I'm sorry, too."

She braved a sideways glance and found him smiling at her. She returned it with one of her own.

Dusty stirred and sat up. He rubbed his eyes. "Emmett?"

Eyes locked with Addie's, Emmett said, "Whatcha need, Dusty?"

"The outhouse."

Emmett and Addie exchanged a grin. Addie pointed. "There's one behind the library. You could use it."

"No. I wanna use *my* outhouse."

Emmett reached into the back and tousled Dusty's dark hair. "All right, buddy, I'll walk you home." He looked at Addie and shrugged. "I should get the seltzer tablets to Paw anyway, then find some men to help me unload these crates. It might be fifteen or twenty minutes before I get back, so I'll say goodbye now."

Addie swallowed a knot of unexpected sadness. She wasn't ready to say goodbye. "That's fine. I hope Dusty's tummy will be okay."

"I'm sure he'll be fine after he, er, visits the outhouse."

Addie's face heated. She looked aside.

Emmett hopped down and, being the perfect gentleman she'd told Mother he was, helped her out. He lifted his brother from the back and draped his hand over Dusty's narrow shoulder. "See you tomorrow at church, Addie."

Thank goodness it didn't seem to bother him for her to come to service with Nanny Fay. After being glared at each Sunday by so many pairs of distrustful eyes, his simple comment was as sweet as a wisteria-laden breeze. She offered him a smile. "Yes, tomorrow. Bye, Emmett. Bye, Dusty."

Dusty flapped a weak wave, and the pair ambled off together.

She started for Nanny Fay's and then turned back. Dusty wasn't the only one who needed the outhouse. She visited the one behind the library. As she headed for the road, she glanced through the library window at the dark space. Emmett planned to unload the crates this evening. If the lamps were lit, it would simplify things for him. She hadn't been able to help lift those crates into the back, but she could certainly help by lighting the lamps.

The library door was closed, but it wouldn't be locked. When Emmett had moved in, he'd removed the string-and-crossbar system and added a doorknob, but the latch kit lacked a locking mechanism. A little hook and latch on the inside secured the door when he closed himself in for the night, but otherwise the building remained accessible to anyone who came along.

Addie opened the door and stepped over the threshold. She blinked rapidly, willing her eyes to adjust so she could find her way to the table, where a lamp and box of matches always waited on the corner. She took a hesitant step in the direction of the table, and her foot connected with something. She stopped and squinted at the floor. A book lay open and facedown in front of her. She blew out a little huff of aggravation. Such a careless thing to do. Addie bent over to pick it up and drew in a horrified gasp. The entire floor was littered with books.

She abruptly straightened and stared at the mess. A groan grew in her chest and emerged as a whimper. "Oh, Bettina . . . Why would you do such a thing?" But she already knew why. Retaliation. Addie shouldn't have gone to Lynch with Emmett.

THIRTY-ONE

Boone's Hollow
Emmett

Lamplight glowed behind the library windows. He hadn't lit those lamps, but he could reason who had. A feeling he couldn't define swooped through him, and his feet sped up without conscious thought. Kermit Gilliam, Ned Belcher, and Preacher Darnell double-stepped to keep up, Gilliam grunting under his breath.

Emmett gave the wagon's side a light slap on his way to the library's stoop. "Gimme a minute, fellows, to decide where to stack these crates in here, and then I'll —"

Addie blocked the doorway. She wrung her hands, and her eyes were sheeny with unshed tears. Another feeling captured him, but this one he recognized. Concern. For her.

"What's the matter?"

She glanced beyond him to the men, then

430

settled her watery gaze on him. "I came in to light the lamps for you, and I . . . I found . . ." Her lower lip sucked in, and she took a slight step to the side.

Emmett peered in, and his heart seemed to fire into his throat. He crossed the threshold, placing his feet in the patches of floor between scattered books and magazines. Whoever'd been in earlier hadn't been so careful. Boot prints marred the covers of several books. Some had lost their covers altogether, and magazine pages littered the floor like the leftovers from a ticker tape parade. A stone seemed to drop into his belly. Dozens of questions cluttered his mind, and he didn't know which to ask first.

"I'm so sorry, Emmett. It's all my fault. If I'd stayed at Nanny Fay's today and helped her make blueberry jam, none of this would have happened."

He paused and looked over his shoulder at Addie, who remained near the doorway, hugging herself. "What are you talking about?"

She blinked several times, and one tear let loose and rolled down her pale cheek. "Bettina. She thought I was trying to steal her beau, so —"

"I already told you I'm not her beau." The harshness in his tone startled him.

Her eyebrows dipped together. "I know, and you know. But I don't think she knows."

The preacher stuck his head in. "Hey, Emmett, I'd like to —" His eyes widened, and he came all the way in. "What happened in here?"

Addie scurried out. Emmett wanted to go after her, to assure her she wasn't to blame. But he couldn't. His legs had turned to concrete and refused to move. Some director he'd turned out to be. Sending out a rider who didn't deliver a single book in ten days of trying. Failing at maintaining peace among the employees. Now allowing the destruction of government-owned materials. He had no business being in charge of anything.

Emmett bent over and picked up a book. The rumpled pages hung by threads. He tucked them back into the binding. "Reckon a storm blew through." He turned his gaze to the preacher. "It'll take me a little while to get this cleaned up, and I can't bring the crates in until it's done. Would you ask Kermit if they can stay on the wagon until tomorrow afternoon?"

Preacher Darnell crossed on tiptoe through the maze of books and put his hand on Emmett's shoulder. "I'm sure sorry about all this, Emmett. You reckon somebody's upset about the new book gal?"

Somebody was upset, all right. He nodded.

The preacher hung his head. "These feuds an' fear gotta end. Nanny Fay's a fine Christian woman. But the people in town have blinders on when it comes to her. I —"

Emmett gave a start. "You think somebody did this because Addie stays with Nanny Fay?"

Preacher Darnell aimed a frown at Emmett. "Isn't that what you're thinkin'?"

Emmett licked his dry lips, his gaze drifting across the carnage. "I don't know for sure." Righteous indignation filled him. "But I can tell you one thing. When I find out who did this, no matter who it is, I'll file charges of vandalism and destruction of government property. I won't be turning the other cheek."

Emmett sat on the edge of one of the crates sent from Georgetown and stared at the stacks of books and magazines covering the table. He needed to open the crates and organize the new materials so he'd have packs ready for the girls to take tomorrow, but his heavy heart held him in place.

He was pretty sure Preacher Darnell's fiery sermon about letting God be the judge

433

instead of taking retribution into one's own hands was a last-minute switch, but his words had poured as eloquently as if he'd practiced them for weeks. A part of the man's emotional talk roared in Emmett's memory.

" 'Dearly beloved, avenge not yourselves, but rather give place unto wrath: for it is written, Vengeance is mine; I will repay, saith the Lord.' Feuds and violence have no place in the Christian's heart or actions! Repent of your hateful attitudes, an' if you've wronged a neighbor, seek their forgiveness an' ask how you can make things right!"

After the service, Emmett had expected half the congregation to flood to the back pew, where Nanny Fay and Addie sat together, but not a one of them even looked their way. A few came to him, though, and pointed their fingers of blame.

Barney Shearer clapped Emmett on the shoulder. "Heard about the mess. Prob'ly someone from Tuckett's Pass done it. They don't got a lib'ary over there, an' the ol' green-eyed monster convinced one of 'em to ruin ours. You know how them Tuckett folks are."

Baylus Landrum shook his gray head and puckered his lips in a sorrowful frown.

"Sure sorry 'bout what happened to them books, Emmett, but reckon it shouldn't come as a surprise. I can't figure why that ol' woman don't take herself to Tuckett's Pass an' let Boone's Holler have some peace."

Even Juny Faulkner, the doctor's wife, approached with her nose in the air. "Just goes to show those hills people don't appreciate anything they're given. If I was you, I'd close the doors an' let 'em find a way to buy books for themselves an' their youngsters. That would teach 'em."

They needed teaching, all right. As did nearly every person who called Boone's Hollow home. He puffed his cheeks and blew, wishing he hadn't lost Addie's story. He didn't know a single person from the area who didn't enjoy a good tale — well, except Paw, who didn't have patience for storytelling. That's why some who weren't exactly religious showed up at church every Sunday. Preacher Darnell had a way of weaving biblical truths into story form. Even Jesus told parables, which were the same as stories. If Emmett picked an evening and made it read-aloud hour at the library, he'd get swarmed. And if he could have read Addie's tale, maybe experiencing ostracism through the eyes and feelings of a book character would finally reach the stubborn, prideful folks.

But sitting here ruminating wouldn't get his work done. He rose and grabbed the hammer he'd borrowed from Kermit and pried the lid off the first crate. As the nails screeched from the wood, someone tapped on the doorframe. He didn't need one more piece of unsolicited advice. He hollered, "Library's closed."

"It's me, Emmett — Addie."

He dropped the hammer and bounded to the door. He flicked the latch and swung the door wide. She'd changed from the pretty yellow-and-white-striped dress she'd worn to church into her overalls, and she held a squat jar of purple jam on her palms the way a crown bearer carried the king's headpiece.

"I brought a peace offering. May I come in?"

"You don't owe me a peace offering. But please come in." He took the jar and gestured her over the threshold. She entered with greater hesitation than he'd ever witnessed, then planted herself near one of the empty shelves and hung her head. She still felt guilty, and she shouldn't. This guilt wasn't hers to carry. He put the jar on the dresser in his living quarters, then faced her, sliding his hands into his trouser pockets. "Listen, Addie, put it out of your mind that you're responsible for what happened here. Because you aren't."

She kept her head low but peeked at him through her eyelashes. "That's kind of you to say, but you know it isn't true. I've made an enemy of Bettina by becoming your friend" —

His pulse skittered.

— "and of the rest of the town by becoming Nanny Fay's friend. They all want me to leave. It makes perfect sense that if the library program has to close, I'll be sent away. So I . . ." She held her hands to the empty shelves. "I caused this."

He hurried to her and took her hands. "No, you didn't. Ignorance did this. Hatred did this. Jealousy did this." He squeezed her hands and dipped his knees, meeting her uncertain gaze. He sent up a silent prayer for her to hear and accept the truth. "Addie, you are none of those things. You're intelligent and caring and giving. Don't blame yourself for someone else's foolish choices, please?"

She sucked in her lips and stared into his eyes for several seconds. She stood so still he wondered if she'd stopped breathing.

Then she gave a little nod. "All right. I'll try."

He stood straight and released her hands. "Attagirl."

She grinned. "Do you need some help? Nanny Fay always sleeps on Sunday afternoons, and she works so hard the rest of the week that I don't like to disturb her. I tried writing in my room, but I'm too restless to sit and write today." She wrinkled her nose. "Besides, I really want to know what's inside those crates."

Emmett laughed. Never had a laugh felt as good as this one. He beckoned with a twitch of his finger. "I was just fixing to open the first one. Come peek."

She skipped to the crate and leaned in as he lifted the lid aside. She yanked away a wad of rumpled paper and squealed. "Picture books!"

He couldn't resist another laugh. Her delight was contagious. He opened the second crate, which contained novels, textbooks, cookbooks, and a variety of nonfiction books, and finally the third, where they found the promised scrapbooking materials, as well as dozens of magazines.

Addie lifted out a blank scrapbook and sank onto the floor. She laid the cloth-covered cardboard book in the crook of her bent legs. "I hope you haven't discarded the magazines we had before. I know they were in pretty sad shape even before they got thrown around like confetti" —

Her choice of words inspired a grin, even though the circumstances weren't funny at all.

— "but that doesn't mean the pages can't be salvaged."

Emmett gestured to the table and the stacks of damaged books and magazines. "I haven't thrown out anything yet. I want to try to fix as many as possible, but some are probably beyond repair." The thought made him sick to his stomach, but a seltzer tablet wouldn't cure his ache.

She flipped the top cover back and forth between her hands and gazed at him, her expression thoughtful. "Before I came here, I stayed with a woman who cut up old clothes and made quilts for the destitute and downtrodden. She taught me to utilize every possible inch of the clothing pieces. If we apply the same technique to the magazine pages, we could fill every one of these scrapbooks and have unique instructional yet fun books to share with the hills people."

Emmett squatted in front of her, his elbows on his knees. "Would you want to take on the project? Be the . . . scrapbook lady?"

She chewed the corner of her lip. "You mean I would spend the whole day making scrapbooks instead of taking books around to folks?"

He nodded.

She lowered her head and traced circles on the scrapbook's cover with her finger. "As much as it pains me to concede defeat, I can't let my stubbornness stand in the way of people receiving items that could educate, inform, and inspire them. They won't take materials directly from me. But I could still have a hand in what they receive if I make the scrapbooks." She looked up and shrugged, a grin quivering at the corners of her rosy lips. "If the boss assigns me to scrapbook duty, I guess I'll become the scrapbook gal instead of a book gal."

"Consider yourself assigned." He stood, took the scrapbook, and set it on top of the closest crate. Then he grabbed her hands and pulled her to her feet. "But for now, since you're willing to help, let's unload these crates, catalog the titles, and fill the shelves. Monday's gonna sneak up, and we need to be ready for it."

A little shiver of delight rattled down Addie's spine. *"We,"* he'd said, as if they were partners. Most likely he meant nothing by it, but the word rolled in the back of her mind while they emptied the crates and categorized the books into neat stacks on the floor. Addie suggested recording the titles, authors, and classifications of the books as they removed them, but Emmett said he'd find it simpler to record them from their alphabetized positions on the shelves. Such a smart idea. She told him so, and his smile of appreciation warmed her from the inside out.

His mother, accompanied by Dusty, knocked on the door at suppertime. Surprise registered on her face when she spotted Addie, but then she chuckled and patted the side of the large woven basket she carried on her arm. "Sure am glad I brung extra. Reckon the Good Lord knew how many mouths needed fed. Didn't reckon Emmett was comin' to the house for supper or goin' to the evenin' service, considerin' what all needs doin' here. I won't pester you none about the service. I think the Lord'll understand. But you do need to eat an' keep up your strength. That goes for you, too, Miss Addie."

Addie might have felt embarrassed or as if she were in the way with anyone else, but Damaris Tharp had such a sweet spirit she put Addie at ease. The table was still cluttered with damaged books, so they sat on the floor, stacks of books standing silent sentinel around them. Emmett offered a short word of grace, and they ate the cheese sandwiches, pickles, and brownies.

Dusty took the last brownie from the basket, and Addie nudged him with her elbow. "I'm glad your tummy's all better. I figured you'd stay away from sweet stuff for days after that licorice gave you such a stomachache."

Damaris's merry laughter rang. "Oh, law, ain't nothin' gonna keep Dusty away from sweets. I tell him he better be careful in a rain shower 'cause sugar melts."

Dusty grinned around a huge bite. "I'm fine. Paw is, too. Said them seltzer tablets did the trick."

Damaris gathered up the plates and wadded napkins and stacked them in her basket, chuckling. "I think he was doin' better even before you brung those tablets to him, 'cause he was spry enough to go traipsin' in the woods a bit. 'Course, bein' out in the trees, huntin' squirrels or castin' a line for trout, always has done Emil good." Her face puckered. "The money from his coal-minin' job has sure blessed this family, but I worry sometimes about what it does to his soul. Bein' underground so much . . . wouldn't that wear on a person?"

Emmett wiped his mouth with his muslin napkin and tossed it into the basket. "I wouldn't worry too much about him, Maw. When he took me to Mine Thirty-One to look around, he told me he appreciates the fresh air and the sun more now than he did before because of his time in the tunnels. Seemed to me being a miner makes the world look brighter to him."

A smile broke over the woman's face. "Well, now, that is a good thing. Not only that he feels it, but that he told you about it. It sure tickled him to share that part o' himself with you, Emmett. He seemed to walk a little prouder them days, bein' able to teach his boy." She stood and scooped up the basket by its twisted handle. "Come along now, Dusty, an' we'll let these two get back to work."

Addie walked Damaris and Dusty to the door, then turned to Emmett. "Your mother is wonderful. She —"

He was sitting on the floor, blue eyes seemingly locked on one of the shelves, his forehead scrunched.

She hurried to him. "Are you all right?"

He blinked twice, as if waking up, and looked at her. "What?"

"Do you have a headache? We have been working for a long time. Maybe you need a break."

He shook his head and stood, his frown intact. "No, I'm fine. Was thinking is all." His chest expanded with a full breath, and the furrows in his brow eased. "Would you mind putting the ruined books in one of the empty crates? I'll decide what to do with them later."

"Of course." Addie crossed to the table and lifted a stack of books. As she turned to place them in the crate, she spotted Emmett in her peripheral vision. He stood still as a statue, staring out the window, as forlorn as if he'd lost his best friend.

THIRTY-TWO

Bettina

Bettina ducked behind the bushes next to the library and unrolled the sleeves on her blouse. She bumped the bruises on her wrist and cringed. Mercy, Pap'd squeezed her hard. Probably bruised her all the way to the bone. It'd be days before the spots faded enough to wear a short-sleeved blouse again. She gritted her teeth, holding in a groan. She had to get out of that house.

The clip-clop of shoed horses came up the street — Glory and Alba. Bettina zipped around to Mule and fiddled with his reins, like something needed fixing, and smiled at the pair. "Hey, gals."

"Hey yourself." Alba looped Biscuit's reins on a straggly branch. "Where was you last night? Everybody else came to my place after service. Maw gave us chocolate cake an' fresh whipped cream."

Bettina's mouth watered.

445

"But you didn't even come to service." Alba's blue eyes glittered. "Emmett didn't neither. Was the two o' you off sparkin' someplace?" She and Glory giggled.

As if she'd tell them she was soaking her bruises in Boone's Creek in a useless attempt to make 'em go away. She tugged at her cuffs and tossed her head. "Ain't nobody's business what I was doin'."

Both girls laughed again, and Glory looked up the street to the livery. "Wonder where Addie's got to. She ain't brung Russet over yet, an' she's gen'rally the first one here."

All at once Emmett was standing next to them. His face looked like thunder. "Girls, c'mon inside. We need to talk." He turned around and went into the building.

Glory and Alba exchanged nervous looks and followed Emmett, but Bettina stayed by Mule. Her stomach whirled. Everybody in Boone's Holler knew about the library getting torn up one end to the other. If she went in there, would Emmett tell her the library was closing? That they wouldn't have jobs no more? That Addie was going back to wherever she lived before? She'd stayed away from him at church yesterday morning, scared he'd read all the hope in her face and be mad. He liked his job. She didn't want him to lose it, but neither did she want him to keep working with Addie. She shifted from foot to foot, but she couldn't make herself go in.

Emmett poked his head out and frowned at her, stern as Pap. "Bettina, we're waiting for you."

She forced her feet to carry her forward. Glory and Alba sat on crates lined up along the front wall. Addie sat at the table. Bettina scowled. How come she was wearing a dress?

Emmett pointed, and Bettina settled next to Alba. He folded his arms and stood in front of them. "First of all, let's clear the air about the damage that happened here Saturday. *Somebody* wants this program to close, but that somebody isn't going to win."

Why was he looking straight at her? Her tummy gave a flip.

"A lot of books were ruined, but thanks to a group of people from Addie's town, we got other books — books of all kinds — to replace them. That means you'll get to go on your routes today like always."

Alba and Glory let out happy little squeals. Bettina couldn't decide if she was happier'n she was sad or the other way around. So she stayed quiet.

"The only thing is it'll be the old routes."

Alba jolted upright and bumped Bettina's arm. Bettina hissed and pulled it against her ribs. Alba didn't say so much as sorry. "How come the old routes?"

Emmett's face kind of said sorry. "I'm pulling Addie from deliveries. We all know that hasn't gone so well."

Bettina leaned forward and looked at Addie. Glory and Alba did, too, and they almost bumped heads. Probably wouldn't have hurt Glory. Her frizzy hair made a good cushion. But it would serve Alba right if it hurt after banging Bettina's arm like she done. Addie watched Emmett the way a mama cat watched her kittens and didn't even seem to notice the other girls.

Bettina jabbed her thumb in Addie's direction. "What's she gonna do? Sit here an' make sheep's eyes at you all day?"

Emmett's scowl got even darker than some Pap'd make.

Bettina shrank back.

"Nobody is going to sit an' make sheep's eyes at anybody. Addie will be making scrapbooks from the torn-up magazine pages so they can still be used." He pointed to three satchels lined up on top of one of the shelves. "Your packs are ready. I tucked in a note with all the stops of your former routes to help you remember. For instance,

Bettina's Monday note says Nanny Fay, Cissell, Froman, Neely, Day, McCash, and Toon."

Bettina toyed with the button on her cuff. He'd said them names to help her. But how she hoped Addie didn't figure out why she needed the help.

"To make it a little easier for you today, I only put in two books for each stop. I hope that'll speed things for you while you get used to doing the longer routes again." He took a big breath and let it out, and he seemed to lose some steam. "I'm sorry we had to go back to the longer routes, but the goal of this program is to put books in people's hands. If that doesn't happen, the government might close us down. I don't want to lose my job. Do you?"

Alba and Glory shook their heads. Bettina ground her teeth together and stared at her knuckles.

"All right, then. Grab your packs and head out. I'll see you this evening."

Glory and Alba snagged their packs and scuttled out the door. Bettina reached for hers and took a little sideways glance at Emmett. He was watching her, his lips set in a line that wasn't smile nor frown. With them glasses on, his hair combed straight back, and wearing his Sunday suit, he sure didn't look much like the Emmett she used to know.

Her stomach did another whirl. She swung her pack over her shoulder and hurried after Glory and Alba. They were already in their saddles. Bettina'd hoped to talk a little bit before they all set out, maybe see if they was as upset about going back to the long routes as she was, but they seemed eager to go. She waved and heaved herself onto Mule's back.

Nanny Fay

The smell of blueberries hung heavy on the porch, covering the smells of grass and earth and the wild wisteria blooming at the edge of the woods. Even though she liked all those smells, Nanny Fay didn't mind them playing second fiddle to the blueberries. Eagle used to get tired of the smells when she'd been canning. Would sometimes grumble that after smelling the food for so long, it didn't even taste good. But Nanny Fay loved the smell of blueberries. Blueberries smelled like happiness.

Rosie's daughter ought to be riding in any minute, and Nanny Fay was ready for her. The books she needed to return waited in a stack on the bench next to her, and she held a jar of jam in her lap. She'd topped the jar with a circle of pink-and-white-checked fabric held in place with a pink ribbon. Rosie'd been fond of pink, and Nanny Fay used to tease her that's how come she'd been named Rosie. She didn't know if Bettina liked pink, but she hoped the color would remind her of her mama.

A pair of turtledoves stopped their pecking and took flight, and moments later Bettina's old mule broke through the brush. Nanny Fay stood, cringing at the catch in her back, and hobbled to the porch railing. She put on a smile, even though Bettina wore her usual frown.

"Mornin'. Ain't it a purty day?" She greeted Bettina like she always did, knowing full well she might not even get a grunt in answer.

Bettina dug in her pouch and pulled out a pair of books. She shoved them at Nanny Fay.

Nanny Fay held out the jar of jam. "Trade you."

Bettina pulled the books back. "Huh?"

Nanny Fay bounced the jar. "Blueberry jam. I figure since you bring me books as reg'lar as clockwork, I should maybe give you a little somethin'. As a thank-you."

Bettina stared at the jar the way little children stared at a Christmas pudding. "I gotta bring you books. It's my job."

"Oh, I know." Nanny Fay wasn't gonna get rattled. She'd got so used to people's scowls and grumbles she didn't hardly see or hear 'em anymore. Besides, wasn't it fine that the girl was actually talking? "But that don't mean I ain't grateful. Here. You have some o' that on your breakfast biscuits." She leaned over the railing and dropped the jar into the pouch draped over the mule's neck, then took the books. "Lemme get you the ones you're s'posed to take back." She shuffled to the bench, grabbed the books, and returned to the railing. "Here you go."

Bettina took them. The button on her cuff popped loose, and her sleeve slid up an inch or so. A circle of purple marks showed on the girl's wrist.

Nanny Fay got whisked backward in time so fast dizziness struck. She closed her eyes. Pictures flashed behind her eyelids. Bettina's wrist, then Rosie's arms. Bettina's wrist, Rosie's legs. Back and forth, back and forth. Bruises. So many bruises. She grabbed the railing and prayed for her head to clear. The images faded. Her balance returned.

She opened her eyes. Bettina was gone. Nanny Fay gripped her throat and moaned, "Oh, Rosie, your little gal . . ."

■ ■ ■ ■

Bettina

Who'd she think she was, giving her presents? Bettina urged Mule up the narrow passage, away from Boone's Holler. Away from Nanny Fay. If it'd been anything but blueberry jam in that jar, Bettina would've throwed it at the old witch lady. But she couldn't throw something made from blueberries. Maw'd liked blueberries best of all the wild fruits growing on the mountain.

She slid her hand inside the pack. Her fingers found the smooth jar and followed it up to the cloth. Pink-and-white-checked cloth. Maw'd wore a pink-and-white-checked dress to Sunday service pret' near all spring and summer long. But it disappeared before Maw died. Bettina never did figure out where it went, though she'd hunted for it more'n once. She'd thought she could maybe wear it. Maw always looked pretty as a rosebud in that dress, and Bettina'd look that pretty, too, wearing it.

Everybody in Boone's Holler said she was the spitting image of Maw. Same build. Same long eyelashes. Same wavy dirt-brown hair and widow's peak. Same freckles. She was proud to look like Maw. Proud to be able to see to the cooking and cleaning and washing so she'd be a good wife someday. If she put on Maw's dress, would Emmett think she was pretty as a rosebud? Would he see her as all growed up and ready to be his wife? She'd look for the dress again after Pap went to sleep tonight.

The Cissell cabin was across the creek, maybe another three hundred yards up the mountain, and already Bettina tasted the sweet apple cider Miz Cissell kept in a jug under the porch, where it stayed cool. "C'mon, Mule, hurry up." She tapped Mule with her heels and kept running her fingers over that soft piece of cloth tied on the jar of blueberry jam. When noontime come, she'd put some of that jam on the bread and butter she'd packed for her lunch and have herself a feast.

Blueberry jam and pink-and-white-checked cloth. How'd Nanny Fay know them were Maw's favorites? Bettina shivered. Pap'd say it was 'cause she was a witch. Bettina wouldn't tell Pap about her present. Nor nobody else. This would be her little secret. Well, hers and Nanny Fay's.

THIRTY-THREE

Addie

One done. It had taken the better part of the day, but she'd filled an entire scrapbook with carefully snipped out pictures of birds. Addie corked the pot of glue, set the glue brush in a cup of water on the windowsill, and stretched her arms over her head. Her muscles went tight, then quivery, and her entire frame shuddered. A sigh eased from her chest. What a good feeling. Both the physical relief of stretching and the satisfaction of completing the first official scrapbook for the Boone's Hollow library.

She turned sideways in the chair and caught Emmett watching her. Heat filled her face. He'd taken one of the empty scrapbooks and used it as a lap desk for his work, giving her the table for her project. He sat with his ankle on his opposite knee, balancing the scrapbook on his bent leg. Given his height and the size of the chair, he probably needed to stretch more than she had.

She stood. "Would you like to trade places for a while?"

"No, this arrangement actually works well for me. I can pull the chair close to the shelf and record an entire line of books without having to get up and down." He tapped his pen on the edge of the inventory page. "These books, Addie . . . I'm astounded by how many your mother and her friends collected. Especially in such a short amount of time. And for them to arrive the same day that so many of our books were destroyed." He swallowed. "Thank you for asking her to organize the book drive. It saved our jobs. I'm sure of it."

Addie wiped away a spot of glue with her finger, her head low. "It's the least I could do after —"

His foot hit the floor with a thud, and Addie jumped. "Didn't I tell you it isn't your fault?"

"Yes, but . . ." The way Bettina had glared that morning when she'd seen Addie sitting at the table was burned into her memory. "I can't shake the feeling that if I'd been more cautious around you, less friendly, then —"

"Look, Addie." He stood and plopped the scrapbook and pen on the chair seat, then ambled to the table. "I'm all for being respectful, for treating people the way we want to be treated. But there's a verse in Ephesians, something like 'Put off falsehood and speak truthfully to your neighbor, for we are all members of one body.' Does it do Bettina any good for us to pretend we don't like each other and let her continue to build a false relationship in her imagination? Isn't honesty a better response?"

Addie stared into his open, honest face. She liked Emmett. She'd liked him from the first moment she saw him at the bonfire. But how did he know? And what should she say now that she knew he liked her, too?

His gaze drifted past her to the pages drying on the table. He inched forward, scanning the pages by turn, a smile lifting the corners of his lips. "Say, these are really well done. They're as nice as any printed magazine pages."

If he was willing to switch to a more comfortable topic, she'd follow him. "Thank you. I kept thinking about the quilts Griselda Ann put together — balancing color and pattern. I think they came out pretty good, too, if you don't mind me bragging on myself a little bit."

He chuckled. "Brag away. You know, I really hope you'll be able to finish your degree. You'll make a fine teacher."

She frowned at him. "Teacher?"

He frowned, too. "Did I remember incorrectly? I thought you said you were enrolled in the College of Education at the university."

She couldn't believe he remembered that. "I was, but . . ." They were friends. He'd admitted he liked her. Could she trust him with her secret? "I don't really want to be a teacher."

He perched on the edge of the table and folded his arms, giving him a scholarly appearance. "Then why were you in the program?"

"Because it was the one that most closely prepared me for what I really want to do." A lot of people didn't think women could be good writers. Would Emmett hold that view? "I hope to be A. F. Penrose, a published author." The pen name honored her parents, but it didn't divulge her gender. She searched his face for signs of humor or derision.

"An author? That's . . . that's . . ." He laughed. "I don't know what to say. Except you'd be wonderful."

Her pulse skipped a beat. "You think so?"

"I do. When I read the story you brought in here, I was amazed at how you pulled me

458

in, as if I were the one living it instead of the character. You're an excellent writer, Addie. You should pursue it."

"Even though I'm a girl?"

"Bosh." He waved his hand as if shooing away her question. "What's that got to do with anything? Do you think when God created humankind, He made a list of special talents for males and another for females? Oh, there are things for which one gender or the other is probably better suited, such as men for hard physical labor or women for nurturing. I think He did that so there'd be a balance in the husband-wife relationship. But I can't imagine God would give you such a special gift and then say you can't use it just because you're a girl. That would be cruel."

No one, besides Mother and Daddy, had been so encouraging and understanding about her desire to write. Joy exploded in her chest and propelled her from her chair. She threw her arms around his neck in a hug of both gratitude and delight. "Thank you, Emmett!"

His arms closed around her, warm and snug, and then he abruptly released her. He cast an apologetic grimace at her. "I'd better finish the inventory list for the nonfiction books. Reports are due the twenty-fifth of each month, and the girls will be back from their routes soon, and . . ." He walked backward to the chair as he spoke, his hands flying around in nervous gestures.

Addie blinked back tears of embarrassment and regret. "I'm sorry. I didn't mean to offend you. I only wanted to thank you for showing such confidence in me. It won't happen again."

He reversed direction so quickly his soles skidded on the floor. He took her hands. "No, I'm sorry. I like you, Addie. More than I've ever liked a girl."

Her heart set up such a thrum it threatened to drown out his voice.

"But we work together. I'm . . . I'm your boss. Every class I took at the university advised against forming relationships in a workplace. It creates conflict within the working environment and can cause not only a breakdown of morale but even bitterness between coworkers." He sighed, letting his head flop back. "I wish I hadn't taken those courses."

She had the same wish. She forced a soft laugh. "I understand."

He lowered his head and gazed earnestly into her upturned face. "Do you really? Because *I* don't want to offend *you*."

"I'm not offended."

His shoulders slumped. "I'm glad."

"But, Emmett, I think there's already bit-terness between coworkers."

He nodded, one slow bob of his head. "You and Bettina."

"Yes." She sighed. "If she's angry enough at me to come in here and destroy books, then morale has broken down completely."

Emmett released her hands and gently gripped her upper arms, leaning down slightly. "Addie, I'm not convinced Bettina tore this place apart."

She raised her eyebrows in surprise. If not Bettina, then whom? How many people were angry enough at her to sabotage the library? Did resentment toward Nanny Fay run so deeply they would demolish some-thing beneficial to the entire community? Emmett had told her ignorance, hatred, and jealousy were behind the destruction. But it felt personal. As if she herself had been at-tacked. It had to be Bettina. She started to tell him so.

"Addie? Emmett?"

Emmett let go of her so quickly she almost stumbled. She turned to the door. Nanny Fay stood just inside the doorway. She held a rumpled bundle of pink gingham in her hands. Anguish contorted her face.

Addie rushed to her. "Nanny Fay, what's

461

happened?" She gave the woman a quick head-to-toe examination and didn't spot signs of blood or trauma.

Nanny Fay held out the wadded-up cloth, her hands trembling. "I been huggin' this all day, prayin', thinkin', stewin', prayin' some more. An' I come to realize I can't carry it all myself. I need help. So here I am, comin' to you."

Emmett reached them in two long strides and took hold of Nanny Fay's elbow. He guided her to the table and eased her into the chair. He braced his hands on his knees and peered into her face, concern creasing his forehead. "What is it? If I can help, I will."

Tears winked in the old woman's faded blue eyes. She hugged the fabric to her chest. "It's about Bettina. We gotta get her out o' that house. 'Cause if we don't, someday Burke's gonna do her in."

Chills attacked Addie's frame. She skittered close and sat on the edge of the crate closest to the table. "You really think her father would hurt her?"

Nanny Fay nodded grimly. "I know he would." She snapped the wad of cloth and held it out, and it took the shape of a dress. The fabric bore rips, grass stains, and brownish smears.

Addie's stomach churned. "Is that blood?"

Another nod.

"Is it Bettina's dress?"

Emmett shook his head. "No. It belonged to Bettina's mother. I remember because my maw always complimented it — said it made her cheeks glow."

A sad smile tipped up the corners of Nanny Fay's lips. "Your maw was right. This dress . . . it was Rosie's favorite. She come to me late one night, a-staggerin', hardly able to stay on her feet. She was wearin' this dress, an' she was bruised from head to toe." Her chin quivered, and tears rolled. She hugged the dress to her chest. "Burke had come home late, drunk as a skunk, an' beat her near senseless 'cause supper'd grown cold."

Nanny Fay's entire frame trembled, and Addie slipped her arm around her shoulders. Nanny Fay leaned in, tipping her head to Addie's temple. "I had her strip down so I could tend to her bruises. Whilst I was seein' to her, my door busted open an' Burke come in, ravin' like a madman. He . . . he knocked me down an' threw her over his shoulder like she was nothin' more'n a sack o' taters. Stormed out with her. I didn't see her after that. But I won't never forget how she was shiverin', part

463

from shock, an' part, I think, 'cause he'd hurt things inside o' her."

Addie gasped.

"I ain't no real doctor, as folks in these parts are all-fired quick to point out, so I can't say for sure. But it only makes sense to me. After that night, folks talked about a hurtin' in her gut that wouldn't go away. Then she sank into a sleepful state, an' she died. Burke blamed me, but . . ." Tears rolled down the old woman's face. "She was such a little gal. Hardly bigger'n a child. An' he beat her with his fists." She sat up and wiped her eyes, sniffing hard. "Now he's doin' it to Bettina."

Emmett drew back. "How do you know?"

"I seen the bruises on her wrists. Seen 'em this mornin' when she brung me my books. They're fresh, as bold purple as —" Her face crumpled, and she began to sob. "As ripe blueberries."

Addie embraced Nanny Fay. Emmett jolted to his feet and paced the length of the library, one fist pressed to his chin. Addie held her friend and followed Emmett with her eyes. Fury pulsated from him, and she didn't blame him. A man who abused his wife and child deserved to be beaten until his body was covered in bold purple bruises. Until his insides caused him pain.

"Emmett, what are you going to do?"

He came to a stop so quickly it appeared he'd collided with a wall. He stood for several seconds, tense as a taut spring, then lowered his hand. A harsh laugh burst from his throat. "To think the people in this town watch Nanny Fay, a harmless elderly woman, and fear what she'll do, but they turn a blind eye to an able-bodied man who batters his family. I can't fathom a father —" He shook his head hard, as if scattering his thoughts. He muttered, almost to himself, "What is wrong with him?"

Addie wanted to comfort him, but she didn't want to leave Nanny Fay without support. The woman continued to cry in whimpering moans and hiccups. Suddenly Bettina's behavior — her resentment, her desire to win Emmett's favor, her jealousy — made sense. Addie rubbed Nanny Fay's quivering back and held Emmett's gaze. "I don't know what's wrong with him or the people in this community, but I think we now know what's wrong with Bettina. And I think we should —"

"Why're you talkin' about me?" Bettina's angry voice blasted from the doorway. She pointed at Nanny Fay. "What's that ol' witch woman doin' here?" Her face drained of color, and her finger took aim at the

465

crumpled gingham. "An' why's she got my maw's dress?"

Emmett took a step toward her. "Bettina, we know what your pap's been doing."

The girl's hazel eyes narrowed to resentment-filled slits. "W-w-what're you talkin' about?"

Emmett stretched his hand to her and gently lifted her cuff. "This."

Bettina thrust her hand behind her back. "I did that myself. Did it choppin' wood."

"Bettina . . ." Emmett spoke so gently that tears stung Addie's eyes. "Those aren't bruises from chopping wood. They're from a hand. From your father's hand. Am I right?"

She balled her fists and glowered at Emmett. "You think I'm stupid enough to let a man put his hands on me? If you think that, you're the stupid one. You, an' you, an' you!" She pointed at each of them by turn, her motions jerky and uncontrolled. She flung the book pack onto the library floor and spun toward the doorway. "An' that blueberry jam tasted like dirt!"

"Bettina!"

Emmett and Addie called her name at the same time, but she raced out of the library, flung herself on Mule's back, and escaped up the street.

THIRTY-FOUR

Bettina

Bettina rode Mule hard. Up the road past the church, past the schoolhouse, all the way through Tuckett's Pass and up where backwood folks hiding from revenuers lived. She would've gone farther, except Mule's sides were heaving and froth bubbled out of his mouth. She might kill him if she kept going, and then what would she do? She stopped and slid from his back.

"C'mon, Mule." She led him into the trees a ways. Little Muddy Creek was here somewhere. Dumb name for a creek. The water was clear as glass. She'd let him get a drink and clean the froth off his nose. The water up high was cold year-round. It'd cool him down fast, and if she dipped her wrists, it'd take some of the pain out. But no creek, no matter how cold, could take the pain out of her heart.

"They know, Mule. They know my pap

467

hates me." She could say it out loud to Mule. He wouldn't tell nobody. Wouldn't laugh. Or, worse, look at her all pitying like. She couldn't stand them looks she got after Maw died, everybody petting her hair and rubbing her shoulder and saying things like, "Poor Bettina. What's she gonna do now that she ain't got no maw?" Wasn't nothing worse than being pitied. She missed Maw. Missed her more'n she ever knew a body could miss someone. But all the pitying in the world wouldn't bring her back. If something didn't do no good, why do it?

Mule bobbed his head up and down and snorted. She took a few more steps, and the trickle of water running over stones met her ears. Mule must've smelled it. She pushed through a little more brush, and there was Little Muddy Creek. Mule plunged his nose in, and she crouched next to the water and watched it flow.

Her muscles unpinched, and she let out a long, slow breath. Listening to the water's music, smelling the clean air and pine and honeysuckle, being there with Mule in the fading light soothed her. Maybe she'd stay up here tonight. Maybe she'd stay up here forever. Not like anybody really cared about her anyway. Pap said she was nothin' more'n a burr under his saddle. Only reason he kept her around was for chores and the money she brought in. She'd been planning on moving out soon as she married Emmett, so —

She lurched upright. Emmett . . . He was nice as nice could be in the library, but only 'cause he felt sorry for her. He hadn't never looked at her that way before. She wouldn't be able to look him in the eyes ever again after seeing his pity. Even if they did get married now, she'd always wonder if he married her out of feeling sorry for her.

Mule shook his head, spraying water over her, then stuck his wet nose against her neck. She stood and curled her arms around his spotted neck. "We ain't goin' back, Mule. For sure not tonight. We'll decide tomorrow if it'll be forever."

Emmett

Emmett drummed his fingers on Burke Webber's dinner table and bounced his knee. The hard dirt under his foot made an annoying grating sound. But he couldn't sit still. Neither could Maw. She was flicking the corners of the pages she'd found in Bettina's room, reading the words. Both of them were as twitchy as a starved man hunting grouse. But they'd sit here until Bettina got home. Even if Burke arrived first.

Emmett watched Maw's face while she read. Despite the nervous *flick-flick-flick,* she was caught up. The same way he'd been when he read the same pages. He'd been uneasy about Maw snooping in Bettina's personal space, but she insisted she had to, saying, "If she packed up an' then skedaddled, we need to not sit an' wait. We need to go searchin' for her." She was right, so he stopped arguing. Then he was glad she went in, because she found Addie's story and what looked like a letter Addie had written to a friend. Maw tucked the letter in her pocket — "That's private an' we shouldn't look at it" — but she was enjoying the story.

He couldn't wait to tell Addie the lost had been found. And the fact that Bettina had taken it made him wonder if she had been the one to wreak havoc in the library. He'd rather it was her than the other person he suspected. Either way, he wouldn't press charges like he'd vowed to do in the heat of anger. But it'd be easier on his heart if Bettina had done it in a jealous fit than if it'd been done by another to personally hurt him.

Maw's thumb stilled. She looked up. "What time is it?"

He checked his timepiece. "Half past six."

"The miners' wagon should be pullin' up

to Belcher's about now." She set the story aside. "Reckon we'll be confrontin' Burke before we see Bettina. Maybe that's best." She shook her head, and tears made her blue eyes brighten. "How could I not've known how Burke was hurtin' her? Rosie was my best friend. I knew how her maw whaled on her, an' I knew Burke spoke rough. Heard him myself an' didn't like her puttin' up with such. I told Rosie so, too." Horror flooded her expression. "You reckon that's why she never told me he was doin' more'n rough talk? 'Cause she thought I blamed her?"

Emmett reached across the table and placed his hands over Maw's. "I reckon she didn't tell you for the same reason Bettina never told anybody. She felt shameful about it and didn't want anyone to know." He closed his eyes for a moment, searching his memory, then looked his mother in the eyes. "In my psychology class, the professor told us that people often don't admit they're being abused because they think they caused it somehow by what they did or didn't do. They don't want others, especially others they admire, to know how worthless they are."

Maw jerked her hands free. "Rosie wasn't worthless! An' neither is Bettina."

He rounded the table and knelt next to Maw. "Of course not. No one's worthless in God's eyes." Not even Burke Webber. The truth drew him up short. He struggled to regain his train of thought. "But when someone treats you bad over and over, you start feeling worthless. That's probably what happened to Rosie and Bettina. They didn't tell you not because they don't trust you but because they admire you and want you to admire them."

Maw gazed into his eyes for several seconds, her brows pulled low and her lips pressed into a thin line. Then she shook her head and sighed. A deep, regretful sigh. "I wish she'd told me, Emmett. Maybe she'd be alive today if she'd just told."

Emmett rose and placed his hand on his mother's shoulder. "We can't do anything more for Rosie, but we can help Bettina. And we will by —"

"Gal, why don't I smell supper cookin'?" The roar came from outside the cabin, and then Burke stormed in. He slid to a stop and aimed his angry glare at Emmett. "What're you doin' in here? Did Bettina let you in?" He tossed his scowl left and right. "Bettina? Where are you, gal? You know better'n to have folks in when I ain't home."

Maw stood. "Burke, stop your bellowin'.

Bettina ain't here. We let ourselves in. The door wasn't locked."

His lips curled into a derisive snarl. "Locked or not, you wasn't invited. That's trespassin'."

"Maybe it is, but least we didn't hurt nobody by comin' in."

Burke growled under his breath.

Emmett had brought Maw for Bettina's sake, but he hadn't expected her to confront Burke. Her love for Rosie and Bettina emboldened her. But she was stoking Burke's fury fire. He stepped between them. "Burke, we're here about Bettina."

He stomped to the standing cupboard in the corner and pawed through it. "She fall off the mule an' hurt herself?"

His lack of concern stirred Emmett's compassion for Bettina and raised his ire at the man. He prayed for calm and patience before answering. "No, she didn't hurt herself. But you've been hurting her."

Burke stopped all movement. Then he slowly turned and sent a menacing glare at Emmett. "What's she been tellin' you?"

"She hasn't said a word. But her bruises speak for themselves."

Burke snorted a laugh. "Oh, law, that?" He turned his attention to the cupboard and pulled out a can. He ambled toward the

473

stove. "Girl's as clumsy as a newborn colt. Always bumpin' into things or droppin' somethin'." He clanked the can onto the iron stove. He dug in his pocket, withdrew a pocketknife, and pried at the can's lid. "I tell you what, though. I might take a stick to her when she gets in tonight. She knows she's s'posed to come on home an' get supper cookin'. She's always been dim witted, but since you took over at the lib'ary, Emmett, she's been downright addlebrained. Needs a good hidin' to knock some sense into her."

Maw pushed Emmett aside. "Is that why you beat Rosie? To knock sense into her?"

He spun toward them, the little knife gripped in his fist. "What happens between a man an' his woman is just that — between them. So you best hush your talk, Damaris."

The knife blade shining in the lamplight gave Emmett chills. He stepped in front of Maw again, but she scuttled around him. Normally as docile and delicate as a hummingbird, now she puffed up like a rooster protecting the henhouse. "Why'd you do it, Burke? Why'd you raise your fists to her? She was such a gentle soul. She didn't deserve what you give her."

Burke threw the knife on the stove, then pointed at Maw. "I ain't gonna put up with no sass in my own home. 'Specially not from some woman who don't know her place." He aimed his coal-blackened finger at Emmett. "Take your maw out o' here before I forget myself. An' tell my moony-eyed, lame-brained excuse for a daughter to get herself home. There's chores waitin'."

"I can't do that, Burke."

The man scrunched his face into a disbelieving scowl. "You forget you're speakin' to one o' your elders, boy? Your pap taught you better'n that."

"Yes, sir, he did." Emmett picked up Addie's story from the table and curled it into a tube. "But I can't send Bettina because I don't know where she is. That's why Maw and I came here — to check on her. And I'll be honest, even if I knew where she was, I wouldn't send her here. Not after knowing that you've been mistreating her."

Burke braced his hand on the stove and leaned, his head tipping at a sharp angle. "I knew Bettina was sweet on you, but I sure never expected you to go soft over her, you bein' a college boy an' all. That girl, she's a looker, same as her maw. I'll give 'er that. But she's dumb as a stick." He straightened and turned his back to them. Knife in hand, he dug at the can's lid. "I'm done talkin'. Go home."

Emmett curled his hand around Maw's elbow and gave her a little tug toward the door, but she dug in her heels.

"What about Bettina?" Maw quivered from head to toe, and her face glowed bright red. "Don't you care at all about where she's at right now? How she's feelin'?"

Burke snatched a small pot from a shelf above the stove and emptied the can's contents into it. "What I'm carin' about right now is gettin' my belly filled after a long day o' work. You might oughta go see to your husband's supper, Damaris."

Maw shot out the door, and Emmett followed. She stomped over the dirt path leading away from the cabin, her lips set tight and her eyes sparking fury. Emmett had never seen his mother so riled, and even though the Bible advised using a soft answer to turn away wrath, he didn't know what to say, so he said nothing. They got as far as the little footbridge across Boone's Creek, and she whirled to face him. "You ain't goin' home. Nor to the lib'ary."

"You want me to try to find Bettina?"

"No. She knows this mountain an' likely has a spot she's gone to before to get away from . . . from . . ." She waved her hand in the direction of the Webber cabin. "She'll come down when she's good an' ready. But

476

when she comes, she'll go home. An' some-body needs to waylay her an' keep her from goin' in. Burke's all wound up. He'll likely soothe himself with some o' his homemade brew when he's done eatin'. If you think Burke's mean when he's sober, you don't wanna see him drunk. If he really gave Rosie a mortal wound with his fists, he might do the same to Bettina. We can't risk it."

Dusk would fall soon. The time when fireflies flickered in the bushes and cicadas started singing. Summer sights and sounds that had always meant good times to Emmett. But this conversation, the reason for it, tainted the promise of a sweet summer evening. "All right, Maw. I'll stay right here and watch for her."

"Good. I'll go by the lib'ary, tell Addie an' Nanny Fay that Bettina's took off somewhere an' they should go on home. Then I need to get myself home an' feed your paw an' Dusty. But soon as we're done eatin', I'll send your paw to keep watch with you. I'll send some supper with him, too, so you don't go hungry."

He wasn't hungry at all. His stomach held too much dread. But he wouldn't turn down Maw's cooking. "Thanks, Maw."

She wrapped him in a hug. "Thank you, Son, for carin' enough to help Bettina. I

477

know she's been a real trial to you, but she's only wantin' to be loved. We gotta feel sorry for her instead o' bein' upset with her." She squeezed his middle, pressing her cheek against his chest. "An' I gotta remind myself that vengeance is God's, 'cause — oh, dear Lord, forgive me — I'm fightin' a terrible urge to find a chunk o' wood an' take aim at Burke Webber's fool head."

THIRTY-FIVE

High on Black Mountain
Bettina

Mule snuffled the back of Bettina's neck and woke her. She rolled over and squinted at him. The trees blocked most of the moonlight, but his white hide glowed like a ghost in the shadows. She rubbed his nose. "You're all right. Least you got supper."

He'd chomped tender grass growing by the creek while she searched for wild onions. But she hadn't found any. Her belly ached from emptiness. She should've brought that jar of blueberry jam Nanny Fay'd gave her. Her mouth watered, remembering its sweetness. Had it broke when she threw her pack? It'd be all over the books if it did. She didn't know if she was more sorry about losing the jam or the books. And she didn't know why she even cared about the books.

She gave Mule's prickly nose another rub. "Quiet now. Go to sleep."

But Mule unfolded his legs and stood, shaking his head and snorting. Bettina stood, too. Mule was smart. If he was nervous, something was prowling. What was hiding in the shadows? A cougar? Maybe a bear? Knowing that wild critters came out to drink at night, she'd took Mule far away from the creek before they bedded down. But maybe she hadn't gone far enough. Or maybe she'd put them right close to a den. Not like she could see, with it being so dark after sundown. Her heart took up such a pounding she thought it might come right on out of her chest. She curled her arms around Mule's neck and held tight, needing the comfort his warm, strong form provided.

Twigs snapped nearby, and men's voices muttered.

"Oh, lawsy, Mule, somebody's out there," she whispered into Mule's pointed ear. She'd for sure picked the wrong place to rest. She didn't smell no sour mash, and she sure knew what it smelled like from visiting Pap's still, but maybe the pine trees covered it up. That's why Pap's was in the high reaches of Black Mountain — he said the strong smell from pine trees could hide most anything.

Would the trees hide Mule's and her smells? Because those voices were getting louder. Closer. Probably moonshiners, and they didn't take to folks snooping around their stills. She and Mule might get shot and buried, and nobody'd ever know what happened to them. She whispered to Mule, "Least if we get killed, I'll get to see Maw again."

That is if God let her come through heaven's gates. She shivered. She pawed until she found Mule's trailing reins. She took hold and pulled. "C'mon, we gotta —"

"Who's there?"

She'd whispered too loud. Now they were coming. Feet crushed dried leaves. More twigs snapped, louder this time. It was dark enough for her to hide, but how to hide Mule? His white coat would stick out no matter where she took him. She danced in place, and Mule made snuffly noises, and before she could find the courage to leave him and run, two men burst through the bushes and pointed rifles at her.

Bettina screamed.

Boone's Hollow
Nanny Fay

Nanny Fay knelt by her bed. Her knees ached. Her back throbbed. Tiredness weighed on her like a load of stove wood. But she wouldn't sleep until she'd found

481

peace. With her elbows braced on the edge of the mattress and her chin on her knuckles, she held herself upright.

"Dear Lord, keep her safe wherever she is." She'd asked at least a dozen times already, but the widow in the Bible asked the judge again and again for justice until he gave it. The judge didn't care one little bit about God, and still he gave in to the widow's request. God, who was very good, wouldn't ignore one of His own. "Please, Father, keep her safe even though she was foolhardy to run off that way. She run away 'cause nobody cares about her now that Rosie's gone. Except You."

And you.

Nanny Fay shook her head and scowled. She was so sleepy her brain was talking to her.

"But I don't know for sure she knows You."

She knows you.

"She goes to church every Sunday, same as Rosie did. But there's a heap o' people sittin' in church pews week after week who don't know You like they oughta. 'Cause they ain't took the time to know Your Son." Her throat went tight, and her nose stung. She pushed the words out even though they warbled. "Oh, dear Lord, she needs to know

482

You. She needs to understand how much You love her. Somehow she's gotta figure out she don't need to go chasin' after Emmett or any other fella to find love. All she's gotta do is turn to Jesus, an' then she'll be Yours an' she'll have all the love she needs."

So tell her.

Nanny Fay's eyes popped open. Why was something inside her head interrupting her prayers? "Tell her? She ain't gonna listen to me."

Then show her.

Nanny Fay's chin slipped off her knuckles and nearly hit the mattress. Her body sagged, but not all from tiredness. The peace she'd been waiting for surged from her middle outward like water seeping through a crack and filled every part of her being. She struggled to her feet. Her stiff muscles groaned, but a smile pulled at her lips. "Yes. Yes. That's what I'll do. I'll show her."

Emmett

"Ain't them crickets ever gonna shut up?"

Emmett jolted. Had he drifted off? He must have. He inwardly berated himself. How would he know when Bettina returned if he couldn't stay awake and listen for her?

He shifted, sitting a little straighter, then

leaned against the rough tree trunk again. The clouds that had been shrouding the moon earlier must have moved on, because a slight amount of light touched Paw's aggravated face. "I dunno. They're noisy, all right."

Paw grunted. "Never have liked crickets. Just chirp, chirp, chirp . . . Good for nothin'. Except fish bait. Catfish'll snatch 'em right up." He nudged Emmett with his elbow. "You remember goin' after catfish one summer when you was a littler feller? Before Dusty was born. You might've been about how old Dusty is now. We went with your Grandpappy McCallister."

Emmett vaguely recalled a fishing trip with Paw and his maw's father before the old man died. "I think so." He forced his tired mind to think back. "Yeah. Yeah, I recall you and Grandpaw gave me a tin can and told me to hunt up crickets. But I don't remember catching any."

"You didn't. 'Cause you didn't look for 'em." Paw laughed, but the sound held a hard edge. "Him an' me found a good spot to drop our lines, got our poles ready, an' waited. Waited some more. Finally he says, 'Best go find him. Prob'ly gonna be like Little Boy Blue sleepin' somewheres.' I went lookin' for you. An' I found you, but you weren't sleepin'."

Suddenly Emmett remembered. Mr. Halcomb had given him a copy of *The Story of Doctor Dolittle* as a prize for winning the end-of-the-year spelling bee. He'd found a comfortable spot on the creek bank to read, and then Paw had come along. Paw hadn't said a word. But he hadn't needed to. The disappointment on his face said it all.

"That's when I knew for sure, you an' me, we was differ'nt." The dry, sad laugh rumbled again. "Ain't no way I'da been caught readin' a book when I could be fishin' or huntin' or doin' anything else outdoors when I was a youngster."

His father's disappointment — his disapproval — stung as much now as it had then. Emmett stared across the deep shadows and forced his tight vocal cords to speak. "I'm sorry, Paw."

The sliver of moonlight disappeared behind another cloud passing over.

"Ain't your fault, I reckon." Paw's voice sounded raspy, too, like maybe he was having a hard time making his words come out. "Your maw's always held a fondness for books an' readin'. She read stories to you before you were out o' the cradle. Reckon them stories reached inside you someplace an' took hold."

485

He smacked his palms together several times, and the crickets fell silent. For a few seconds. Then one started chirping, another joined in, and pretty soon the chorus filled the night again.

Paw sighed. "Fool crickets. Guess we had them few days, though, didn't we?"

Emmett didn't follow. "Few days?"

"Workin' the mine . . ."

Ah. Yes. Emmett hung his head. "Those were good days, Paw. I don't regret them."

"They was awful short."

Emmett swallowed. There was something he'd pondered. Something he needed to know but was afraid to know. He didn't want to see his father's expression when he asked. If hurt showed in Paw's eyes, he'd never forgive himself. But the cover of darkness gave him a chance to ask. "Is that why you tore up the books in the library?"

Paw's rump scooting on the dried leaves sounded loud. Loud enough to still the crickets for a few seconds. "How'd you know?" Paw's warm breath, scented with the corned beef hash they'd eaten for supper, hit Emmett's cheek.

Misery twined through his gut. "I didn't. Not for sure. But I got to thinking. About how much it pleased you to have me working at the mine with you. About how much

486

it upset you when I took the library job. And then Maw said you'd gone traipsing the day it happened, and I wondered if . . ." He swallowed again. "Well, I wondered."

Paw scooted some more, and his shoulder bumped Emmett. "I didn't go there to tear things up. Went to talk to you. To ask if you might change your mind. 'Cause you're right, I liked havin' you at the mine with me. Seemed like there wasn't nothin' else we had in common, but at least we had that, an' then it was gone. But you wasn't there, an' I got to lookin' at those books, an' all o' sudden it felt like they was what had kept us apart all these years. I reckon I took out my mad on them." The cloud uncovered the moon, and Emmett got a peek at his father's remorseful expression. "I'm sorry. It was a fool thing to do. Afterward, I wished I could take it back. But there wasn't no fixin' it."

Emmett put his hand over Paw's. "You fixed it right now, Paw, by telling me." It would ease Addie's mind to know she wasn't the target. "I like books and book learning. I always have, and I likely always will. It's a part of who God made me to be. I *like* books . . . but I *love* you. You're my father. Just because we aren't alike in every way doesn't mean we can't do things together. Like fishing."

487

He lifted Paw's hand and squeezed it. "In fact, since the crickets are bothering us so much, maybe I can catch about half that choir and early some morning you, Dusty, and me can go to Boone's Creek and catch us a catfish breakfast."

Paw chuckled. "That sounds good, Emmett. I'd —"

The crickets hushed.

Paw yanked his hand free and sat up. "There's a horse comin'."

Emmett heard it, too. But it sounded like more than one. He pushed himself to his feet, and Paw stood beside him. He made out three riders, Bettina on her white mule between the other two. He waited until they were within a few feet and then called, "Bettina, are you all right?"

All three animals stopped. Rifles hissed from scabbards, the sound threatening. Bettina's form leaned forward, as if she was trying to find him. "Emmett? Is that you?" Her voice quavered and had a nasal tone. She'd been crying.

"Yeah, it's me and my paw."

"Whoever's there, come out where we can see you."

The authoritative voice didn't belong to anyone Emmett knew. He and Paw moved out from under the tree. Emmett went to

Mule's side. He squinted up at the other riders. Both men, both wearing Stetson-type hats. They held their rifles with the barrels pointed skyward. "My name's Emmett Tharp. Over there's my father, Emil. Who're you?"

"They're revenuers." Bettina spat the title.

"We found this girl up on the mountain." The man who'd ordered Emmett and Paw to make themselves seen spoke. "You know her?"

"Her name's Bettina Webber," Paw answered. "Her an' her pap live in the cabin on the other side o' the creek behind me."

Bettina clamped her hand on Emmett's shoulder. "They found me sleepin', an' they wouldn't lemme be. Said I must be a boot-legger hidin' out up there."

"Bootlegger?" Paw snorted and came up close. "I've known Bettina her whole life. She ain't no bootlegger. She's a gal who knows the mountain, that's all. Ain't no crime in spendin' a summer night out under the moon, is there?"

The second fellow braced his elbow on his knee and scowled at Paw. "What're you two fellers doin' out here in the middle o' the night? You sure you ain't runnin' moon-shine?"

Paw laughed as if someone had told a

joke. "*Pffft.* We're huntin' crickets." He slid his hands into his pockets and rocked on his boot heels. "Me an' my son plan to do some fishin'. Mighty fine catfish in this creek, an' they like crickets more'n any other bait. Before you come along, we had a good bead on 'em, but now they've quit singin'." He shrugged. "Reckon we'll head home."

Emmett took hold of Mule's reins. "I'll escort Bettina to her cabin. Since she hasn't done anything worth being taken in for."

The pair looked at each other for several seconds. Then the one who'd done most of the talking slid his rifle into its scabbard. "All right. She can go. But we'll be askin' about you when we get to the sheriff's office in Lynch. An' we'll be back if your names show up on any lists."

Paw grinned. "Only place you'll find both o' us listed is on the membership roster for the low Baptist church."

The two lawmen turned their horses, and the animals carried them into the trees. As soon as they'd disappeared from sight, Bettina slid off Mule's back and fell against Emmett. She gripped handfuls of his shirt and buried her face against his front.

He gave her shoulders a few awkward pats. "Reckon you've had quite a scare."

She nodded without pulling loose. "I'm still scared. Scared to go home. Pap . . . he's gonna be all-fired mad."

Emmett believed her. "Don't worry. You're going to my folks' place. My paw'll take you to my maw, and she'll see to you tonight."

Bettina lifted her face and gazed at him. "She will?"

Emmett transferred her to Paw. "We'll decide tomorrow where you'll go from there. But you won't be going back to your pap. We won't let him hurt you again, Bettina. I promise you that."

Paw helped Bettina onto Mule's back and led the animal to the road. Bettina clung to the mule's neck and sent Emmett a wobbly smile of appreciation over her shoulder.

He waited until Paw and Bettina disappeared around the bend, and then he hurried in the direction the revenuers had taken. Bettina hadn't done anything that warranted being arrested, but her pap sure had. The lawmen probably wouldn't care about Burke Webber using his fists on his wife and daughter, but they'd be interested in the still up the mountain. He'd break the Don't Ask, Don't Tell code of the hills' folk by telling, but keeping Bettina safe was more important than keeping the code.

THIRTY-SIX

Addie

Addie bit the inside of her lip and tried to
rein in her active imagination as she walked
to the library Tuesday morning. Nanny Fay
walked alongside her, countenance serene,
as if she didn't have a worry in the world.
Addie wished she could set aside her worries, but after yesterday afternoon's dramatic
end — wouldn't Felicity enjoy hearing
about it? — she wasn't sure what to expect
once she got to the library.

She couldn't forget Bettina's stricken
expression as she raced out the door. And
she couldn't fathom a father beating his
child. But she couldn't fathom parents trad-
ing their child to a strange man for gunpow-
der, either. Why did some children suffer
so? She didn't know, but these revelations
increased her admiration for Penrose and
Fern Cowherd, and she would do her best
to convey her feelings when she spoke to

her parents next.

They reached the little slope leading to the road, and Addie gestured for Nanny Fay to precede her. Nanny Fay moved sideways, using the tree roots extending from the eroded dirt as steps, then stopped at the edge of the street. She pointed. "Lib'ary door's propped open. Emmett must be up an' ready for the day." She took off as if fired from a cannon.

Addie trotted to catch up, then offered her hand and helped Nanny Fay onto the stoop. Nanny Fay called "Yoo-hoo" as she crossed the threshold, and Addie followed her in.

Emmett rose from the table and met them near the door. He took Nanny Fay's hands. "This is a surprise. Are you going to help Addie with the scrapbooks today?"

Nanny Fay laughed softly. "I'm here to check on Bettina. Seein' her mama's dress gave her such a shock. I owe her an apology, an' I aim to give it."

Addie had worn her overalls in case Emmett needed her to take Bettina's route. His mention of scrapbooks answered that question. Another question begged an answer, though. "So she's back?"

He nodded. "Showed up somewhere around two this morning."

Nanny Fay's frame gave a little shudder. "Is she with Burke?"

"No." Emmett glanced at Addie over the old woman's snow-white head. "She's at my folks' place. And as for Burke . . . he's gone."

Addie drew back. Emmett had been so angry when he left the library. Her imagination conjured possibilities again. "Gone . . . for good?"

"I don't know." Emmett released Nanny Fay's hands and crossed to the table. "Some revenuers brought Bettina down from the mountain, and then they went to Burke's cabin. But he wasn't there. Maw and I saw him at suppertime, and Paw and I weren't twenty yards from his cabin door for hours afterward, and we never saw him leave. He must have sneaked out and gone up the mountain. I was at the wagon this morning with Paw when the miners left, and Burke wasn't on it. I don't know where he is."

Emmett had met the miners' wagon? Concern smote her. "Did you get any sleep at all last night?"

A soft smile graced his face. "I'll be fine. We Tharps are tough. Just ask my paw. And I reckon you'll sleep a little easier when I tell you I know who vandalized the library. It had nothing to do with you, Addie. Or you, Nanny Fay. It was directed at me, but

494

we've got it all worked out and it won't happen again." He turned his back to them and sorted through a stack of papers on the table.

Addie wanted to ask more, but something in his expression as he'd talked — a blend of pain and relief — held her tongue. Maybe later, if they had a moment alone, she'd dig for more information.

"And there's this." He turned and held up several pages the way a warrior held a shield.

She gasped and lunged for them. "My story! Oh, Emmett, you got it back!"

He grinned. "Maw found it."

Addie scanned the lines of penciled words, her heart dancing in her chest. "Oh, it's like being reunited with a friend. Please thank her for me."

"I will." Emmett sat on the edge of the table and folded his arms. "She also found what she thought was a letter you'd been writing, but she didn't read it. It's tucked at the back of the story."

Addie peeked. Sure enough, her letter to Felicity was there, too. How odd. The story and her letter had been misplaced in different locations, yet apparently, Damaris had found them in the same place. Curiosity built in her chest, and she turned to Emmett. "Where —" The query got lost beneath the tender gaze she found aimed at her. Another question formed. *Why are you looking at me the way I imagine Eagle looked at Nanny Fay on their wedding day?* But female chatter intruded, and the question remained unasked.

Glory and Alba burst in. Community gossip must not have traveled far yet, because neither said a word about Bettina. They said hello to Addie, skirted around Nanny Fay, grabbed their packs, and headed out the door. The third pack remained on the shelf. Addie stared at it, a fuzzy idea taking shape in the back of her mind.

She edged up to it and placed her hand on it. "Emmett, would you let me take Bettina's route today? I think I can find all the houses."

His brows dipped. "Are you sure that's a good idea? You know how . . . well . . ."

"I know. But I might have found a way to endear myself to the people of Boone's Hollow, and I'd like to at least give it a try." She lifted the pack and cradled it against her stomach. "Bettina likely needs a day to recover from her difficult night, so I want to go, if you'll let me."

He stood unmoving for several seconds, indecision flashing in his blue eyes, but then the sweet tenderness returned, and he nodded. "All right. Go ahead. Bettina's mule is tethered behind our cabin. If you take him, he'll help guide you. He could probably deliver the books on his own."

Both she and Nanny Fay laughed. Addie entrusted her story to Emmett's keeping, kissed Nanny Fay on the cheek, and scurried out the door.

Bettina

Bettina trudged down the hill toward town. When she'd seen Emmett last night, she'd been so relieved to be free of them two lawmen she hadn't thought about anything else. But now, knowing she'd have to face him in the light of day, her insides quivered. Miz Tharp had told her she didn't need to worry. Still, Bettina wasn't so sure. Miz Tharp was real nice, but she was a woman. Emmett was a man. He'd never acted anything like Pap, but she'd never acted so all-fired dumb with him before. She might've poked his angry spot. Would he holler?

The library door was open, but she didn't walk right in. She sneaked up next to the stoop and peeked around the corner. Then she whisked back out. Nanny Fay was in there with Emmett. The two of them were sitting at the table, talking soft and chummy.

497

Her palms started to sweat. Bad enough to face Emmett, but if he started hollering and Nanny Fay heard it all, Bettina'd run to the hills and never come back.

She pulled in a big breath of the morning air, smoothed her hands down her rumpled britches — she didn't have no clothes to put on except the ones she'd worn yesterday and slept in last night, since nobody'd let her go to her cabin — and gave her head a little toss. Somehow the gesture didn't perk her like it usually did. She puffed her cheeks and blew out the air, then zipped around the corner and pasted on a big smile. "Mornin'."

Emmett and Nanny Fay both turned. Both smiled. Emmett patted the back of Nanny Fay's hand and stood. He leaned down to the old lady. "I'll be praying." Then he headed for Bettina.

She instinctively shrank a little, but he stopped a couple or so feet away and slid his hands into his pockets.

"Addie took your route today, so you'll be cutting flower pictures from the magazines for a scrapbook. Before you get started, though, you've got a visitor." He nodded his head toward Nanny Fay. "I'll let you two talk." He went out the door.

Bettina gawked after him, her heart

pounding like a woodpecker driving its beak into a tree. Why'd he go and leave her all alone with the old witch lady? Was he getting even by letting Nanny Fay cast a spell on her? She stayed frozen in place, afraid to move in case something bad happened.

Nanny Fay screeched the second chair from the table, and Bettina near jumped out of her britches. "Come sit down, Bettina. I ain't gonna hurt you."

She sure talked soft. Nice. The way she did on her porch when Bettina brought her books. The way Damaris Tharp talked. The way Maw had talked. The remembrances urged Bettina across the floor, but she gave a wide berth and slid into the chair's seat from the opposite side. She pressed her palms together and jammed them between her knees, then hunched her shoulders, making herself as small as possible. She cleared her dry throat. "Whatcha want with me?"

Nanny Fay fixed her pale blue eyes on Bettina. They looked watery. Sad. "I wanna tell you I'm sorry."

Bettina jerked. She scrunched her eyebrows. "Sorry . . . for what?"

"For havin' your maw's dress in my hands when you come in yesterday. I reckon that gave you a real start."

It sure had. "Where'd you get it, anyway?"

"It got left at my cabin one night."

Bettina eyeballed the woman through squinty eyes. "That don't make sense. Why would my maw go to your cabin?"

Nanny Fay wiggled around in her chair and put her hands on the table. She laced her fingers together, and if she didn't for all the world look like she was fixing to pray. "Bettina, you might not wanna believe this, but me an' your maw was real good friends."

Bettina shot her eyebrows high. "What? Nuh-uh."

The old lady chuckled. "Oh, yes. She was just a little bitty thing, not even half your age now, when she come to my place the first time. She'd took a fall, skinned up her knees an' the heels of her hands. She was bleedin', an' she was upset an' scared."

Probably scared 'cause she'd come face to face with a witch.

"I cleaned her wounds an' put some soothin' oil on 'em, then bandaged her up. When I did, I noticed . . . I noticed . . ."

The water in her eyes started dripping down her face. Tears. Was she crying? Bettina gulped and hunched a little lower, but she couldn't take her eyes off Nanny Fay's tears.

"I noticed she had marks. Bruises, Bettina.

She had bruises."

Cold shivers attacked. Bettina's arms broke out with gooseflesh.

"Some old, some newer. Somebody'd hurt her again an' again. Like to broke my heart."

"Who done it?" Bettina didn't even realize she'd spoke aloud until she heard her voice.

Nanny Fay tipped her head to the side, like she was all of a sudden too weary to hold it up. "Honey, her mama did it. But I didn't find that out for a long time, 'cause Rosie — your maw — didn't want me to know." She sighed, looked down at her hands for a few seconds, then set her watery gaze on Bettina again. "But after that day, she kept a-turnin' up at my place. Not every day. Sometimes not for weeks at a time. But I'd be doin' my chores or sittin' on my porch readin' my Bible, an' there she'd be. For years she come visitin'. Even after she married your pap. Even after you was born she came."

Bettina shook her head. "She couldn'ta done that. Pap, he wouldn'ta let her."

Two more tears went rolling. And Bettina knew without a doubt this lady wasn't no witch. Everybody knew witches were too dried up to shed tears. Pap'd been wrong.

"You're right that your pap didn't want

her seein' me. That's why when you got big enough to put words together, she quit comin'. She was scared if you said where she'd been, there'd be trouble. But you got big enough to go to school. When you was at the schoolhouse an' your pap was at work, she'd come. Her an' me, we made blueberry jam together."

More goose bumps popped up, but these were a different kind. She whispered, "Blueberries . . ."

Nanny Fay unfolded her hands and touched Bettina's wrist with one finger. Hardly a touch at all, like a butterfly lighting, but it made Bettina go warm all over. "When I seen them bruises on you yesterday, I remembered your maw. I remembered her bruises. I remembered her mama wasn't the only one who hurt her. An' I knew I had to tell you somethin'."

Without even meaning to, Bettina leaned closer to the woman. "Tell me what?"

"You're loved, Bettina. You're loved by God, who wants to be your Father. You're loved by the Savior, who wants to forgive your sins. I know you're huntin' for love. I've seen you lookin' for it, tryin' to earn it from your pap, tryin' to coax it out o' Emmett. An', honey, you don't gotta keep earnin' or coaxin'. All you gotta do is look

502

to heaven an' ask Jesus for it, an' it'll be yours."

Bettina stared into Nanny Fay's teary eyes. Something glowed in there. Something Bettina hadn't seen in four years . . . love. Then she couldn't see very good anymore because her own eyes were all watery.

She sniffed and rubbed her nose. "Ain't no way God loves me. Not like He did Maw. Or He does Emmett or . . . or Addie." Or maybe even Nanny Fay. "I'm too stupid an' clumsy. I ain't worth —"

"You're worth everything to God, Bettina, an' don't you forget it. He wove you together in your maw's womb, an' in His eyes you are wonderfully made. You don't have to believe me. You can see it in the Bible your own self."

Bettina hung her head. She could look at the words, but they wouldn't say nothing to her. They never had.

A warm hand cupped her chin and lifted her face. Her gaze met Nanny Fay's tender smile. "Honey, I know you have the same trouble your maw did. Letters, they didn't make no sense to her. But I read those words to her when she was a little thing, an' she believed 'em. I want you to believe 'em, too."

Bettina swallowed. She nodded.

503

"An' somethin' else. Your maw's gone, but a part o' her is livin', an' if I can, I wanna help her little gal." Nanny Fay's hand dropped away. "If you'll let me."

Bettina wrapped her arms over her middle. Her stomach was jumping like a whole creek full of frogs was inside there. "Whadda you wanna do?"

"You shouldn't stay with somebody who hurts you. I got room in my cabin. I want you to move in with me. I ain't young anymore, an' I don't know how long I got 'til the Lord calls me home. I don't got children to pass my cabin an' plunder to, but I loved your maw — loved her like she was my own little gal — an' I'd like you to have those things when I'm put in the ground."

Bettina's mouth fell open. "Why would you go an' give me your cabin? I never did nothin' nice to you. Never really talked to you or . . . or . . ." She hung her head. If she'd known Nanny Fay had been so good to Maw, would she have treated the old lady better? Shame fell over her. No. She wouldn't have risked having the townsfolk look at her the way they looked at Nanny Fay. The way Pap looked at her, like she wasn't even worth seeing.

Nanny Fay put her hand on Bettina's arm.

"I want you to have it, Bettina."

Bettina hunched her shoulders so tight she thought she might close up like a pill bug. "I don't deserve you bein' nice to me."

"I don't deserve God bein' nice to me, but He is. He sent me your maw when I was needin' a child to love. He's give me lots o' grace. Least I can do is show grace to you."

Bettina lifted her head. "What's that mean — grace?"

"Grace is what God does best. It's showin' love an' forgiveness, even to folks who don't deserve it."

Bettina fiddled with a new tear in her sleeve. She probably got it last night when she was pushing Mule through brambles and trees. Her insides felt all tore up, too. But somehow, what Nanny Fay said made her feel like maybe some things inside were mending. Why hadn't she ever noticed how kindly Nanny Fay was? Most folks talked bad about her, wouldn't give her so much as a howdy-do, but if somebody was ailing and needed help, she gave 'em her cures. Nanny Fay gave grace. And she'd loved Maw.

Bettina looked up into Nanny Fay's eyes. "I wanna come stay with you."

Nanny Fay made a happy gasp, and she

505

pressed her palms to her heart. "Oh, honey . . ."

Maw used to call her honey. The name made Bettina go all warm inside. She wanted to help Nanny Fay feel that way, too. She'd said lots of mean things, but she could fix at least one of 'em.

"Nanny Fay? That blueberry jam didn't taste like dirt. It tasted like happiness."

THIRTY-SEVEN

Black Mountain
Addie

"Yoo-hoo in the house!" Addie held tight to Mule's reins and kept him at the edge of the woods. She'd learned not to enter people's yards unless they invited her. But a person was allowed to holler for attention. Mother wouldn't approve of a lady yelling across a yard, but things were different here in the hills.

The cabin door creaked open, and Mrs. Hinson stepped out. A teenage girl and two little boys came, too. The littlest boy climbed the railing and clung to the post cut from a sapling's trunk. He reminded Addie of a little monkey. Mrs. Hinson's hands went to her hips. She was a big-boned woman, and the pose gave her a fierce appearance.

"You again? Didn't I tell you not to bring no books here?"

"Yes, ma'am, you did. And I didn't bring

507

you books."

The little boy on the railing hopped down and stomped his foot. "Aw, Maw!"

She cupped the back of his head with her large hand and propelled him toward the door. "Git inside, Jamie. Mercy, Sam, you go in, too." The children obeyed, casting curious looks toward Addie over their shoulders. The woman glared at Addie again. "Then what you doin' here?"

"I came to ask a question."

Mrs. Hinson moved to the edge of the porch. "What question?"

Addie sent up a silent prayer of gratitude for the woman's interest. "May I come up a little closer so I don't have to yell?" She patted Mule's neck. "This old fellow doesn't much like me yelling in his ear."

The mule twitched his ears as if adding agreement.

Mrs. Hinson waved her hand. "C'mon up, then, but stay on your mule's back. I only got time for a short talk."

Addie grinned. "Yes, ma'am."

Boone's Hollow
Emmett

Emmett propped himself against the library doorjamb and watched for Mule. As soon as Addie got back, he'd drop into his cot

508

and sleep until tomorrow morning. Well, he'd sleep after he had a chance to talk with Addie. She needed a warning before she returned to Nanny Fay's.

Mule — being ridden and not led — came clopping from around the bend at the head of the road. Addie sat on his back, as regal as a princess on a tasseled litter. She must have spotted him, because she raised her hand high and waved, smiling big. The corners of his lips tugged upward of their own accord, and he stepped off the stoop and met the mule on the patch of ground outside the library.

Addie handed him the bulky pack. "Were you worried about me?"

"Not so much worried as curious." He flopped the pack over his shoulder. The thing was heavy. He patted it, offering her a sympathetic grimace. "Did you bring 'em all back?"

She laughed and slid to the ground. "Sort of. I brought back some of what you sent today, but I retrieved some that had been delivered previously."

He jolted in surprise. The motion unbalanced him, and he took a stumbling sideways step, gaping at her. "Some folks traded with you?"

She nodded, smiling so big her cheeks

were like rosy apples. "Mm-hmm!" She slipped her hand through his elbow and guided him to the library, jabbering as animatedly as Glory or Alba did with the other. "Mrs. Hinson swapped with me, which made her little Jamie turn cartwheels. Mrs. Woodward and Mrs. Petty wouldn't let me come in their yards, but Mrs. Retzel, Mrs. Grimes, and Mrs. Harp all traded with me *and* agreed to help me with my project."

Emmett emptied the pack onto the table. "Project? What project?"

Addie's eyes sparkled like a firefly's flash at midnight. "When you showed me the story I'd written about Nanny Fay this morning, I was so thrilled. Her life, her ability to overcome hardship, is such an inspiration." She paced back and forth, her hands stirring the air. "I started thinking . . . every life is a story. And the lives of these folks who live on Black Mountain are so unique, so rich in tradition. Someone should record the stories for future generations. It was almost as if God bopped me over the head and instructed me to use my love of writing to benefit the community."

He followed her with his gaze, listening not only to her words but also to her passion. Seeing not only her enthusiasm but also her heart.

510

She spun to face him and threw her arms wide. "Think of it, Emmett. The collected memories of the folks who call Boone's Hollow and Tuckett's Pass their home could be compiled in a book and kept here in the library. Friends, neighbors — enemies, even — could read one another's stories and learn from them. If they understand one another, won't they be more accepting? More compassionate? More . . ." Her arms fell to her sides. Her smile faded. She scuffed to a chair and plopped into it. "You think it's silly, don't you?"

Her question stole his ability to remain upright. He yanked out the second chair and sat. "No. No, Addie, not at all. Why would you say that?"

"You're staring at me as if I've suddenly broken out with green spots."

He laughed. "Green spots are good. Especially on that one dress you have. Or is it a green dress with white spots? I don't remember now. But you're really pretty in it." He must be overly tired to let something like that come out of his mouth. He grinned at the pink flush climbing her cheeks. He took her hand. "Addie, I don't think it's silly. I think it's a wonderful idea. I'd actually considered the benefit of hosting a weekly story night. At the time, I was bemoaning the absence of the story you'd written about Nanny Fay."

She tipped her head and examined him. "Really?"

"Really. I'd like to talk more about it with you, but right now I'm very sleepy and trying hard to stay awake."

She stood. "I should go, then. But may I start writing down people's stories?" She cringed. "I probably should have asked that before I brought it up to the folks on Bettina's route. I guess I got carried away."

He tugged her hand, and she sat again. "You said it seemed as if God gave you the idea. He's a much higher authority than I am, so you need to heed His directions."

She blew out a breath, and her smile returned. "Oh, good. Mrs. Retzel, especially, was excited to tell me about her family. That's why I was late coming in. She wanted to start right away."

"Then I think you should." He yawned and idly ran his thumb back and forth on her knuckles. "You know, Addie, this library program was started to give jobs to people who were having a hard time finding them because of the country's financial hardships."

She nodded. "I know."

"Which means . . ." He hoped he could

keep his thoughts together long enough to get them all said before he fell asleep. She was starting to look fuzzy around the edges. "When the economy improves, the program will end. This economic depression can't last forever."

"I should hope not!"

He held up his hand in a mute bid for her silence. "But there are a little over a hundred families living in and around Boone's Hollow and Tuckett's Pass. If you plan to write all their stories, you might need to stay here even after the library program closes."

She bit the corner of her lip and stared at him, her expression pensive.

"You might need to make Boone's Hollow your home. Or at least have a tie to it that brings you back again and again, until all the memories are collected." He put his elbow on the table and rested his chin in his hand. "Do you understand what I'm saying?" His eyelids felt as heavy as a filled book satchel. They refused to stay open. "What I'm saying, Addie, is . . ." He yawned. "Is . . ."

He slumped forward and laid his head on his bent arm. He'd finish telling her his thoughts later. When he could remember what they were.

Addie

Addie closed the library door behind her and caught hold of Mule's reins. "C'mon, big fellow, I'll take you with me to Nanny Fay's tonight. She'll feed you some supper, and she's got a nice little shed where you can sleep. It'll be comfortable for you." More comfortable than the library table, where Emmett was sleeping. She stifled a giggle. She'd never seen anyone drop off so quickly and in such an odd position. She hoped he didn't end up sleeping there all night or his neck might be permanently slumped.

The yellow glow behind Nanny Fay's cabin windows was a welcoming beacon. The front door stood open, and light painted a path across the porch floor. Aromas, both sweet and savory, carried on the evening breeze, and Addie's stomach growled.

She looped Mule's reins over the porch railing and gave the animal a rub on his forelock. "Sorry, but I'm going to get my supper first. Then I'll come see to you." She bounded up on the porch and into the house, calling Nanny Fay's name. But then she stopped and stared, hardly able to believe what she was seeing. Bettina Webber setting the dining table? "B-Bettina?"

The girl sent Addie a sheepish glance. "Hey, Addie."

Nanny Fay bustled from the stove, carrying a steaming pot of something. "Adelaide, didn't Emmett come with you?"

Confusion mounting, Addie crossed to the table and held on to the back of the chair she generally sat in. "No. Was he supposed to?"

Nanny Fay shook her head, tsk-tsking. "He was s'posed to tell you Bettina was here, an' he was s'posed to come have supper. I made rabbit stew an' a blueberry pie for dessert. He said he'd for sure come."

Bettina put spoons and forks next to the fourth plate, then scurried to the kitchen. Addie stared after her. "Emmett fell asleep at the table in the library." She might be sleeping, too, and dreaming this entire scene. After the way Bettina spoke about Nanny Fay, what was the girl doing here?

Nanny Fay set the pot in the middle of the table, then put her hand on Addie's arm. "He was s'posed to let you know Bettina's movin' in. I can see you're flummoxed by her bein' here." She spoke barely above a whisper, worry glimmering in her

515

eyes. "I'm thinkin' now I shoulda asked you first, seein' as how you're payin' for a room, but I couldn't let her go back to Burke. Not knowin' how he's treatin' her. But you don't gotta worry. She'll sleep with me."

Addie shook her head slowly, absorbing Nanny Fay's words. "No. No, she won't."

Bettina approached the table. She carried a basket of biscuits and kept her head low.

Nanny Fay sent a worried look at the girl, then hung her head. "Well, Adelaide, you was here first. So, I reckon if you're firm set against it, I should oughta —"

"She can't stay with you. Not at night." Addie swallowed the chortle building in her throat. "Because she'll never get any rest. Nanny Fay, you snore."

Both Bettina and Nanny Fay jerked upright and stared at Addie.

Addie let the grin pulling at her cheeks have its way. "She'd better stay with me instead."

Bettina's mouth dropped open. "You'd share your room with me after I . . . I . . ."

Addie rounded the table and put her hand on the younger girl's shoulder. "Bettina, may I be honest?"

Hesitance showed in her hazel eyes, but she gave a little nod.

"There are two things I've been praying

for since I got to Boone's Hollow. The first is that I would make friends. The second is that people in town would be kindlier to Nanny Fay." She offered a smile to the old woman and then returned her attention to Bettina. "I think your being here is an answer to both of those prayers."

Tears shimmered in the corners of Bettina's eyes. She didn't speak, but the gratitude and wonder in her expression spoke more loudly than words.

Addie squeezed Bettina's shoulder and lowered her hand. She shifted to include Nanny Fay. "And now, since both of you are in the same place, I'd like to ask a favor."

Nanny Fay shrugged. "If I can."

Bettina licked her lips. "What is it?"

"I have a new job." Addie explained her intention to record the stories of each of the families and put them in a collection in the library. "Would you mind if I interviewed the two of you so I can write Rosie's story first? Someone as special as your maw shouldn't be forgotten."

Tears welled up in Bettina's eyes. Nanny Fay put her arm around the young woman's shoulders and smiled at her. Bettina nodded. "I'd like that, Addie. Thank you. An' . . ." She gulped, chin quivering. "Thanks for showin' me grace."

EPILOGUE

Addie held the lit match to the last candle. The wick caught, the flame flared, and a tiny flicker danced at the end of the wick. The scent of bayberry filled the library — a festive aroma. She blew out the match, then paused for a moment, smiling at the row of candles set off by fresh-cut boughs of holly on the front windowsill. Such a perfect touch, considering the season.

She turned and caught Bettina on her knees in front of the decorated Christmas tree, rearranging the wrapped packages. Again. Stifling a laugh, she dropped the extinguished match in a little bowl next to the lit lamp, crossed to the tree, and crouched next to the packhorse librarian. "When I was a little girl, my mother told me every time I messed with the gifts under

518

the tree, one of them would fly up the chimney and go to someone else's house."

Bettina shot her a crinkle-nosed grin. "Since there ain't no chimney in the lib'ary, I'm not too worried about that." She sighed and sat back on her heels, looking at the presents. "Miz West had cocoa an' cookies for people at Christmastime last year, an' quite a few folks come by. With folks knowin' their youngsters'll get their very own book to carry home, we'll likely see every family from Boone's Hollow an' Tuckett's Pass come through here tonight. I been countin', an' I'm afraid there won't be enough."

Addie's heart swelled. Bettina's concern showed how much the girl's compassion had grown in the past months of living with Nanny Fay. She gave Bettina a one-armed hug. "Emmett carefully calculated how many we'd need, and the church ladies from Georgetown made sure they sent a few more books than he requested." They'd even graciously wrapped the books and tagged them with an appropriate age range before shipping the crate to Lynch. Mother had become invested in what she continued to call Addie's ministry, and Addie couldn't be more grateful. "Don't worry. We should be all right."

Bettina sent a furtive glance over her shoulder, as if ascertaining they were alone, then leaned in close to Addie. "I wanna tell you somethin'."

She spoke in such a soft whisper that Addie had to strain to hear. The two of them had shared many secrets, but Bettina's solemn expression made Addie suspect this one would be more serious than previous ones. Addie whispered, too. "What is it?"

"You know how the week after I moved out, my pap got took in for havin' that still up the mountain?"

Addie nodded and curled her hand around Bettina's wrist. The whole town had jabbered for days after Burke Webber's arrest. He might've been let off with a warning if he hadn't aimed a rifle at one of the officers and threatened to blow the man's brains to kingdom come.

"Well, he ain't gonna be back. Least not for years. So my folks' cabin is sittin' empty."

Sadness flooded Addie's middle. "Are you moving back to your cabin?" She would miss her late-night chats with her friend.

Bettina shook her head. "Nuh-uh. But I'm gonna see if Emmett wants to live in it." She puckered her face as if she'd tasted a sour pickle. "If he's fixin' to take a bride, he ain't gonna wanna share that itty-bitty space

520

here in the lib'ary. He's gonna need a real house."

Addie drew back. "A . . . a bride?" Funny how much the thought of Emmett marrying bothered her. She bit her inner lip for a moment, gathering courage. "Who's he marrying?"

Bettina huffed a little disbelieving laugh. "You, silly."

Addie gasped, a little squeak accompanying the intake of breath. "Me?"

"Well, sure. Who else would he marry up with 'cept you?"

Addie shook her head. Over their months of working together, she and Emmett had discovered an ease of cooperation fostered by respect, appreciation, and common values. Her feelings for him had grown beyond mere friendship into something deeper, but given his determination to avoid personal relationships in the workplace, Addie had kept her feelings a secret.

She sighed. "Emmett told me he can't get involved with an employee. You're mistaken, Bettina."

Bettina's expression turned sly. "I reckon when a feller's in love, he finds ways around such silly rules. An' before you ask how I know he's in love with you, I seen enough movies to reckanize when a feller's got his sights set on a gal. He loves you."

Addie held her breath, hardly daring to believe Bettina's words.

"An' when you have your weddin' day, it'd make me plumb proud if you wore the purty dress I bought at the Lynch store." Bettina snickered, the sound mischievous. " 'Course, we'll hafta stitch somethin' extra around the hem to make it long enough for you, seein' as how you're so much taller'n me, but I reckon Miz Tharp'll know how to fix it." She searched Addie's eyes, her expression so hopeful it brought the sting of tears. "Will you wear it, Addie? It'd let me know you really have forgave me for all the mean things I did."

Addie embraced the younger woman. She'd prayed for a friend, and God couldn't have sent a better one. "Everything's forgiven, Bettina, and I'd be honored to wear your dress." She pulled back. "But Emmett's never said a thing to me about marriage. This might all be your imagination."

Impishness glittered in Bettina's hazel eyes. "It ain't my 'magination. You wait an' see."

The door opened, allowing in a rush of cold air, and Alba and Glory burst into the room, giggling. Emmett followed them. He closed the door with his foot and then put his hands on his waist. "If you two don't stop laughing at me, you'll find coal in your stockings this year." They laughed harder and crossed to the table. "And stay out of those cookies. They're for the guests."

"My maw's the one who baked 'em all," Glory said, "so I reckon I can eat 'em if I want to." She snapped a sugar-dusted cookie in half and shared it with Alba, grinning.

Addie stood. After Bettina's statement about Emmett's being in love, Addie was half-afraid to meet his gaze. She looked at his new suit instead. Oh, how handsome and professional he appeared in the charcoal-gray broadcloth. Her heart rolled over. But then she realized something was wrong. "Why aren't you wearing the Santa costume?" Daddy had dressed as Santa for the Georgetown bank's Christmas party for as far back as Addie could remember. He'd sent the suit with the books for their library Christmas gathering, stipulating only that Addie bring it back with her when she came home for Christmas. He wanted to don it on Christmas Eve and give out token gifts to the other boarders at Fee's. Always giving . . . Her parents set such a wonderful example of charity.

Emmett made a face and pointed with his

thumb at Glory and Alba. "That's what they're teasing me about. I couldn't fit into the suit. I was too tall. Maw talked Paw into wearing it, and he'll play Santa tonight."

Addie gaped at him in amazement. "Your paw is coming . . . as Santa?"

Emmett grinned. "I know. I reckon he's mellowing some." He leaned down a bit. "His biggest concern was Dusty figuring out who was underneath the beard and spoiling it for all the kids. I sure hope he can sneak over here without Dusty putting two and two together."

After Bettina's bold speculations, having Emmett so close did funny things to Addie's pulse. She took a step sideways and forced a smile. "Dusty will be too excited to notice who's underneath the Santa hat."

"I hope you're right." He flicked a nervous glance out the window. "And I hope he hurries. We said the door would open at seven, but folks'll probably start showing up earlier, and we can't leave them standing out in the cold."

"If Santa makes a grand entrance, it will add to the festivities rather than detract."

The creases in his forehead didn't relax.

She nudged him lightly. "Stop worrying. This is going to be the best Christmas party the town's ever seen."

Townsfolk began arriving at a few minutes before seven. The surprise and excitement of those who were in the building when Santa Claus came through the door at five minutes past thrilled Addie. She whispered to Emmett that they'd probably talk about it each Christmas for the next twenty years.

With Bettina, Glory, and Alba's help, Santa distributed books to every child age twelve and younger, and they sneaked a few to older kids, too. People came and went, but the room was crowded the entire hour and a half Emmett had set aside for the open house. Nanny Fay and Addie worked together to keep the cookie platters filled. A few people drew back when they realized who was serving them, but none refused a cookie — a Christmas miracle, Addie declared to herself.

Emmett mingled, exchanging a few words with each family that came through the doors. Although he wandered the floor, somehow every time Addie looked up, she spotted him no matter where he stood in the room. Her heart gave a little flutter when his head turned and his blue-eyed gaze connected with hers.

Someone tugged her sleeve, and she looked to find Dusty standing close. He quirked his finger for her to bend down.

She leaned close, and he curled his hand along her jaw. "Guess what, Addie?" His warm breath tickled her ear. "My paw is Santa Claus. The real Santa Claus! But don't tell, okay? It's a secret."

She tapped her finger to her lips and winked, and he scampered off with a cookie — maybe his sixth? — in his hand. She chuckled under her breath. Dusty would never forget this Christmas. And neither, she ventured to guess, would Mr. Tharp.

As Addie had predicted, Emmett planned correctly. They had enough books to go around, with three left over, but all that remained on the cookie trays were crumbs when the last family departed with cries of "Merry Christmas!" Glory helped Alba stack the cookie plates and carry them out. Addie took a broom and began sweeping up the cookie crumbs and discarded bits of wrapping paper. Bettina and Nanny Fay blew out all the candles and then headed for the cabin Bettina now claimed as home. Addie called after them, "I'll be there after I've finished sweeping."

But as soon as the door closed behind them, Emmett plucked the broom from her hand. "You've done enough."

She pointed silently to the crumbs littering the floor.

He shook his head, smiling. "It'll keep. Maw said she'd help with the cleaning tomorrow. Don't you need to pack for your trip to Georgetown?"

All at once the joy of the evening faded. Addie wanted to see her parents and Preacher Finley and her friends from Georgetown. But leaving Emmett, Nanny Fay, Bettina, and the other girls — not to mention several townsfolk — for even a short time would hurt. She'd truly grown to love all of them. She swallowed a knot of sorrow. "I can't pack until I have the Santa costume from your paw."

"Well, then, let's go to my folks' place and get it. I reckon he's out of it by now. He said it was itchy. Then I'll walk you to Nanny Fay's." He paused, a bashful grin twitching on the corners of his lips. "If that's all right?"

She'd never turn down time with Emmett. She nodded.

He helped her into her coat, and they set out. The town was quiet, but lamplight behind windows in every house and cabin gave the mountainside a cheery glow. The breeze had calmed, and although the air was cold enough to show their breath, she wasn't uncomfortably cool. But some of her warmth came from within. She enjoyed walking by starlight with Emmett.

He led her across the street and followed the pathway behind the general merchandise store. Emmett gestured to the Barr place as they passed it. "I'm sure glad Jennie brought her youngsters to the party. Those books are probably the only presents her kids will get this year." He smiled down at her. "Your mother is wonderful. Please tell her how much I appreciate her."

"I will." Addie pushed her hands into her pockets. "I won't be surprised if she sends me back with more books and magazines. Since word got out, people who don't even attend church with her and Daddy have made donations. Even in these hard times, people want to give. It's love in action, and it's such a beautiful thing to see."

" 'Doubt thou the stars are fire, doubt that the sun doth move, doubt truth to be a liar, but never doubt' " — Emmett's eyes glittered — " 'I love.' "

A chill wiggled down her spine, hope rising at the meaning behind his words.

"Shakespeare's statement from *Hamlet* could be your mother's."

Disappointment fell. "Yes. Yes, it fits her well." She shifted her attention to the pathway leading to the Tharps' cabin.

Damaris opened the door to them and

greeted Addie with a big hug. Then she pressed the neatly folded Santa costume into her arms. "You have a good Christmas, Addie. We'll see you after the first of the year." Mr. Tharp also wished Addie a merry Christmas, and she and Emmett set out again.

The walk to Nanny Fay's took them through the trees, and it seemed cooler there. She hugged Daddy's velvet costume for warmth. The smell of woodsmoke from fireplaces hung on the air — a pleasant aroma. Other than the crunch of leaves beneath their feet, the world was completely silent. One of them should say something. She'd be in Georgetown for almost two weeks, enough time to help Mother and Daddy settle into the two-bedroom bungalow they'd found to rent. Her folks couldn't afford telephone service yet, which meant she wouldn't be able to even make a telephone call to Boone's Hollow. Shouldn't she and Emmett take advantage of the minutes together now? Why didn't he —

"Addie?"

She released a little squeak of surprise. "Yes?"

"How many stories do you think you've written so far?"

She wouldn't have chosen the topic of her

memory collecting. They could talk about it anytime. Shouldn't alone time be for something more personal? But at least he'd spoken. She shrugged. "Twelve so far. And thirty-eight more families are waiting their turns."

"So . . ." His tone sounded musing. "Two stories per month? Is that the pace you're keeping?"

Mathematically he was correct. She nodded. "Yes. I could probably get more covered if I was writing all day, but using only the evening hours slows me down." Her own story writing had been set aside, but she didn't regret it. These people's histories were more important than her fictional characters' tales.

They broke through the trees into the clearing around Nanny Fay's cabin. The familiar glow behind the windows and a curling line of smoke from the rock chimney beckoned Addie, but Emmett maintained a slow, leisurely pace. She matched it.

"Would you like to do the writing full time?"

She frowned up at him. "I can't do that. I have to earn a wage." Although she'd paid her college bill, Mother and Daddy would need her help in covering the expenses of their new little house. Daddy also wanted her to start a savings account, setting aside some funds with the hope of finishing her degree someday.

He placed his hand on her spine and guided her to the porch, to the bench Eagle had built for Nanny Fay, and he sat. He patted the open spot, and she perched next to him, puzzled by the serious expression on his face. "Did you know that the WPA has hired photographers to make a pictorial account of the nation's hardships?"

She hadn't heard, but she liked the idea. Someday, when things were easier, people would need to remember the hardworking folks who survived these difficult times. Pictures would personalize what they'd had to overcome.

"Pictures are good, but they need words to go with them." Emmett's blue eyes, lit by the lamplight behind the glass, remained fixed on her face. "As well as you write, I think you should consider submitting some of your family stories to the committee in Washington. They might very well hire you to record the history of the folks living on Black Mountain. Then you could commit your full days to it, and when all was done, you'd have a publishing credit to your name."

Being paid to write these families' histories

stirred excitement in her chest. But at the same time, worry nibbled. "If I was hired, though, I'd have to give up working at the library. No more . . . working alongside you." She swallowed. "Is that what you want?"

"What I want is for you to fully use the abilities God has given you." Fervency glowed in his eyes. "You have a special gift for words, Addie. You're spending so many hours recording these stories, and it would be nice if you were recompensed for your effort. If you were writing full time, you could complete more than two a month. At the rate you're going, it'll be more than a year before you can write the one I really want to read."

"Which one is that?"

His lips curved into a sweet smile. "Ours."

She drew back, raising her eyebrows. "Ours?"

He nodded. "Think about it while you're in Georgetown. And when you come back, I'll ask you again about creating a you-and-me story."

Her heart pattered, and eagerness thrummed in her veins. "Why don't you ask me now?"

"It wouldn't be fair. You haven't been home with all the things the city offers. You need to know for sure that your story belongs here in these hills with me." He reached through the folds of red velvet and took her hands. "Go home. Have time with your parents. Do a lot of praying and thinking. And when you come back, we'll talk. All right?"

Always the businessman, wanting to plan first and act later. She smiled. "All right. But, Emmett? You need to know that if I write a you-and-me story, it'll be a fairy tale with a happily-ever-after ending."

He leaned down slightly and touched his forehead to hers. "I wouldn't expect anything less."

READERS GUIDE

1. Addie was looking forward to a carefree summer when a meeting with the dean of students pulled the rug from beneath her feet and changed the trajectory of her life. Was this happenstance or divine intervention? Has what you perceived as a negative situation ever resulted in a positive life change for you? How can we know whether unexpected events are merely circumstances or God's means of sending us on a God-designed pathway?

2. Bettina suffered from an undiagnosed condition that prevented her from being able to read and write. How did she compensate for her inability to understand "book learnin' "? Did you find it strange that she set her sights on marrying someone who'd earned a college degree? Why do you think she was so determined to marry Emmett?

3. Emmett and Addie both had mothers who read to them, and they both liked books from an early age. Emmett's love of reading created a rift between him and his father. In addition to Emmett's studious nature, what distanced father and son? Do you think their relationship in the future will be better? Why or why not?

4. Nanny Fay had a difficult childhood and then a difficult adult life because of the superstitions and generational grudges held by people in Boone's Hollow. How was she able to maintain a kind nature despite the many snubs? What do you think it meant to her when Addie chose to rent a room in her cabin?

5. Miss West told Addie, "A book takes one into another person's thoughts and emotions. . . . Stories can stir compassion, can inspire integrity, can show different lifestyles and problem-solving skills. Books, Addie, have the power to change people for the better." Has a book ever influenced your view of a real-life person or situation? In what way?

6. Emmett fell in love with Addie, but he didn't immediately ask her to marry him. For what reasons did he delay proposing? Did you find his decision wise or unwise? Why?

7. Addie decided to record the life stories of the people living in the hills around Boone's Hollow and Tuckett's Pass. What inspired this desire? What did she hope to accomplish? Have you ever written your life's story? Would you consider doing so to pass your life lessons to the next generation?

ACKNOWLEDGMENTS

Daddy and Connie — our trip to Black Mountain and the communities of Cumberland, Lynch, and Benham was such fun. I will always treasure the memories of our "traipsin'," even though I was sure I would either sweat to death or plunge to my death on one of those winding mountain roads! You made my first research trip without Mom a time of laughter and pleasant moments to cherish. I love you both.

My Sunday school and Lit & Latte ladies — your prayers and support are so appreciated, and I know they bolstered me as I completed this story. You all are a blessing in my life. Thank you.

Shannon, Christina, Abby, Kathy, and the team at WaterBrook — thank you for your support, suggestions, and efforts to make this story the best it can be. I appreciate being part of your team.

Most importantly, *God* — how would I

navigate this world without You? Thank You for taking my hard times and making them work for my good and Your glory. You are the author of my life, and I pray the words I pen always share Your love and truth. May any praise or glory be reflected directly back to You.

ABOUT THE AUTHOR

In 1966, **Kim Vogel Sawyer** told her kindergarten teacher that someday people would check out her book in libraries. That little-girl dream came true in 2006 with the release of *Waiting for Summer's Return.* Since then, Kim has watched God expand her dream beyond her childhood imaginings. With more than fifty titles on library shelves and more than 1.5 million copies of her books in print worldwide, she enjoys a full-time writing and speaking ministry. Kim and her retired military husband, Don, are empty nesters living in a small town in Kansas, the setting of many of Kim's novels. When she isn't writing, Kim stays active serving in her church's women's and music ministries, crafting quilts, petting cats, and spoiling her quiverful of granddarlings. You can learn more about Kim's writing at www.kimvogelsawyer.com.